PENGUIN BOOKS

THE PENGUIN BOOK OF
MODERN WOMEN'S SHORT STORIES

Susan Hill was born in Scarborough in 1942, and educated at grammar schools there and in Coventry. She read English at King's College, London, of which she is now a fellow. Her novels include *I'm the King of the Castle* (Somerset Maugham Award), *The Albatross* (John Llewellyn Rhys Prize), *Strange Meeting*, *The Bird of Night* (Whitbread Award), *In the Springtime of the Year*, *Air and Angels* and *The Service of Clouds*. She has written three volumes of short stories, including *A Bit of Singing and Dancing*, two ghost novels, *The Woman in Black* and *The Mist in the Mirror*, and a number of stories for children. Her autobiographical books are *The Magic Apple Tree* and *Family*, and she has also edited three volumes of women's short stories for Penguin.

Susan Hill lives in a Gloucestershire farmhouse, from where she runs her own small publishing company, Long Barn Books, and edits and publishes the quarterly journal *Books and Company*. She is married to the Shakespeare scholar Stanley Wells, and they have two daughters. Further information about Susan Hill and her books can be found on the following websites:

www.susan-hill.com   www.booksandcompany.co.uk
www.thewomaninblack.com

The Penguin Book of MODERN WOMEN'S SHORT STORIES

≈

Edited by SUSAN HILL

PENGUIN BOOKS

PENGUIN BOOKS

Published by the Penguin Group
Penguin Books Ltd, 80 Strand, London WC2R 0RL, England
Penguin Putnam Inc., 375 Hudson Street, New York, New York 10014, USA
Penguin Books Australia Ltd, Ringwood, Victoria, Australia
Penguin Books Canada Ltd, 10 Alcorn Avenue, Toronto, Ontario, Canada M4V 3B2
Penguin Books India (P) Ltd, 11 Community Centre, Panchsheel Park, New Delhi – 110 017, India
Penguin Books (NZ) Ltd, Cnr Rosedale and Airborne Roads, Albany, Auckland, New Zealand
Penguin Books (South Africa) (Pty) Ltd, 24 Sturdee Avenue, Rosebank 2196 South Africa

Penguin Books Ltd, Registered Offices: 80 Strand, London WC2R 0RL, England

www.penguin.com

This collection first published in Great Britain as *The Parchment Moon*
by Michael Joseph 1990
Published under this title in Penguin Books 1991
14

This selection and introduction copyright © Susan Hill, 1990
All rights reserved

The acknowledgements on p. vii constitute
an extension of this copyright page

Printed in England by Clays Ltd, St Ives plc

Contents

vi

Acknowledgements

For permission to reprint the stories specified we are indebted to:

The Estate of Elizabeth Taylor and A. M. Heath & Co. Ltd for 'The Devastating Boys' by Elizabeth Taylor (Chatto & Windus, 1972);

William Heinemann Ltd for 'Slaves to the Mushroom' from *Dreams of Dead Women's Handbags* by Shena Mackay (1987);

Hamish Hamilton Ltd for 'Some Retired Ladies on a Tour' from *A Nail on the Head* by Clare Boylan (1983);

The Peters Fraser & Dunlop Group Ltd for 'Hassan's Tower' from *Winter's Tales* by Margaret Drabble (Macmillan, 1966);

The Estate of Elizabeth Bowen and Jonathan Cape Ltd for 'The Visitor' from *The Collected Stories of Elizabeth Bowen* (1980);

Sara Maitland and Brilliance Books for 'A Fall From Grace' from *Weddings and Funerals* by Aileen Latourette & Sara Maitland (1984)

Methuen & Co. Ltd for 'The Tulip Plate' from *People for Lunch* by Georgina Hammick (1987);

David Higham Associates Ltd for 'The Black Madonna' from *The Go-Away Bird* by Muriel Spark (Macmillan, 1958);

A. S. Byatt and Chatto & Windus Ltd for 'The July Ghost' from *Sugar and Other Stories* by A. S. Byatt (1987);

Elizabeth Jane Howard and Jonathan Cape Ltd for 'Summer Picnic' from *Mr Wrong* by Elizabeth Jane Howard (1975);

Curtis Brown London on behalf of Patricia Ferguson for 'Indefinite Nights' © Patricia Ferguson from *Indefinite Nights* by Patricia Ferguson (1987);

Felicity Bryan for 'The Weighing Up' from *Such Visitors* by Angela Huth (Heinemann and Mandarin, Copyright 1989);

The Executors of the Sylvia Townsend Warner Estate and Chatto & Windus Ltd for 'A Love Match' from *The Selected Stories of Sylvia Townsend Warner* edited by Clare Harman (1988);

George Weidenfeld & Nicolson Ltd for 'Savages' from *A Fanatic Heart* by Edna O'Brien (1985);

Hamish Hamilton Ltd for 'The New People' from *The Garden of the Villa Mollini* by Rose Tremain (1987);

The Peters Fraser & Dunlop Group Ltd for 'Miss Anstruther's Letters' by Rose Macaulay from *London Calling* edited by Storm Jameson (Harper, 1942);

Helen Harris and the Arts Council of Great Britain for 'The Man Who Kept the Sweet Shop at the Bus Station' by Helen Harris from *New Stories 5* (1980);

William Heinemann Ltd for 'Addy' from *Goodnight, Sweet Ladies* by Caroline Blackwood (1988);

Jessie Kesson and Chatto & Windus Ltd for 'Stormy Weather' from *Where the Apple Ripens* by Jessie Kesson (1986);

Faber & Faber Ltd for 'Passages' from *The Way Paver* by Anne Devlin (1986);

The Estate of Jean Rhys and Anthony Sheil Associates Ltd for 'Mannequin' from *The Left Bank* by Jean Rhys (Jonathan Cape, 1927);

Ruth Fainlight for 'Another Survivor' (Copyright Ruth Fainlight 1978) from *Twelve Stories by Famous Women Writers* edited by Denys val Baker (W. H. Allen, 1978);

Murray Pollinger Ltd for 'Nothing Missing But the Samovar' from *Pack of Cards* by Penelope Lively (William Heinemann, 1986);

Hamish Hamilton Ltd for 'Stone Trees' from *The Pangs of Love* by Jane Gardam (1983);

Fay Weldon and Hodder & Stoughton Ltd For 'Weekend' from *Watching Me, Watching You* by Fay Weldon (1981).

*

Introduction

An editor can, simply by the act of selection and omission, make an anthology appear to support any particular critical point of view. But in fact, what it primarily reflects is simply personal taste. I have compiled a collection of stories of the kind I most like reading, and which reflect life and human beings in a way that interests and engages me.

I enjoyed every one of these stories the first time I read them. They stayed in my mind and I reflected upon them, phrases and scenes kept coming back to me to be relished, and I enjoyed them even more on second and subsequent readings. and any editor – any reader, for that matter – wants to communicate enthusiasm, to introduce as many other people as possible to writing that has meant so much to them.

But I did more than enjoy: I admired profoundly. I think the stories are all outstanding examples of their kind. There is not a weak link, no story I would not be prepared to defend on the grounds of literary merit although, of course, I could have tripled or quadrupled the length of the volume without any difficulty and I have had to leave out much that I would love to have included. I hope that it will therefore serve as a taster, to introduce the reader to the entire body of stories by the individual writers included here (most of whom have published collections of short stories) and so lead them on to explore the whole rich territory of short fiction written by women in this country, during this century and particularly since the war.

The stories I have chosen are not overtly political nor geographically wide-ranging; they do not deal with 'global concerns'. They are no less important as a result. They are quiet, small-scale, intimate stories – a tone which suits the form best. They are about everyday but not trivial matters, about the business of being human and about the concerns of the human heart. I do not believe that, in the last resort, fiction is, or even should be, about anything else. I did not set out to look for stories with any particular theme, within this wider context. But now that these stories are collected together, it is clear that certain themes do stand out and recur. Indeed, they were themes which I came upon repeatedly in numerous other stories I read.

Women alone, women emotionally (and sometimes also physically) isolated, constantly reappear. Often, as in the stories by Rose Tremain and Jane Gardam, they have been isolated by bereavement. In both of these, the women are expressing a desperate longing and need to be able to communicate, with the beloved other person, in the old way.

Most poignantly, as in A. S. Byatt's 'The July Ghost', the loss by death is of a child. This is a ghost story and a rare example of the form which is saying something deeply serious, as well as being one of rare literary merit. I think it is one of the finest ghost stories written this century. But it is also immediately accessible, and speaks on a direct level to 'the ordinary reader'. In that sense, it fulfils my aim that every story included should be both artistically excellent, and of a kind that the average, interested reader can appreciate.

Isolation is often both the result and the cause – in a dreadful vicious circle – of eccentricity. Edna O'Brien, Sara Maitland and Caroline Blackwood all brilliantly portray women at whom fingers are pointed and knowing looks directed, because their behaviour is in some way unacceptably peculiar, and as a result they are set outside the confines of normal human society, becoming, as a means of defence, even more eccentric. Yet the consequences are by no means wholly negative: the isolated one is not necessarily portrayed as the loser.

Inevitably, the theme of childhood is a dominant one and it is the children themselves, not their parents or others related to them, who hold centre stage. No one has written better in this century about the strangeness and frequent loneliness of being a child, and the obtuseness of adult understanding of them, than Elizabeth Bowen, both in her novels and short stories. 'The Visitor' is a poignant account of time spent by a small boy, with well-meaning but uncomprehending strangers, while his mother is dying at home.

Elizabeth Taylor's devastatingly funny story 'The Devastating Boys' is about children in a very different context, though they, too, are cut off from home among well-meaning strangers; and as well as being perceptive about the two refugees, it is gently ruthless in laying bare the loneliness within a marriage.

Non-communication between married partners begins even on the honeymoon, in Margaret Drabble's coolly analytical 'Hassan's Tower'. But Fay Weldon's view of married life, in her small masterpiece 'Weekend', is far bleaker and more bitter. And no one writes with greater trenchancy and insight of the north London middle classes.

'Weekend' is the only story that could be called overtly feminist. Yet in one sense, the whole collection might be described so because we are left in no doubt that these women writers are wholly and inevitably *on the side* of women. Here are girls growing up within their own secret, yearning worlds, in the stories of Helen Harris and Jessie Kesson, and a perfect overview of a girl growing up and a woman growing old in a story by Elizabeth Jane Howard which I admire most for its wonderful atmosphere of tranquil wisdom, and for presenting the whole cycle of female life, in microcosm, on a single day.

Relationships are not only married ones. There is a curious, tender story of a brother and sister from Sylvia Townsend Warner, and I could well have included several others by different writers, on the same theme. Rose Tremain's story is vaguely sapphic, but Georgina Hammick's women friends are very separate, and the gulf between them becomes horribly obvious in the course of the story.

Women grow up, marry and have their children; they are bereaved, grow old, die. They also work, and it is working women who are the subject of the stories by Patricia Ferguson and Shena

Mackay. Theirs, the nurse and the mushroom picker, are members of that great army of underpaid and exploited, and so, in a very different context, are the young mannequins in Jean Rhys's classic and utterly typical Parisian sketch.

Food, the getting and eating of meals, takes up a large part of most women's lives, and when they are unhappy or betrayed it often preoccupies them, as they either starve themselves ruthlessly or overeat, like the heroine of Angela Huth's 'The Weighing Up', the best piece of fiction on the theme since Caroline Blackwood's novella *The Stepdaughter*. But sex is only incidentally referred to, and it is treated, in Fay Weldon and Clare Boylan's stories, very matter-of-factly, and with a certain disgust – eroticism is wholly absent.

There is humour in flashes, and much verbal wit throughout, but the jokes, and the comedy, are mainly black, nowhere more so than in Muriel Spark's marvellous, idiosyncratic piece 'The Black Madonna', one of the finest stories from this prolific mistress of the form.

And lest it be supposed that women do not write well about men, or at least succeed in doing so only from a woman's point of view, Penelope Lively and Ruth Fainlight have a young and an elderly hero each, and the world is seen through their eyes with complete conviction.

These stories are about anger and bitterness, love and loss, loneliness, growing, waste, change, oppression, nostalgia, grief, endurance, war, fear, death. They move one to tears, to laughter, to pity, to despair, and to admiration at fine writing. But perhaps most importantly, they move the reader to give a cry of recognition and understanding – yes, this is what it feels like to be human in this way – time and time again.

It goes without saying that they may equally well be read and enjoyed by both sexes, but perhaps they do speak, at a certain level, very particularly to other women.

Susan Hill
1990

*

The Devastating Boys

Laura was always too early; and this was as bad as being late, her husband, who was always late himself, told her. She sat in her car in the empty railway-station approach, feeling very sick, from dread.

It was half-past eleven on a summer morning. The country station was almost spellbound in silence, and there was, to Laura, a dreadful sense of self-absorption – in herself – in the stillness of the only porter standing on the platform, staring down the line: even – perhaps especially – in inanimate things; all were menacingly intent on being themselves, and separately themselves – the slanting shadows of railings across the platform, the glossiness of leaves, and the closed door of the office looking more closed, she thought, than any door she had ever seen.

She got out of the car and went into the station walking up and down the platform in a panic. It was a beautiful morning. If only the children weren't coming then she could have enjoyed it.

The children were coming from London. It was Harold's idea to have them, some time back, in March, when he read of a scheme to give London children a summer holiday in the country. This he might have read without interest, but the words 'Some of the children will be coloured' caught his eye. He seemed to find a slight tinge of warning in the phrase; the more he thought it over, the more he was convinced. He had made a long speech to Laura about children being the great equalizers, and that we should learn from them, that to insinuate the stale prejudices of their elders into their fresh, fair minds was such a sin that he could not think of a worse one.

He knew very little about children. His students had passed beyond the blessed age, and shades of the prison-house had closed about them. His own children were even older, grown-up and gone away; but, while they were young, they had done nothing to destroy his faith in them, or blur the idea of them he had in his mind, and his feeling of humility in their presence. They had been good children carefully dealt with and easy to handle. There had scarcely been a cloud over their growing-up. Any little bothers Laura had hidden from him.

In March, the end of July was a long way away. Laura, who was lonely in middle-age, seemed to herself to be frittering away her days, just waiting for her grandchildren to be born: she had agreed with Harold's suggestion. She would have agreed anyway, whatever it was, as it was her nature – and his – for her to do so. It would be rather exciting to have two children to stay – to have the beds in Imogen's and Lalage's room slept in again. 'We could have two boys, or two girls,' Harold said. 'No stipulation, but that they must be coloured.'

Now *he* was making differences, but Laura did not remark upon it. All she said was, 'What will they do all the time?'

'What our own children used to do – play in the garden, go for picnics . . .'

'On wet days?'

'Dress up,' he said at once.

She remembered Imogen and Lalage in her old hats and dresses, slopping about in her big shoes, see-sawing on high heels, and she had to turn her head away, and there were tears in her eyes.

Her children had been her life, and her grandchildren one day would be; but here was an empty space. Life had fallen away from her. She had never been clever like the other professors' wives, or managed to have what they called 'outside interests'. Committees frightened her, and good works made her feel embarrassed and clumsy.

She *was* a clumsy person — gentle, but clumsy. Pacing up and down the platform, she had an ungainly walk — legs stiffly apart, head a little poked forward because she had poor sight. She was short and squarely-built and her clothes were never right; often she looked dishevelled, sometimes even battered.

This morning, she wore a label pinned to her breast, so that the children's escort would recognize her when the train drew in; but she felt self-conscious about it and covered it with her hand, though there was no one but the porter to see.

The signal dropped, as if a guillotine had come crashing down, and her heart seemed to crash down with it. Two boys! she thought. Somehow, she had imagined girls. She was used to girls, and shy of boys.

The printed form had come a day or two ago and had increased the panic which had gradually been gathering. Six-year-old boys, and she had pictured perhaps eight or ten-year-old girls, whom she could teach to sew and make cakes for tea, and press wild flowers as she had taught Imogen and Lalage to do.

Flurried and anxious entertaining at home; interviewing headmistresses; once — shied away from failure — opening a sale-of-work in the village — these agonies to her diffident nature seemed nothing to the nervousness she felt now, as the train appeared round the bend. She simply wasn't good with children — only her own. *Their* friends had frightened her, had been mouse-quiet and glum, or had got out of hand, and she herself had been too shy either to intrude or clamp down. When she met children — perhaps the small grandchildren of her acquaintances, she would only smile, perhaps awkwardly touch a cheek with her finger. If she were asked to hold a baby, she was fearful lest it should cry, and often it would, sensing lack of assurance in her clasp.

The train came in and slowed up. Suppose that I can't find them, she thought, and she went anxiously from window to window, her label uncovered now. And suppose they cry for their mothers and want to go home.

A tall, authoritative woman, also wearing a label, leaned out of a window, saw her and signalled curtly. She had a compartment full of little children in her charge to be delivered about Oxfordshire. Only two got out on to this platform, Laura's two, Septimus Smith and Benny Reece. They wore tickets, too, with their names printed on them.

Benny was much lighter in complexion than Septimus. He was obviously a half-caste and Laura hoped that this would count in Harold's eyes. It might even be one point up. They stood on the platform, looking about them, holding their little cardboard cases.

'My name is Laura,' she said. She stooped and clasped them to her in terror, and kissed their cheeks. Sep's in particular, was extraordinarily soft, like the petal of a poppy. His big eyes stared up at her, without expression. He wore a dark, long-trousered suit, so that he was all over sombre and unchildlike. Benny had a mock-suède coat with a nylon-fur collar and a trilby hat with a feather. They did not speak. Not only was she, Laura, strange to them, but they were strange to one another. There had only been a short train-journey in which to sum up their chances of becoming friends.

She put them both into the back of the car, so that there should be no favouritism, and drove off, pointing out – to utter silence – places on the way. 'That's a café where we'll go for tea one day.' The silence was dreadful. 'A caff,' she amended. 'And there's the little cinema. Not very grand, I'm afraid. Not like London ones.'

They did not even glance about them.

'Are you going to be good friends to one another?' she asked.

After a pause, Sep said in a slow grave voice, 'Yeah, I'm going to be a good friend.'

'Is this the country?' Benny asked. He had a chirpy, perky Cockney voice and accent.

'Yeah, this is the countryside,' said Sep, in his rolling drawl, glancing indifferently at some trees.

Then he began to talk. It was in an aggrieved sing-song. 'I don't go on that train no more. I don't like that train, and I don't go on that again over my dead body. Some boy he say to me, "You don't sit in that corner seat. I sit there." I say, "You don't sit here. I sit here." "Yeah," I say, "You don't own this train so I don't budge from here." Then he dash my comic down and tore it.'

'Yep, he tore his comic,' Benny said.

'"You tear my comic, you buy me another comic," I said. "Or else." "Or *else*," I said.' He suddenly broke off and looked at a wood they were passing. 'I don't go near those tall bushes. They full of snakes what sting you.'

'No they ain't,' said Benny.

'My Mam said so. I don't go.'

'There aren't any snakes,' said Laura, in a light voice. She, too, had a terror of them, and was afraid to walk through the bracken. 'Or only little harmless ones,' she added.

'I don't go,' Sep murmured to himself. Then, in a louder voice, he went on. 'He said, "I don't buy no comic for you, you nigger," he said.'

'He never said that,' Benny protested.

'Yes, "You dirty nigger," he said.'

'He never.'

There was something so puzzled in Benny's voice that Laura immediately believed him. The expression on his little monkey-face was open and impartial.

'I don't go on that train no more.'

'You've got to. When you go home,' Benny said.

'Maybe I don't go home.'

'We'll think about that later. You've only just arrived,' said Laura, smiling.

'No, I think about that right now.'

Along the narrow lane to the house, they were held up by the cows from the farm. A boy drove them along, whacking their messed rumps with a stick. Cow-pats plopped on to the road and steamed there, zizzing with flies. Benny held his nose and Sep, glancing at him, at once did the same. 'I don't care for this smell of the countryside,' he complained in a pinched tone.

'No, the countryside stinks,' said Benny.

'Cows frighten me.'

'They don't frighten me.'

Sep cringed against the back of the seat, whimpering; but Benny wound his window right down, put his head a little out of it, and shouted, 'Get on, you dirty old sods, or else I'll show you.'

'Hush,' said Laura gently.

'He swore,' Sep pointed out.

They turned into Laura's gateway, up the short drive. In front of the house was a lawn and a cedar tree. From one of its lower branches hung the old swing, on chains, waiting for Laura's grandchildren.

The boys clambered out of the car and followed her into the hall, where they stood looking about them critically; then Benny dropped his case and shot like an arrow towards Harold's golf-bag and pulled out a club. His face was suddenly bright with excitement and Laura, darting forward to him, felt a stab of misery at having to begin the 'No's' so soon. 'I'm afraid Harold wouldn't like you to touch them,' she said. Benny stared her out, but after a moment or two gave up the club with all the unwillingness in the world. Meanwhile, Sep had taken an antique coaching-horn and was blowing a bubbly, uneven blast on it, his eyes stretched wide and his cheeks blown out. 'Nor that,' said Laura faintly, taking it away. 'Let's go upstairs and unpack.'

They appeared not at all overawed by the size of this fairly large house; in fact, rather unimpressed by it.

In the room where once, as little girls, Imogen and Lalage had slept together, they opened their cases. Sep put his clothes neatly and carefully into his drawer; and Benny tipped the case into his — comics, clothes and shoes, and a scattering of peanuts. I'll tidy it later, Laura thought.

'Shall we toss up for who sleeps by the window?' she suggested.

'I don't sleep by no window,' said Sep. 'I sleep in *this* bed; with *him*.'

'I want to sleep by myself,' said Benny.

Sep began a babyish whimpering, which increased into an anguished keening. 'I don't like to sleep in the bed by myself. I'm scared to. I'm real scared to. I'm scared.'

This was entirely theatrical, Laura decided, and Benny seemed to think so, too; for he took no notice.

A fortnight! Laura thought. This day alone stretched endlessly before her, and she dared not think of any following ones. Already she felt ineffectual and had an inkling that they were going to despise her. And her brightness was false and not infectious. She longed for Harold to come home, as she had never longed before.

'I reckon I go and clean my teeth,' said Sep, who had broken off his dirge.

'Lunch is ready. Afterwards would be more sensible, surely?' Laura suggested.

But they paid no heed to her. Both took their tooth-brushes, their new tubes of paste, and rushed to find the bathroom. 'I'm going to bathe myself,' said Sep. 'I'm going to bathe all my skin and wash my head.'

'Not *before* lunch,' Laura called out, hastening after them; but they did not hear her. Taps were running and steam clouding the window, and Sep was tearing off his clothes.

'He's bathed three times already,' Laura told Harold.

She had just come downstairs, and had done so as soon as she heard him slamming the front door.

Upstairs, Sep was sitting in the bath. She had made him a lacy vest of soap-froth, as once she had made them for Imogen and Lalage. It showed up much better on his grape-dark skin. He sat there, like a tribal warrior done up in war-paint.

Benny would not go near the bath. He washed at the basin, his sleeves rolled up: and he turned the cake of soap over and over uncertainly in his hands.

'It's probably a novelty,' Harold said, referring to Sep's bathing. 'Would you like a drink?'

'Later perhaps. I daren't sit down, for I'd never get up again.'

'I'll finish them off. I'll go and see to them. You just sit there and drink this.'

'Oh, Harold, how wonderfully good of you.'

She sank down on the arm of the chair, and sipped her drink, feeling stunned. From the echoing bathroom came shouts of laughter, and it was very good to hear them, especially from a distance. Harold was being a great success, and relief and gratitude filled her.

After a little rest, she got up and went weakly about the room, putting things back in their places. When this was done, the room still looked wrong. An unfamiliar dust seemed to have settled all over it, yet, running a finger over the piano, she found none. All the same, it was not the usual scene she set for Harold's home-coming in the evenings. It had taken a shaking-up.

Scampering footsteps now thundered along the landing. She waited a moment or two, then went upstairs. They were in bed, in separate beds; Benny by the window. Harold was pacing about the room, telling them a story: his hands flapped like huge ears at the side of his face; then he made an elephant's trunk with his arm. From the beds, the children's eyes stared unblinkingly at him. As Laura came into the room, only Benny's flickered in her direction, then back at once to the magic of Harold's performance. She blew a vague, unheeded kiss, and crept away.

'It's like seeing snow begin to fall,' said Harold at dinner. 'You know it's going to be a damned nuisance, but it makes a change.'

He sounded exhilarated; clashed the knife against the steel with vigour, and started to carve. He kept popping little titbits into his mouth. Carver's perks, he called them.

'Not much for me,' Laura said.

'What did they have for lunch?'

'Fish cakes.'

'Enjoy them?'

'Sep said, "I don't like that." He's very suspicious, and that makes Benny all the braver. Then he eats too much, showing off.'

'They'll settle down,' Harold said, settling down himself to his dinner. After a while, he said, 'The little Cockney one asked me just now if this were a private house. When I said "Yes", he said, "I thought it was, because you've got the sleeping upstairs and the talking downstairs." Didn't quite get the drift.'

'Pathetic,' Laura murmured.

'I suppose where they come from it's all done in the same room.'

'Yes, it is.'

'Pathetic,' Harold said in his turn.

'It makes me feel ashamed.'

'Oh, come now.'

'And wonder if we're doing the right thing – perhaps unsettling them for what they have to go back to.'

'My dear girl,' he said. 'Damn it, those people who organize these things know what they're doing.'

'I suppose so.'

'They've been doing it for years.'

'Yes, I know.'

'Well then . . .'

Suddenly she put down her knife and fork and rested her forehead in her hands.

'What's up, old thing?' Harold asked, with his mouth full.

'Only tired.'

'Well, they've dropped off all right. You can have a quiet evening.'

'I'm too tired to sit up straight any longer.' After a silence, lifting her face from her hands, she said, 'Thirteen more days! What shall I do with them all that time?'

'Take them for scrambles in the woods,' he began, sure that he had endless ideas.

'I tried. They won't walk a step. They both groaned and moaned so much that we turned back.'

'Well, they can play on the swing.'

'For how long, how *long*? They soon got tired of that. Anyhow, they quarrel about one having a longer turn than the other. In the end, I gave them the egg-timer.'

'That was a good idea.'

'They broke it.'

'Oh.'

'Please God, don't let it rain,' she said earnestly, staring out of the window. 'Not for the next fortnight, anyway.'

The next day, it rained from early morning. After breakfast, when Harold had gone off, Laura settled the boys at the dining-room table with a snakes-and-ladders board. As they had never played it, she had to draw up a chair herself, and join in. By some freakish chance, Benny threw one six after another, would, it seemed, never stop; and Sep's frustration and fury rose. He kept snatching the dice-cup away from Benny, peering into it, convinced of trickery. The game went badly for him and Laura, counting rapidly ahead, saw that he was due for the longest snake of all. His face was agonized, his dark hand, with its pale scars and scratches, hovered above the board; but he could not bring himself to draw the counter down the snake's horrid speckled length.

'I'll do it for you,' Laura said. He shuddered, and turned aside. Then he pushed his chair back from the table and lay, face-down on the floor, silent with grief.

'And it's not yet ten o'clock,' thought Laura, and was relieved to see Mrs Milner, the help, coming up the path under her umbrella. It was a mercy that it was her morning.

She finished off the game with Benny, and he won; but the true glory of victory had been taken from him by the vanquished, lying still and wounded on the hearth-rug. Laura was bright and cheerful about being beaten, trying to set an example; but she made no impression.

Presently, in exasperation, she asked, 'Don't you play games at school?'

There was no answer for a time, then Benny, knowing the question wasn't addressed to him, said, 'Yep, sometimes.'

'And what do you do if you lose?' Laura asked, glancing down at the hearth-rug. 'You can't win all the time.'

In a muffled voice, Sep at last said, 'I don't win *any* time. They won't let me win any time.'

'It's only luck.'

'No, they don't *let* me win. I just go and lie down and shut my eyes.'

'And are these our young visitors?' asked Mrs Milner, coming in with the vacuum-cleaner. Benny stared at her; Sep lifted his head from his sleeve for a brief look, and then returned to his sulking.

'What a nasty morning I've brought with me,' Mrs Milner said, after Laura had introduced them.

'You brought a nasty old morning all right,' Sep agreed, mumbling into his jersey.

'But,' she went on brightly, putting her hands into her overall pockets. 'I've also brought some lollies.'

Benny straightened his back in anticipation. Sep, peeping with one eye, stretched out an arm.

'That's if Madam says you may.'

'They call me "Laura".' It had been Harold's idea and Laura had foreseen this very difficulty.

Mrs Milner could not bring herself to say the name and she, too, could foresee awkwardnesses.

'No, Sep,' said Laura firmly. 'Either you get up properly and take it politely, or you go without.'

She wished that Benny hadn't at once scrambled to his feet and stood there at attention. Sep buried his head again and moaned. All the sufferings of his race were upon him at this moment.

Benny took his sweet and made a great appreciative fuss about it.

All the china had gone up a shelf or two, out of reach, Mrs Milner noted. It was like the old days, when Imogen's and Lalage's friends had come to tea.

'Now, there's a good lad,' she said, stepping over Sep, and plugging in the vacuum-cleaner.

'Is that your sister?' Benny asked Laura, when Mrs Milner had brought in the pudding, gone out again, and closed the door.

'No, Mrs Milner comes to help me with the housework – every Tuesday and Friday.'

'She must be a very kind old lady,' Benny said.

'Do you like that?' Laura asked Sep, who was pushing jelly into his spoon with his fingers.

'Yeah, I like this fine.'

He had suddenly cheered up. He did not mention the lolly, which Mrs Milner had put back in her pocket. All the rest of the morning, they had played excitedly with the telephone – one upstairs, in Laura's bedroom; the other downstairs, in the hall – chattering and shouting to one another, and running to Laura to come to listen.

That evening, Harold was home earlier than usual and could not wait to complain that he had tried all day to telephone.

'I know, dear,' Laura said. 'I should have stopped them, but it gave me a rest.'

'You'll be making a rod for everybody's back, if you let them do just what they like all the time.'

'It's for such a short while – well, relatively speaking – and they haven't got telephones at home, so the question doesn't arise.'

'But other people might want to ring you up.'

'So few ever do, it's not worth considering.'

'Well, someone did today. Helena Western.'

'What on earth for?'

'There's no need to look frightened. She wants you to take

the boys to tea.' Saying this, his voice was full of satisfaction, for he admired Helena's husband. Helena herself wrote what he referred to as 'clever-clever little novels'. He went on sarcastically, 'She saw you with them from the top of a bus, and asked me when I met her later in Blackwell's. She says she has absolutely *no* feelings about coloured people, as some of her friends apparently have.' He was speaking in Helena's way of stresses and breathings. 'In fact,' he ended, 'she rather goes out of her way to be extra pleasant to them.'

'So she does have feelings,' Laura said.

She was terrified at the idea of taking the children to tea with Helena. She always felt dull and overawed in her company, and was afraid that the boys would misbehave and get out of her control, and then Helena would put it all into a novel. Already she had put Harold in one; but, luckily, he had not recognized his own transformation from professor of archaeology to barrister. Her simple trick worked, as far as he was concerned. To Harold, that character, with his vaguely left-wing opinions and opinionated turns of phrase, his quelling manner to his wife, his very appearance, could have nothing to do with him, since he had never taken silk. Everyone else had recognized and known, and Laura, among them, knew they had.

'I'll ring her up,' she said; but she didn't stir from her chair, sat staring wearily in front of her, her hands on her knees – a very resigned old woman's attitude; Whistler's mother. 'I'm *too* old,' she thought. 'I'd be too old for my own grandchildren.' But she had never imagined *them* like the ones upstairs in bed. She had pictured biddable little children, like Lalage and Imogen.

'They're good at *night*,' she said to Harold, continuing her thoughts aloud. 'They lie there and talk quietly, *once* they're in bed. I wonder what they talk about. Us, perhaps.' It was an alarming idea.

In the night she woke and remembered that she had not telephoned Helena. 'I'll do it after breakfast,' she thought.

But she was still making toast when the telephone rang, and the boys left the table and raced to the hall ahead of her. Benny was first and, as he grabbed the receiver, Sep stood close by him, ready to shout some messages into the magical instrument. Laura hovered anxiously by, but Benny warned her off with staring eyes. 'Be polite,' she whispered imploringly.

'Yep, my name's Benny,' he was saying.

Then he listened with a look of rapture. It was his first real telephone conversation, and Sep was standing by, shivering with impatience and envy.

'Yep, that'll be O.K.,' said Benny, grinning. 'What day?'

Laura put out her hand, but he shrank back, clutching the receiver. 'I got the message,' he hissed at her. 'Yep, he's here,' he said, into the telephone. Sep smiled self-consciously and drew himself up as he took the receiver. 'Yeah, I am Septimus Alexander Smith.' He gave his high, bubbly chuckle. 'Sure I'll come there.' To prolong the conversation, he went on, 'Can my friend, Benny Reece come, too? Can Laura come?' Then he frowned, looking up at the ceiling, as if for inspiration. 'Can my father, Alexander Leroy Smith come?'

Laura made another darting movement.

'Well, no, he can't then,' Sep said, 'because he's dead.'

This doubled him up with mirth, and it was a long time before he could bring himself to say goodbye. When he had done so, he quickly put the receiver down.

'Someone asked me to tea,' he told Laura. 'I said, "Yeah, sure I come."'

'And me,' said Benny.

'Who was it?' Laura asked, although she knew.

'I don't know,' said Sep. 'I don't know *who* that was.'

When later and secretly, Laura telephoned Helena, Helena said, 'Aren't they simply *devastating* boys?'

'How did the tea-party go?' Harold asked.

They had all arrived back home together – he, from a meeting; Laura and the boys from Helena's.

'They were good,' Laura said, which was all that mattered. She drew them to her, one on either side. It was her movement of gratitude towards them. They had not let her down. They had played quietly at a fishing game with real water and magnetized tin fish, had eaten unfamiliar things, such as anchovy toast and brandy-snaps without any expression of alarm or revulsion: they had helped carry the tea things indoors from the lawn. Helena had been surprisingly clever with them. She made them laugh, as seldom Laura could. She struck the right note from the beginning. When Benny picked up sixpence from the gravelled path, she thanked him casually and put it in her pocket. Laura was grateful to her for that and proud that Benny ran away at once so unconcernedly. When Helena praised them for their good behaviour, Laura had blushed with pleasure, just as if they were her own children.

'She is really very nice,' Laura said later, thinking still of her successful afternoon with Helena.

'Yes, she talks too much, that's all.'

Harold was pleased with Laura for having got on well with his colleague's wife. It was so long since he had tried to urge Laura into academic circles, and for years he had given up trying. Now, sensing his pleasure, her own was enhanced.

'When we were coming away,' Laura said, 'Helena whispered to me, "Aren't they simply *dev*astating?"'

'You've exactly caught her tone.'

At that moment they heard from the garden, Benny also exactly catching her tone.

'Let's have the bat, there's a little pet,' he mimicked, trying to snatch the old tennis-racket from Sep.

'You sod off,' drawled Sep.

'Oh, my dear, you shake me rigid.'

Sep began his doubling-up-with-laughter routine; first, in silence, bowed over, lifting one leg then another up to his chest, stamping the ground. It was like the start of a tribal dance, Laura thought, watching him from the window; then the pace quickened, he skipped about, and laughed, with his head thrown back, and tears rolled down his face. Benny looked on, smirking a little, obviously proud that his wit should have had such an effect. Round and round went Sep, his loose limbs moving like pistons. 'Yeah, you shake me rigid,' he shouted. 'You shake me entirely rigid.' Benny, after hesitating, joined in. They circled the lawn, and disappeared into the shrubbery.

'She *did* say that. Helena,' Laura said, turning to Harold. 'When Benny was going on about something he'd done he said, "My dear, you shake me entirely rigid."' Then Laura added thoughtfully, 'I wonder if they are as good at imitating *us*, when they're lying up there in bed, talking.'

'A sobering thought,' said Harold, who could not believe he had any particular idiosyncrasies to be copied. 'Oh, God, someone's broken one of my sherds,' he suddenly cried, stooping to pick up two pieces of pottery from the floor. His agonized shout brought Sep to the french windows, and he stood there, bewildered.

As the pottery had been broken before, he hadn't bothered to pick it up, or confess. The day before, he had broken a whole cup and nothing had happened. Now this grown man was bowed over as if in pain, staring at the fragments in his hand. Sep crept back into the shrubbery.

The fortnight, miraculously, was passing. Laura could now say, 'This time next week.' She would do gardening, get her hair done, clean all the paint. Often, she wondered about the kind of homes the other children had gone to – those children she had glimpsed on the train; and she imagined them staying on farms, helping with the animals, looked after by buxom farmers'-wives – pale London children, growing gratifyingly brown, filling out, going home at last with roses in their cheeks. She could see no difference in Sep and Benny.

What they had really got from the holiday was one another. It touched her to see them going off into the shrubbery with arms about one another's shoulders, and to listen to their peaceful murmuring as they lay in bed, to hear their shared jokes. They quarrelled a great deal, over the tennis-racket or Harold's old cricket-bat, and Sep was constantly casting himself down on the grass and weeping, if he were out at cricket, or could not get Benny out.

It was he who would sit for hours with his eyes fixed on Laura's face while she read to him. Benny would wander restlessly about, waiting for the story to be finished. If he interrupted, Sep would put his hand imploringly on Laura's arm, silently willing her to continue.

Benny liked her to play the piano. It was the only time she was admired. They would dance gravely about the room, with their bottles of Coca-Cola, sucking through straws, choking, heads bobbing up and down. Once, at the end of a concert of nursery-rhymes, Laura played *God Save the Queen*, and Sep rushed at her, trying to shut the lid down on her hands. 'I don't like that,' he keened. 'My Mam don't like *God Save the Queen* neither. She say "God save *me*".'

'Get out,' said Benny, kicking him on the shin. 'You're shaking me entirely rigid.'

On the second Sunday, they decided that they must go to church. They had a sudden curiosity about it, and a yearning to sing hymns.

'Well, take them,' said liberal-minded and agnostic Harold to Laura.

But it was almost time to put the sirloin into the oven. 'We did sign that form,' she said in a low voice. 'To say we'd take them if they wanted to go.'

'Do you *really* want to go?' Harold asked, turning to the boys, who were wanting to go more and more as the discussion went on. 'Oh, God!' he groaned – inappropriately, Laura thought.

'What religion are you, anyway?' he asked them.

'I am a Christian,' Sep said with great dignity.

'Me, too,' said Benny.

'What time does it begin?' Harold asked, turning his back to Laura.

'At eleven o'clock.'

'Isn't there some kids' service they can go to on their own?'

'Not in August, I'm afraid.'

'Oh, God!' he said again.

Laura watched them setting out; rather overawed, the two boys; it was the first time they had been out alone with him.

She had a quiet morning in the kitchen. Not long after twelve o'clock they returned. The boys at once raced for the cricket-bat, and fought over it, while Harold poured himself out a glass of beer.

'How did it go?' asked Laura.

'Awful! Lord, I felt such a fool.'

'Did they misbehave, then?'

'Oh, no, they were perfectly good – except that for some reason Benny kept holding his nose. But I knew so many people there. And the Vicar shook hands with me afterwards and said, "We are especially glad to see *you*." The embarrassment!'

'It must have shaken you entirely rigid,' Laura said, smiling as she basted the beef. Harold looked at her as if for the first time in years. She so seldom tried to be amusing.

At lunch, she asked if the boys had enjoyed their morning.

'Church smelt nasty,' Benny said, making a face.

'Yeah,' agreed Sep. 'I prefer my own country. I prefer Christians.'

'Me, too,' Benny said. 'Give me Christians any day.'

'Has it been a success?' Laura asked Harold. 'For them, I mean.'

It was their last night – Sep's and Benny's – and she wondered if her feeling of being on the verge of tears was entirely from tiredness. For the past fortnight, she had reeled into bed, and slept without moving.

A success for *them*? She could not be quite sure; but it had been a success for her, and for Harold. In the evenings, they had so much to talk about, and Harold, basking in his popularity, had been genial and considerate.

Laura, the boys had treated as a piece of furniture, or a slave, and humbly she accepted her place in their minds. She was a woman who had never had any high opinions of herself.

'No more cricket,' she said. She had been made to play for hours – always wicket-keeper, running into the shrubs for lost balls while Sep and Benny rested full length on the grass.

'He has a lovely action,' she said to Harold one evening, watching Sep take his long run up to bowl. 'He might be a great athlete one day.'

'It couldn't happen,' Harold said. 'Don't you see, he has rickets?'

One of her children with rickets, she had thought, stricken.

Now, on this last evening, the children were in bed. She and Harold were sitting by the drawing-room window, talking about them. There was a sudden scampering along the landing and Laura said, 'It's only one of them going to the toilet.'

'The *what*?'

'They ticked me off for saying "lavatory",' she said placidly. 'Benny said it was a bad word.'

She loved to make Harold laugh, and several times lately she had managed to amuse him, with stories she had to recount.

'I shan't like saying good-bye,' she said awkwardly.

'No,' said Harold. He got up and walked about the room, examined his shelves of pottery fragments. 'It's been a lot of work for you, Laura.'

She looked away shyly. There had been almost a note of praise in his voice. 'Tomorrow,' she thought. 'I hope I don't cry.'

At the station, it was Benny who cried. All the morning he had talked about his mother, how she would be waiting for him at Paddington station. Laura kept their thoughts fixed on the near future.

Now they sat on a bench on the sunny platform, wearing their name-labels, holding bunches of wilting flowers, and Laura looked at her watch and wished the minutes away. As usual, she was too early. Then she saw Benny shut his eyes quickly, but not in time to stop two tears falling. She was surprised and dismayed. She began to talk brightly, but neither replied. Benny kept his head down, and Sep stared ahead. At last, to her relief, the signal fell, and soon the train came in. She handed them over to the escort, and they sat down in the compartment without a word. Benny gazed out of the further window, away from her, rebukingly; and Sep's face was expressionless.

As the train began to pull out, she stood waving and smiling; but they would not glance in her direction, though the escort was urging them to do so, and setting an example. When at last Laura moved away, her head and throat were aching, and she had such a sense of failure and fatigue that she hardly knew how to walk back to the car.

It was not Mrs Milner's morning, and the house was deadly quiet. Life, noise, laughter, bitter quarrelling had gone out of it. She picked up the cricket-bat from the lawn and went inside. She walked about, listlessly tidying things, putting them back in their places. Then fetched a damp cloth and sat down at the piano and wiped the sticky, dirty keys.

She was sitting there, staring in front of her, clasping the cloth in her lap, when Harold came in.

'I'm taking the afternoon off,' he said. 'Let's drive out to Minster Lovell for lunch.'

She looked at him in astonishment. On his way across the room to fetch his tobacco pouch, he let his hand rest on her shoulder for a moment.

'Don't fret,' he said. 'I think we've got them for life now.'

'Benny cried.'

'Extraordinary thing. Shall we make tracks?'

She stood up and closed the lid of the keyboard. 'It was awfully nice of you to come back, Harold.' She paused, thinking she might say more; but he was puffing away, lighting his pipe with a great fuss, as if he were not listening. 'Well, I'll go and get ready,' she said.

*

Slaves to the Mushroom

'*Overalls*, ladies!'

That was the signal for the work-force to peel off its rubber gloves, remove its protective clothing and down tools and hurry across to the new canteen, where the wearing of overalls was forbidden.

'And gentleman,' added the supervisor, catching the offended eye of Robbo, the only male worker who wore one of the firm's issue green and white gingham nylon smocks, his crinkly hair tied back in a matching checked bandeau.

The morning break lasted ten minutes and workers were faced with a choice of visiting the cloakroom or the canteen; the buildings were several hundred yards apart and although there might just be time to queue for a cup of tea, after a visit to the toilet there would not be time to drink it. Robbo and his friend Billy headed for the cloakroom, jumping over the trough of disinfectant that everybody was supposed to walk through on leaving the shed.

Some people had been working all night and were due to knock off for the day. Others had started their shifts at seven or eight o'clock, and the canteen served a good breakfast menu; toast, eggs, bacon, sausages, tinned tomatoes, fruit juice, tea and coffee. The workers sat at yellow formica-topped tables and flicked their cigarette ash into silver-foil ashtrays. Although the food was cheap, some workers, those Asian women for example who did not prefer to huddle in the cloakroom, brought their own food and thermos flasks.

Sylvia carried her tray over to the nearest table where a

group of people who had just started that week sat together and, finding herself opposite a black man with an artificial hand, saw an opportunity to tell the story of how, when hunting as a girl, a hound had bitten off her nipple. He was unimpressed, stirring his tea arrogantly with the spoon held in a sort of pincer.

'They're called dogs,' he said.

'Well, this was definitely a hound,' replied Sylvia huffily. 'I should know.'

The canteen was clean and warm; outside the aluminium-framed windows sleet was whipped about a dirty-looking sky. Spanish words and laughter from a table of black-haired women chalked up the most decibels and was rivalled by Urdu or some such from the large sari-ed contingent, who were bussed in by their own coach. Sylvia decided to forgive the man, and give him and his fellow newcomers a friendly word of warning. She lowered her voice.

'You have to watch those Asians,' she said. 'They take your mushrooms if you don't keep an eye on them. Lean right across the beds and grab all the best ones. Work in gangs, they do, go up and down cutting the big ones. No wonder they always get such big bonuses. We don't stand a chance. You've got to watch them.'

'How long have you been working here?' a girl asked.

'Fortnight pay day.'

The supervisors whistled up their teams and tea break was over. A drift of icing sugar lay over the leaves and a flash of February sun gilded the icy puddles in the gravel as they crunched back in their wellies to the sheds, throwing half-smoked cigarettes into the bin of sand outside the door.

Green Star Mushrooms Limited was a member of a large group of companies and supplied chains of pizza restaurants, stores and supermarkets as well as having numerous smaller outlets for its white cultured fungi. It consisted of an administration block, a building that housed generators and machinery, storage and packaging depots and six vast windowless sheds like aircraft hangars where the mushrooms grew. Each shed was divided into four sections, and each section housed four long bays, each in four tiers, like aluminium bunk beds packed with compost. To pick from the lowest bed, workers had to crouch on the floor; aluminium stepladders were used to reach the second and third levels, and the top bed was attained by a central flight of steps, and when all the pickers were installed up there, a section of the walkway was slid over the entrance and nobody could come down again until it was removed. A long polythene wind-tunnel was suspended just above their heads. Swinging about like monkeys was frowned on. The sheds seemed dark until you became accustomed to the electric light.

'Right. Everybody into number thirteen,' Shirley the supervisor called.

'Lucky for some,' said Robbo.

Sylvia stuck her number on the boxes and baskets she had picked and unhooked her ladder and tray and bucket and made for the door. She was dismayed to see the heaps and piles of boxes and baskets the Asians were staggering along with. That pretty little girl who had started on the same day as she smiled at her as she put down her pyramid. They had been friends for a morning until she had been enveloped in the silken cluster of her own kind, and now unless she smiled Sylvia could not recognize her. They all looked alike with their long black plaits down their backs, except those whose plaits were grey.

'Hello, Sheila,' said Sylvia, thinking again that it was a sensible English-sounding name.

'Hi, Sylvia,' said Shreela. 'How many pounds have you picked this morning?'

'Enough,' said Sylvia, standing on tiptoe to hoist her heavy bucket of stalks and broken mushrooms and compost and empty it into the huge polythene sack on a frame provided for waste. She could see who was going to get a bonus and who wasn't. Shirley and an assistant stood at the door weighing them and noting down each person's pickings.

*

No mushrooms were allowed to be taken from one room to another; neither was any equipment without first being sterilized. Stepladders had to be dunked into a vat of disinfectant, first one way up, and then the other, likewise trays and knives. The floor was awash with suds and stalks and bits of mushroom; there were men whose job it was to keep the floors clean, and to empty the rubbish sacks. Sylvia wondered what became of the stalks, wondered if they were utilized in some way. It seemed such a waste; surely they could be used to make packet soup or something; great vats of grey soup ladled out to the homeless and hungry. She had decided not to ask, since her enquiry as to what the compost was made of was met with the short answer 'shit'. It was better not to think about that; the crumbly dark compost smelled of mildew and nothing worse, but she imagined it was shovelled out from battery houses where chickens were kept in cruel and grotesque captivity; she had seen one once on a visit to a farm and the smell had been overpoweringly disgusting. The battery was not unlike this place, she thought.

'At least we've got room to turn around and flap our wings,' she remarked to the women waiting to dunk their ladders.

'Pardon?'

'Sylvia, you're dreaming again. Get on with it.' Shirley had materialized in her white official wellies. Sylvia's knife slipped from her fingers and fell to the bottom of the vat. She had to roll up her sleeve and plunge her arm in, but she couldn't reach the bottom. She panicked, flapping her wet arms about. This was total disaster. She didn't know whether to run away, out of the shed into the bleak countryside never to return, or to try to manage without her knife, but there was no way she could break the stalks off as neatly as she could cut them. She was elbowed out of the way and was making desperate bids to reach the knife, leaning right over the murky water until she almost fell in, her face scraping the surface. Someone grasped her ankles. Sylvia screamed, flailing about, certain that she was to be drowned. Then she felt the ground beneath her feet and turned to scream at her attacker. It was Dexter towering over her, grinning.

'Looking for something?'

She would have given him a piece of her mind but she saw Shirley approaching.

'My knife,' she gasped. 'I dropped it.'

Dexter reached down and effortlessly brought out the knife, his brown arm dripping dirty pearls. Sylvia could have kissed it. She scuttled off to number thirteen, her ladder with her rack hooked over it and a pile of boxes and baskets clanking behind her. She had been late clocking on, having to change into her wellies, and the only ladder left had been this rusty job with one wheel. Funny how she always got lumbered with the leftovers. As now, when she arrived in the shed, everybody else had nabbed the best places. She was confronted with a sparse sprinkling of tiny mushrooms in the only vacant bed.

'What are we picking?' she asked the woman next to her, who with her friend formed a deadly team. They had been there only as long as Sylvia but had already chalked up fat bonuses and were due to be promoted to Valerie's team of skilled pickers. Sylvia would have to wait the statutory six weeks before promotion and the rate she was going, might not achieve it even then.

'Down to 5p,' said the woman. Sylvia received the news glumly. It took her forever to fill a box with these hateful buttons. The closed mushrooms were categorized according to size – 5p, 10p and 50p, large and extra large. 'If we got five pence for each mushroom we picked, that would work out at more than £2.30 an hour, wouldn't it?'

Nobody answered.

'Fives into £2.30 goes – forty-six. So that's forty-six mushrooms per hour, I mean pence per mushroom we ought to get, isn't it, Marie?'

Again Marie didn't bother to answer Batty Sylvia, who went on happily with her calculations while her basket remained empty.

'Fifty pence per mushroom, now that would be, um, £2.30 divided by fifty equals, knock off the noughts and that's $4\frac{3}{5}$ per mushroom, we ought to get . . .'

'Something a bit wrong with your calculations, gel.'

It was that Dexter strutting along in his tight jeans like a cockerel in a yard of hens.

'Don't you gel me,' said Sylvia crossly, then she remembered he had retrieved her knife.

'Dexter! Sylvia! Get on with your work.'

Someone made a ribald noise.

Sylvia blushed. Having her name shouted out like that as if she was a naughty little girl in school, by a chit of a girl half her age. She bowed her head over the bed and started cutting mushrooms, but her heart was thudding as she saw Shirley approach.

'I dread it when I see those white wellies coming,' muttered Robbo who was working the opposite side of her bed, where she could see great clusters of fifty-pence mushrooms disappearing under his knife. Sylvia liked best the open mushrooms, big as saucers, big as elephant's ears: half a dozen of them filled a basket; they were more like the mushrooms she had found in the fields as a girl in the early morning or the evening with the rough grass silvered and wet with dew.

'What are these?' Shirley was shaking the box.

'My buttons,' said Sylvia.

'Why are they in a box? You know buttons go in a basket. Where are your ten pences?'

'Here,' Sylvia held out a green plastic box. A few mushrooms rolled about on the bottom.

'You've got your open and your closed mixed up. And they're supposed to be of uniform size. Get them sorted out, and get your act together.'

Act? Sylvia's back felt as if it was breaking, her knees creaked as she crouched. She lapsed on to her knees, feeling wet mud seep through her trousers. She picked until she had exhausted that bed and then unhooked her rack from the side of the bed, folded up her ladder and carried them, with her boxes and baskets to another bed. She had forgotten her numbers, a roll of sticky labels that had to be stuck on every box and basket that she picked, so that her quota could be assessed. She found them lying in a muddy pool. Everything was so mucky, the fingers of her rubber gloves were engrained with sticky black mould, her sleeve stinking of disinfectant, her wellies bleared, her overall had a wet dirty patch right across the stomach and there was a smear of compost on her cheek. Some people managed to look quite neat and composed at the end of the day; not Sylvia. She was wrecked by dinner time. If you didn't wear your rubber gloves your fingers were stained and your nails packed with black mould that a scrubbing brush could not remove. Like the supermarket trolley which inevitably Sylvia got, the one with the squeak and the wheels that went in the wrong direction, her ladder was unstable and her rack hung at a perilous angle, endangering her mushrooms. Pull, slice off the stalk, mushroom in box or basket, stalk in bucket, stoop, bend, up the ladder, stretch, pull, cut, down the ladder, empty bucket. Nobody was talking much today, except the Asian women who talked incessantly. It was amazing that anybody could have so much to say. To Sylvia's eye they moved like a flock of brightly coloured locusts leaving the beds bare behind them.

'It's not fair,' she complained to Shirley. 'They're picking all the mushrooms.'

'That's what they're paid to do.'

Talk about inverted prejudice.

Later, however, she was pleased to hear Shirley telling them off for indiscriminate picking, dropping everything into their baskets regardless of size, and appointing two of their number to sort them out. Downright cheating.

Getting her act together: Sylvia saw all the mushroom pickers in a Busby Berkeley-style sequence, turning their buckets upside down and beating them like drums, swarming up the aluminium supports like sailors in the rigging, kicking out their arms and legs starwise, their green and white gingham overalls twirling as they tap-danced in their wellies, juggling mushrooms and flashing knives, spreading out the pink palms of their rubber gloves as they fell on one knee behind Shirley, the star in her white wellies.

'Where's your radio, Sharon?' she called.

'Pardon?'

'I said, where's your wireless today?'

'I left it in the toilet.'

'Go and get it then.'

'I can't.'

'Go on.'

'You go and get it if you're so keen.'

Sylvia knew there was no way she could leave the shed. On her first morning she had heard someone who asked to go to the toilet told that she should have gone at tea break.

'"Radio Mercury, the heart of the South,"' she sang in compensation, and then,

> 'You and me, we sweat and strain
> Bodies all achin', racked with pain
> Tote dat barge, lift dat bale –
> Get a little drunk and you lands in jai-aal.'

Robbo joined in in a surprising bass voice, given the overall and bandeau, and then he and Billy dissolved into cackles. It wasn't that funny, thought Sylvia, but she was glad she had made them laugh. Sometimes this place was like a morgue with everyone silently picking, lost in their own thoughts and in the smell of mildew. Then Shirley came along and detailed Sylvia and a silent lad named Gary to clear one of the beds that had been picked. People were supposed to clear the beds as they went along, but this one was full of a debris of broken stalks and deformed mushrooms and frail thin toadstools, illegal immigrants who had sneaked in somehow. Gary didn't mind, he mooned through the day, pale as a mushroom, just achieving his quota and never thinking of a bonus, but Sylvia was seething on the top step of her rickety ladder as she grubbed out the leftovers, losing valuable picking time while others filled their baskets with mushrooms that should have been hers.

'What's for dinner, Stewart?' called Marie.

Stewart couldn't read or write but he always knew the menu off by heart.

'Sausage, beans and chips. Quiche and salad. Macaroni cheese. Fruit slice and custard or ice cream.' He spoke thickly as though his mouth was already crammed with bangers and beans.

Sylvia looked at her watch. It had drowned in the disinfectant and presented a bloated, dead face.

'Right, bring your mushrooms to be checked and go to dinner.'

The newcomers who had not yet been issued with gloves had to scrub their hands in the trough in the passage. Sylvia hurried past them, through the footbath and into the fresh freezing air, narrowly missing a forklift truck, and lighting a cigarette as she went and joined the queue in the canteen. Maintenance men and the other workers were already seated at some of the tables. She carried her tray over to an empty table where she was joined by Marie and her mate, Dexter, Stewart and Sharon.

'Ooooh, my back. It's killing me. When I took this job I'd no idea there'd be so much heavy lifting.'

'And carrying. And climbing.'

'What did you do before?' Marie asked Sylvia.

'Oh, all sorts of things. Shop work, bar work, kennel maid . . .'

'I'm surprised you wanted to work with dogs, after what that hound did to you.'

'Oh well, it didn't mean any harm. Just got overexcited.'

A guffaw of crude laughter greeted this. Sylvia concentrated on threading a piece of macaroni on each of the tines of her fork. She hated vulgarity, and besides the incident had not happened to her but to somebody else she had heard of.

'I was working in a Christmas-cracker factory up until a few weeks ago.'

'Why'd you give it up?'

'Oh, the novelty wore off.'

She might have added that she had a job in a balloon factory, but she blew it, and that she used to work in a pub until she was barred, she had been a postwoman but she got the sack, and that she had worked on a newspaper but it folded. That hadn't been her fault; she was just the tea lady. She had to work, Jack couldn't and she had to support them both. She didn't like leaving him alone all day, but it couldn't be helped.

'I picked fifty-eight pounds this morning,' she heard someone say. 'What did you do?'

'Fifty-three.'

You could buy mushrooms cheap, if you wanted, on Friday afternoons, but to do that would have meant Sylvia's missing the firm's minibus which dropped her at the top of her road. Anyway she hadn't felt like eating a mushroom since she started this job; even a mug of mushroom soup brought on a bout of nausea. She had had a narrow escape on her first morning. Shirley had come up to her and said, 'You're not eating mushrooms are you?'

'No, I'm chewing gum.'

'Well, you're not really supposed to eat in here at all.'

'Sorry.'

Phew. A few minutes before, she had been eating mushrooms, popping the little white buttons into her mouth as she worked, just as one eats strawberries when strawberry picking. Now the nasty monopods clodhopped through her dreams, and the smell of the compost was enough to turn her up. One old bloke, with one eye, did eat the mushrooms, but he was the only one, and she was sure Shirley turned a blind eye.

★

Just before the half-hour was up, Sylvia made a dash for the cloakroom. She didn't bother with make-up any more, or to comb her hair. Every pair of trousers she possessed was stained at the knees with brown marks that wouldn't wash out, and she was too tired to care. After her first day, her arms had been so stiff that she could hardly move them, her back felt as if it was broken and her legs felt as heavy as trees. She was getting used to it now, and managing quite well with just the fractured spine. As she emerged from the ladies' cloakroom she encountered Robbo and Billy coming giggling out of the gents'.

'What have you two been up to?' she asked in a friendly fashion, but they didn't answer. Nevertheless she was pleased to follow them because she had forgotten which shed they were in, and they all looked alike to her. There had been the awful time she had left her numbers in the canteen and had to gallop back to get them, only to find they had been put in the dinner waste, and she had had to rake through a refuse sack of banana skins and cigarette butts and slimy yoghurt cartons and half-eaten sandwiches to find them, and then she had run back to the wrong shed and wandered for what seemed like hours like a lost soul through all the wrong sheds opening doors on silent beds of ghostly mushrooms, and throbbing machinery and men hosing down the floors. She was crying when she finally found her team. She was supposed to be working on the top stage and the trap door had been shut, and people had had to move all their ladders and baskets and boxes to let her in, and of course all those people who worked in gangs and pairs had grabbed all the best places.

Half-way through the afternoon they had to change sheds again, so racks were unhooked, ladders folded and perilous pyramids of boxes and baskets carried to be weighed. Sylvia had done a bit better since lunch and was feeling quite pleased with herself as she dunked her stepladder in the disinfectant, first this way, then that. Sharon had brought her radio and the afternoon was passing quite pleasantly until Billy started teasing Stewart about living in a hostel.

'What sort of a hostel is it then?' he kept saying.

'It's for the handicapped,' Stewart said.

'Why d'you live there then, Stewart?'

'Leave him alone,' someone shouted.

'Pick on someone your own size,' suggested somebody else and everybody laughed. Billy was a slender five feet two, and Stewart was a lumbering six feet, bursting out of his cardigan. Then Billy started jostling Stewart and knocked a basket of his mushrooms to the floor. Stewart gave a howl as they rolled away in the mess of muddy compost and stalks and lunged at Billy with his knife. The man with the artificial arm leaped forward and seized the knife in a lightning pincer grasp. Stewart fell to his knees snuffling as he gathered up his dirty mushrooms, like precious jewels, and replaced them in his basket.

'It'd serve you right if I had an epileptic fit,' he told Billy.

'Robbo, Billy. Outside.' Shirley's white wellies had sped silently down the aisle. Robbo and Billy followed them out to the tune of 'Rat in the Kitchen' from Sharon's radio.

'They're for the chop,' said Dexter. 'Tippling on the job again.'

In the administrative block Robbo and Billy faced the boss in her white cap with the Green Star insignia. Robbo had removed his bandeau and his hair spread out on the shoulders of his green and white overall.

'By the way,' he said, 'remember when I cut myself with my knife?'

'You'd had your tetanus jabs,' interrupted Shirley.

'It bled quite a lot if you remember, all over the place . . . all over my mushrooms.'

'Well?'

'Well, I just wondered if I should have mentioned that I was AIDS positive . . .?'

He and Billy departed laughing to pick up their cards, leaving the two women to ponder the credibility and implications of his statement.

★

'Five o'clock people, pack up your things.'

As she carried her things to the door Sylvia saw little Sheila's silky trousers coming down the steps from the top bed. That was all she could see of her, so hung about with brimming baskets and piled with full green boxes was she. It was unbelievable. Sylvia had worked really hard, and Sheila's efforts made it look as though she hadn't tried at all.

'You've done well, Sheila,' said Sylvia. 'Let me give you a hand with some of those.'

She put down her own poor pickings and took some of Shreela's from her.

'Oh, thank you, Sylvia. If you just take these for me I'll go and get the rest.' The rest. Sylvia knelt quickly and peeled off Shreela's numbers from four of the boxes and stuck on her own. Then she piled them on top of her boxes and carried them to be weighed. She could see that Shirley was impressed as she wrote down the amount. Then she went back to help Shreela with the rest of her load. She joined the queue to wash the stepladder, wash the rack, stack them up, then dashed to the cloakroom for her coat. No time to change out of her wellies. The minibus was waiting. If Fred was driving, you were allowed to smoke; if the other Fred was driving, you weren't.

As the Green Star minibus snouted out into the lane Sylvia reflected that she would have lots to tell Jack when she got home – Billy and Robbo getting the chop, Dexter rescuing her knife, her bumper crop; and he would tell her all about his day, the tussle with a spray of millet, hard pecking on the cuttlefish, conversations with himself in the mirror. She wondered what to have for tea; whatever it was it wouldn't be mushrooms on toast. Behind them in the sheds, thousands of tiny white nodules no bigger than a pin's head starring the black compost were starting to swell.

CLARE BOYLAN

*

Some Retired Ladies on a Tour

'There's a man,' Alice said. 'She's with a man.' She scrubbed the bus window with a bunched-up brown stretch glove. May sat down heavily beside her, still probing a blasted peppermint. She leaned forward, her menthol breath ruining all Alice's work on the glass.

They could make him out through the window mist, a tall, pale figure, his garments worried by wind and rain. Mrs Nash was holding his hand. The thing that bothered them speechless was an aspect of his stance that was a confirmation of youth. They couldn't see him properly but he was definitely young. 'She's a nutting,' May said. 'She's nutting but thrash.'

It wasn't the first time they had talked about Mrs Nash. She turned up at the slide-illustrated lecture and told them all she had a stall at Birkenhead Market. It was a tour for retired ladies. She was the only one of them who hadn't retired although she was of an age for it. 'Mention my name and you'll get a cut,' she told them, to get pally.

Doris Moore had a laugh about that. Up to the summer she had been a manageress at Imperial Meats. 'Mention my name and you'll get a cut,' she said with a wink that pleated her turquoise eyeshadow like a quilt.

Forty years she had been with Imperial. When she left they gave her a set of cut sherry glasses. She put them out on the kitchen table at home and filled them each to the brim with whisky. Not a drop was spilled when she drank them. She was quite proud of that. Out of the blue she had a vision of her first day at Imperial. She was fourteen when she stepped through the metal doors and began a novice's jiggle against the chill. They were all looking at her bow-tied blouse that was the colour of red-currants. The men wore aprons covered with blood. The women, their noses blue under powder, wore mountains of jumpers and folded their arms over their wombs to protect any life that might be there. Not that many of them married. There was a habit that came with working in the cold, of not changing underwear every day.

By the time she was thirty, Doris realized that she hadn't bothered to look for a man. She had been too busy looking for jumpers. Her big achievement was learning to knit. She came to look on the cold as a constant; warmth and sunshine were interruptions. At the slide-illustrated lecture, she was the one who asked if the hotels had central heating. 'That's all right, then,' she said, when the man apologized for the fact that they had not.

She was the youngest of the ladies but retired all the same. At fifty she woke moaning with rheumatism. She developed a cough that wouldn't go away. At fifty-four she got pleurisy and the doctor ordered her to leave Imperial. After he had tapped on her chest she put back on her jumpers and sat in front of him crying. She couldn't go and work in an office or a shop, not with the central heating. He helped her to get a disability pension. She managed with that and the home knitting, which wasn't taxed. It was quite nice, really. She began to do up her face and to wear fancy knits.

Alice and May had latched up with Doris from the start. They all took a drink and could enjoy a laugh. Doris was something of a star. She had discovered quite late a talent for making people laugh out loud. It was her appearance of not giving a damn. Few people realized that deep down she really didn't give a damn.

She sat in a seat in front of Alice and May. She had actually seen Mrs Nash and her man before the others but she didn't let on. She didn't want to watch Alice's glove fretting him into sharp relief. She preferred looking at him through the condensation on the window, thinking his beige outline like a young Alan Ladd; thinking the way he held on to Mrs Nash was more like a blind person than a beau; thinking that of all of them he was most of an age with her. She watched until they started to move towards the bus and then she tossed her head back so that the tassel on her purple knitted hat boxed May playfully on the cheek. 'Mention her name and you'll get a cut,' she said loud enough for the whole bus to hear because she knew that everyone had been looking. When Mrs Nash stepped on to the bus the retired ladies were all laughing. She laughed delightedly with them and then trailed off, uncertain, because they stopped laughing quite abruptly.

They were looking at the man. Unless your taste was in your mouth you'd have to admit he was handsome, Doris said later. He was about forty-five with light curly hair and a boyish, diffident smile. The ones who were most aware of him glared huffily and looked away. The motherly ones smiled to make him at ease. Mrs Nash could see they were admiring him. She grinned proudly under her green Crimplene turban. 'She has a nice smile,' Alice said, easily wooed by a show of good cheer. May clicked on her mint reprovingly. Mrs Nash held up the man's hand as if he was a winner in a boxing match or else an item for auction. 'This is Joe,' she said. 'He's my son.'

The drive was a disappointment. They had expected the driver to be a comedian who would take them all on, call them darling, sing over the microphone so they could join in and jolly up the shy ones. Instead there was a snivelling young pup who got his thrills speeding around corners and wouldn't stop to let them go to the toilet. By the time they got to the first resort the outgoing ones were bored and bad-tempered. The eldest ladies were purple and rigid with misery.

He pushed them out of the bus and disappeared into a pub. They found themselves teetering on the edge of a cliff and stood there shivering, staring down at the sand that curved in a thin ribbon around the base, yellow in the twilight, like custard poured on a pudding. 'Bloody hell, where's our hotel?'

carped May. 'Across the road, you daft old toad,' Doris
guffawed, her sharp eyes picking out the 'Cliff Palace' as
specified in the brochure, although the description they had
been given did not tally with the outward appearance of the
hotel, which looked fat and pink and putrefied.

The younger ones marched across the road with loud com-
plaints and laughter, purposefully heading for the bar. The
older ones shuffled and scuttled and snuffled and grumbled.
Mrs Nash looked hopefully at the first batch and guiltily at the
second. She and Joe walked to the hotel alone, holding on to
each other.

At reception there was a bit of commotion that made them
forget all about the dismal journey. Mrs Nash was having a
row with the receptionist. There'd been a mistake, she said.
Her son had been put in a separate bedroom.

The blotched young woman behind the desk pressed her
fingers on the edge of the wood in desperation and clung on
with her thumbs. A man in a suit came down the stairs and the
girl gave him an imploring look. 'She wants to sleep with her
son,' she blurted, making it sound much worse than the young
couples that came in the season. The manager looked at the
agitated sea of post-sexual female flesh, at the shrivelled face
under the potty green hat. Christ. He couldn't have cared less
if she wanted to sleep with a Marmoset monkey. He wondered
about the bloke though.

He sidled warily past the grannies and crouched beside the
girl at reception, his closeness making fresh blotches on her
complexion. 'They can have thirty-seven,' he said, with a glance
at the book. He took a key from a hook on the wall and held it
out to Mrs Nash on his little finger. She took it with a grateful
smile but Doris Moore had noticed his sneer. 'Any notion of
rooms for us or are you going to make us sleep on our feet like
blasted horses?' she said, loudly and rudely, causing a titter
among the ladies. Doris had the knack all right. 'Not until
you've had your oats, dear,' said the manager, quick as you like,
and those who understood shrieked with delight.

Dinner was very nice. There was a lovely mushroom soup followed by roast turkey and a choice of trifle or bread and butter pudding with cheese as an extra. Alice was finished first and she took her cup of tea into the residents' lounge because she wanted a seat by the fire. As she left she had the impression of something dark scuttling behind her like a spider. She turned to find herself gazing at the green turban. 'A drink! You've got to have a drink,' Mrs Nash said, grinning triumphantly as if it was a forfeit. Joe, behind her, seemed a transparent creature, a daddy-long-legs, but her cordiality was echoed in his smile. Alice knew what May would think but her mouth was watering for a gin and orange. 'All right, then, while I'm waiting for my friend,' she said.

'Friends are very nice,' Mrs Nash said, when she was settled into the fire, sucking her port. 'I haven't got many friends. Account of Joe.' 'Oh, yes?' Alice said with a kindly look at Joe who seemed miles distant from them, smiling at the flames and taking sips at his glass of lager. Alice was having a very nice time. The drink was a large and she was going to be the one who would tell the others about Mrs Nash and her man.

On his way to work, Joe had fallen down with a clot, Mrs Nash told Alice. He was brought home in a bread van and she remembered noting a stack of coconut cream sponges and having a silly urge to buy one for when he came to. A clot, the doctor said, which was working its way to his brain. You couldn't tell when it would strike. Next time he'd be a goner. She ought not to let him out of her sight.

She had watched him asleep on the sofa. His feet were up on the olive green Dralon that she was paying off at nine pounds a month. It was the sofa that reminded her Joe was the only thing that had ever actually belonged to her. She wasn't about to let him go to a clot. The clot wouldn't dare strike while she was around.

Alice fished a slice of orange out of her empty glass and severed the flesh from the rind slickly with her false teeth. She was planning how she would tell May that you could never judge on the face of things. She didn't have long to wait. As she tipped the glass on her tongue to catch the tantalizing residual taste of alcoholic boiled sweeties, May stormed in, making demolition noises as she crunched on her peppermints in a rage.

'I hope I'm not interrupting something,' she said savagely. Alice didn't know where to put herself. 'I told Mrs Nash I was waiting for you,' she entreated. 'She's been telling me about her son.' She could only hope the implications would sink in and have a soothing effect. May was too hopping mad to hear. There was malice in the way she munched on her mints. Mrs Nash pawed gently at the sleeve of the fawn woollen cardigan that covered her son. 'Is it time you went to the lav?' she said. Joe returned from his dreams without any perceptible change to his expression. He drained his lager and stood up, holding hands with his mother. 'We're going to the toilet,' he smiled at the ladies.

Doris, who had just come into the lounge with the stragglers, couldn't restrain herself. 'Enjoy yourselves,' she called out. When the two of them were gone Doris went into a fit of indrawn croaks that in a girl would have passed for giggles. 'He winked at me,' she squawked when the fit had subsided. Alice couldn't tell if he had or not but she was cross with Doris for taking the good out of what she had to say and May's sulk was making her edgy.

'Don't be silly,' she snapped. 'That was just a reflex – like a chicken running about when its head's been cut off.'

Doris was off again, creaking like a wheelbarrow left out in the rain. 'That's right,' she said. 'Cut off his head. Cut off everything while you're at it. Mention her name and you'll get a . . .' And the residents' lounge was filled with exhausted titters.

There was no getting any good out of her when she was in that sort of mood. Alice went and switched on the television and sat in silence through half of a film about Vikings. Most of the ladies had gone to bed by ten. A few of them fell asleep in

soft armchairs, which was a problem for management to deal
with. Mrs Nash and Joe did not return at all. When Alice and
May had the fire to themselves Alice lashed out on two gins
and settled down to trade her latest piece of intelligence for a
return to her friend's favour. 'I've got news for you,' she said.
'Concerning what?' May said, moodily. 'Concerning Mrs Nash
and her son,' Alice wheedled.

May drained her glass in a gulp, screwing up her face against
the sting. She snatched her white PVC handbag, which seemed
to be writhing in some private torment on the arm of her chair
as the firelight explored its folds. 'Listen to nutting she says,'
she hissed, before marching off, leaving Alice alone with the
task of forgiving everybody.

For those who could remember or to whom it concerned,
the beginning of the holiday was like the first days at boarding
school. Things got better with each day that passed. The
ladies formed into gaggling groups and saved places at table for
their special friends. The bad bits turned into laughing matters.
They made jokes about the brat of a bus driver and the three
days spent in a boarding house in Cornwall that was run by a
widower. At breakfast they came down to plates of cold prunes
and custard. After dinging the pristine plastic façade of chilly
vanilla sauce with their spoons one or two of the ladies chewed
on the fruit, which had not been properly soaked, before
sliding a ragged brown mess out under cover of a paper napkin
and immersing it as best they could beneath the custard. Next
morning the prunes and custard were back again. They could
tell it was yesterday's breakfast because of the breaks in the
custard.

When the same brown and yellow preparation came up as a
proper pudding on day five in a different location, Doris Moore
whispered across the tables, 'He sent them on,' and the dining
room shivered with mirth. The waitress, who had legs the
colour and shape of sausages of salami, couldn't for the life of
her see that prunes and custard were a laughing matter.

In the evenings there were concerts. Alice, who used to do a turn in amateur dramatics, recited a monologue entitled *If I was a lady, but then I'm not*. Most of the ladies sang a song, which was a sort of exquisite agony. They knotted their fingers in their laps and became marble-eyed with nostalgia. Their voices sailed up at the light bulb, as fragile and dreary as moths. A Mrs Dunbarr accompanied on the piano. That was the nice thing about seaside hotels, always a piano. For her role as concert pianist, Mrs Dunbarr brought a black moiré gown with batwing sleeves that flowed and billowed over her brittle mauve fingers as they plundered the keys for Old Favourites.

Mrs Nash had a repertoire of love songs which she sang to her son, gazing into his face as if he was Nelson blooming Eddy. The real surprise was Joe. You couldn't get him to speak, never mind sing. But he responded to his mother's serenade with a song about a fellow in love with two girls, rocking back and forth, as earnest as a schoolboy. There was a line that went: 'One is my mother, God bless her, I love her.' He would pause and purse his nicely-made lips to kiss the crumpled pink sponge clumsily parcelled in green. Nothing could come up to that. The ladies clapped until their fingers pained them. Joe, strained by the excitement would crown it by announcing to all that they were going to the toilet. 'Enjoy yourselves,' the ladies called, made bold by Doris Moore and their alcoholic treats, sluiced with lime or lemon or orange.

Aside from that, nobody took much notice of Mrs Nash. She didn't seem to fit. She courted Alice at a distance with gin and orange sent via the waitress. Alice was torn. You couldn't budge May, though. That blasted, savage gnashing of peppermints when her back was up was not a thing you could ignore.

By the end of the week, just when Alice was beginning to enjoy herself, she found she was also getting homesick. For two nights she had slept in a room with a curiously shaped alcove that prevented the bed from fitting flush with the wall. The bed head was missing and her pillows fell off in the middle of the night, which woke her up. She lay alert in the dawn, heartbroken for the weight of her cats on her feet and the mingled smells of mould and ivy that were the breath of the house where she had lived from birth. She found herself worrying about Doris Moore.

You could go off Doris, she discovered. No longer tired and frightened, the ladies lacked incentive for communal mirth and Doris looked for new means of drawing attention to herself. She went on and on about Joe. He winked at her. He got her in a corner and told her she was his type. He no longer looked at his mother when he sang his song, but at her. May thought it was a joke, a laugh at the lad. Alice found it got her goat, even though she didn't say as much. She could only consider the mental betrayal of her friend as a flaw in herself and it gnawed at her in the small hours, a pain as sharp as wind.

It was the second last day of the holiday. Alice was up at seven, tormented by the bed and her nagging conscience. She allowed herself a cardigan under her woolly dressing-gown and shuffled to the window in slippers to watch the sun come up. She didn't find it poetic. She was too old. Alice didn't like the violent orange globe that thrust out of the sea. The ocean ought to be the colour of an army blanket, not pink or blue like paraffin. She dressed as slowly as possible, adding a brooch to the bodice of her frock, some peculiar purplish rouge to her cheeks. Time dawdled along with her. It was only half past seven when she went down to annoy the staff for breakfast.

The first thing to hit her in the eye when she entered the dining room was the green hat. After the relief at not being first down, there came the pleasurable anticipation of forbidden fruit. She hurried to join the lone diners. 'Joe and me likes an early breakfast,' said Mrs Nash through mouthfuls of fried bread and bacon. 'We're not too gone on all them others,' she confided. 'You're all right though.' She embraced Alice with a loving glance and added affectionately: 'You're looking desperate.' Alice told her about the faulty bed and her lack of sleep, though not about Doris Moore, which was just as well because Doris sashayed through the swing doors just then, togged out to the teeth in maroon angora.

'Enjoying the worms?' she said in a preoccupied fashion, all eyes for Joe. Alice looked at her doubtfully. 'It's rashers,' Mrs Nash said, giving no quarter. She shrugged impatiently and sat down, snatching up the menu in an ill-tempered fashion. Joe glanced at her several times and began to titter. 'I get it,' he whispered. 'The early bird catches the worm.' 'You're soft,' she said in a gently mocking way that was not like her.

Mrs Nash and Alice were deep in conversation. Alice was beginning to think of her as a buddy. At her age she couldn't afford to be class conscious. When she got back home she might give May the bullet. Mrs Nash made much of her, made her feel like somebody. She wanted to give Alice her bed-head and was promising to bring it around in the night. Alice, feeling the holiday needed a climax, said she would have a noggin of gin in the room so they could have a party – a midnight feast. She felt a twinge of guilt at not having included Doris but she needn't have worried. There was no trace of umbrage in the cracked moon face framed with fluffy wine-coloured wool. The silly thing was in a world of her own, muttering and creaking, making a perfect fool of herself with Joe Nash.

Doris hadn't got anything in particular in mind, though like Alice, she felt the holiday hadn't reached its peak. There was drinking during the day. They could afford to lash out with the holiday almost at an end. She was a bit tiddly that night when she went to bed at eleven. Undressing proved a difficult business so she hung up the maroon angora, patting it with her hand on the hanger, and left it at that. She fell asleep thinking of Joe; his nice hair, his admiring eyes, knowing full well it was the only way to have a man, where you wouldn't have to come face to face with his resentments.

At twelve she was awake again, pitched into alertness by a hellish noise that came from the end of the corridor – a scraping and rattling loud enough to wake the dead. Doris sat up, allowing the freezing air to invade the pinhole ventilations in her wool vest. The first twinge of rheumatism brought her

back to earth. She swung out of bed, cursing, groped in the
dark for a hairy grey dressing-gown and roped herself into it.
In the middle of knotting the cord she was taken with a fit of
laughing. It dawned on her; it was Mrs Nash and her blooming
bed-head.

She tiptoed to the door and opened it a crack. Mrs Nash was
in the corridor, dragging her burden as valiant as an ant. Doris
had to stuff a hand over her mouth. She thought she would die.
Over a lavishly flower-printed pair of pyjamas, Mrs Nash had
on the green hat. A bloody sheikh!

When the shuffling and scraping receded, Doris let herself
out into the corridor, shutting the door without a sound. If
anyone should see her she was on her way to the toilet.
Actually she was going to visit Joe. In fifty-four years she had
not been kissed – not properly – by a man. It would make the
holiday. She wouldn't tell May and Alice and them. They
would say 'Be your age!' When she got home she would ask
round the girls from the factory, break open a bottle and give
them all a laugh.

She knew the room. She tapped at the door and walked
straight in. 'Joe,' she called, not able to see in the dark. She felt
between two single beds for a locker and switched on the lamp
that was there.

Joe was curled up in his blankets like a child, fast asleep,
worlds away. She touched his hair with her fingers, a curious,
damp, disturbing feel. 'Joe!' He opened his eyes and looked at
her in alarm, immediately turning his gaze to the bed that had
become his mother's by occupation. 'Your Mam's gone to see
Alice,' she explained. 'I thought I'd come and keep you company.'

'I was asleep,' he said. 'Mother gave me a pill.' Doris was
disappointed with his reaction and her bare feet were frozen
solid. 'Hey, why are you latched on to her all the time?' she
said. Her voice came out a bit sharp. 'Are you cold?' he asked
her. 'Bloody frozen.' She dabbled her toes on the hurtful, shiny
floorcover.

He threw back a portion of bed-covers, showing himself respectably covered in nice striped pyjamas. 'You better get in.' Doris gave him her hard-bitten grin. She didn't want more on her plate than she could handle but there was nothing in his approach to suggest anything underhand. She undid her dressing-gown and laid it on his mother's bed before clambering into the small, warm space beside him.

He was leaning on his elbow, not quite sitting or lying, and smiling at her. She couldn't think of a damn thing to say. His hand rested lightly on her waist, a soft, woolly hump of flesh. She was wary but as far as she could tell there was no harm in it. He took his hand from her hip and touched her lips, pressing them with a finger as if to kill an insect. He kissed her; patted her mouth with lips as warm and soft as bath towels. Doris relaxed. She sighed with relish. Romance was something, by heck it was.

They lay in silence, not speaking, just touching enough to warm one another. From the corner of her eye she saw it coming but alarm was too far from her mind to be summoned. Something reared up and launched itself at her like a dervish. 'Joe!' she cried, as if calling to him for help.

Joe had pinned her down with his bones. His tongue went into her mouth. He ran his hands over her body, under her vest and bloomers, going to places that weren't allowed. His foraging hands found her breasts, warm round cotton cannonballs.

As soon as his mouth was off hers, Doris dug her fingers into his hair and wrenched back his head. 'Here you! What the hell do you think you're at?' she hissed, not wanting to shout and wake up the whole hotel. He waited until her shuddering lessened and began arranging the peroxide curls on her forehead. 'You mustn't mind me,' he said gently. 'I'm a bad boy. That's why my Mam sticks with me.' He was smiling in that pleasing, diffident way but she was too close to him to be fooled. Even in the dim light she could see that his eyes were cold as lumps of haddock. Doris summoned up her old self and slapped on a smile. 'You're a fast operator, you are,' she said. 'I'm not that sort of girl, you know. I only came in here to get warm.' She could see his face misting over again, that suffusion of sex that made him look like the living dead. Bloody hell! The last thing to do was remind him of herself. She took a deep breath. 'Your Mam seems a good sort,' she said. 'I'd say she's a most unusual woman. You know, the way she stays with you, thick and thin.'

'The doctor said she had to,' he said pleasantly.

She rumpled his irresistible curls and began to feel capable again. 'Poor old Joe,' she cooed. 'Not well, are you?'

'Haven't you heard?' he said. 'My mother tells everyone. A clot that's working its way to my brain? I could drop down dead any minute.' His fingers reached for the sympathy of her breasts. Doris didn't care for that but she felt she had an advantage now and could handle him. 'Well you'll have to cut this class of caper for a start,' she said lightly. 'You could wreck your health.'

She attempted to remove his hands but he thrust her away and was kneading her greedily. His breathing had gone funny again and Doris could feel her heart trying to escape from beneath the monstrous hands that were squeezing private parts of her body as if they were lumps of wet washing. He began to laugh. She could feel his pleasure in her fright. 'My Mam's a liar,' he said. 'There was never a clot. There was a body.'

Doris tried to think about her maroon dress, so sad on its hanger, like a little woolly beast put outside the door for the night. She drove her mind into the chill closets of Imperial. Nothing could stop the chill that was growing inside her, strangling her guts, and threatening to stop her heart, feeding the pleasure of this strange man perched so incongruously on her stomach.

He kept rubbing himself on her. She felt he was sharpening himself to do her an injury. He was giggling. 'The judge sent me up for five years for treatment. Doctor didn't want to let

me out. He didn't think it was safe. My Mam swore she'd
never let me out of her sight if they let me go. And the woman
was dead. There was no bringing her back.'

Doris began to scream. The scream came from deep inside
her, a place that was not obedient to her mind, so that even
though her brain knew it was better to die than have the
whole hotel gallivanting in to find you in bed with a man, her
lungs sent out foghorn signals of fright. The manager was first
to arrive. Mrs Nash scuttled past him with her green hat
askew in a nest of pins and hair as grey and rusty as an old
Brillo. Her little black eyes darted about like insects. Splat! She
clapped hands with authority. Doris's mouth slammed shut.
The monster glided off her and cringed against his pillows. He
looked about anxiously. The green hat was a beacon. He
searched beneath it and found what he was looking for. The
minuscule mouth, like a rubber band on a bunch of flowers,
stretched up and up in a smile. By the light of a boarding-
house bulb, Joe's returning smile, gluey with tears, was that of
a four-year-old.

The whole bus was there to witness the reconciliation, the
driver leering like a gorilla as Doris Moore slid out of bed and
buried her shameful body in the grey dressing-gown. When
Doris had brazened it as far as the door Mrs Nash turned and
grinned at the retired ladies in a most menacing fashion.
'Nightie-night, now,' she said cheerily. They fled.

Early in the morning she left with Joe. They went home all
the way in a taxi. They got no breakfast. The ladies knew that
because those who couldn't sleep for excitement came down
breathless and bleary at seven. They were shunted off back to
bed like children on Christmas morning. 'Jesus save me from
geriatrics,' said one frowzy scullion to another in full hearing of
the ladies. 'Leaping from bed to bed in the night, down at six
with their daft sons for taxis to Liverpool and banging about
for breakfast at seven. Roll on the summer couples with more
on their minds than breakfast!'

Doris Moore had more on her mind than breakfast. The

coach had been revving a full five minutes and those with bad memories of the outward trip were wanting to go back and spend a penny when she appeared at the hotel entrance. She was wearing her purple, that she had on the first day. She was a big woman. Two heavy suitcases dangled from her hands like balloons.

She set down the cases and spent a long time smoothing her knitted gloves. The leaden day hung on her for colour. The wind whipped her blonde curls about in a flirty manner like scraps of paper in the street. Her woolly fingers retrieved her luggage and she stepped out briskly. When she boarded the bus the ladies jostled for a look, feeling nervous and foolish as if she was the queen. She pretended to be hell-bent on finding a seat. Her cherry-coloured lips drooped. Alice wanted to make a space for her. She attempted to move her heavy coat and her paper carrier bag of gifts and mementoes which were on the seat in front but May's hand shot out to restrain her. 'Don't you lift a hand for that hussy,' she threatened. 'Don't do nutting for the likes of her.'

Doris jerked her chin up and glared at May. Her eyes were glittering. Behind the sullen mask there was a look of triumph to them. She was lording it over them as a woman of experience.

She sat in the place that was saved for Alice's bag in spite of May. After hefting her own cases on to the overhead rack she shoved Alice's things to one side and shimmied her large knitted shape into the seat in an insolent fashion.

The bus was paralysed into quiet. When the vehicle whistled around corners the ladies rattled from side to side, uncomplaining. No one rustled a mag., sucked on their teeth, rendered down a peppermint. 'Well, you never can tell,' was what Doris said when their waiting was over. Everyone looked at their laps in order to ignore her properly. Doris speculated upon her knitted fingers with a rueful sneer. 'He seemed a nice enough lad, I mean.' The ladies looked out of the windows, observing Doris only through cracks in their conscience. 'People like him

should be locked up for their own good. Stark, staring, raving
. . .' She succeeded in luring a few watery eyes from under
fragile shells. She sighed, genuinely perturbed. She could tell
what they were thinking; that if such things had to happen it
was better that they should happen to little silly seventeen-
year-olds who really couldn't be expected to know better. She
snorted. 'He killed a woman once. He could've done me in.'
Doris's face burrowed into her gloves. She had unwittingly
revived the demons of the night. She was fed up. It occurred to
her that after all there wasn't much to tell. She wanted things
to be like they were at the start, with her as the star and
everyone in top form enjoying her jokes and getting in the
mood for a drink when they stopped for lunch. All she had
done was to make them miserable and herself look a prize
blooming fool into the bargain.

She started to sing. 'Show me the way to go home –' a stern
hymnal beat, voice like a vacuum cleaner. 'I'm tired and I want
to go to bed . . .' From nowhere, another voice – a *man's* voice.
The ladies' faces twitched towards the driver in unison, eyes
wide with astonishment. His virile tones surged through the
bus like central heating. He took his eyes off the road to leer
round at Doris. 'Come on, darling,' he encouraged, beckoning
with a hand. Doris shimmied up the aisle, singing loudly,
clapping her hands in time. She sat beside the driver, boldly
taking the microphone from its stand and pressing the switch.
'WEEE-WON'T go home 'til morning,' she led off afresh
with deafening volume, grinning coarsely into the knowing
features of the youth.

Alice's feet began to move. She couldn't help it. They
always got a life of their own when there was music. She
hadn't realized that she was actually singing until May's white
handbag rocketed into her ribs. By then it was too late. The
whole busload had been infected. A frail, chalky choir of
celebration, hermetically sealed into the luxury bus, pledged
that it wouldn't go home 'til morning.

Home. The word died on her lips with such suddenness that

it left a picture. It was her little house with its smells of mould and ivy, its two cats which received with democratic indifference her argument or endearment; and rising now like thick brown soup to soak up these familiar images and even the sounds of merriment on the bus, its silence. 'I don't want to go home,' Alice thought in a panic. 'I'm lonely.'

She tried to remind herself of the price people pay for companionship; the dreadful shame of Mrs Nash's secret, Doris Moore's damaged reputation. 'It's a bargain!' was all she could think. But she pulled herself together very quickly and sang out. 'We won't go home 'til morning!'

And so say all of us.

MARGARET DRABBLE

✱

Hassan's Tower

'*If,*' she said, 'I could be *sure* they were free, then I would eat them.'

'They must be free,' he said, 'when you look at the price of the drink.'

'But supposing, just *supposing,*' she said, 'they turned out to be as ludicrously expensive as the drink? If you can pay twelve shillings for one gin and tonic, just *think* what you might have to pay for those.'

He was silenced, for he too had been thinking this thought, though unwilling to admit it to her, unwilling to display before her the full extents of his mercenary fear; and he was annoyed with her for voicing it, for in her such thoughts were merely niceties, whereas to him they were daily bread. He stared glumly at the little squares of toast, with their sadly appetising decorations of sardine, shrimp, and olive, and wondered how much, in the fantastic and unreal financial system which he had entered, they could possibly cost. What, he wondered, was the absolute ceiling for each of those squares? Five shillings? Ludicrous, ludicrous, but alas surely not impossible? Seven and six? Now seven and six was truly impossible. By no stretch even of the Moroccan five-star imagination could they possibly cost seven and six each. So if she were to eat them all (and be assured that she would eat them all, if any, her appetite being as it now appeared insatiable), that would cost him over three pounds. But what was three pounds, after all, amongst friends? Or between bride and bridegroom, rather? Nothing, it would appear. To his continuing amazement, even he thought that it was nothing. Although, of course, so much too much for the article. And then, of course, there was the chance, the probability, that they might be free, thrown in, as it were, with the shocking price of the gins. It would be a shame to leave them, if they were free. But then again, if they weren't free, and she ate them, and then set off towards the lift and the hotel bedroom on the assumption of non-payment, what would happen then? Would the barman in his foolish fez nip deftly out from behind his bar and pursue him? Or would the cost be added, discreetly, amongst the price of sundries on their anyway colossal hotel bill? Really, he was caught by inexperience between two brands of meanness: he hated to leave them if they were free, and he hated equally to eat them if they cost more than they ought. And he was, moreover, irritated by her luxurious, gratuitous hesitations: what had he married her for, but to decide about such things?

He reached out and took one, then pushed the little plate over to her. She took one, to his annoyance, independently, almost absent-mindedly, showing no gratitude for his decisive action, her face blank as though her mind had left his trifling crisis far behind. As indeed, when she spoke, he found that she had.

'I do so *wish*,' she said, in her quietly strident, heavily over-inflected tones, 'that you wouldn't get in such a panic when people try to sell you things. I mean, that man in that souk place this afternoon. There was no need to get so worked up about it, surely?'

'What do you mean, worked up?'

'Well, there was no need to *shout* at him, was there?'

'I didn't shout,' he said. 'I hardly raised my voice. And anyway, if you don't shout, they go on pestering.'

'You should ignore them,' she said.

'How can I ignore them, when they're hanging on to my coat sleeve?'

'Well then,' she said, changing her tack, 'why don't you just laugh? That's what other people do, they just laugh.'

'How do you know they laugh?'

'Because I see them. That French couple we saw in Marrakesh, with all those children pestering them, they were just laughing.'

'I don't find it funny,' he said. 'I wish they'd just leave me alone, so I could look at things in peace.'

'They don't mean any harm,' she said. 'They're just trying it on.'

'Well, I wish they wouldn't try it on me.'

'What you would like,' she said, 'is a country without any people in it. With just places. And hotels.'

'Nonsense,' he said. 'I don't mind people, I just wish they'd stop trying to sell me things I don't want. I just want to be left alone.'

'I find them all quite amusing,' she said, with a determined little lift of her chin: and he hated her for saying it, because he knew they didn't amuse her at all. On the contrary, they scared the life out of her, all these foreign jugglers and mountebanks, these silent hooded robed men, and the only reason why she did not like him to shout at them was that she was afraid he would provoke some reciprocal violence or offence. She wanted him to laugh in order to placate them: she was so nervous that if left to herself she would buy their horrible objects, their ill-stitched toy camels, their horrid little woolly caps, their rings set with fake, crude-faceted stones. And yet if he were to buy them she would despise him for it, as she would have despised him had he left, through fear of ignorance, the shrimps and the olives. It was just like her, to accuse him of her own fears; yet there had been a time, surely, when they might have in some way shared their alarms, and a time not so far distant at that. Even during their long and grinding engagement there had been moments of unison, moments when he could sneer at her family and she mock at his with some forgiveness, but in the last two weeks, since their wedding, their antagonism, so basic, so predictable, had found time to flower and blossom, and their honeymoon had been little more than a deliberate cultivation of its ominous growth. He had hoped that in leaving England they would have left behind some of their more evident differences, differences that should be of no importance in a foreign setting, but instead they had found themselves steadily isolated in a world of true British conflict, where his ways and hers had become monstrously exaggerated, as though they were on show, a true British couple, for all of Morocco to observe. Things which he had been able to tolerate in her at home, and which he had seen merely as part of her background, now seemed part of the girl herself: and similarly, in himself, he could feel his own defects magnified beyond all proportion, his behaviour distorted by foreign pressures into a mockery of itself. He began to see some reason for leaving sex until the honeymoon, for at least its problems would have diverted him from other more gloomy forebodings. It was a mistake to come to Morocco, but where else could they have gone, in their position, with so much money, and in so cold a month?

It was the money, truly, that created the worst of their problems, and it was Morocco that cast so nasty a shade upon the money. He knew quite well that were he not earning what he himself daily considered to be a truly astonishingly high salary, he would never have dared to marry a girl with so much money of her own, because of what people might say: and thus between them, she with a small inherited fortune, and he with money earned by the sweat of his brow writing idle articles for a paper, they were really rather well off. And the subject of their finances was an endless source of bitterness. Both suffered from guilt, but hers was inherited, his acquired: when he attacked her for hers, he could not but see how much more guilty he himself was, for he had had a choice. It was no defence to say that he had not sought the money but the job itself, for there were certainly less lucrative branches of journalism than the one into which he had, however respectably and innocently, drifted. He must have wanted it, just as he had wanted her, although, like the money, she had so many

connotations which he despised. But in England the money
had at least seemed necessary as well as wickedly desirable: all
her friends had it, all his friends, being clever, were beginning
to acquire it, and in fact he sometimes found himself wondering
how his own parents had so dismally failed to have it. Here in
Morocco, however, things were very different. To begin with,
every penny they spent was pure unnecessity (although he had
hopes of recovering a little on the tax by writing a judicious
article). Nobody saw them spending it, and the conditions of
expense he found sickening in the extreme. He had not bar-
gained for such poverty and squalor, and the rift between rich
and poor, between hotel and medina, made his head split in
efforts of comprehension. As a student, years ago, he had
travelled in a different style, and almost as far afield as this: he
had been to Tangier, with a few pounds in his pocket, suffering
from appalling stomach disorders, hunger, filth, and painful
blisters, and he had sat in dirty cafés with seedy expatriates,
staring at the glamour of more elegant tourists, and desiring
their beds and their meals, and yet at the same time confident
that he was happy, and that they were not capable of seeing, as
he had seen, the city rising white in the morning out of the sea,
in the odourless distance, and all the more beautiful for the
cramped and stinking night. In those days he had been permitted to see, and because he now could not see, was it not logical
to suppose that the money had ruined his vision?

The truth was that perhaps in those old days he had been
able to pretend that he too was poor, as these Arabs were poor,
and he had seen that their life was possible. He had not winced
at the sight of their homes, and nobody had thought it worth
while to pester him with toy camels and fake rubies. But now,
on this painful honeymoon, every time he went out of the
hotel a boy at the door would leap jabbering at him, jabbering
about his shoes, and could he clean the gentleman's shoes, and
please could he clean the gentleman's shoes, and he could speak
English, for listen, he could sing the songs of the Beatles. He
lay there in wait, this boy, and every time Kenneth ventured

through the great revolving doors — and they even swung the doors for him, they wouldn't allow him the pleasure of revolving his own exit — this wretched, grinning, monkey-faced, hardly human creature would pounce on him. He was unbelievably servile, and yet at the same time increasingly brazen: when Kenneth had declined for the tenth time to have his shoes cleaned, the boy had pointed out that in fact his shoes *needed* cleaning, and that they were a disgrace to any respectable, hotel-dwelling tourist. And Kenneth, gazing at his own feet, could not but admit that his shoes were dirty, as they usually were, for he disliked cleaning them, he disliked the smell of polish, he disliked getting his hands dirty. And yet he could not let this hatefully leering, intimately derisive child do them, for it was not in him to stand while another pair of hands dirtied themselves for money on his behalf. So that each time he entered or departed from the hotel, the boy at the door would chant some little jingle in French about the English miser with muddy shoes, and Chloe would stiffen coldly by his side.

He looked at her now, as she sat there, sipping her gin, and eating idly the pricy small squares: her face, as ever, was plain in repose, a little blank and grim, and the fatigue of sightseeing let the coarse dullness of her skin show through her make-up. He was continually amazed by how plain she really was, how featureless, for when he had first known her she had seemed to him beautiful, exotic, and obviously to be admired; now, knowing her better, he could see that it was animation only that lent her a certain feverish grace. The grace was real enough, but more rarely bestowed on him. When still, she was nothing, and her face, which had once dazzled and frightened him, now merely touched him. One day, months ago, at the beginning of their engagement, she had shown him in a moment of confidence a photograph of herself as a schoolgirl, and the sight of her stolid, blank, fat face, peering miserably at the camera from amongst her smaller-featured, more evidently acceptable school friends had filled him with despair, for she

appeared to him for the first time as pathetic, and if there was
anything he hated it was the onslaughts of pathos. But by then
it was too late, and he was no more able to refuse the
temptations of pity than he had been able, earlier, to refuse
those of an envious admiration. More and more, as his first
clear impressions of her dissolved into a confusing blur of
complications, he found himself harking back to what others
had said of her, as though their estimate of her value must be
more just, as though it could not be possible that he should
have married such a woman through a sense of obligation.
Others found her beautiful, so beautiful she must be, and it
was his fault only if he had ceased to see it.

When she had finished the gin, and all but one of the little
squares (he could not even to himself call them canapés, so
deeply did the word offend his sense of style, but then there
was no word in his background for such an object, for in his
background such objects did not exist, so what was one to call
them but canapés?) she leant back in her chair, letting her
headsquare fall to the ground, and not even acknowledging it
when a hovering uniformed boy handed it back to her. She
looked tired, and the gin had affected her; she had a weak head.
He was not surprised when she said,

'Let's have dinner here in the hotel tonight, I haven't the
strength to go out again. Let's have dinner in their panoramic
restaurant, shall we?'

And he agreed, relieved that he would not have to pass once
more that day the grinning familiar bootboy, and they went up
to their room and changed, and then they went up to the vast
glassy restaurant on the top floor, and looked out over the city
as they silently ate, and she complained about her steak, and
he got annoyed when the head waiter came and wrenched from
him his orange, saying that he would prepare it, as though a
man could not peel his own orange (and in fact he disliked
peeling oranges, almost as much as he disliked cleaning his own
shoes, he disliked the juice in his fingernails, and the pith that
he was obliged through laziness to devour) and she got annoyed

with him for getting annoyed with the head waiter, and they silently left the restaurant and went silently to bed, disturbed only by the uncontrollable whine of the air-conditioning, which neither of them had been able to subdue. In Marrakesh, oranges had hung upon the trees by the roadside, and thudded warmly from time to time at their feet, and the walls and buildings had been orange too, and beautiful against the distant icy snows of the Atlas mountains, where lions walk, but not beautiful to him, and they had quarrelled there, quarrelled bitterly, because they could not find the Bahia Palace, and because he would not take – not trusting them – a guide, and because they had both been frightened of the mobbing children.

In the morning they went to Rabat. They did not particularly want to go to Rabat, but it was necessary to go somewhere, and they had heard that Rabat was worth a visit. When they got there, they did not know what to see, so they looked at the tediously modern-looking palace, and wondered at the vast numbers of local sightseers, until they bought a paper and discovered, though imperfectly, that there was some day of national holiday in progress. They sat in a French café, and looked at the paper, and wondered where to have lunch, and he thought once more that money, instead of enlarging prospects, confined them and made choice pointless. There seemed to be an expensive enough restaurant called after something called the Tower of Hassan, so they went and had lunch there and he was foolishly taken in yet again by the charm of the idea of eating horrible semolina, which remained horrible however cooked, and then they wondered what to do next, and she said:

'Well, let's go and see Hassan's tower.'

'Do you really want to go and see Hassan's tower?' he asked irritably. 'You know what it'll be like, just some crumbly great incomprehensible lump of brickwork, crawling with guides and postcard sellers and pickpockets. And on a festival too. It'll be even more horrid than usual.'

'It might be nice,' she said. 'You never know, it might be nice.' Though he could see that she took his point, and that she too quailed.

'It won't be nice,' he said, 'and anyway we'll never find it.'

'It must be on the map,' she said, and produced from her handbag the little chart which the hotel had given her, on which all the streets were misnamed, and which was so badly drawn that it was impossible to follow. And it was not on the map.

'Oh Lord,' she said, 'if we just drive around a little we're sure to see it. I mean to say, it must be *important*, or it wouldn't have restaurants named after it.'

'That's what you said about the Bahia Palace,' he said.

'But this is different,' she said. 'It's a tower. It must, well, it must kind of stick up. One ought to be able to see it over the *top* of things.'

'What do you expect me to do, then?' he asked. 'Just get in the car and drive around until I see something that might be the Tower of Hassan? Eh?'

This, it turned out, was just what she did expect, so, with a suspension of disbelief, of much the same order as when he would embark, at home, so continually to drive through the London rush hour, he got into the car and they started to drive around looking for a tower. Driving was hazardous, because he had not grasped the principle that those making right-hand turns have the right of way, and consequently his estimate of the Moroccan character could not but be lowered by his experiences at junctions. However, somewhat to his surprise, they did very shortly locate something that could only be the tower after which their restaurant had been named, and so they parked the car and got out to look at it. It was, as he had foretold, incomprehensible: a square red block, decorated in some system which they did not understand, and baffling in its solid lack of beauty.

'Well,' she said, after they had stared at it in silence for some time from the safety of the road, 'I suppose it must be very old.'

'It looks old,' he conceded.

'There must be a good view from the top,' she ventured. 'Look, there are people on top.'

And there were, indeed, people on top.

'We could go up,' was the next thing she said.

'What?' he exclaimed, with a violence that was only half assumed. 'What? All the way up that thing? And I bet there isn't even a lift. I'm not climbing all the way up there just to get my pocket picked. And I bet it'd cost us a fortune even to get in.'

She did not answer, but wandered slowly forward on to the short scrubby turf of the surrounding open space. He followed her, watching her movements with a grudging pleasure: she was wearing a navy wool skirt and jersey, and in the bright light they had a heavy absorbent matt dull warmth that curiously suited her skin. On the turf, she stopped, without turning to him, and said,

'I should like to go up.'

'Nonsense,' he said, but he followed her to the foot of the tower, nonetheless. He knew that she had made her mind up, and he was too alarmed by the country to let her go alone, and also ashamed that she, though afraid, had the bravado to continue. It annoyed him to know that although she was wholly impelled by timidity, her actions would belie her motives: she would climb the tower, though trembling in every limb through fear of rape, whereas he, alone, and afraid only for his pocket and his sensibilities, would probably not venture.

There was no lift, and no doorkeeper or entrance fee either: access was free. She stepped first out of the sunlight and into the gloom of the doorway: there was just a broad, square, mounting path, without steps.

'Come on,' she said.

'It'll be a long way,' he said, 'and probably smelly.'

'I don't mind the smells,' she said. 'If you wait for me here, I'll go up by myself. I want to see what it's like.'

'There won't be anything to see,' he said, but he started to follow her just the same, being genuinely unable to let her go alone; and moreover, having got so far, there was something irresistible about the idea of ascent. So, with a sense of humiliating risk, he began to climb. They had made several turns of the tower, and had already risen a good few yards above ground level, before he became nervously aware that none of the other people either ascending or descending were tourists: they were all Arabs, and there was not a guide-book in sight. It was worse than he had expected. He closed his hand tightly in his pocket over his passport and his wad of traveller's cheques, and wondered whether he should draw Chloe's attention to the situation, but she was a yard or two ahead of him, walking slowly and evenly, and not apparently suffering from the breathlessness that threatened him. So, not wishing to make himself conspicuous by calling out in his foreign tongue, he was obliged to follow. None of the Arabs so far, it was fair to say, seemed to be paying him much attention, and nobody had so much as offered him a packet of postcards, so he relaxed a little, as much as the rigour of climbing would allow, and concentrated on watching the glimpses of gradually increasing panorama through the arrow slits on each side of the wall. He wondered if there might, after all, be a view from the top. There were certainly enough people coming and going, and they must be coming and going for something, he assumed: they all seemed to be in a happy holiday mood. He began, gradually, to feel pleased that there had been no lift, no rich man's way up, no European approach. His pleasure was marred at one point by sudden panic, as he heard above and ahead of him a great deal of high-pitched screaming: he looked anxiously for Chloe, but she was out of sight, round the next bend, and he started to run up the absurdly high incline after her when the source of the screaming hurled itself harmlessly down the tower, and proved to be nothing but a group of very small children, who had climbed to the top simply in order to run breathlessly and hilariously down. Down they rushed, banging

into people as they came, losing their footing, falling, rolling, scrambling up again, to be met by amused indulgence
from the ascending adults. The men shook their heads and
smiled, the women laughed behind their veils. It was clearly
a well-established pastime, such usage of Hassan's tower, and
welcomed in the dearth of parks, fairs and playgrounds.

When he reached the top, the sudden glare of the sun
dazzled him, and he could not at first see Chloe. She was
standing at one corner of the wide square block, gazing out
over the estuary towards the sea: the view was, as she had
foreseen, breathtaking. In silence they stared at it, and he
thought that it was very beautiful but somehow depressing
because totally, totally unimportant, and pointless in a way
that beautiful landscapes somehow are, and yet there was
Chloe staring at it in exaggerated affected passion as though it
mattered, as though it meant something, staring in fact as he
had stared at early-morning Tangier ten years ago, and after a
moment or two he could stand the sight of her rapture no
longer, and he went and sat down on one of the stone parapets,
his knees weak from the climb, his breath short, and his spirits
unbelievably low from some dreadful bleak sightless premoni-
tion of middle age. And as he sat there, it seemed to him that
what he felt for her was something quite dangerously near to
dislike: he disliked her hypocrisy, her affectations of bravery
and transport, her nervous gestures of well-born vivacity, and
all the unsuspecting ignorances of her class. And the thought of
disliking his bride, and in such a lovely place, and upon his
honeymoon, and in the cool moodless light of his maturity,
was too depressing to be borne. He could not bear it. Erect,
unstooping, he could not bear it. And yet it was this that he
was beginning, at that moment, to bear.

He sat there, quietly, and he watched his mind trying
to heave up this stony problem, this weight of suffering,
these solid years. At first it could get no leverage; it could
not edge itself beneath so much as a corner. But he was not
a man to give in; he was a self-made man, a man self-bred to

determination. And after a while, he forced himself to say to himself: she is not affected, she is not hypocritical, she is quite possibly as sincerely stirred by a stretch of glittering water and a few white houses as I myself was, in those other days. I was sincere then, and why should not she be now? I had no monopoly of sincerity. She is younger than me, and she enjoys things that I no longer enjoy: it is to her credit that she climbed this tower, to her credit that she makes an effort not to be frightened of the snake charmers. Other girls do not make such an effort; other girls do not aim even their hypocrisies in such admirable directions. These things are to her credit. I absolve her of hypocrisy.

And there, panting and sweating a little from the strain of justice, he for a few moments stayed. So much he had shouldered; so much, indeed, was true.

When he had accustomed himself to taking this, he went on. He said: it is unjust for me to reproach her for her class, to feel her suspicions, to notice things that she cannot by her inheritance notice. She does not notice when servants pick up her gloves and hand her her bag and hold open doors before her, because she was bred not to notice them. But her nature pays attention, although her past does not. And there is some distinction, some small distinction. And it was for her nature that I married her, and not for her past — and if it was for her past, and for her parents, and for her voice and clothes and certainty, then I myself am culpable, I myself am to blame, for espousing those things that are in her. It cannot be true that I married such things, because I remember that what I felt for her was love, and it was because we loved each other that I married her, and not for any other reason. I loved her passionately once, before we were married, before we were engaged, and that is as much and more than some people ever love anyone. So far as love goes, I have not missed out completely. It is unfortunate that it does not last, but it is generally held that it does not last, and at least I felt it once, I had my share. I am no worse off than a man who is forced to admit, after ten years of marriage, that he no longer loves his wife. So far as love goes, I have not done too badly. I have finished with love, just as I have finished with scenery. But I know something of it, and I must try not to resent its absence in me, nor its presence in others, just as I must try not to resent and envy her superior joy, her more rejoicing eye.

She said once that I did not enjoy life much, and God knows perhaps she was right.

It appears, he said to himself, that love is a thing that does not last for very long, and that my marriage will have to get along without it.

And having, finally, come to that, he found that he had heaved the whole thing on to his back, and that he was braced, like snowy Atlas, to bear it. It was weighty, but it was certainly not intolerable. He breathed, he lived. And he would continue to do so. He had married the wrong woman (or so, he thought, he might put it to himself, if the phrase did not falsely presuppose a right one) but he would not therefore cease to live. He could not have said that he was happy, but he could concede that at some distant time the pleasure of success-ful labour and heroically prolonged weight-lifting might be transformed into something like happiness: not the happiness of innocence, of passion, or of violence, but a kind of happiness nevertheless. And the sensation which came from the stiffening of the moral fibre, while not perhaps as appropriate to a honeymoon as the stiffening of other fibres, was not without its satisfactions. He felt that in future he would expect less from life, and suffer it more; he would expect less of Chloe, and await no more revelations. He hoped that she would bear with him with equal resolution. Resolution had once seemed to him but a poor substitute for desire, but now he felt that he would be grateful if they could achieve it, and that it might, through familiarity, prove to have a beauty of its own.

Though beauty was a dangerous concept, he was resolved to expect little in the way of beauty.

After he had delivered to himself this final warning, he

seemed to have finished with the subject. He could think of no more to think, so he stopped thinking. His knees were no longer wobbling, his breath had regulated itself, and his eyes had grown accustomed to the glare and the light. He wondered if he should have presented his mental efforts to himself in terms of accent, and not in terms of support; on the whole he thought not, because it was after all not a view that he had gained, but a burden. Chloe was his burden: a small eight-stone navy-blue cashmere burden. He looked after her, but she was still gazing resolutely away from him; either her rapture or her disaffection was long-lived. In galleries, she had an annoying habit of staring for hours at one painting, and she would take all afternoon to go round an exhibition. He could never imagine what thoughts she managed to think on such occasions. When he asked her, she would lecture him on the poverty of his visual responses, so he no longer asked her.

In one hand she held a bunch of marigolds that she had picked in the morning on the way, and some eucalyptus leaves that a small boy had thrust through the car window. The orange flowers looked pretty on the dark wool, like a coloured picture in a child's book. And Chloe was pretty, after all, at the very worst pretty, and Morocco had its charms, and not for nothing did flowers grow and the sun shine in the winter. It was cold comfort, but the sun was after all faintly hot. It seemed to be coming from a long way off, through a great deal of clear and frozen air, but it was reaching him. He stretched out his legs, and rolled up the sleeves of his jersey, and began, idly to look round.

The more he looked, the more he realized that the people on top of the tower were in their own way as astonishing a view as the more evidently panoramic vistas. The whole of the top of the tower was thick and covered with people: small children were crawling about, mothers were feeding babies, young men were holding the hands of girls and indeed the hands of other young men, boys were sitting on the very edge and dangling their feet into space, and old women who would need a day to recover from the climb were lying back in the sun, for all the world as though they were grandmothers on a beach in England. And a beach in England was what the scene most of all resembled; he saw there the very groups and attitudes that he had seen years ago as a child at Mablethorpe, and as he gazed he felt growing within him a sense of extraordinary familiarity that was in its own way a kind of illumination, for he saw all these foreign people keenly lit with a visionary gleam of meaning, as startling and breathtaking in its own way as Tangier had once been. He saw these people, quite suddenly, for what they were, for people, for nothing but or other than people; their clothes filled out with bodies, their faces took on expression, their relations became dazzlingly clear, as though the details of their strangeness had dropped away, as though the terms of common humanity (always before credited in principle, but never before perceived) had become facts before his eyes. It was as though he had for a few moments seen through the smoky blur of fear that convinces people that all foreigners are alike, and had focused beyond it upon the true features and distinctions of separate life: there they stood, all of them, alive and separate as people on a London street, brothers and sisters, cousins, the maiden aunt with the two small children, the pretty fast girl with nylons under her long gown and a lipsticked mouth under her pale-green lace veil, the fat woman with her many operations, the student with his Arabic Dostoevsky. Even their garments, hitherto indistinguishably strange, took upon themselves distinctions, and from their bodies and in their faces humanity spoke with one and many voices. They were many and various, and because they were many and various they were one, and he was admitted. And it seemed to him that it was not he himself that was for the first time seeing, but rather that perception had descended upon him, like a gift, like a sign, like a bird. He could see: he wanted to cry out that he could see, and that five minutes earlier he had resigned himself to blindness. And the vision before him now was of a promise and a hope far fuller than any of the passions of his youth, because it was no longer a lonely knowledge: it had a hundred different faces. The world was not empty, as he had feared, nor had he come to the end of what was interesting in it, and the romantic solitary clinch of wedlock was nothing, nothing, compared with all these other people, these children, these mothers, these nieces, uncles, grandmothers, doctors, carpenters, politicians, idiots, waiters, cobblers and pavement artists. Ten years ago he could surely not have told the one from the other, and now he began to know, he began to tell, and even when the brightness of illumination faded he knew that he would be left with at least the faith and grounds of knowledge. And he felt, watching these people, a most simple pleasure and delight, and he was on holiday in their holiday, and he wondered how he could ever have imagined that they might pick his pocket. That they might well have picked his pocket was irrelevant: he should not have imagined such a thing. And as he watched them, he suddenly became aware that one of the young men at whom he was staring was none other than the bootboy from the hotel. And he stared at the bootboy, and the bootboy stared at him, and their eyes met with recognition, but with no acknowledgement: neither of them smiled, neither of them moved, for there was no way, in that place, of expressing their mutual degradations. Such a past they, in their common and equal courtesy, consented to ignore. And he saw, too, that the bootboy was with a small woman who was his mother, and that by one hand he held his little brother, who was wearing a best red shiny holiday shirt, and who was about four years old.

Elizabeth Bowen

*

The Visitor

Roger was awakened early that morning by the unfamiliar sound of trees in the Miss Emerys' garden. It was these that had made the room so dark the previous evening, obscuring the familiar town lights that shone against the wall above his bed at home, making him feel distant and magnificently isolated in the Miss Emerys' spare-room. Now, as the sky grew pale with sunless morning, the ceiling was very faintly netted over with shadows, and when the sun washed momentarily over the garden these shadows became distinct and powerful, obstructive; and Roger felt as though he were a young calf being driven to market netted down in a cart. He rolled over on his back luxuriously, and lay imagining this.

But the imagination-game palled upon him earlier than usual, defeated by his returning consciousness of the room. Here was he alone, enisled with tragedy. The thing had crouched beside his bed all night; he had been conscious of it through the thin texture of his dreams. He reached out again now, timidly, irresistibly to touch it, and found that it had slipped away, withdrawn into ambush, leaving with him nothing of itself, scarcely even a memory.

He had never slept before in anybody's spare-room; theirs at home had been wonderful to him: a port, an archway, an impersonal room with no smell, nothing of its own but furniture; infinitely modifiable by the personality of brushes and sponge-bags, the attitude of shoe-trees, the gesture of a sprawling dress across a chair.

The Miss Emerys' spare-room had long serious curtains that

hung down ungirt beside the window, fluted into shadows. One never touched the curtains; if one wanted to make the room dark, one drew a blind that had a lace edge and was stamped all over with a pattern of oak-leaves. Miss Emery, when she brought Roger up to bed last night, tried to do this, laid one hand on the acorn of the blind-cord, but Roger prayed her to desist and she desisted. She understood that no one liked to see the sky from bed. She was a sympathetic woman, and made Roger increasingly sorry for all the things he used to think about her blouses.

The furniture was all made of yellow wood, so shiny and one knew so yielding, that one longed to stab and dint it. There were woollen mats that Miss Dora Emery had made – she had even promised to teach Roger. She had promised this last night, while Roger sat beside her in a drawing-room that positively rocked and shimmered in a blinding glare of gaslight. A half-finished rug lay across her knee and rolled and slid noiselessly on the floor when she moved; the woolly, half-animate thing filled Roger with a vague repulsion. 'I'm doing the black border now,' she had explained, tweaking the clipped strands through the canvas with a crochet hook and knotting them with a flick of her wrist. 'Soon I'll be coming to the green part, the pattern, and I shall work in some touches of vermilion. You really must watch then, Roger, it will be so pretty, you'll really be amused.' Roger wondered if she would have come to the vermilion, even to the green, by the time his mother died. Miss Emery was not a quick worker. 'How much more black will there be before the pattern?' he inquired. 'Three inches,' said Miss Emery, and he measured out the distance with his finger.

There were paintings on the spare-room wall of moors with Scotch cattle, and over the chest of drawers there was a smaller picture in a green-and-gold frame called 'Enfin – Seuls.' French. It depicted a lady and gentleman holding each other close and kissing in a drawing-room full of palms; they seemed to be glad of something. The paper had a pattern on it, although Roger's father and mother had said that patterned wall-papers were atrocious. Roger looked at it, and jumped with his mind from clump to clump – they were like islands of daisies – pretending he was a frog who had been given a chance of just eight jumps to get away from a dragon.

A clock ticked out in the passage; it must be a very big one, perhaps a stationmaster's clock, given the Miss Emerys by a relation. It had no expression in its voice; it neither urged one on nor restrained one, simply commented quite impartially upon the flight of time. Sixty of these ticks went to make a minute, neither more nor less than sixty, and the hands of the clock would be pointing to an hour and a minute when they came to tell Roger what he was expecting to hear. Round and round they were moving, waiting for that hour to come. Roger was flooded by a desire to look at the face of the clock, and still hearing no one stirring in the house he crept across to the door, opened it a crack, quite noiselessly, and looking down the passage saw that the clock had exactly the same expression, or absence of expression, as he had imagined. Beyond the clock, a rich curtain of crimson velvet hung over the archway to the stairs, and a door painted pale blue stood open a little, showing the bathroom floor.

Roger had never believed that the Miss Emerys or any of the people he and his mother visited really went on existing after one had said good-bye to them and turned one's back. He had never expressed this disbelief to his mother, but he took it to be an understood thing, shared between them. He knew, of course, with his *brain*, that the Miss Emerys (as all the other people in the roads round them) went on like their clocks, round and round, talking and eating and washing and saying their prayers; but he didn't *believe* it. They were, rather, all rolled up swiftly and silently after one's departure and put away for another occasion, and if one could jump round suddenly, taking God by surprise, one would certainly find them gone. If one met a Miss Emery on one's walks, one assumed she must have sprung up somewhere just out of sight, like a mushroom, and that after one had passed her, nothingness would swing down to hide her like a curtain. Roger *knew* that all the doors round the Miss Emerys' landing opened on to rooms, or would do so if he walked through them when he was expected. But if he opened a door when he was not expected, would there be anything beyond it but the emptiness and lightness of the sky? Perhaps even the sky would not be there. He remembered the fairy tale of Curdie.

The spare-room opened off a very private little corridor that had no other door along it but the bathroom's. The Miss Emerys could not fully have realized the charm of this, or they would have taken the room for their own. Roger had an imaginary house that, when it was quite complete in his mind, he was some day going to live in: in this there were a hundred corridors raying off from a fountain in the centre; at the end of each there was a room looking out into a private garden. The walls of the gardens were so high and smooth that no one could climb over into anybody else's. When they wanted to meet, they would come and bathe together in the fountain. One of the rooms was for his mother, another for his friend Paul. There were ninety-seven still unappropriated, and now it seemed there would be ninety-eight.

Somebody in a room below pulled a blind up with a rush, and began to sweep a carpet. Day was beginning in a new house.

The Miss Emerys' breakfast-room was lovely. By the window, they had a canary in a cage, that sprang from perch to perch with a wiry, even sound. Outside, the little early-morning wind had died; the trees were silent, their leaves very still. Since there was no sun this morning, the breakfast table held without competition all the brightness, to radiate it out into the room. No sun could have been rounder or more luminous than the brass kettle genially ridiculous upon a tripod, a blue flame trembling beneath it. There were dahlias, pink and crimson, and marmalade in a glass pot shaped like a barrel cast a shadow of gold on the table-cloth. There was a monstrous tea-cosy, its frill peaked intelligently; and Miss Emery smiled at Roger over the top of it. There were parrots printed on the cosy – they battled with one another – so brilliant one could almost hear them screech. Could a world hold death that held that cosy? Miss Emery had pinned a plaid bow-tie into the front of her collar. Could she have done this if what Roger expected must soon happen to Roger? Must it happen, mightn't it be a dream?

'Come in, dear,' said Miss Emery, while he revolved this on the threshold, and Miss Dora Emery, who had not come to help him to dress (perhaps she was not allowed to), forced a lump of sugar quickly between the bars of the canary's cage, and came round the table to greet him. Roger eyed her cheek uncertainly; it was pink as a peach, and against the light its curve showed downy: he wondered what was expected of him. They eyed one another with a fleeting embarrassment, then Miss Dora jerked away a chair from the table, said 'And you sit there, in Claude's place,' and pushed back the chair with him on it, pausing over him for a second to straighten a knife beside his plate.

On the table, the hosts of breakfast were marshalled into two opposing forces, and a Miss Emery from either end commanded each. The toast, eggs, bacon, and marmalade had declared for Miss Dora; but the tea-pot and its vassals, the cruet and the honeycomb – beautifully bleeding in flowered dish – were for Miss Emery to a man. The loaf, sitting opposite to Roger, remained unabashedly neutral. Roger looked from one Miss Emery to the other.

'Plenty of milk? I expect so; Claude always liked plenty of milk in his tea. What I always say is – little boys like what's good for them, don't you worry, grown-ups!'

'Two pieces of bacon? Look, if this egg's too soft, mop it up with your bread; I should. They *say* it isn't polite, but – '

'Yes, please,' said Roger, and 'thank you very much, I will.' What jolly ladies the Miss Emerys were!

They were looking at him anxiously; were they afraid he was not quite pleased and comfortable? Perhaps they did not often have a visitor. They were aunts; they had once had a nephew called Claude, but he had grown up and gone to India, leaving only some fishing-tackle behind him and a book about trains which had been given to Roger. Were they looking piteously at him in the pangs of baffled aunthood? But were they perhaps wondering if he *knew*, how much he knew, and whether they ought to tell him? They were ladies with bright eyes that would fill up easily with emotion, white, quick hands and big bosoms. Roger could hear them saying, 'Little mother-less boy, poor little motherless boy!' and they would snatch him and gather him in, and each successively would press his head deep into her bosom, so deep that perhaps it would never come out again.

Roger shrank into himself in fearful anticipation: he must escape, he must escape, he must escape . . . Yesterday had been one long intrigue for solitude, telling a fib and slipping away from his little sisters, telling a fib and slipping away from his father. Father didn't go to work now but walked about the house and garden, his pink face horribly crinkled up and foolish-looking, lighting cigarettes and throwing them away again. Sometimes he would search anxiously for the cigarette he had thrown away, and when he had picked it up would look at it and sigh desolately to find it had gone quite out. Father was an architect: he would go into this study, tweak a drawing out of a portfolio, run to his desk with it, pore over it, score it through; then start, look back at the door guiltily, return to stare and stare at the drawing, push it away, and go on walking about. Up and down the room he'd go, up and down the room, then dart sideways as though at a sudden loophole and disappear through the door into the garden. But he always came back again to where Roger was; he couldn't let one alone. His presence was a torment and an outrage. Roger disliked people who were ridiculous, and he had never cared to look long at his father. Father had dark-brown hair, all fluffy like a baby's, that stood out away from his head. His face was pink and always a little curly, his eyebrows thick and so far away from his eyes that when one came to them one had forgotten they ought to be there. Lois and Pamela loved him; they thought he was beautiful, so it was all quite fair; and Roger thought *she* was wonderful, the way she had always tolerated him and allowed him to kiss her. Always the best hour of the day for her and Roger had been when the little girls had gone to bed, and *he* had not yet come in. Now the pink face was curled up tight, and the eyes were scared and horrible, and the hands always reaching out to Roger to grab him with 'Come on, old man, let's talk. Let's talk for a bit.' And they had nothing to say, nothing. And at any moment this man who had no decency might begin talking about *her*.

Now, suppose the Miss Emerys were beginning to – no, the thing was unthinkable. And besides, perhaps they didn't even know.

'What's Roger going to do today?' Miss Emery asked her sister.

'We-ell,' said Miss Dora, considering. 'He could help you garden, couldn't he? you know you wanted somebody to help you sort the apples. You know you were saying only yesterday, *"If only I had somebody to help me sort the apples!"* Now I wonder if Roger likes sorting apples?'

'Well, I never have,' said Roger, 'but I expect it would be very nice.'

'Yes, you'd love it,' said the Miss Emerys with enthusiasm. 'Claude loved it, didn't he, Doodsie?' added Miss Dora. 'Do you remember how he used to follow you about at all times of the year, even in March and April, saying, "Aunt Doodsie, mightn't I help you sort the apples?" How I did tease him: I used to say, "Now then, Mister, I know what you're after! Is it the sorting, or the apples?" Claude was very fond of apples,' said Miss Dora, very earnest and explanatory, 'he liked apples very much. I expect you do too?'

'Yes, very much, thank you.'

'Do you look forward to going back to school?' asked Miss Emery, and her voice knew it was saying something dangerous. Back to school . . . When Mother had died, Father would send him away to school with all the other ugly little boys with round caps. Father said it was the best time of one's life; Father had liked school, he had been that kind of little boy. School *now* meant a day-school, where one painted flowers and mothers came rustling in and stood behind one and admired. They had a headmistress, though they were more than half of them little boys, and there were three older than Roger. Father said this wasn't the sort of school for a grown man of nine. This was because Father didn't like the headmistress; she despised him and he grew fidgety in her presence.

'Which school?' said Roger disconcertingly, when he had swallowed his mouthful of bread and honey.

'We-ell,' hesitated Miss Dora, 'the one you're at now, of course,' she said, gathering speed. 'It seems to me a very nice school; I like to see you going out to games; and that nice girl behind you with the red hair.'

'Yes,' said Roger, 'that's Miss Williams.' He masticated silently, reflecting. Then he said provocatively, 'I should like to stay there always.'

'Oooh!' deprecated Miss Dora, 'but not with little girls. When you're a bigger boy you'll think little girls are silly; you won't want to play with little girls. Claude didn't like little girls.'

'How long *do* you think I'll stay?' asked Roger, and watched her narrowly.

'As long as your father thinks well, I expect,' said Miss Dora, brightly evasive – 'Doodsie, do call poor Bingo in – or shall I? – and give him his brekky. I can hear him out in the hall.'

Roger ignored the liver-coloured spaniel that made a waddling entrance and stood beside him, sniffing his bare knees.

'*Why* my father?' he pressed on, raising his eyebrows aggressively at Miss Dora.

' — Bingo-Bingo-Bingo-Bingo-*Bingo*!' cried Miss Dora suddenly, as in convulsive desperation, clapping her hands against her thighs. The spaniel took no notice of her; it twitched one ear, left Roger, and lumbered over to the fireplace, where it sat and yawned into the empty grate.

Roger spent the morning with Miss Emery, helping her sort the apples and range them round in rows along the shelves of the apple-room, their cheeks carefully just not touching. The apple-room was warm, umber and nutty-smelling; it had no window, so the door stood open to the orchard, and let in a white panel of daylight with an apple tree in it, a fork impaled in the earth, and a garden-hat of Miss Dora's hanging on the end of the fork, tilted coquettishly. The day was white, there were no shadows, there was no wind, never a sound. Miss Emery, her sleeves rolled up, came in and out with baskets of apples that were too heavy for a little boy to carry. Roger, squatting on the ground, looked them over for bruises — a bruised apple would go bad, she said, and must be eaten at once — and passed up to her those that were green and perfect, to take their place among the ranks along the shelves . . . 'That happy throng' . . . It *was* like the Day of Judgment, and the shelves were Heaven. Hell was the hamper in the musty-smelling corner full of bass matting, where Roger put the Goats. He put them there reluctantly, and saw himself a kind angel, with an imploring face turned back to the Implacable, driving reluctantly the piteous herd below.

The apples were chilly; they had a blue bloom on them, and were as smooth as ivory — like dead faces are, in books, when people bend to kiss them. 'They're cooking apples,' said Miss Emery, 'not sweet at all, so I won't offer you one to eat. When we've finished you shall have a russet.'

'I'd rather, if I might,' said Roger, 'just bite one of these. Just bite it.'

'Well, bite then,' said Miss Emery. 'Only don't take a big one; that would be only a waste, for you won't like it.'

Roger bit. The delicate bitter juice frothed out like milk; he pressed his teeth deep into the resisting whiteness till his jaws were stretched. Then in the attentive silence of the orchard he heard steps beginning, coming from the house. Not here, O God, not here! Not trapped in here among Miss Emery and the apples, when all he wanted when *that* came was to be alone with the clock. If it were here he would hate apples, and he would hate to have to hate them. He looked round despairingly at their green demi-lunes of faces peering at him over the edge of the shelves. His teeth met in his apple, and he bit away such a stupendous mouthful that he was sealed up terrifyingly. The fruit slipped from his fingers and bumped away across the floor. Not a bird or a tree spoke; Miss Emery, standing up behind him on a chair, was almost moveless — listening? The steps came slowly, weighted down with ruefulness. Something to hold on to, something to grip! . . . There was nothing, not even the apple. The door was darkened.

'The butcher *did* come, Miss. Are there any orders?' . . .

But that settled it — the apples were intolerable. Roger asked if he might go now and play in the garden. 'Tired?' said Miss Emery, disappointed. 'Why, you get tired sooner than Claude — he could go on at this all day. I'm afraid that apple disappointed you. Take a russet, dearie, look, off that corner shelf!'

She was kind; he had no heart to leave behind the russet. So he took it, and walked away among the trees of the orchard, underneath the browning leaves. One slid down through the air and clung against the wool of Roger's jersey; a bronze leaf with blue sheen on it, curled into a tired line. Autumn was the time of the death of the year, but he loved it, he loved the smell of autumn. He wondered if one died more easily then. He had often wondered about death; he had felt in *her* the same curiosity; they had peered down strangely together, as into a bear-pit, at something which could never touch them. She was older; she ought to have known, she ought to have known . . .

The grass was long and lustreless; it let his feet pass through reluctantly. Suppose it wove itself around them, grew into them and held them — Somebody's snare. He began the imagination game.

Miss Dora was leaning over the gate talking to some ladies; a mother and daughter, pink and yet somehow hungry-looking. They turned their heads at the sound of his footsteps in the grass; he dropped his eyes and pretended not to see them. They drank him in, their voices dropped, their heads went closer together. He walked past them through the trees, consciously visible, oh, every line of him conscious — this was how a little boy walked while his mother was dying . . . Yes, they had been great companions, always together. Yes, she was to die at any moment — poor little boy, wouldn't it be terrible for him! . . . He turned and walked directly away from them, towards the house. Their observation licked his back like flames.

Then he hated himself: he did like being looked at.

After lunch, Miss Dora took him down to the High Street with her to buy wool. His mouth was still sleek with apple-dumpling, his stomach heavy with it, though they had given him a magazine with horses in it, and sent him off for half an hour to digest. Now they walked by a back way; Miss Dora didn't want to meet people. Perhaps it was awkward for her being seen about with a little boy who half had a mother and half hadn't.

She walked and talked quickly, her hands in a muff; a feather nodded at him over the edge of her hat, the leaves rustled round her feet. He wasn't going to remember last autumn, the way the leaves had rustled . . . running races, catching each other up. He barred his mind against it, and bit his lip till he was quite sick. He wouldn't remember *coming in to tea* — not that.

'What's the matter, darling,' said Miss Dora, stopping short concernedly. 'Do you want to go somewhere? Have you got a pain?'

'No, oh no,' said Roger. 'I was just imagining those white

mice. How awful losing them, how awful. Do go on about them, Miss Dora, go on about Claude.'

'– And when he was packing up to go back to school, *there* was the little nest, at the bottom of his play-box, and the little mother mouse, curled up, and Claude said . . .' Miss Dora continued the Saga.

When they got to the town they saw far down at the other end of the High Street the two scarlet tam-o'-shanters of Lois and Pamela, bobbing along beside the lady who had taken *them*. Somebody had given Lois a new hoop; she was carrying it. Pamela was skipping on and off the kerb, in and out of the gutter. She didn't look as if she minded about Mother a bit. Pamela was so young; she was six. He wanted to go and tell Pamela that what she was doing was wrong and horrible, that people must be looking at her out of all the windows of the High Street, and wondering how she could.

'There are the little *sisters*, Roger – rrrrun!'

People would all say, 'There are those poor little children, meeting one another!' and tell each other in whispers, behind the windows of the High Street, what was going to happen. He didn't want to be seen talking to his sisters, a little pitiful group.

'Go – on, rrrrun!'

He hung back. He said he would go round and see them after tea, he thought. 'Shy of Mrs Biddle?' asked Miss Dora swiftly. He allowed her to assume it. 'Well, of course she *is* a little . . . I mean she isn't quite . . .' said Miss Dora. 'But I expect the little girls like her. And I didn't think you were a shy little boy.'

Back at the Miss Emerys' by half-past three, Roger found that it was not tea-time, and that there was nothing to do, nothing to escape to. That walk with Miss Dora had shattered the imagination game; it wouldn't come back to him till tomorrow, not perhaps for two days. He leaned against an apple tree, and tried sickly to imagine Claude. A horrid little boy, a dreadful little boy; he would have pulled Roger's hair and chaffed him about playing with his mother. Mercifully, he had passed on irrecoverably into the middle years; he was grown up now and would smile down on Roger through the mists of Olympus. Roger didn't get on with other little boys, he didn't like them; they seemed to him like his father, noisy outside and frightened in. Bullies. The school he was going to would be full of these little boys. He wondered how soon he would go to school; perhaps his father was even now writing to the schoolmaster – while Mother lay upstairs with her eyes shut, not caring. Roger thought Father would find this difficult; he smiled at the thought in leisurely appreciation. 'Dear Mr Somebody-or-other, my wife is not dead yet, but she soon will be, and when she is I should like to send my little boy to your school . . . If it is not too expensive; I am not a rich man.' Roger's father often said, 'I am not a rich man,' with an air of modest complacency.

Home was not so far away from Roger as he stood in the Miss Emerys' garden. It was twenty minutes round by the road; from the top of an apple tree one should be able to see the tall white chimneys. There had been something wonderful – once – about those chimneys, standing up against the distant beech trees, dimming the beech trees, on a quiet evening, with their pale, unstirring smoke. From up high, here, one would be able to see the windows of the attics; see whether the windows were black and open, or whether the white blinds were down. If he sat from now on, high in an apple tree, he could watch those windows. Night and day, nothing should escape him. When the blinds came down gently and finally to cover them, Roger would know. There would be no need to tell him, he would be armoured against that. Then he could run upstairs to the Miss Emerys' landing, and be alone with the clock. When they came up after him, puffed with a deep-drawn breath to impart *that*, he could just turn round and say calmly, rather tiredly, 'Oh, it's all right, thank you, I do know.' Then they would look mortified and go away. Really-kind Miss Emery, really-kind Father *would* look mortified; they wouldn't like having the thing snatched away from them.

Roger gazed up into the apple tree. The branches were big and far apart, the bark looked slippery. 'I'm afraid,' he thought, and tried to drown it. He was a little boy, he was afraid of the pain of death. 'I don't dare go up, and I don't dare go back to the house. I *must* know, I can't let them tell me. Oh, help me, let them not have to come and tell me! It would be as though they saw me see her being killed. Let it not have to be!'

And now it would be and it must be, even while he deliberated and feared. Roger saw his father open the gate of the orchard and stand hesitatingly, looking round at the trees. He was hatless, his face was puckered up and scared – Oh, to run, to run quickly to somebody who would not know, who would think his mother was still alive, who need never know she was not! To be with somebody comfortable and ignorant, to grasp a cork handle through which this heat couldn't come blazing at him. Horrible footsteps, horrible grey figure coming forward again, and now pausing again desolately among the trees. 'Roger?' called the voice, 'Roger!'

Roger pressed back. He too was grey like the tree-trunks, and slimmer than they; he urged himself against one, hopelessly feigning invisibility, trying to melt. 'Roger!' came the voice continuously and wearily, 'Old man? Roger!'

Now he was coming straight towards one, he couldn't fail to see. He would drink one in and see one defenceless, and draw a big breath and say IT. No Miss Emery, no cook, no death, no refuge, and the tree shrinking away from before one.

'*Ah*, Roger!'

He thrust his fingers into his ears. 'I *know*, I *know*!' he screamed. 'Go away, I can't bear it. I know, I tell you.'

The pink face lengthened, the scared eyes of his father regarded him, as he stood there screaming like a maniac. A voice was raised, did battle with the din he made, and was defeated. Roger leaned with his arms flung round the girth of the apple tree, grinding his forehead into the bark, clamouring through the orchard. When his own voice dropped he heard how silent it was. So silent that he thought his father was dead too, lying in the long grass, till he turned and saw him beside him, holding something towards him, still standing.

He was holding out a picture-postcard; he meant Roger to take it. 'Steady, old man,' he was saying; 'steady, Roger, you're all jiggy: steady, old man!'

'What, what, what?' said Roger, staring wildly at the postcard. It was glazed and very blue; blue sea, infinitely smooth and distant, sky cloudless above it; white houses gathered joyously together by the shore, other white houses hurrying from the hills. Behind the land, behind everything, the clear fine line of a mountain went up into the sky. Something beckoned Roger; he stood looking through an archway.

'It came for you,' said Father, 'it's from Aunt Nellie; it's the Bay of Naples.'

Then he went away.

This was the blue empty place, Heaven, that one came out into at last, beyond everything. In the blue windlessness, the harmony of that timeless day, Roger went springing and singing up the mountain to look for his mother. He did not think again of that grey figure, frightened, foolish, desolate, that went back among the trees uncertainly, and stood a long time fumbling with the gate.

*

A Fall From Grace

Those years the children – in Brittany, Bordeaux and the Loire Valley, even as far away as the Low Countries, Andalusia and the Riviera – missed their acrobats. In the Circus the dingy wild animals, the clowns, illusionists and freaks remained, but earthbound. Gravity held the Circus, and the mud, the stench and the poverty were more evident. The magic-makers, the sequinned stars that flashed and poised and flew and sparkled through the smoke above the watchers' heads, the death-defiers who snatched the Circus from the mud and turned it into flowers and frissons, were gone.

Gone away to the strange camp on the Champs de Mars where they were needed to help Monsieur E. build his beautiful tower. Oh, the local residents might tremble in their beds with fear at the fall from heaven; intellectuals and artists might protest that 'Paris is defaced by this erection'. But the Circus people, the artists of body and philosophers of balance (with wild libidinous laughs at so unfortunate and accurate a turn of phrase), they understood; the acrobats – without words and with a regular fifty centimes an hour – knew. They alone could comprehend the vision. They knew in the marrow of their bones and the tissue of their muscles the precise tension – that seven million threaded rods, and two and a half million bolts could, of course, hold fifteen thousand steel girders in perfect balance. With sinews and nerves and cartilage they did it nightly: that tension and harmony against gravity was their stock-in-trade. Their great delight was that Monsieur E., a gentleman, a scientist, knew it too, and knew that they knew and needed them to translate his vision. High above Paris they swooped and caracoled, rejoicing in the delicacy and power of that thrust, upwards, away from the pull of the ground. And so they left their Circuses, sucked towards Paris by a dream that grew real under their authority – and for two years the acrobats and trapeze artists and highwire dancers and trampolinists abandoned their musical illusions to participate in historical, scientific reality.

Eva and Louise too came to Paris. Not that they were allowed to mount up ever higher on the winches, hanging beside the cauldrons which heated the bolts white hot; not that they were permitted to balance on the great girders, shifting their weight so accurately to swing the heavy strands of lace into place. Their skill, as it happens, was not in doubt, but they were women. They drifted northwards, almost unthinkingly, with their comrades and colleagues, simply because the power of Monsieur E.'s vision was magnetic and all the acrobats were drawn inwards by it and Eva and Louise were acrobats. And they lived with the other acrobats on the Champs de Mars, poised between aspiration and reality, and the city of Paris went to their heads and they were, after a few months, no longer who they had been when they came.

Their Circus had been a disciplined nursery for such children. Born to it, they had known its rhythms, its seductions and its truths from the beginning. Precious to their parents because identical twins are good showbusiness, they were only precious inasmuch as they worked and made a show. With each lurching move of the travelling caravans they had had to re-create the magic from the mud. Only after the hours of sweat and struggle with the tent, with the law, with the unplanned irregularities of topography, and with costumes which had become muddy or damp or creased or torn – only then were they able to ascend the snaking ladders and present the New Creation, where fear and relief were held in perfect tension; where the immutable laws of nature – gravity and pendula arches, weight, matter and velocity – were apparently defied but in fact bound, utilized, respected and controlled; where hours of dreary practice, and learning the capacities and limits of self and other, where the disciplines of technique and melodrama and precision were liberated suddenly and briefly into glamour and panache. And still were only a complete part of a delicately balanced and complete whole which included the marionette man, the clowns, the seedy lions and the audience itself.

But Paris, and a Paris in which they could not do what they were trained to do, was a holiday, a field day, where the rewards were quick and detached from the labour. As the tower grew so did Eva and Louise, but the tower was anchored and they were free-floating. They learned to cross the laughing river and seek out the *boîtes* of Montmartre. Here, their white knickers and petticoats frothed easily in the hot water now available to them, they learned to dance the new dance – the Cancan. Here their muscularity, their training, their athleticism stood them in good stead. They were a hit: with the management who paid them to come and show off round bosoms, shapely legs, pink cheeks and bleached petticoats; with the clientele whose oohs and ahhs were more directly appreciative than those of any Circus audience.

Yes, the beauty and the energy of them as they danced and pranced and watched the tower grow and watched their comrades labour upwards. They walked under the spreading legs of the tower and laughed at the jokes called down to them; they ran among the tents and teased the labourers; they turned the odd trick here and there for affection and amusement, although they could get better paid across the river where the rich men lived. Monsieur E., coming each day to see how his dream was developing, soon learned their names and would stop and smile for them, and they smiled back, arms entwined with each other, but eyes open for everything that was going on in the world. And they reassured him of his beauty, his virility, his potency, all of which he was manifesting in his tower which broke the rules of nature by the authority of science and the power of men. One day he told them, for the simple pleasure of saying it, for he knew they were simple girls and simply would not understand, that when his tower was finished it would weigh less than the column of air that contained it. The girls laughed and wanted to know why then it would not fly away, and he laughed too, indulgently, and explained, paternally, about displacement. But from then on the idea of the tower simply, ooh-la-la, flying away with them was fixed in Eva and Louise's minds and it made them laugh because of course they knew that it was impossible.

And walking in the streets and parks they learned new styles of dressing and new styles of living; and their eyes were wide and bright with delight. Having little to do all day they wandered here and there, through boulevards and over bridges. In the flower markets they were overcome by the banks of sweetness, the brilliance of colours; in the antique-shop windows they saw the bright treasures from China and Egypt, from far away and long ago; and in the cafés they smelled new smells and heard raffish conversations about things they had not even dreamed of. And everywhere they went, because they looked so alike and smiled so merrily and were always together, people came to recognize them and smile at them, and they felt loved and powerful and free as they had never felt before. All Paris was their friend and the city itself was their Paradise.

They were a hit too in the *Salons des Femmes*, where the strange rich women, who dressed like men and caressed Eva and Louise like men too, were delighted by their health and energy and innocence. And by their professional willingness to show off. Louise enjoyed these evenings when they drank tiny glasses of jewel-coloured drinks and performed – dances, tumbles, stage acrobatics – and were petted and sent home in carriages. But Eva felt nervous and alarmed; and also drawn, excited, elated and it was not just the coloured concoctions that made her giggle all the way back to the Champs de Mars and swear that they would not go again. In the dark warmth of the bed they shared, Eva's arms would wind round Louise as they had done every night since they were conceived, but her fingers crackled with new electricity and she wondered and wanted and did not want to know what she wanted.

And of course they did go again, because it was Paris and the Spanish chestnut flowers stood out white on the streets like candles and the air was full of the scent of them, giddy, dusty, lazy. At night the city was sparkling and golden and high above it the stars prickled, silver and witty. And Monsieur E.'s tower, taut and poised was being raised up to join the two together. In the hot perfumed houses they were treated as servants, as artists and as puppy dogs, all together, and it confused them, turned their heads and enchanted them. One evening, watching them, the Contessa della Colubria said to her hostess, 'Well, Celeste, I think they won't last long, those two. They'll become tawdry and quite spoiled. But they are very charming.' 'I don't know,' Celeste said, 'they are protected. By their work of course, but not that; it must be primal innocence to love, to be one with another person from the beginning, with no desires, no consciousness.' 'Innocence? Do you think so? Perhaps it is the primal sin, to want to stay a child, to want to stay inside the first embrace, the first cell.' The Contessa's eyes glittered like her emeralds. 'Do you think it might be interesting to find out?' Celeste turned away from her slightly, watching Eva and Louise across the salon; she said quickly, 'Ah, *ma mie*, leave them be. They are altogether too young for you to bother with.' The Contessa laughed, 'But, Celeste, you know how beguiled I am by innocence. It attracts me.'

She was mysterious, the Contessa della Colubria, strange and fascinating; not beautiful *mais très chic*, clever, witty, and fabulously wealthy. She had travelled, apparently everywhere, but now lived alone in Paris, leaving her husband in his harsh high castle in Tuscany and challenging the bourgeois gossips with her extravagance, her outré appearance and the musky sensation of decadence. Rumour followed her like a shadow, and like a shadow had no clear substance. It was known that she collected the new paintings, and Egyptian curios and

Chinese statues; it is said that she also collected books which respectable people would not sully their homes with, that she paid fabulous sums to actresses for ritual performances, that she slid along the side of the pit of the unacceptable with a grace that was uncanny. But she had created a social space for herself in which the fear, the feeling, that she was not nice, not quite safe, became unimportant.

She took Eva and Louise home in her carriage that night. Sitting between them, her arms around each neck, her legs stretched out, her long narrow feet braced against the floor, her thin face bland, only her elongated ophidian eyes moving. The sharp jewel she wore on her right hand cut into Louise's neck, but she did not dare to say anything. The Contessa told them stories.

'You see the stars,' she said, and they were bright above the river as the carriage crossed over it. 'Long ago, long long ago, it was thought that each star was a soul, the soul of a beautiful girl, too lovely to die, too bright to be put away in the dark for ever. The wild gods of those times did not think that so much beauty should be wasted, you see. Look at that star up there, that is Cassiopeia, she was a queen and so lovely that she boasted she was more beautiful than the Nereides, the sea-nymphs, and they in their coral caves were so jealous and angry that they made Neptune their father punish her. But the other gods were able to rescue her and throw her up to heaven and make her safe and bright.

'And those stars there, those are Ariadne's crown; it was given to her by Bacchus who was the god of wine and passion, not an orderly god, not a good god at all, but fierce and beautiful. Ariadne loved Theseus first, who was a handsome young man, and she rescued him from a terrible monster called the Minotaur who lived in a dark maze and ate people. Ariadne gave her lover a thread so he could find his way out and a sword so he could kill the monster. But he wasn't very grateful, as men so seldom are, and he left her on an island called Naxos.'

'I know those ones,' said Louise, pointing, breaking the soft flow of the Contessa's voice with an effort, 'those ones up there, those are the Seven Sisters who preferred to be together.'

'The Pleiades, yes, how clever you are. And you see that one of them is dimmer than the others. That is Meriope, and her star is faint because she married, she married a mortal, but the rest are bright and shiny.'

Louise's neck hurt from the Contessa's sharp ring. She felt tired and uneasy. She wanted to sit with Eva, their arms around each other, tight and safe. She did not understand the Contessa. But Eva liked the stories, liked the arm of the Contessa resting warm against her skin, admired the sparkling of emeralds and eyes and was lulled, comfortable and snug, in the smooth carriage.

The balance shifted. They knew about this. As Eva leaned outwards and away, away from the centre, then Louise had to move lower, heavier, tighter, to keep the balance. As Louise pulled inward, downward, Eva had to stretch up and away to keep the balance. On the tightrope they knew this; but it was a new thing for them. There was another way, of course; their parents had had an act based on imbalance, based on difference, based on his heavy grounding and her light flying, the meeting-place of the weighty and the floating. But they had not learned it. Even in the gravity-free place where they had first learned to dance together, in the months before they were born, it had been turning in balance, in precise sameness. It was the poise of symmetry that they knew about; the tension of balance. And it was foolhardy always to change an act without a safety net and with no rehearsals. They did not know how to discuss it. The difference was painful, a tightening, a loss of relaxation, of safety. The acrobat who was afraid of falling would fall. They knew that. But also the acrobat who could not believe in the fall would fall. They knew that too.

The Contessa took them to a smart pâtisserie on the Champs-Elysées. She bought them frothing hot chocolate, and they drank it with glee, small moustaches of creamy foam forming on their pink upper lips. They were laughing and happy. 'Which of you is the older,' she asked, 'which was born first?' 'We don't know,' said Eva and giggled. 'No one knows. We tumbled out together and the woman who was supposed to be with my mother was drunk and she got muddled up and no one knows.' 'If they did it would not matter,' said Louise. 'Our mother says we were born to the trade, we dived out with elegance.' Eva and Louise were pleased with themselves today, with the distinction of their birth, with their own inseparability, with the sweetness of the chocolate and the lightness of the little apricot tartlets. The smart folk walked by on the pavement outside, but they were inside and as pretty as any grand lady. And in the bright spring sunlight the Contessa was not strange and dangerous, she was beautiful and glamorous, she was like something from a fairy story who had come into their lives and would grant them wishes and tell them stories.

The Contessa came in her new toy, her automobile, roaring and dangerous, to seek them out on the Champs de Mars. She was driven up in her bright new chariot, and stopped right between the legs of the tower. The acrobats swarming up and down, labouring, sweating and efficient, swung aside to make space for her, as she uncoiled herself from the seat and walked among them. And she knew Monsieur E. and gave him a kiss and congratulated him on his amazing edifice. Louise did not like to see her there, but she invited them into her car and they rode off to the admiring whistles of their friends. 'In Russia,' the Contessa told them, 'the people ride in sleighs across the snow and the wolves howl at them, but it does not matter because they are snugly wrapped in great furs and the horses pull them through the dark, because it is dark all winter in Russia, and the motion of the sleigh is smooth and the furs are warm and they fall asleep while the horses run and the night is full of vast silences and strange noises so that they hang bells on the horses' bridles, and all the nobility speak in French, so that people will know how civilized they are, and not mistake them for the bearded warriors who live in snow houses beyond the northern stars. And even the women of these people wear high leather boots and ride with the men on short-legged, fierce horses. They ride so well up in that strange land that ordinary people have come to believe that they and their horses are one: they call them Centaurs, horses with human heads and trunks and arms. Long, long ago there were real Centaurs who roamed in Anatolia and knew strange things and would sometimes take little babies and train them in their ways and they would grow up wise and strong and fit to be rulers, because the Centaurs taught them magic, but for ordinary people the Centaurs were very dangerous because they were neither people nor animals, but monsters.'

And they rode in the Contessa's car round the Bois and she took them back to her house and taught them how to sniff up a white powder through slender silver straws and then they could see green-striped tigers prowling across the Contessa's garden with eyes like stars, and butterflies ten feet across with huge velvet legs that fluttered down from the trees like falling flowers. And when they went home they found they could believe that Monsieur E.'s tower could fly, and they could fly on it, away away to a warm southern place, but they did not want to leave Paris, so they waved to the tower and they were laughed at for being drunk, and they did not tell anyone about the white powder.

One day at a party, in a new beautiful strange house where they had been invited to do a little show, the Contessa sought out Eva for one brief moment when she was alone and said, 'I have a pretty present for you.' 'Yes, madame.' 'See it is earrings.' She held out her long, thin, dry hand, the palm flat and open, and there was a pair of earrings, two perfect little gold apples. 'These are golden apples from the garden of the Hesperides; Juno, the queen of all the Gods, gave them to Jupiter, the king of all the Gods, for a wedding present. They grow in a magical garden beyond the edge of the world and they are guarded by the four beautiful daughters of Atlas who carries the world on his back. And around the tree they grow on lies a huge horrible dragon who never sleeps. So you see they are very precious.' Eva looked at them, amused; she had little interest in their value, but liked their prettiness. 'One for me and one for Louise, madame?' she asked. 'No, both are for you. But you will have to come by yourself one evening to my house and collect them.' 'But madame, we always go together, you know that.' 'Eva,' smiled the Contessa, 'I'll tell you a little story: once there was a woman and she was expecting a baby, and she wished and wished good things for her baby and especially that it would grow up to have good manners. Well, her pregnancy went on and on, and on and on, and still the baby was not born. And none of the wise doctors could make any sense of it. And in the end, ever more pregnant, after many many years, as a very ancient lady she died of old age. So the doctors who were of course very curious opened her up and they found two little ladies, quite more than middle-aged, sitting beside the birth door saying with perfect good manners, "After you," and, "No, no, my dear, after *you*". *C'est très gentil*, but what a waste, what a waste, don't you think?' Eva giggled at the silly story, covering her mouth with her hand like a child. She did not care about the earrings but she knew that if she went to the Contessa she would find out, she would find out what it was she did not know, what it was that made her nervous and elated. She could feel too the weight of Louise, the weight of Louise inward on both of them, the weight swinging out of balance. She had to correct that inward weight with an outward one. Had to remake the balance, the inward weight with an outward one. Also she wanted to know, and if she went she would know that and something else perhaps.

'Yes, madame,' she said, 'yes, I will come.'

And the Contessa smiled.

She did not know how to tell Louise. She could not find any words for what and why; they have never needed words before, they have not rehearsed any. Next Tuesday she would go to visit the Contessa. This week she had to find words to tell Louise. Instead she drank. Louise, who knew she was excited but could not feel why, could not understand, could not pull Eva back to her, drank too. Their comrades on the Champs de Mars thought it was funny to see the girls drunk; they plied them with brandy and wine. Drunk, Eva and Louise showed off, they performed new tricks, leaping higher, tumbling, prancing; they do not stumble or trip, they cannot stumble or trip. They are beautiful and skilful. This is their place. The men clap for them, urging them on. In the space under the tower they dance and frolic. They start to climb, swinging upwards; from each other's hands they ascend. Somersaulting, delighting, they follow the upward thrust of the tower; its tension, its balance is theirs. The voices of the men fade below. Once, as they rise above seven hundred feet, they falter. 'It's your fault,' says Eva, 'you lean in too hard.' 'No,' says Louise, 'it is you, you are too far out.' But they find their rhythm again, trusting the rhythm of the tower that Monsieur E. and their hard-worked colleagues below have structured for them. On the other side of the river they can see Paris, spread out for them now, the islands in the Seine floating on the dark water, the gay streets shining with golden lights. Above, the sky is clear: the moon a bright dying fingernail, the constellations whizzing in their glory. The tower seems to sway, sensitive to their need. It is not quite finished, but as they approach the top they are higher than they have ever been, they are climbing and swinging and swooping upwards. Suddenly both together they call out to one another, 'It was my fault, I'm sorry.' The rhythm is flowing now, their wrists linked, trusting, knowing, perfect. It is their best performance ever. Down below the men still watch, although it is too dark to see. They know they will never see another show like this. They know these two are stars. They make no error. They do not fall. They fly free, suddenly, holding hands, falling stars, a moment of unity and glory.

But it is three hundred yards to the ground and afterwards no one is able to sort out which was which or how they could be separated.

*

The Tulip Plate

'There's a man I often see here,' Nell said, as she walked round the lake with her weekend visitor. 'No matter what time of day I choose – on Saturdays and Sundays, that is – he's nearly always here too.'

'How romantic,' said her visitor, whose name was Margaret and who was interested in men. 'What sort of man? Perhaps he has conceived a passion for you.'

'No,' Nell said, referring to the words romantic and passion. 'I don't know what sort of man. It's his dog I'm interested in – you don't see so many white bull-terriers about these days.'

Margaret said she wouldn't know a bull-terrier if she met one. She had to be honest about it, she'd never liked dogs or trusted them. Presumably, if it was fully white, it must be albino and have pink eyes?

Nell said yes to this and notched up one more thing they didn't have in common. To prove the point she called out 'Hurry up, Dearest!' to her own dog who was busy in the reeds, looking for water rats.

They had to keep moving because of the cold. The lake was a large one for southern England and, with its inlets and varied vegetation, gave the appearance of being natural, when it was man-made. Three quarters of the way round it ran a metalled path-cum-roadway, wide enough for single motor traffic, on the waterside of which creosoted wood stumps, like dwarf telegraph poles, had been set at intervals to deter cars from parking on the bank. They were having to stick to this path and not venture into the woods that bordered its other side because

Nell, writing to confirm train times, had omitted to tell Margaret to bring boots.

'I should have told you to bring some boots,' she said, 'so that we could walk in the woods.'

'I don't own any boots,' Margaret said. 'I never walk at home if I can help it – except to go to the shops, of course. But I'm quite enjoying this,' she added, understanding suddenly that her truthfulness, of which ordinarily she was not ashamed, might just occasionally be mistaken for rudeness. 'It reminds me of the Round Pond in Kensington Gardens.'

'North America, more like' – Nell was astounded by such inaccuracy – 'or Canada to be precise. Look.' She stopped, and Margaret stopped, and they both stared beyond a slatted landing stage across the dull water to where nameless waterfowl skied and flapped, and to where, in the far distance, little boats with coloured sails raced in the wind. On the opposite bank a mixed forest, dominated by giant pines or firs, climbed into the sky, and beneath it, right on the shore line, they could just make out a log cabin with a flagpole jutting from its roof. This was the sailing club, Nell explained. 'You see,' she said, 'it's not like England at all. It makes me think – especially when the sky's a really bright blue – of those photographs in the *National Geographic*.' She was pleased with this piece of observation, and used some version of it to the infrequent visitors she brought to the lake, most of whom were in wholehearted agreement.

'So it is! How clever of you!'

'You're absolutely right – we could be on Golden Pond! Did you see that film, by the way?'

Margaret, however, merely shivered and nodded in the direction of the boats and remarked, 'Red sails in the sunset,' in a dry voice.

'Have you had enough?' Nell felt she had to ask. Margaret's clothes were too thin and smart for a cold country walk. But what was she going to do with her if they turned back so soon? Tea would be a bit of a diversion, but after that? They had no friends in common anymore. What would they find to talk about for the rest of the evening?

The night before, the day of Margaret's arrival and first visit for nearly twenty years, they had talked shop. Or rather Margaret – following Nell from sitting room to kitchen, from kitchen to cellar, from fridge to cooker, while breathing down her neck or standing on her toes (and Nell was a claustrophobe) had talked shop, and Nell had interjected the odd 'yes, but,' or 'don't you think –'. But if there is a limit to how long two persons – the one a librarian, the other a bookseller, the former doing most of the talking, the latter most of the listening – can maintain an enthusiastic discourse on stock-control systems and library cuts, Public Lending Right and the Net Book Agreement, they had reached it; if there is a point when analysis of sales and borrowings, a debate on the problem of unreturned books and shoplifting ('They're both theft, mind you, straightforward theft, and should be punished as such,' Margaret had exclaimed, with a jerk of her elbow that had sent a china candlestick flying), becomes less than enthralling, then ditto. Even the topics they were agreed upon – the rudeness of customers, the inefficiency of publishers, the vanity of authors ('They never come into the shop to buy, you know,' Nell said when she could get a word in, 'merely to check that their own dreary books are on the shelf') – had lost their edge by midnight. 'Must hit the hay now, folks,' Margaret had announced in what she thought of as an American accent, 'or I won't have gotten my beauty sleep.'

For Nell, the worst aspect of the evening had been the discovery that Margaret did not drink or smoke. She'd made one small glass of sherry last nearly two hours, drumming the table lightly with manicured fingers each time Nell reached for the whisky bottle or for her cigarettes. On the other hand – and it seemed odd in one so thin and birdlike – she had an enormous appetite for food. Nell had imagined the cottage pie would do at least two meals, but Margaret – 'Do you mind if I do? It seems a pity to waste it' – had helped herself three times until nothing remained but a spoonful of mashed potato. The fruit salad had disappeared likewise. When Margaret finally put down her spoon, a solitary slice of banana was left swimming in the bowl.

The problem of what to have for supper now beset Nell as they passed two umbrellas, all that could be seen of two fishermen wedged below them on the bank. Perhaps if she were to open a tin of baked beans and another of mushrooms, and fry an onion or two . . .

'I'm game to go a bit further,' Margaret said. She always made the best of things. And she felt no inducement to return to Nell's freezing house and sit, as they had yesterday evening and this morning, in Nell's squalid sitting room in front of Nell's pathetic fire. Also, Nell had threatened her with a tour of the garden. It was incomprehensible to Margaret how gardeners could stand around in cold and mud and enthuse – and expect others to enthuse – over a collection of dead and indistinguishable twigs. 'Do you enjoy cooking?' she asked, to cover the loudness of her shoes and Nell's boots on the tarmac. The digestion of a pub lunch of bread and cheese was not being helped by the memory of last night's grey mince, and what could only have been instant mashed potato.

'Not in the ordinary way,' Nell said. She stopped briefly to pierce a last year's oak leaf with the spike of her walking stick. 'But I like doing it for special occasions.'

Margaret wondered which category her own visit came into. 'I love it,' she said, with an emphasis that made it sound a virtue. 'I enjoy my food, I'm not ashamed to admit. Planning meals, shopping for them, preparing them – surely one of the great pleasures of life.'

Nell yawned and said nothing.

'Is that your man?' Margaret asked, as they stepped to the verge to avoid collision with a young-looking father and two children in red anoraks. The bigger child, his head thrust forward and over the handlebars, made motorbike noises and zig-zagged his tricycle; the smaller one hung over the side of his pushchair and scraped a stick along the tarmac.

'Aggression starts early in the male,' Nell said to no one in particular. 'No, he's always alone – except for his bull-terrier, that is. He's not my man, incidentally.' They climbed down from the bank, but Margaret lingered for a moment in the road, looking over her shoulder and repeating 'Boys will be boys' in an admiring voice.

They walked on in silence. A pale sunshine, that had been struggling all day with the clouds, gave up, and the afternoon grew increasingly dark and wild. It was the end of March and officially spring, but there was no sign yet of green and growing things. Margaret folded her arms and hugged the chest of her Country Casuals coat. She was ready to go back. Not back to Nell's, but back on the train to her own tidy and centrally-heated flat, and the prospect of supper – sole *bonne femme*, perhaps, with croquette potatoes and braised celery hearts.

'That's it – we'll have to turn round now,' Nell said, eyeing Margaret's shoes. A few yards ahead of them the road dwindled into a waterlogged track, winding between alders bent double in the wind. She swung the dog lead round her head and whistled for Dearest who was doing her best to follow a squirrel into a tree.

It was after they'd turned round, with the wind in their backs now instead of their faces, that things began to improve between them.

'Do you remember Miss Benson?' Nell suddenly asked.

'Miss Benson,' Margaret repeated, 'Miss Benson? *Joan* Benson. Oh dear. I never thought to hear that name again.' And she started to laugh.

'She was in love with Elaine Crabtree,' Nell went on, 'when Elaine was hockey captain and head girl.' Nell remembered this because she'd been in love with Elaine Crabtree herself. Elaine had had an oval, freckled face and untidy eyebrows she combed in front of the glass with a pocket comb kept for the purpose. Margaret, who hadn't loved anyone at school apart from Shelley, didn't remember this detail, but she could see

Miss Benson and Elaine, in particular the former's thighs as she belted down the pitch, blowing her whistle and shouting, 'Reds, get free! Mark your opponent, Sally!'

'Miss Benson was sacked, you know,' Nell said, 'shortly after we left. I can't remember who told me. She was found on the hockey field in the middle of the night, dead drunk apparently and singing bawdy songs.'

'You're making it up,' Margaret said. But she was pleased with the turn their conversation had taken.

The memory of Miss Benson led them on to other members of staff and other girls, to school buildings and classrooms and dormitories, to the prefects' study and 'Pre's Teas' of cold baked beans and condensed milk sucked from the tin. Prompting and correcting each other, they were able to conjure up the jacaranda trees that bordered the drive, the wood smoke ('That smell,' Nell said, 'I keep it here, at the back of my nose'), curling into the sky from the staff bandas that lay below the games fields in an exclusive cluster out of sight of the main block. They recalled mornings that, because they were six thousand feet above sea level, remained coldly misted until midday, afternoons so wiltingly hot that failure to wear a hat was punished by an order mark or with sunstroke.

'She must be dead now,' Margaret said. She was speaking of the biology mistress, whose luxuriant moustache and habit of throwing chalk at her pupils they had just been dissecting. 'Very probably, they're all dead. It's nearly forty years ago, you realize.'

This terrible truth brought them both to a halt. What have I done with my life? Nell thought, What have I got to show for all these years? On an impulse, she put her arm through Margaret's, regretted it at once, and had to leave it there.

'Quiz time, now,' Margaret said, encouraged by the intimacy Nell's arm betokened. 'What did we sing in that inter-school choral comp we were expected to win and came bottom of?'

'A La-a-ake and a faer-ie boat,' Nell sang, 'and something else. Can't remember what. Oh yes I can — in Hans' old mill his five black cats — '

'Three black cats.'

' – his three black cats watch the bins for the thieving rats – Jekyll and Jessup, and o-one eye-eyed – help.'

'Jill,' Margaret said.

'Jill. Cats are never Jill though, are they. Supposing they were, someone called Hans would have cats called Gretchen or Gertrud. Why are children made to sing such nonsense? A lake and a fairy boat – I ask you.'

'We are walking beside a lake,' Margaret pointed out, 'and the fairy boats are over there.' But when they scanned the water, the boats were somewhere beyond a promontory and hidden from them by the trees.

A sudden cloudburst of hailstones sent them running down the bank to a rustic bench and the shelter of a yew tree. The yew formed a black tent above their heads, and they sat cosily together watching the hailstones tear the surface of the lake.

'What's that scent you're wearing?' Nell said. It came from Margaret's silk scarf, and the collar of her coat. It was strong, and in some way unsettling: she never wore scent herself.

'*Jolie Madame*,' Margaret said. 'How do we stop your dog whining? Does he do it all the time?' Nell picked up Dearest and held her on her knee, where she dug her claws in and trembled and continued to whine. A reek of wet dog displaced the *Jolie Madame*.

'Odeur de wet dog,' Margaret said. She turned her head away. She turned back to Nell. 'You weren't very nice at school,' she confided, poking her in the ribs. 'I hated you at the beginning.'

'*We* thought *you* were too big for your boots,' Nell said, recalling how Margaret, whose father had been a major or colonel in some regiment sent out from England to put down the Mau Mau, had arrived in the middle of a Lent term and gone – at only fifteen – straight into the sixth form. She'd made the rest of them – settlers' daughters like herself, whose parents farmed in remote up-country places, District Commissioners' daughters, daughters of doctors and dentists and government officials in Nairobi – feel that 'colonial' equalled not just naive and unsophisticated, but stupid. Nell couldn't remember now how they'd ever become friends. Perhaps on her own side, it had been a question of finding when you couldn't beat someone, that it might be expedient to join them.

Margaret reminded Nell that she's never owned any boots. She asked if Nell missed Africa in general, and the farm at Hoey's Bridge in particular, and Nell said she did, and more and more as she got older. But she'd never go back, she said, never. They talked about Hoey's Bridge for a while. Margaret remembered playing pingpong in the creamery and how green and cold it was in there compared to outside, and how they'd been caught once by Nell's mother dipping their fingers in the vats. She had a clear picture of Nell's mother, she said, in men's brown trousers and an aertex shirt and bush hat; in fact she was prepared to swear Nell's mother hadn't worn anything else during the whole of her visit, which must have been three weeks. She remembered being woken every morning by the shamba boys sweeping the tennis court and singing, if you could call it that; and she remembered a tennis party with twin brothers who'd come from Kitale for the weekend, and how rude and cocky they were, especially the smaller one who had ginger hair.

Nell wondered if it was working in a library that made Margaret talk so much. She watched the storm ending. Like a cine film run backwards, the hail was drawn off the lake and back up into the clouds. Afterwards the banks, the bushes and the rough grass at the water's edge were left with a granular coating, like imitation snow.

'Behold, a white dog,' Margaret said when they were back on the roadway. 'It must be your man at last.'

'Yes, that's him.' A long way off, a man and a dog could just be seen heading in their direction. 'Since you're so interested in what you insist on calling *my* man, I dare you,' said Nell, on whom all this chat about school and childhood had had the effect of making her feel frivolous and fifteen, 'to say something when we meet. Engage him in conversation.'

'Whatever for?' said Margaret. But she was intrigued, nevertheless.

'Because,' said Nell, 'because it would be amusing. I'd like to know what his voice is like. I imagine it to be Scots – Edinburgh, not Glasgow.'

Margaret said it would make more sense if Nell spoke to him because she was the one who saw him all the time. But Nell said no. She didn't explain that it was too late to speak to anyone with whom she had not even exchanged nods. He always looked preoccupied and unapproachable, his eyes on the ground or on the lake. Even their dogs avoided each other. She had no grounds for approaching him. But Margaret didn't care who she said Boo to. 'You could say "Good evening",' Nell told her, 'and perhaps something about his dog. You could say "that's a handsome dog – is he a Staffordshire bull-terrier?" – I happen to know that he is, but it's a legitimate question to dog owners. We enjoy compliments and enquiries,' she added pointedly.

'I'm not fond of dogs, as you know,' Margaret said. As she spoke, and as if to confirm her opinion, Dearest defecated hugely and wetly on the grass beside them, afterwards stretching out her back legs and kicking up a shower of slush and mud.

'Talk about the weather then,' Nell said. 'If you do it,' she encouraged, 'if you can keep him talking for at least five minutes, I'll let you have the tulip plate.'

The evening before, Margaret had admired the plate that had contained her cottage pie. It had a pattern of intertwined red and yellow tulips round the rim, and in the centre, once the mince and potato and watery beans had been forked up, she'd discovered a wicker basket with red and yellow tulips springing from it. 'What a very pretty plate!' she'd said. 'Is it part of a set?' Nell, who thought the design feeble and the colours crude, had merely shrugged and smiled.

Nell's offer acted as a spur to Margaret. If the plate were hers – she'd even decided this as Nell took it away and put it in the sink – it would hang on the sitting-room wall. She had just the right spot for it, in a little alcove above the bookcase. And it would go with the curtains which, while neither red nor yellow, had splashes of both in their multicoloured pattern.

'I'll see then,' she said to Nell. 'I won't promise, but I might.' A sense of conspiracy quickened their footsteps. As her quarry came nearer, Margaret tried to size him up, but he kept getting lost behind the trees, or hidden by a curve in the lake, and when he was visible she couldn't see his face because he was looking at the ground. He'd evidently not sheltered from the storm, for as he came into focus she could see that his hair was sopping and flattened to his scalp. The dog was wet through, also: a pink piggy skin showed through his saturated coat. A hideous creature, surely, even by dog lovers' standards: tiny pink eyes, a pink belligerent nose, wet fat slapping as he rolled rather than walked –

It was at this moment, when they were perhaps fifty yards from certain encounter, that a car, going too fast for the place and the weather, overtook them, its tyres sending out a burst of grit and slush. Margaret's camel coat, her twelve denier tights, her tan court shoes, took the worst of it. Cursing, she bent down to examine the damage. Nell seized her by the elbow.

'Don't bother with that now,' she said. 'It'll brush off when it's dry.' But Margaret was no longer in the mood for schoolgirl games. She kept swivelling to see the back of her coat. It was wrecked; from what she could see of it, a major disaster.

'Go on, go on, cowardy custard,' Nell said out of the side of her mouth. But as they came face to face with 'her' man, it was Nell who was the coward. She stepped well clear of the confrontation and made for the trees with Dearest, neck fur up and tail down between her legs, at her heels. Abandoned on the tarmac, Margaret hesitated for a moment, and then went up to the man and stood in front of him so that he was forced to stop and look at her. He had pale blue eyes and a tired face, but it was a much younger face than Margaret had been expecting. Nell had said nothing about his being a young man. He couldn't have been more than thirty, at the most.

'Good afternoon,' she began, and stopped. Out of the corner of her eye she could see Nell, some way ahead and out of earshot, pretending an interest in a larch cone she'd found in the grass. A question about the bull-terrier, at that moment sniffing her shoes and ankles and the hem of her coat, a comment on the freakishness of the storm, half formed themselves, retreated, evaporated altogether. She had nothing to say to this fellow at all. She opened her mouth. 'Tell me, how is Mary?' she heard herself say.

The man looked at her, and it was a look more curious than surprised. He swivelled his head and looked up at the sky, and then back at Margaret. To her alarm, his eyes filled with large, blistery tears.

'Not so good today,' he said in a sad, flat voice. 'It can't be long now, she's very weak.' He blinked, and the tears tipped out of his eyelids and broke on his cheeks. He brushed them away with the back of his hand. 'She sleeps most of the day, when the pain lets her.' He nodded towards the bull-terrier. 'I'm taking a little breather with Tray.'

'I'm so sorry,' Margaret said, appalled. She'd never seen a man cry.

'If only she'd fought more,' the man said, 'if only she'd put up a proper fight –' his voice tailed off. He clenched his fists and stared out at the lake. 'But you know Mary,' he said, turning back to Margaret with a sad smile, 'she's always been a fatalist. She just accepts things.'

'I'm so sorry,' Margaret said.

'Thank you,' the man said. 'I suppose you work at the Centre,' he added – and it seemed to Margaret to be not a question, but a statement requiring only her confirmation – 'with Janet and the others.'

'Yes,' Margaret nodded, 'yes I do.'

'Janet has been a particular help,' the man said. His emphasis made Margaret feel that she herself had not been. 'She's sitting with Mary now, reading to her, holding her hand.'

'That's good,' Margaret said. 'I'm glad about that.' She stepped backwards and then sideways, to give him a chance to walk on, but he didn't take it.

'Give her my love, please,' she said. She put out a hand and touched his sleeve. It was soaking. 'Goodbye,' she said. 'God bless you.'

'Whom shall I say?' the man called after her. 'Whose love shall I give?'

'Alison's,' Margaret said, over her shoulder, without looking back.

'Alison's,' the man repeated, 'Alison's.' He watched her walk slowly away from him, her shoulders hunched, her head bowed, the posture – at once reverent and self-conscious – of one who has just left the altar rail after receiving Communion.

'Well,' Nell said impatiently, coming out of her ambush, 'you've won the tulip plate, I see. You were hours – I nearly died of cold.'

'It was awful,' Margaret said, more to herself than to Nell. 'I walked into some sort of family tragedy.'

'Must be his wife who's dying,' Nell said when Margaret, haltingly, and omitting the 'Alison' and the 'God bless you' her thirty-year-old atheism was still smarting from, had re-counted the conversation. 'Cancer, I should think, from the sound of it.'

All lies, Margaret murmured wonderingly to herself, one lie after another, I told him nothing but lies.

'Or one of his children,' Nell said. 'The Centre could be a day nursery, or a clinic, or a home for handicapped children.' And she was silent, trying to imagine what it would be like to have a child; a healthy child, a sick child, a child you loved and who loved you; a child who died. If it was me dying, she thought suddenly, who would weep? Would anyone?

'I still don't understand,' she began as they reached the car, 'what —' She was going to say, what made you ask about *Mary*?, but knew that however she phrased it, it would sound like the question that really occupied her, which was: How could something so strange happen to someone as insensitive as Margaret? And why should a man she'd seen countless times on her walks, and who'd never so much as glanced in her direction, choose Margaret, of all people, to tell his troubles to?

She opened the rear door to find her shoes, and then leant against the car while she took off her boots. Margaret got into the passenger seat without saying a word, and did up her seat belt.

Nell didn't like this silent Margaret. Silence was the prerogative of the imaginative. Moreover, this silence had a secret, exclusive feel. 'A cup of tea is what we need, Meg,' she said, switching on the engine. 'It'll cheer you up. I hope.'

But Margaret did not cheer up. (Something momentous had happened, something that would alter her life. She had been chosen, she knew. But for what? For what?) She sat stiffly in her ruined coat, and stared ahead as the windscreen wipers raked and squeaked.

'Just going to see if they've got any tea-cakes, then,' Nell said crossly, pulling up without warning outside the village shop — an action which provoked a swerve, a blast on the horn and a rude gesture from the driver behind.

MURIEL SPARK

*

The Black Madonna

When the Black Madonna was installed in the Church of the Sacred Heart the Bishop himself came to consecrate it. His long purple train was upheld by the two curliest of the choir. The day was favoured suddenly with thin October sunlight as he crossed the courtyard from the presbytery to the church, as the procession followed him chanting the Litany of the Saints: five priests in vestments of white heavy silk interwoven with glinting threads, four lay officials with straight red robes, then the confraternities and the tangled columns of the Mothers' Union.

The new town of Whitney Clay had a large proportion of Roman Catholics, especially among the nurses at the new hospital; and at the paper mills, too, there were many Catholics, drawn inland from Liverpool by the new housing estate; likewise, with the canning factories.

The Black Madonna had been given to the church by a recent convert. It was carved out of bog oak.

'They found the wood in the bog. Had been there hundreds of years. They sent for the sculptor right away by phone. He went over to Ireland and carved it there and then. You see, he had to do it while it was still wet.'

'Looks a bit like contemporary art.'

'Nah, that's not contemporary art, it's old-fashioned. If you'd ever seen contemporary work you'd *know* it was old-fashioned.'

'Looks like contemp—'

'It's old-*fashioned*. Else how'd it get sanctioned to be put up?'

'It's not so nice as the Immaculate Conception at Lourdes. That lifts you up.'

Everyone got used, eventually, to the Black Madonna with her square hands and straight carved draperies. There was a movement to dress it up in vestments, or at least a lace veil.

'She looks a bit gloomy, Father, don't you think?'

'No,' said the priest, 'I think it looks fine. If you start dressing it up in cloth you'll spoil the line.'

Sometimes people came from London especially to see the Black Madonna, and these were not Catholics; they were, said the priest, probably no religion at all, poor souls, though gifted with faculties. They came, as if to a museum, to see the line of the Black Madonna which must not be spoiled by vestments.

The new town of Whitney Clay had swallowed up the old village. One or two cottages with double dormer windows, an inn called The Tyger, a Methodist chapel, and three small shops represented the village; the three shops were already threatened by the Council; the Methodists were fighting to keep their chapel. Only the double dormer cottages and the inn were protected by the Nation and so had to be suffered by the Town Planning Committee.

The town was laid out like geometry in squares, arcs (to allow for the by-pass), and isosceles triangles, breaking off, at one point, to skirt the old village which, from the aerial view, looked like a merry doodle on the page.

Manders Road was one side of a parallelogram of green-bordered streets. It was named after one of the founders of the canning concern, Manders' Figs in Syrup, and it comprised a row of shops and a long high block of flats named Cripps House after the late Sir Stafford Cripps who had laid the foundation stone. In flat twenty-two on the fifth floor of Cripps House lived Raymond and Lou Parker. Raymond Parker was a foreman at the motor works, and was on the management committee. He had been married for fifteen years to Lou, who was thirty-seven at the time that the miraculous powers of the Black Madonna came to be talked of.

Of the twenty-five couples who lived in Cripps House five were Catholics. All, except Raymond and Lou Parker, had children. A sixth family had recently been moved by the Council into one of the six-roomed houses because of the seven children besides the grandfather.

Raymond and Lou were counted lucky to have obtained their three-roomed flat although they had no children. People with children had priority; but their name had been on the waiting list for years, and some said Raymond had a pull with one of the Councillors who was a director of the motor works.

The Parkers were among the few tenants of Cripps House who owned a motor-car. They did not, like most of their neighbours, have a television receiver, from being childless they had been able to afford to expand themselves in the way of taste, so that their habits differed slightly and their amusements considerably, from those of their neighbours. The Parkers went to the pictures only when the *Observer* had praised the film; they considered television not their sort of thing; they adhered to their religion; they voted Labour; they believed that the twentieth century was the best so far; they assented to the doctrine of original sin; they frequently applied the word 'Victorian' to ideas and people they did not like – for instance, when a local Town Councillor resigned his office Raymond said, 'He had to go. He's Victorian. And far too young for the job'; and Lou said Jane Austen's books were too Victorian; and anyone who opposed the abolition of capital punishment was Victorian. Raymond took the *Reader's Digest*, a magazine called *Motoring* and the *Catholic Herald*. Lou took the *Queen*, *Woman's Own*, and *Life*. Their daily paper was the *News Chronicle*. They read two books apiece each week. Raymond preferred travel books; Lou liked novels.

For the first five years of their married life they had been worried about not having children. Both had submitted themselves to medical tests as a result of which Lou had a course of

injections. These were unsuccessful. It had been a disappointment since both came from large sprawling Catholic families.
None of their married brothers and sisters had less than three
children. One of Lou's sisters, now widowed, had eight; they
sent her a pound a week.

Their flat in Cripps House had three rooms and a kitchen.
All round them their neighbours were saving up to buy houses.
A council flat, once obtained, was a mere platform in space to
further the progress of the rocket. This ambition was not
shared by Raymond and Lou; they were not only content,
they were delighted, with these civic chambers, and indeed
took something of an aristocratic view of them, not without a
self-conscious feeling of being free, in this particular, from the
prejudices of that middle class to which they as good as
belonged. 'One day,' said Lou, 'it will be the thing to live in a
council flat.'

They were eclectic as to their friends. Here, it is true, they
differed slightly from each other. Raymond was for inviting
the Ackleys to meet the Farrells. Mr Ackley was an accountant
at the Electricity Board. Mr and Mrs Farrell were respectively
a sorter at Manders' Figs in Syrup and an usherette at the
Odeon.

'After all,' argued Raymond, 'they're all Catholics.'

'Ah well,' said Lou, 'but now, their interests are different.
The Farrells wouldn't know what the Ackleys were talking
about. The Ackleys like politics. The Farrells like to tell jokes.
I'm not a snob, only sensible.'

'Oh, please yourself.' For no one could call Lou a snob, and
everyone knew she was sensible.

Their choice of acquaintance was wide by reason of their
active church membership: that is to say, they were members
of various guilds and confraternities. Raymond was a sidesman,
and he also organized the weekly football lottery in aid of the
Church Decoration Fund. Lou felt rather out of things when
the Mothers' Union met and had special Masses, for the
Mothers' Union was the only group she did not qualify for.

Having been a nurse before her marriage she was, however, a member of the Nurses' Guild.

Thus, most of their Catholic friends came from different departments of life. Others, connected with the motor works where Raymond was a foreman, were of different social grades to which Lou was more alive than Raymond. He let her have her way, as a rule, when it came to a question of which would mix with which.

A dozen Jamaicans were taken on at the motor works. Two came into Raymond's department. He invited them to the flat one evening to have coffee. They were unmarried, very polite and black. The quiet one was called Henry Pierce and the talkative one, Oxford St John. Lou, to Raymond's surprise and pleasure, decided that all their acquaintance, from top to bottom, must meet Henry and Oxford. All along he had known she was not a snob, only sensible, but he had rather feared she would consider the mixing of their new black and their old white friends not sensible.

'I'm glad you like Henry and Oxford,' he said. 'I'm glad we're able to introduce them to so many people.' For the dark pair had, within a month, spent nine evenings at Cripps House; they had met accountants, teachers, packers, and sorters. Only Tina Farrell, the usherette, had not seemed to understand the quality of these occasions: 'Quite nice chaps, them darkies, when you get to know them.'

'You mean Jamaicans,' said Lou. 'Why shouldn't they be nice? They're no different from anyone else.'

'Yes, yes, that's what I mean,' said Tina.

'We're all equal,' stated Lou. 'Don't forget there are black Bishops.'

'Jesus, I never said we were the equal of a Bishop,' Tina said, very bewildered.

'Well, don't call them darkies.'

Sometimes, on summer Sunday afternoons Raymond and Lou took their friends for a run in their car, ending up at a riverside road-house. The first time they turned up with

Oxford and Henry they felt defiant; but there were no objections, there was no trouble at all. Soon the dark pair ceased to be a novelty. Oxford St John took up with a pretty red-haired book-keeper, and Henry Pierce, missing his companion, spent more of his time at the Parkers' flat. Lou and Raymond had planned to spend their two weeks' summer holiday in London. 'Poor Henry,' said Lou. 'He'll miss us.'

Once you brought him out he was not so quiet as you thought at first. Henry was twenty-four, desirous of knowledge in all fields, shining very much in eyes, skin, teeth, which made him seem all the more eager. He called out the maternal in Lou, and to some extent the avuncular in Raymond. Lou used to love him when he read out lines from his favourite poems which he had copied into an exercise book.

> Haste thee, nymph, and bring with thee
> Jest and youthful jollity,
> Sport that . . .

Lou would interrupt: 'You should say jest, jollity – not yest, yollity.'

'Jest,' he said carefully. 'And laughter holding both his sides,' he continued. '*Laughter* – hear that, Lou? – *laughter*. That's what the human race was made for. Those folks that go round gloomy, Lou, they . . .'

Lou loved this talk. Raymond puffed his pipe benignly. After Henry had gone Raymond would say what a pity it was such an intelligent young fellow had lapsed. For Henry had been brought up in a Roman Catholic mission. He had, however, abandoned religion. He was fond of saying, 'The superstition of today is the science of yesterday.'

'I can't allow,' Raymond would say, 'that the Catholic Faith is superstition. I can't allow that.'

'He'll return to the Church one day' – this was Lou's contribution, whether Henry was present or not. If she said it in front of Henry he would give her an angry look. These were the only occasions when Henry lost his cheerfulness and grew quiet again.

Raymond and Lou prayed for Henry, that he might regain his faith. Lou said her rosary three times a week before the Black Madonna.

'He'll miss us when we go on our holidays.'

Raymond telephoned to the hotel in London. 'Have you a single room for a young gentleman accompanying Mr and Mrs Parker?' He added, 'a coloured gentleman.' To his pleasure a room was available, and to his relief there was no objection to Henry's colour.

They enjoyed their London holiday, but it was somewhat marred by a visit to that widowed sister of Lou's to whom she allowed a pound a week towards the rearing of her eight children. Lou had not seen her sister Elizabeth for nine years.

They went to her one day towards the end of their holiday. Henry sat at the back of the car beside a large suitcase stuffed with old clothes for Elizabeth. Raymond at the wheel kept saying, 'Poor Elizabeth – eight kids,' which irritated Lou, though she kept her peace.

Outside the Underground station at Victoria Park, where they stopped to ask the way, Lou felt a strange sense of panic. Elizabeth lived in a very downward quarter of Bethnal Green, and in the past nine years since she had seen her Lou's memory of the shabby ground-floor rooms with their peeling walls and bare boards, had made a kinder nest for itself. Sending off the postal order to her sister each week she had gradually come to picture the habitation at Bethnal Green in an almost monastic light; it would be bare but well-scrubbed, spotless, and shining with Brasso and holy poverty. The floor boards gleamed. Elizabeth was grey-haired, lined, but neat. The children were well behaved, sitting down betimes to their broth in two rows along an almost refectory table. It was not till they had reached Victoria Park that Lou felt the full force of the fact that everything would be different from what she had imagined. 'It may have gone down since I was last there,' she said to Raymond who had never visited Elizabeth before.

'What's gone down?'

'Poor Elizabeth's place.'

Lou had not taken much notice of Elizabeth's dull little monthly letters, almost illiterate, for Elizabeth, as she herself always said, was not much of a scholar.

James is at another job I hope thats the finish of the bother I had my blood presiure there was a Health visitor very nice. Also the assistance they sent my Dinner all the time and for the kids at home they call it meals on Wheels. I pray to the Almighty that James is well out of his bother he never lets on at sixteen their all the same never open his mouth but Gods eyes are not shut. Thanks for P.O. you will be rewarded your affect sister Elizabeth.

Lou tried to piece together in her mind the gist of nine years' such letters. James was the eldest; she supposed he had been in trouble.

'I ought to have asked Elizabeth about young James,' said Lou. 'She wrote to me last year that he was in a bother, there was talk of him being sent away, but I didn't take it in at the time, I was busy.'

'You can't take everything on your shoulders,' said Raymond. 'You do very well by Elizabeth.' They had pulled up outside the house where Elizabeth lived on the ground floor. Lou looked at the chipped paint, the dirty windows, and torn grey-white curtains and was reminded with startling clarity of her hopeless childhood in Liverpool from which, miraculously, hope had lifted her, and had come true, for the nuns had got her that job; and she had trained as a nurse among white-painted beds, and white shining walls, and tiles, hot water everywhere, and Dettol without stint. When she had first married she had wanted all white-painted furniture that you could wash and liberate from germs; but Raymond had been for oak, he did not understand the pleasure of hygiene and new enamel paint, for his upbringing had been orderly, he had been accustomed to a lounge suite and autumn tints in the front

room all his life. And now Lou stood and looked at the outside
of Elizabeth's place and felt she had gone right back.

On the way back to the hotel Lou chattered with relief that it
was over. 'Poor Elizabeth, she hasn't had much of a chance. I
liked little Francis, what did you think of little Francis, Ray?'

Raymond did not like being called Ray, but he made no
objection for he knew that Lou had been under a strain.
Elizabeth had not been very pleasant. She had expressed
admiration for Lou's hat, bag, gloves, and shoes which were all
navy blue, but she had used an accusing tone. The house had
been smelly and dirty. 'I'll show you round,' Elizabeth had said
in a tone of mock refinement, and they were forced to push
through a dark narrow passage behind her skinny form till
they came to the big room where the children slept. A row of
old iron beds each with a tumble of dark blanket rugs, no
sheets. Raymond was indignant at the sight and hoped that
Lou was not feeling upset. He knew very well Elizabeth had a
decent living income from a number of public sources, and was
simply a slut, one of those who would not help themselves.

'Ever thought of taking a job, Elizabeth?' he had said, and
immediately realized his stupidity. But Elizabeth took her
advantage. 'What d'you mean? *I'm* not going to leave my kids in
no nursery. *I'm* not going to send them to no home. What kids
need these days is a good home-life and that's what they get.'
And she added, 'God's eyes are not shut,' in a tone which was
meant for him, Raymond, to get at him for doing well in life.

Raymond distributed half-crowns to the younger children
and deposited on the table half-crowns for those who were out
playing in the street.

'Goin' already?' said Elizabeth in her tone of reproach. But
she kept eyeing Henry with interest, and the reproachful tone
was more or less a routine affair.

'You from the States?' Elizabeth said to Henry.

Henry sat on the edge of his sticky chair and answered, no,
from Jamaica, while Raymond winked at him to cheer him.

'During the war there was a lot of boys like you from the States,' Elizabeth said, giving him a sideways look.

Henry held out his hand to the second youngest child, a girl of seven, and said, 'Come, talk to me.'

The child said nothing, only dipped into the box of sweets which Lou had brought.

'Come talk,' said Henry.

Elizabeth laughed. 'If she does talk you'll be sorry you ever asked. She's got a tongue in her head, that one. You should hear her cheeking up to the teachers.' Elizabeth's bones jerked with laughter among her loose clothes. There was a lopsided double bed in the corner, and beside it a table cluttered with mugs, tins, a comb and brush, a number of hair curlers, a framed photograph of the Sacred Heart, and also Raymond noticed what he thought erroneously to be a box of contraceptives. He decided to say nothing to Lou about this; he was quite sure she must have observed other things which he had not; possibly things of a more distressing nature.

Lou's chatter on the way back to the hotel had a touch of hysteria. 'Raymond, dear,' she said in her most chirpy West End voice, 'I simply *had* to give the poor dear *all* my next week's housekeeping money. We shall have to starve, darling, when we get home. That's *simply* what we shall have to do.'

'O.K.,' said Raymond.

'I ask you,' Lou shrieked, 'what else could I do, what *could* I do?'

'Nothing at all,' said Raymond, 'but what you've done.'

'My own *sister*, my dear,' said Lou; 'and did you see the way she had her hair bleached? – All streaky, and she used to have a lovely head of hair.'

'I wonder if she tries to raise herself?' said Raymond. 'With all those children she could surely get better accommodation if only she –'

'That sort,' said Henry, leaning forward from the back of the car, 'never moves. It's the slum mentality, man. Take some folks I've seen back home –'

'There's no comparison,' Lou snapped suddenly, 'this is quite a different case.'

Raymond glanced at her in surprise; Henry sat back, offended. Lou was thinking wildly, what a cheek *him* talking like a snob. At least Elizabeth's white.

Their prayers for the return of faith to Henry Pierce were so far answered in that he took a tubercular turn which was followed by a religious one. He was sent off to a sanatorium in Wales with a promise from Lou and Raymond to visit him before Christmas. Meantime, they applied themselves to Our Lady for the restoration of Henry's health.

Oxford St John, whose love affair with the red-haired girl had come to grief, now frequented their flat, but he could never quite replace Henry in their affections. Oxford was older and less refined than Henry. He would stand in front of the glass in their kitchen and tell himself, 'Man, you just a big black bugger.' He kept referring to himself as black, which of course he was, Lou thought, but it was not the thing to say. He stood in the doorway with his arms and smile thrown wide: 'I am black but comely, O ye daughters of Jerusalem.' And once, when Raymond was out, Oxford brought the conversation round to that question of being black *all over*, which made Lou very uncomfortable and she kept looking at the clock and dropped stitches in her knitting.

Three times a week when she went to the black Our Lady with her rosary to ask for the health of Henry Pierce, she asked also that Oxford St John would get another job in another town, for she did not like to make objections, telling her feelings to Raymond; there were no objections to make that you could put your finger on. She could not very well complain that Oxford was common; Raymond despised snobbery, and so did she, it was a very delicate question. She was amazed when, within three weeks, Oxford announced that he was thinking of looking for a job in Manchester.

Lou said to Raymond, 'Do you know there's something *in* what they say about the bog-oak statue in the church.'

'There may be,' said Raymond. 'People say so.'

Lou could not tell him how she had petitioned the removal of Oxford St John. But when she got a letter from Henry Pierce to say he was improving, she told Raymond, 'You see, we asked for Henry to get back the Faith, and so he did. Now we ask for his recovery and he's improving.'

'He's having good treatment at the sanatorium,' Raymond said. But he added, 'Of course we'll have to keep up the prayers.' He himself, though not a rosary man, knelt before the Black Madonna every Saturday evening after Benediction to pray for Henry Pierce.

Whenever they saw Oxford he was talking of leaving Whitney Clay. Raymond said, 'He's making a big mistake going to Manchester. A big place can be very lonely. I hope he'll change his mind.'

'He won't,' said Lou, so impressed was she now by the powers of the Black Madonna. She was good and tired of Oxford St John with his feet up on her cushions, and calling himself a nigger.

'We'll miss him,' said Raymond, 'he's such a cheery big soul.'

'We will,' said Lou. She was reading the parish magazine, which she seldom did, although she was one of the voluntary workers who sent them out, addressing hundreds of wrappers every month. She had vaguely noticed, in previous numbers, various references to the Black Madonna, how she had granted this or that favour. Lou had heard that people sometimes came from neighbouring parishes to pray at the Church of the Sacred Heart because of the statue. Some said they came from all over England, but whether this was to admire the art-work or to pray, Lou was not sure. She gave her attention to the article in the parish magazine:

> While not wishing to make excessive claims . . . many prayers answered and requests granted to the Faithful in an exceptional way . . . two remarkable cures effected, but medical evidence is, of course, still in reserve, a certain lapse of time being necessary

to ascertain permanency of cure. The first of these cases was a child of twelve suffering from leukaemia . . . The second . . . While not desiring to create a *cultus* where none is due, we must remember it is always our duty to honour Our Blessed Lady, the dispenser of all graces, to whom we owe . . .

Another aspect of the information received by the Father Rector concerning our 'Black Madonna' is one pertaining to childless couples of which three cases have come to his notice. In each case the couple claim to have offered constant devotion to the 'Black Madonna,' and in two of the cases specific requests were made for the favour of a child. In *all* cases the prayers were answered. The proud parents . . . it should be the loving duty of every parishioner to make a special thanksgiving . . . . The Father Rector will be grateful for any further information . . . .

'Look, Raymond,' said Lou. 'Read this.'

They decided to put in for a baby to the Black Madonna.

The following Saturday, when they drove to the church for Benediction, Lou jangled her rosary. Raymond pulled up outside the church. 'Look here, Lou,' he said, 'do you want a baby in any case?' – for he partly thought she was only putting the Black Madonna to the test – 'Do you want a child, after all these years?'

This was a new thought to Lou. She considered her neat flat and tidy routine, the entertaining with her good coffee cups, the weekly papers and the library books, the tastes which they would not have been able to cultivate had they had a family of children. She thought of her nice young looks which everyone envied, and her freedom of movement.

'Perhaps we should try,' she said. 'God won't give us a child if we aren't meant to have one.'

'We have to make some decisions for ourselves,' he said. 'And to tell you the truth if *you* don't want a child, *I* don't.'

'There's no harm in praying for one,' she said.

'You have to be careful what you pray for,' he said. 'You mustn't tempt Providence.'

She thought of her relatives, and Raymond's, all married with children. She thought of her sister Elizabeth with her eight, and remembered that one who cheeked up to the teachers, so pretty and sulky and shabby, and she remembered the fat baby Francis sucking his dummy and clutching Elizabeth's bony neck.

'I don't see why I shouldn't have a baby,' said Lou.

Oxford St John departed at the end of the month. He promised to write, but they were not surprised when weeks passed and they had no word. 'I don't suppose we shall ever hear from him again,' said Lou. Raymond thought he detected satisfaction in her voice, and would have thought she was getting snobbish as women do as they get older, losing sight of their ideals, had she not gone on to speak of Henry Pierce. Henry had written to say he was nearly cured, but had been advised to return to the West Indies.

'We must go and see him,' said Lou. 'We promised. What about the Sunday after next?'

'O.K.,' said Raymond.

It was the Saturday before that Sunday when Lou had her first sick turn. She struggled out of bed to attend Benediction, but had to leave suddenly during the service and was sick behind the church in the presbytery yard. Raymond took her home, though she protested against cutting out her rosary to the Black Madonna.

'After only six weeks!' she said, and she could hardly tell whether her sickness was due to excitement or nature. 'Only six weeks ago,' she said – and her voice had a touch of its old Liverpool – 'did we go to that Black Madonna and the prayer's answered, see.'

Raymond looked at her in awe as he held the bowl for her sickness. 'Are you sure?' he said.

She was well enough next day to go to visit Henry in the sanatorium. He was fatter and, she thought, a little coarser: and tough in his manner, as if once having been nearly disembodied he was not going to let it happen again. He was leaving the country very soon. He promised to come and see them before he left. Lou barely skimmed through his next letter before handing it over to Raymond.

Their visitors, now, were ordinary white ones. 'Not so colourful,' Raymond said, 'as Henry and Oxford were.' Then he looked embarrassed lest he should seem to be making a joke about the word coloured.

'Do you miss the niggers?' said Tina Farrell, and Lou forgot to correct her.

Lou gave up most of her church work in order to sew and knit for the baby. Raymond gave up the *Reader's Digest*. He applied for promotion and got it; he became a departmental manager. The flat was now a waiting-room for next summer, after the baby was born, when they would put down the money for a house. They hoped for one of the new houses on a building site on the outskirts of the town.

'We shall need a garden,' Lou explained to her friends. 'I'll join the Mothers' Union,' she thought. Meantime the spare bedroom was turned into a nursery. Raymond made a cot, regardless that some of the neighbours complained of the hammering. Lou prepared a cradle, trimmed it with frills. She wrote to her relatives; she wrote to Elizabeth, sent her five pounds, and gave notice that there would be no further weekly payments, seeing that they would now need every penny.

'She doesn't require it, anyway,' said Raymond. 'The Welfare State looks after people like Elizabeth.' And he told Lou about the contraceptives he thought he had seen on the table by the double bed. Lou became very excited about this. 'How did you know they were contraceptives? What did they look like? Why didn't you tell me before? What a cheek, calling herself a Catholic, do you think she has a man, then?'

Raymond was sorry he had mentioned the subject.

'Don't worry, dear, don't upset yourself, dear.'

'And she told me she goes to Mass every Sunday, and all the kids go excepting James. No wonder he's got into trouble with an example like that. I might have known, with her peroxide hair. A pound a week I've been sending up to now, that's fifty-two pounds a year. I would never have done it, calling herself a Catholic with birth control by her bedside.'

'Don't upset yourself, dear.'

Lou prayed to the Black Madonna three times a week for a safe delivery and a healthy child. She gave her story to the Father Rector who announced it in the next parish magazine. 'Another case has come to light of the kindly favour of our "Black Madonna" towards a childless couple . . . .' Lou recited her rosary before the statue until it was difficult for her to kneel, and, when she stood, could not see her feet. The Mother of God with her black bog-oaken drapery, her high black cheekbones and square hands looked more virginal than ever to Lou as she stood counting her beads in front of her stomach.

She said to Raymond, 'If it's a girl we must have Mary as one of the names. But not the first name, it's too ordinary.'

'Please yourself, dear,' said Raymond. The doctor had told him it might be a difficult birth.

'Thomas, if it's a boy,' she said, 'after my uncle. But if it's a girl I'd like something fancy for a first name.'

He thought, Lou's slipping, she didn't used to say that word, fancy.

'What about Dawn?' she said. 'I like the sound of Dawn. Then Mary for a second name. Dawn Mary Parker, it sounds sweet.'

'Dawn. That's not a Christian name,' he said. Then he told her, 'Just as you please, dear.'

'Or Thomas Parker,' she said.

She had decided to go into the maternity wing of the hospital like everyone else. But near the time she let Raymond change her mind, since he kept saying, 'At your age, dear, it might be more difficult than for the younger women. Better book a private ward, we'll manage the expense.'

In fact, it was a very easy birth, a girl. Raymond was allowed in to see Lou in the late afternoon. She was half asleep.

'The nurse will take you to see the baby in the nursery ward,' she told him. 'She's lovely, but terribly red.'

'They're always red at birth,' said Raymond.

He met the nurse in the corridor. 'Any chance of seeing the baby? My wife said . . .'

She looked flustered. 'I'll get the Sister,' she said.

'Oh, I don't want to give any trouble, only my wife said –'

'That's all right. Wait here, Mr Parker.'

The Sister appeared, a tall grave woman. Raymond thought her to be short-sighted for she seemed to look at him fairly closely before she bade him follow her.

The baby was round and very red, with dark curly hair.

'Fancy her having hair. I thought they were born bald,' said Raymond.

'They sometimes have hair at birth,' said the Sister.

'She's very red in colour.' Raymond began comparing his child with those in the other cots. 'Far more so than the others.'

'Oh, that will wear off.'

Next day he found Lou in a half-stupor. She had been given a strong sedative following an attack of screaming hysteria. He sat by her bed, bewildered. Presently a nurse beckoned him from the door. 'Will you have a word with Matron?'

'Your wife is upset about her baby,' said the matron. 'You see, the colour. She's a beautiful baby, perfect. It's a question of the colour.'

'I noticed the baby was red,' said Raymond, 'but the nurse said –'

'Oh, the red will go. It changes, you know. But the baby will certainly be brown, if not indeed black, as indeed we think she will be. A beautiful healthy child.'

'Black?' said Raymond.

'Yes, indeed we think so, indeed I must say, certainly so,' said the matron. 'We did not expect your wife to take it so badly when we told her. We've had plenty of dark babies here, but most of the mothers expect it.'

'There must be a mix-up. You must have mixed up the babies,' said Raymond.

'There's no question of mix-up,' said the matron sharply. 'We'll soon settle that. We've had some of *that* before.'

'But neither of us are dark,' said Raymond. 'You've seen my wife. You see me —'

'That's something you must work out for yourselves. I'd have a word with the doctor if I were you. But whatever conclusion you come to, please don't upset your wife at this stage. She has already refused to feed the child, says it isn't hers, which is ridiculous.'

'Was it Oxford St John?' said Raymond.

'Raymond, the doctor told you not to come here upsetting me. I'm feeling terrible.'

'Was it Oxford St John?'

'Clear out of here, you swine, saying things like that.'

He demanded to be taken to see the baby, as he had done every day for a week. The nurses were gathered round it, neglecting the squalling whites in the other cots for the sight of their darling black. She was indeed quite black, with a woolly crop and tiny negroid nostrils. She had been baptized that morning, though not in her parents' presence. One of the nurses had stood as godmother.

The nurses dispersed in a flurry as Raymond approached. He looked hard at the baby. It looked back with its black button eyes. He saw the name-tab round its neck, 'Dawn Mary Parker.'

He got hold of a nurse in the corridor. 'Look here, you just take that name Parker off that child's neck. The name's not Parker, it isn't my child.'

The nurse said, 'Get away, we're busy.'

'There's just a *chance*,' said the doctor to Raymond, 'that if there's ever been black blood in your family or your wife's, it's coming out now. It's a very long chance. I've never known it happen in my experience, but I've heard of cases, I could read them up.'

'There's nothing like that in my family,' said Raymond. He thought of Lou, the obscure Liverpool antecedents. The parents had died before he had met Lou.

'It could be several generations back,' said the doctor.

Raymond went home, avoiding the neighbours who would stop him to inquire after Lou. He rather regretted smashing up the cot in his first fury. That was something low coming out in him. But again, when he thought of the tiny black hands of the baby with their pink fingernails he did not regret smashing the cot.

He was successful in tracing the whereabouts of Oxford St John. Even before he heard the result of Oxford's blood test he said to Lou, 'Write and ask your relations if there's been any black blood in the family.'

'Write and ask *yours*,' she said.

She refused to look at the black baby. The nurses fussed round it all day, and came to report its progress to Lou.

'Pull yourself together, Mrs Parker, she's a lovely child.'

'You must care for your infant,' said the priest.

'You don't know what I'm suffering,' Lou said.

'In the name of God,' said the priest, 'if you're a Catholic Christian you've got to expect to suffer.'

'I can't go against my nature,' said Lou. 'I can't be expected to –'

Raymond said to her one day in the following week, 'The blood tests are all right, the doctor says.'

'What do you mean, all right?'

'Oxford's blood and the baby's don't tally, and –'

'Oh, shut up,' she said. 'The baby's black and your blood tests can't make it white.'

'No,' he said. He had fallen out with his mother, through his inquiries whether there had been coloured blood in his family. 'The doctor says,' he said, 'that these black mixtures sometimes occur in seaport towns. It might have been generations back.'

'One thing,' said Lou. 'I'm not going to take that child back to the flat.'

'You'll have to,' he said.

Elizabeth wrote her a letter which Raymond intercepted:

'Dear Lou Raymond is asking if we have any blacks in the family well thats funny you have a coloured God is not asleep. There was that Flinn cousin Tommy at Liverpool he was very dark they put it down to the past a nigro off a ship that would be before our late Mothers Time God rest her soul she would turn in her grave you shoud have kept up your bit to me whats a pound a Week to you. It was on our fathers side the colour and Mary Flinn you remember at the dairy was dark remember her hare was like nigro hare it must be back in the olden days the nigro some ansester but it is only nature. I thank the almighty it has missed my kids and your hubby must think it was that nigro you was showing off when you came to my place. I wish you all the best as a widow with kids you shoud send my money as per usual your affec sister Elizabeth.'

'I gather from Elizabeth,' said Raymond to Lou, 'that there *was* some element of colour in your family. Of course, you couldn't be expected to know about it. I do think, though, that some kind of record should be kept.'

'Oh, shut *up*,' said Lou. 'The baby's black and nothing can make it white.'

Two days before Lou left the hospital she had a visitor, although she had given instructions that no one except Raymond should be let in to see her. This lapse she attributed to the nasty curiosity of the nurses, for it was Henry Pierce come to say good-bye before embarkation. He stayed less than five minutes.

'Why, Mrs Parker, your visitor didn't stay long,' said the nurse.

'No, I soon got rid of him. I thought I made it clear to you that I didn't want to see anyone. You shouldn't have let him in.'

'Oh, sorry, Mrs Parker, but the young gentleman looked so upset when we told him so. He said he was going abroad and it was his last chance, he might never see you again. He said, "How's the baby?", and we said, "Tip-top."'

'I know what's in your mind,' said Lou. 'But it isn't true. I've got the blood tests.'

'Oh, Mrs Parker, I wouldn't suggest for a minute . . .'

'She must have went with one of they niggers that used to come.'

Lou could never be sure if that was what she heard from the doorways and landings as she climbed the stairs of Cripps House, the neighbours hushing their conversation as she approached.

'I can't take to the child. Try as I do, I simply can't even like it.'

'Nor me,' said Raymond. 'Mind you, if it was anyone else's child I would think it was all right. It's just the thought of it being mine, and people thinking it isn't.'

'That's just it,' she said.

One of Raymond's colleagues had asked him that day how his friends Oxford and Henry were getting on. Raymond had to look twice before he decided that the question was innocent. But one never knew. . . . . Already Lou and Raymond had approached the adoption society. It was now only a matter of waiting for word.

'If that child was mine,' said Tina Farrell, 'I'd never part with her. I wish we could afford to adopt another. She's the loveliest little darkie in the world.'

'You wouldn't think so,' said Lou, 'if she really was yours. Imagine it for yourself, waking up to find you've had a black baby that everyone thinks has a nigger for its father.'

'It *would* be a shock,' Tina said, and tittered.

'We've got the blood tests,' said Lou quickly.

Raymond got a transfer to London. They got word about the adoption very soon.

'We've done the right thing,' said Lou. 'Even the priest had to agree with that, considering how strongly we felt against keeping the child.'

'Oh, he said it was a good thing?'

'No, not a *good* thing. In fact he said it would have been a good thing if we could have kept the baby. But failing that, we did the *right* thing. Apparently, there's a difference.'

A. S. BYATT

*

The July Ghost

'I think I must move out of where I'm living,' he said. 'I have this problem with my landlady.'

He picked a long, bright hair off the back of her dress, so deftly that the act seemed simply considerate. He had been skilful at balancing glass, plate and cutlery, too. He had a look of dignified misery, like a dejected hawk. She was interested.

'What sort of problem? Amatory, financial, or domestic?'

'None of those, really. Well, not financial.'

He turned the hair on his finger, examining it intently, not meeting her eye.

'Not financial. Can you tell me? I might know somewhere you could stay. I know a lot of people.'

'You would.' He smiled shyly. 'It's not an easy problem to describe. There's just the two of us. I occupy the attics. Mostly.'

He came to a stop. He was obviously reserved and secretive. But he was telling her something. This is usually attractive.

'Mostly?' Encouraging him.

'Oh, it's not like *that*. Well, not . . . Shall we sit down?'

They moved across the party, which was a big party, on a hot day. He stopped and found a bottle and filled her glass. He had not needed to ask what she was drinking. They sat side by side on a sofa: he admired the brilliant poppies bold on her emerald dress, and her pretty sandals. She had come to London for the summer to work in the British Museum. She could really have managed with microfilm in Tucson for what little manuscript research was needed, but there was a dragging love affair to end. There is an age at which, however desperately happy one is in stolen moments, days, or weekends with one's married professor, one either prises him loose or cuts and runs. She had had a stab at both, and now considered she had successfully cut and run. So it was nice to be immediately appreciated. Problems are capable of solution. She said as much to him, turning her soft face to his ravaged one, swinging the long bright hair. It had begun a year ago, he told her in a rush, at another party actually; he had met this woman, the landlady in question, and had made, not immediately, a kind of *faux pas*, he now saw, and she had been very decent, all things considered, and so . . .

He had said, 'I think I must move out of where I'm living.' He had been quite wild, had nearly not come to the party, but could not go on drinking alone. The woman had considered him coolly and asked, 'Why?' One could not, he said, go on in a place where one had once been blissfully happy, and was now miserable, however convenient the place. Convenient, that was, for work, and friends, and things that seemed, as he mentioned them, ashy and insubstantial compared to the memory and the hope of opening the door and finding Anne outside it, laughing and breathless, waiting to be told what he had read, or thought, or eaten, or felt that day. Someone I loved left, he told the woman. Reticent on that occasion too, he bit back the flurry of sentences about the total un-expectedness of it, the arriving back and finding only an envelope on a clean table, and spaces in the bookshelves, the record stack, the kitchen cupboard. It must have been planned for weeks, she must have been thinking it out while he rolled on her, while she poured wine for him, while . . . No, no. Vituperation is undignified and in this case what he felt was lower and worse than rage: just pure, child-like loss. 'One ought not to mind places,' he said to the woman. 'But one does,' she had said. 'I know.'

She had suggested to him that he could come and be her lodger, then; she had, she said, a lot of spare space going to waste, and her husband wasn't there much. 'We've not had a lot to say to each other, lately.' He could be quite self-contained, there was a kitchen and a bathroom in the attics; she wouldn't bother him. There was a large garden. It was possibly this that decided him: it was very hot, central London, the time of year when a man feels he would give anything to live in a room opening on to grass and trees, not a high flat in a dusty street. And if Anne came back, the door would be locked and mortice-locked. He could stop thinking about Anne coming back. That was a decisive move: Anne thought he wasn't decisive. He would live without Anne.

For some weeks after he moved in he had seen very little of the woman. They met on the stairs, and once she came up, on a hot Sunday, to tell him he must feel free to use the garden. He had offered to do some weeding and mowing and she had accepted. That was the weekend her husband came back, driving furiously up to the front door, running in, and calling in the empty hall, 'Imogen, Imogen!' To which she had replied, uncharacteristically, by screaming hysterically. There was nothing in her husband, Noel's, appearance to warrant this reaction; their lodger, peering over the banister at the sound, had seen their upturned faces in the stairwell and watched hers settle into its usual prim and placid expression as he did so. Seeing Noel, a balding, fluffy-templed, stooping thirty-five or so, shabby corduroy suit, cotton polo neck, he realized he was now able to guess her age, as he had not been. She was a very neat woman, faded blonde, her hair in a knot on the back of her head, her legs long and slender, her eyes downcast. Mild was not quite the right word for her, though. She explained then that she had screamed because Noel had come home unexpectedly and startled her: she was sorry. It seemed a reasonable explanation. The extraordinary vehemence of the screaming was probably an echo in the stairwell. Noel seemed wholly downcast by it, all the same.

★

He had kept out of the way, that weekend, taking the stairs two at a time and lightly, feeling a little aggrieved, looking out of his kitchen window into the lovely, overgrown garden, that they were lurking indoors, wasting all the summer sun. At Sunday lunch-time he had heard the husband, Noel, shouting on the stairs.

'I can't go on, if you go on like that. I've done my best, I've tried to get through. Nothing will shift you, will it, you won't *try*, will you, you just go on and on. Well, I have my life to live, you can't throw a life away . . . can you?'

He had crept out again on to the dark upper landing and seen her standing, half-way down the stairs, quite still, watching Noel wave his arms and roar, or almost roar, with a look of impassive patience, as though this nuisance must pass off. Noel swallowed and gasped; he turned his face up to her and said plaintively,

'You do see I can't stand it? I'll be in touch, shall I? You must want . . . you must need . . . you must . . .'

She didn't speak.

'If you need anything, you know where to get me.'

'Yes.'

'Oh, well . . .' said Noel, and went to the door. She watched him, from the stairs, until it was shut, and then came up again, step by step, as though it was an effort, a little, and went on coming, past her bedroom, to his landing, to come in and ask him, entirely naturally, please to use the garden if he wanted to, and please not to mind marital rows. She was sure he understood . . . things were difficult . . . Noel wouldn't be back for some time. He was a journalist: his work took him away a lot. Just as well. She committed herself to that 'just as well'. She was a very economical speaker.

So he took to sitting in the garden. It was a lovely place: a huge, hidden, walled south London garden, with old fruit trees at the end, a wildly waving disorderly buddleia, curving beds full of old roses, and a lawn of overgrown, dense rye-grass.

Over the wall at the foot was the Common, with a footpath running behind all the gardens. She came out to the shed and helped him to assemble and oil the lawnmower, standing on the little path under the apple branches while he cut an experimental serpentine across her hay. Over the wall came the high sound of children's voices, and the thunk and thud of a football. He asked her how to raise the blades: he was not mechanically minded.

'The children get quite noisy,' she said. 'And dogs. I hope they don't bother you. There aren't many safe places for children, round here.'

He replied truthfully that he never heard sounds that didn't concern him, when he was concentrating. When he'd got the lawn into shape, he was going to sit on it and do a lot of reading, try to get his mind in trim again, to write a paper on Hardy's poems, on their curiously archaic vocabulary.

'It isn't very far to the road on the other side, really,' she said. 'It just seems to be. The Common is an illusion of space, really. Just a spur of brambles and gorse-bushes and bits of football pitch between two fast four-laned main roads. I hate London commons.'

'There's a lovely smell, though, from the gorse and the wet grass. It's a pleasant illusion.'

'No illusions are pleasant,' she said, decisively, and went in. He wondered what she did with her time: apart from little shopping expeditions she seemed to be always in the house. He was sure that when he'd met her she'd been introduced as having some profession: vaguely literary, vaguely academic, like everyone he knew. Perhaps she wrote poetry in her north-facing living-room. He had no idea what it would be like. Women generally wrote emotional poetry, much nicer than men, as Kingsley Amis has stated, but she seemed, despite her placid stillness, too spare and too fierce – grim? – for that. He remembered the screaming. Perhaps she wrote Plath-like chants of violence. He didn't think that quite fitted the bill, either. Perhaps she was a freelance radio journalist. He

didn't bother to ask anyone who might be a common acquaintance. During the whole year, he explained to the American at
the party, he hadn't actually *discussed* her with anyone. Of
course he wouldn't, she agreed vaguely and warmly. She knew
he wouldn't. He didn't see why he shouldn't, in fact, but went
on, for the time, with his narrative.

They had got to know each other a little better over the next
few weeks, at least on the level of borrowing tea, or even
sharing pots of it. The weather had got hotter. He had found
an old-fashioned deck-chair, with faded striped canvas, in the
shed, and had brushed it over and brought it out on to his
mown lawn, where he sat writing a little, reading a little,
getting up and pulling up a tuft of couch grass. He had been
wrong about the children not bothering him: there was a
succession of incursions by all sizes of children looking for all
sizes of balls, which bounced to his feet, or crashed in the
shrubs, or vanished in the herbaceous border, black and white
footballs, beach-balls with concentric circles of primary colours,
acid yellow tennis balls. The children came over the wall:
black faces, brown faces, floppy long hair, shaven heads, respectable dotted sun-hats and camouflaged cotton army hats from
Milletts. They came over easily, as though they were used to
it, sandals, training shoes, a few bare toes, grubby sunburned
legs, cotton skirts, jeans, football shorts. Sometimes, perched
on the top, they saw him and gestured at the balls; one or two
asked permission. Sometimes he threw a ball back, but was apt
to knock down a few knobby little unripe apples or pears.
There was a gate in the wall, under the fringing trees, which
he once tried to open, spending time on rusty bolts only to
discover that the lock was new and secure, and the key not in
it.

The boy sitting in the tree did not seem to be looking for a
ball. He was in a fork of the tree nearest the gate, swinging his
legs, doing something to a knot in a frayed end of rope that
was attached to the branch he sat on. He wore blue jeans and

training shoes, and a brilliant tee shirt, striped in the colours of
the spectrum, arranged in the right order, which the man on
the grass found visually pleasing. He had rather long blond
hair, falling over his eyes, so that his face was obscured.

'Hey, you. Do you think you ought to be up there? It might
not be safe.'

The boy looked up, grinned, and vanished monkey-like over
the wall. He had a nice, frank grin, friendly, not cheeky.

He was there again, the next day, leaning back in the crook
of the tree, arms crossed. He had on the same shirt and jeans.
The man watched him, expecting him to move again, but he
sat, immobile, smiling down pleasantly, and then staring up at
the sky. The man read a little, looked up, saw him still there,
and said,

'Have you lost anything?'

The child did not reply: after a moment he climbed down a
little, swung along the branch hand over hand, dropped to the
ground, raised an arm in salute, and was up over the usual
route over the wall.

Two days later he was lying on his stomach on the edge of
the lawn, out of the shade, this time in a white tee shirt with a
pattern of blue ships and water-lines on it, his bare feet and
legs stretched in the sun. He was chewing a grass stem, and
studying the earth, as though watching for insects. The man
said, 'Hi, there,' and the boy looked up, met his look with
intensely blue eyes under long lashes, smiled with the same
complete warmth and openness, and returned his look to the
earth.

He felt reluctant to inform on the boy, who seemed so
harmless and considerate: but when he met him walking out of
the kitchen door, spoke to him, and got no answer but the
gentle smile before the boy ran off towards the wall, he
wondered if he should speak to his landlady. So he asked her,
did she mind the children coming in the garden. She said no,
children must look for balls, that was part of being children.
He persisted – they sat there, too, and he had met one coming

out of the house. He hadn't seemed to be doing any harm, the boy, but you couldn't tell. He thought she should know.

He was probably a friend of her son's, she said. She looked at him kindly and explained. Her son had run off the Common with some other children, two years ago, in the summer, in July, and had been killed on the road. More or less instantly, she had added drily, as though calculating that just *enough* information would preclude the need for further questions. He said he was sorry, very sorry, feeling to blame, which was ridiculous, and a little injured, because he had not known about her son, and might inadvertently have made a fool of himself with some casual reference whose ignorance would be embarrassing.

What was the boy like, she said. The one in the house? 'I don't – talk to his friends. I find it painful. It could be Timmy, or Martin. They might have lost something, or want . . .'

He described the boy. Blond, about ten at a guess, he was not very good at children's ages, very blue eyes, slightly built, with a rainbow-striped tee shirt and blue jeans, mostly though not always – oh, and those football practice shoes, black and green. And the other tee shirt, with the ships and wavy lines. And an extraordinarily nice smile. A really *warm* smile. A nice-looking boy.

He was used to her being silent. But this silence went on and on and on. She was just staring into the garden. After a time, she said, in her precise conversational tone,

'The only thing I want, the only thing I want at all in this world, is to see that boy.'

She stared at the garden and he stared with her, until the grass began to dance with empty light, and the edges of the shrubbery wavered. For a brief moment he shared the strain of not seeing the boy. Then she gave a little sigh, sat down, neatly as always, and passed out at his feet.

After this she became, for her, voluble. He didn't move her after she fainted, but sat patiently by her, until she stirred and sat up; then he fetched her some water, and would have gone away, but she talked.

'I'm too rational to see ghosts, I'm not someone who would see anything there was to see, I don't believe in an after-life, I don't see how anyone can, I always found a kind of satisfaction for myself in the idea that one just came to an end, to a sliced-off stop. But that was myself; I didn't think *he* – not *he* – I thought ghosts were – what people *wanted* to see, or were afraid to see . . . and after he died, the best hope I had, it sounds silly, was that I would go mad enough so that instead of waiting every day for him to come home from school and rattle the letter-box I might actually have the illusion of seeing or hearing him come in. Because I can't stop my body and mind waiting, every day, every day, I can't let go. And his bedroom, sometimes at night I go in, I think I might just for a moment forget he *wasn't* in there sleeping, I think I would pay almost anything – anything at all – for a moment of seeing him like I used to. In his pyjamas, with his – his – his hair . . . ruffled, and, his . . . you said, his . . . that *smile*.

'When it happened, they got Noel, and Noel came in and shouted my name, like he did the other day, that's why I screamed, because it – seemed the same – and then they said, he is dead, and I thought coolly, *is* dead, that will go on and on and on till the end of time, it's a continuous present tense, one thinks the most ridiculous things, there I was thinking about grammar, the verb to be, when it ends to be dead . . . And then I came out into the garden, and I half saw, in my mind's eye, a kind of ghost of his face, just the eyes and hair, coming towards me – like every day waiting for him to come home, the way you think of your son, with such pleasure, when he's – not there – and I – I thought – no, I won't *see* him, because he is dead, and I won't dream about him because he is dead, I'll be rational and practical and continue to live because one must, and there was Noel . . .

'I got it wrong, you see, I was so *sensible*, and then I was so shocked because I couldn't get to want anything – I couldn't *talk* to Noel – I – I – made Noel take away, destroy, all the photos, I – didn't dream, you can will not to dream, I didn't

... visit a grave, flowers, there isn't any point. I was so sensible. Only my body wouldn't stop waiting and all it wants is to – to see that boy. *That* boy. That boy you – saw.'

He did not say that he might have seen another boy, maybe even a boy who had been given the tee shirts and jeans afterwards. He did not say, though the idea crossed his mind, that maybe what he had seen was some kind of impression from her terrible desire to see a boy where nothing was. The boy had had nothing terrible, no aura of pain about him: he had been, his memory insisted, such a pleasant, courteous, self-contained boy, with his own purposes. And in fact the woman herself almost immediately raised the possibility that what he had seen was what she desired to see, a kind of mix-up of radio waves, like when you overheard police messages on the radio, or got BBC 1 on a switch that said ITV. She was thinking fast, and went on almost immediately to say that perhaps his sense of loss, his loss of Anne, which was what had led her to feel she could bear his presence in her house, was what had brought them – dare she say – near enough, for their wavelengths to mingle, perhaps, had made him susceptible ... You mean, he had said, we are a kind of emotional vacuum, between us, that must be filled. Something like that, she had said, and had added, 'But I don't believe in ghosts.'

Anne, he thought, could not be a ghost, because she was elsewhere, with someone else, doing for someone else those little things she had done so gaily for him, tasty little suppers, bits of research, a sudden vase of unusual flowers, a new bold shirt, unlike his own cautious taste, but suiting him, suiting him. In a sense, Anne was worse lost because voluntarily absent, an absence that could not be loved because love was at an end, for Anne.

'I don't suppose you will, now,' the woman was saying. 'I think talking would probably stop any – mixing of messages, if that's what it is, don't you? But – if – *if* he comes again' – and here for the first time her eyes were full of tears – 'if – you must promise, you will *tell* me, you must promise.'

He had promised, easily enough, because he was fairly sure she was right, the boy would not be seen again. But the next day he was on the lawn, nearer than ever, sitting on the grass beside the deck-chair, his arms clasping his bent, warm brown knees, the thick, pale hair glittering in the sun. He was wearing a football shirt, this time, Chelsea's colours. Sitting down in the deck-chair, the man could have put out a hand and touched him, but did not: it was not, it seemed, a possible gesture to make. But the boy looked up and smiled, with a pleasant complicity, as though they now understood each other very well. The man tried speech: he said, 'It's nice to see you again,' and the boy nodded acknowledgement of this remark, without speaking himself. This was the beginning of communication between them, or what the man supposed to be communication. He did not think of fetching the woman. He became aware that he was in some strange way *enjoying the boy's company*. His pleasant stillness – and he sat there all morning, occasionally lying back on the grass, occasionally staring thoughtfully at the house – was calming and comfortable. The man did quite a lot of work – wrote about three reasonable pages on Hardy's original air-blue gown – and looked up now and then to make sure the boy was still there and happy.

He went to report to the woman – as he had after all promised to do – that evening. She had obviously been waiting and hoping – her unnatural calm had given way to agitated pacing, and her eyes were dark and deeper in. At this point in the story he found in himself a necessity to bowdlerize for the sympathetic American, as he had indeed already begun to do. He had mentioned only a child who had 'seemed like' the woman's lost son, and he now ceased to mention the child at all, as an actor in the story, with the result that what the American woman heard was a tale of how he, the man, had become increasingly involved in the woman's solitary grief, how their two losses had become a kind of *folie à deux* from which he could not extricate himself. What follows is not what he told the American girl, though it may be clear at which points the bowdlerized version coincided with what he really believed to have happened. There was a sense he could not at first analyse that it was improper to talk about the boy – not because he might not be believed; that did not come into it; but because something dreadful might happen.

'He sat on the lawn all morning. In a football shirt.'

'Chelsea?'

'Chelsea.'

'What did he do? Does he look happy? Did he speak?' Her desire to know was terrible.

'He doesn't speak. He didn't move much. He seemed – very calm. He stayed a long time.'

'This is terrible. This is ludicrous. There *is no boy*.'

'No. But I saw him.'

'Why you?'

'I don't know.' A pause. 'I do *like* him.'

'He is – was – a most likeable boy.'

Some days later he saw the boy running along the landing in the evening, wearing what might have been pyjamas, in peacock towelling, or might have been a track suit. Pyjamas, the woman stated confidently, when he told her: his new pyjamas. With white ribbed cuffs, weren't they? and a white polo neck? He corroborated this, watching her cry – she cried more easily now – finding her anxiety and disturbance very hard to bear. But it never occurred to him that it was possible to break his promise to tell her when he saw the boy. That was another curious imperative from some undefined authority.

They discussed clothes. If there were ghosts, how could they appear in clothes long burned, or rotted, or worn away by other people? You could imagine, they agreed, that something of a person might linger – as the Tibetans and others believe the soul lingers near the body before setting out on its long journey. But clothes? And in this case so many clothes? I must be seeing your memories, he told her, and she nodded fiercely, compressing her lips, agreeing that this was likely, adding, 'I am too rational to go mad, so I seem to be putting it on you.'

He tried a joke. 'That isn't very kind to me, to imply that madness comes more easily to me.'

'No, sensitivity. I am insensible. I was always a bit like that, and this made it worse. I am the *last* person to see any ghost that was trying to haunt me.'

'We agreed it was your memories I saw.'

'Yes. We agreed. That's rational. As rational as we can be, considering.'

All the same, the brilliance of the boy's blue regard, his gravely smiling salutation in the garden next morning, did not seem like anyone's tortured memories of earlier happiness. The man spoke to him directly then:

'Is there anything I can *do* for you? Anything you want? Can I help you?'

The boy seemed to puzzle about this for a while, inclining his head as though hearing was difficult. Then he nodded, quickly and perhaps urgently, turned, and ran into the house, looking back to make sure he was followed. The man entered the living-room through the french windows, behind the running boy, who stopped for a moment in the centre of the room, with the man blinking behind him at the sudden transition from sunlight to comparative dark. The woman was sitting in an armchair, looking at nothing there. She often sat like that. She looked up, across the boy, at the man; and the boy, his face for the first time anxious, met the man's eyes again, asking, before he went out into the house.

'What is it? What is it? Have you seen him again? Why are you . . .?'

'He came in here. He went – out through the door.'

'I didn't see him.'

'No.'

'Did he – oh, this is so *silly* – did he see me?'

He could not remember. He told the only truth he knew.

'He brought me in here.'

'Oh, what can I do, what am I going to *do*? If I killed myself
– I have thought of that – but the idea that I should be with
him is an illusion I . . . this silly situation is the nearest I shall
ever get. To him. He was *in here with me*?'

'Yes.'

And she was crying again. Out in the garden he could see
the boy, swinging agile on the apple branch.

He was not quite sure, looking back, when he had thought he
had realized what the boy had wanted him to do. This was
also, at the party, his worst piece of what he called bowdlerization, though in some sense it was clearly the opposite of
bowdlerization. He told the American girl that he had come to
the conclusion that it was the woman herself who had wanted
it, though there was in fact, throughout, no sign of her
wanting anything except to see the boy, as she said. The boy,
bolder and more frequent, had appeared several nights running
on the landing, wandering in and out of bathrooms and bedrooms, restlessly, a little agitated, questing almost, until it
had 'come to' the man that what he required was to be re-
engendered, for him, the man, to give to his mother another
child, into which he could peacefully vanish. The idea was so
clear that it was like another imperative, though he did not
have the courage to ask the child to confirm it. Possibly this
was out of delicacy – the child was too young to be talked to
about sex. Possibly there were other reasons. Possibly he was
mistaken: the situation was making him hysterical, he felt
action of some kind was required and must be possible. He
could not spend the rest of the summer, the rest of his life,
describing non-existent tee shirts and blond smiles.

He could think of no sensible way of embarking on his venture,
so in the end simply walked into her bedroom one night. She
was lying there, reading; when she saw him her instinctive

gesture was to hide, not her bare arms and throat, but her book. She seemed, in fact, quite unsurprised to see his pyjamaed figure, and, after she had recovered her coolness, brought out the book definitely and laid it on the bedspread.

'My new taste in illegitimate literature. I keep them in a box under the bed.'

Ena Twigg, Medium. The Infinite Hive. The Spirit World. Is There Life After Death?

'Pathetic,' she proffered.

He sat down delicately on the bed.

'Please, don't grieve so. Please, let yourself be comforted. Please . . .'

He put an arm round her. She shuddered. He pulled her closer. He asked why she had had only the one son, and she seemed to understand the purport of his question, for she tried, angular and chilly, to lean on him a little, she became apparently compliant. 'No real reason,' she assured him, no material reason. Just her husband's profession and lack of inclination: that covered it.

'Perhaps,' he suggested, 'if she would be comforted a little, perhaps she could hope, perhaps . . .'

For comfort then, she said, dolefully, and lay back, pushing Ena Twigg off the bed with one fierce gesture, then lying placidly. He got in beside her, put his arms round her, kissed her cold cheek, thought of Anne, of what was never to be again. Come on, he said to the woman, you must live, you must try to live, let us hold each other for comfort.

She hissed at him 'Don't *talk*' between clenched teeth, so he stroked her lightly, over her nightdress, breasts and buttocks and long stiff legs, composed like an effigy on an Elizabethan tomb. She allowed this, trembling slightly, and then trembling violently: he took this to be a sign of some mixture of pleasure and pain, of the return of life to stone. He put a hand between her legs and she moved them heavily apart; he heaved himself over her and pushed, unsuccessfully. She was contorted and locked tight: frigid, he thought grimly, was not the word. *Rigor mortis*, his mind said to him, before she began to scream.

He was ridiculously cross about this. He jumped away and said quite rudely, 'Shut up,' and then ungraciously, 'I'm sorry.' She stopped screaming as suddenly as she had begun and made one of her painstaking economical explanations.

'Sex and death don't go. I can't afford to let go of my grip on myself. I hoped. What you hoped. It was a bad idea. I apologize.'

'Oh, never mind,' he said and rushed out again on to the landing, feeling foolish and almost in tears for warm, lovely Anne.

The child was on the landing, waiting. When the man saw him, he looked questioning, and then turned his face against the wall and leant there, rigid, his shoulders hunched, his hair hiding his expression. There was a similarity between woman and child. The man felt, for the first time, almost uncharitable towards the boy, and then felt something else.

'Look, I'm sorry. I tried. I did try. Please turn round.'

Uncompromising, rigid, clenched back view.

'Oh well,' said the man, and went into his bedroom.

So now, he said to the American woman at the party, I feel a fool, I feel embarrassed, I feel we are hurting, not helping each other, I feel it isn't a refuge. Of course you feel that, she said, of course you're right – it was temporarily necessary, it helped both of you, but you've got to live your life. Yes, he said, I've done my best, I've tried to get through, I have my life to live. Look, she said, I want to help, I really do, I have these wonderful friends I'm renting this flat from, why don't you come, just for a few days, just for a break, why don't you? They're real sympathetic people, you'd like them, I like them, you could get your emotions kind of straightened out. She'd probably be glad to see the back of you, she must feel as bad as you do, she's got to relate to her situation in her own way in the end. We all have.

He said he would think about it. He knew he had elected to

tell the sympathetic American because he had sensed she would be – would offer – a way out. He had to get out. He took her home from the party and went back to his house and landlady without seeing her into her flat. They both knew that this reticence was promising – that he hadn't come in then, because he meant to come later. Her warmth and readiness were like sunshine, she was open. He did not know what to say to the woman.

In fact, she made it easy for him: she asked, briskly, if he now found it perhaps uncomfortable to stay, and he replied that he had felt he should move on, he was of so little use . . . Very well, she had agreed, and had added crisply that it had to be better for everyone if 'all this' came to an end. He remembered the firmness with which she had told him that no illusions were pleasant. She was strong: too strong for her own good. It would take years to wear away that stony, closed, simply surviving insensibility. It was not his job. He would go. All the same, he felt bad.

He got out his suitcases and put some things in them. He went down to the garden, nervously, and put away the deck-chair. The garden was empty. There were no voices over the wall. The silence was thick and deadening. He wondered, knowing he would not see the boy again, if anyone else would do so, or if, now he was gone, no one would describe a tee shirt, a sandal, a smile, seen, remembered, or desired. He went slowly up to his room again.

The boy was sitting on his suitcase, arms crossed, face frowning and serious. He held the man's look for a long moment, and then the man went and sat on his bed. The boy continued to sit. The man found himself speaking.

'You do see I have to go? I've tried to get through. I can't get through. I'm no use to you, am I?'

The boy remained immobile, his head on one side, considering. The man stood up and walked towards him.

'Please. Let me go. What are we, in this house? A man and a woman and a child, and none of us can get through. You can't want that?'

He went as close as he dared. He had, he thought, the intention of putting his hand on or through the child. But could not bring himself to feel there was no boy. So he stood, and repeated,

'I can't get through. Do you want me to stay?'

Upon which, as he stood helplessly there, the boy turned on him again the brilliant, open, confiding, beautiful desired smile.

ELIZABETH JANE HOWARD

*

Summer Picnic

The illusion that eating in the open air constitutes at least one aspect of the simple life is ancient and enduring, but now, if the contents of all three cars were unloaded on to the lawn and somebody who didn't know about the picnic was asked what it was all for, they might equally have thought that it was the blitz, or a bazaar, or the result of some mysterious crisis like the *Mary Celeste*. Apart from immense quantities of provisions, the parents and their friends took rugs and mackintoshes, dark glasses, cameras and alcohol, cigarettes, writing paper and newspapers, a trug and a trowel for moss-collecting (they were going to a wood), an air cushion and a collapsible bath-chair, and a huge umbrella like a vulture which opened inside or out with impartial difficulty. The nannies took shopping baskets filled with white emergency baby equipment and slow constructive things like knitting. The children (divided roughly into two groups) took a tent, electric torches, books whose lives hung on a single linen thread, butterfly nets, pen-knives that would either never open or never shut, wine gums, a few ravenous caterpillars in a biscuit tin, a bottle filled with sea water and marked POYSIN, and a very battered game of Monopoly. The younger children and the babies took some string, a bunch of dandelion heads, and the number of stuffed animals that their nannies thought good for them. The dogs were not allowed to bring anything.

Lalage, who had not had to prepare either children or food, who was not responsible for the weather or for the motor-cars, who had, in fact, arrived at the perfect picnic age of seventeen,

had spent two delicious hours hovering between a white dress
and a yellow: brushing her yellow hair, polishing her Spanish
sandals, and painting her nails; telling herself continually that
she must remain calm, perfectly calm, and that it could not
possibly rain, at least not before they had all met everybody
from the other house.

Now she wandered restlessly from room to room watching
the car being methodically packed by one of her parents, and
as methodically disarranged and re-packed by the other: waiting
for the exact moment to appear when she would neither be
subjected to torturing minutes of heat in an immobile car, nor
squeezed in unmercifully because she had been forgotten . . .
but she felt they would be hours yet. The rooms already had
that empty sunlit air, when a bluebottle or even a butterfly
trapped between the sashes of the windows seemed to make an
enormous noise, and heavy petals fell momentously on to
tables of mahogany and satinwood, exposing the charming
freckled hearts of midsummer roses . . .

Lalage's mother edged her back cautiously against the tree
which she had chosen rather because it commanded the scene
than afforded her comfort, and extracted a drowning insect
from her cider. Her chief anxieties were over: food was
unpacked; banks of sandwiches were being demolished; little
pools of salt and of lemonade lay on the groundsheets; hard-
boiled eggs and leaves of cos lettuce winked and wilted on the
elegant turf. Nannies were manoeuvring the significant contents of sandwiches into the petulant and indiscriminate
mouths of their charges; and the children – Lalage's mother
glanced at the little sunbaked clearing where they had elected
to picnic, shuddered, and thought very hard about Andrew
Marvell's restoring poem.

Lalage, on the other hand, lay on a mossy bank of dark
delicious green, with her hands clasped behind her golden
head, while that nice young man who drove too fast peeled her
a nectarine, and told her about motor-cars. Suddenly, Lalage's
mother remembered reclining in a punt on the Thames (oh the

agony with one's corsets until one had adjusted the seat either bolt upright, or almost flat) in her best white flannel skirt and poplin blouse, and her boater tipped over her eyes in a way that Mamma had condemned as unbecoming, while another nice young man had broken off an enthusiastic monologue about horses to stammer that she was so splendid to talk to, and might he, could he, could he possibly call her Lillian? He had only enjoyed the delectable advantage for one afternoon: Lillian's Mamma had hurriedly sent her to Scotland, where she was expected to fly as high as the grouse and marry a peer. But she had married a commoner, and her Mamma had acquiesced (after all there were five daughters and no means). Mamma was now possibly asleep. The fact that she sat upright in her bath-chair meant nothing. She had lunched off cold turtle soup and Bath Oliver biscuits, and was now immobile; reeking gently of white violets, and with her diamond rings glaring on her cold, freckled fingers – she was always cold . . . Her eyes were shut.

The young man leapt to his feet, held out a hand to Lalage, and pulled her up beside him. The sudden ease of the impulse made them both smile faintly at one another, as they stood for a moment before strolling away down one of the bridle-paths. Lillian glanced apprehensively at her Mamma, and then at the children, who appeared to be on the brink of a quarrel, which, considering the conditions in which they were picnicking, was hardly surprising. They had pitched a dark brown tent on a baked cart-track. Inside, swathed in car-rugs, they were eating, and playing Monopoly, a game which its perpetrators would barely have recognized – so personal and complex had it become. Occasionally, a younger child would be sent for reinforcements of food. It was sweating so profusely, and so incapacitated by its car-rug, that it was hopelessly inefficient. Lillian had suggested to one of them that they might like to explore the wood, but it had looked at her with purple streaming contempt, and hobbled away. At frequent intervals the tent collapsed upon its occupants and any incipient quarrel was shelved while they feverishly restored their airless gloom.

One of the babies began to cry. He had lunched lightly off dandelion heads, some milk chocolate, and a Monopoly card, and was now quite properly resisting any further nourishment. He was hurried away into the wood by a nurse, but not, Lillian feared, before he had had ample opportunity to waken Mamma . . .

Lalage's grandmother, however, was awake, although since lunch she had successfully persuaded everybody to the contrary. In reality her mind had played upon the scene before her and receded into the past, very much as the chequered streaking sunlight trembled and shifted over the leaves on their branches on the trees, and apparently back into the woods. So she reflected upon the people she could see, and more that she could remember; upon present and past picnics, and the unchanging behaviour of picnickers – pretending the moment they arrived in some romantic or beautiful place that they were in fact at home, only in houses without furniture, which made them either somnolent and dull, or grumpy and restless. The men were almost all asleep, and the women were clearing the debris of the meal. In her young days – sixty-odd years ago – one had really eaten luncheon in the open air. Picnic food had been properly exotic; had by no means degenerated to the mere sandwich. She remembered very young broad beans cooked and frozen in their butter; little tailor-made cold roast birds; delicious claret cup; elaborate galantine; cold *soufflés*; an entire Stilton; trifle such as those poor children in the tent had never seen; and quantities of fruit the perfection of which seemed mysteriously to have vanished today – with the handsome man and good dinner-table conversation. It was better now to be very old, or the age of that granddaughter escaping into the woods to discover whether she liked being kissed.

She remembered doing exactly the same thing on a picnic, only then it was far more difficult, and consequently exciting; and afterwards telling her younger, plainer, sister (Oh Laura! How could you? Oh Laura!): and she remembered that she had been far more excited at telling about it than at the event itself. She had had to escape from the party with its perimeter of servants and ponies, and stroll away up the glen path picking wood anemones which were certain to die even before they reached the carriages which awaited their return down on the road. She had walked, and picked her anemones, until she could no longer hear the party but only the cool frenzied rush of the stream pouring down the glen, below her path. Then the effort of carrying her flowers and her parasol had seemed too great, and she had selected a clean grey boulder in the shade on which to settle carefully. She had hovered for hours that morning between a white frock and a yellow, and had chosen the white muslin as more becoming; but already her skirts were marked with green round the hem from bruised bluebell leaves.

He had surprised her exactly when she had expected him; and she had confirmed her imagination of his kissing her to the accompaniment of a hectic streaking kingfisher, and the faint seductive smell of wild garlic. Their promises had seemed as endless as the golden silver stream: but the following week he had been sent to India with his regiment; and she had never heard what became of him. She had married a gentle impoverished baronet . . . And here was Lalage returned with her young man; both in an elaborate state of flushed indifference . . .

In the car going home, Lalage's grandmother suddenly gave her an immense diamond ring.

Lalage held the hand that wore the ring with the hand that didn't for the rest of the journey, and wondered whether any picnic could be more perfect than this picnic, which had, in fact, altered her whole life, only nobody would understand that, any more than they remembered or understood that she was now seventeen . . .

Lillian, driving another car home – not too fast because it was overloaded, but fast enough to allow the child who was always sick in cars to be sick at home for a change, wondered in an exhausted manner why people described anything difficult or nerve-racking as 'no picnic'.

Lalage's grandmother, after giving away her ring, settled to pretending to be asleep; reflecting sadly on the sad and lonely thought that there was nobody left alive to stare at the ringless finger and say, 'Oh Laura! How could you? Oh Laura!'

*

Indefinite Nights

'Here,' he whispered. 'I was dreaming about you.'

'Oh yes?' I said.

'Yeah, we were on an escalator, we were going down and the walls were going up, these sort of great big granite blocks.'

'Which side was it last time, this one?'

'Mm, just a sec.'

'Okay. Here it comes. Waggle your toes.'

'Mr Haldane was there too, with one of those spotty dogs, you know, a dalmatian, he was carrying it, it was looking at me over his shoulder.'

'Is this sore?'

'No. It's okay. How many more nights you got to do?'

'Four, this stint.'

'Bump night tonight then.'

'Yes, all downhill after tonight.'

'Your name's Christine, isn't it?'

'Christina. Are you warm enough like that?'

'Yeah. Who's on this morning, is it Pam's lot?'

'Why, they your favourite?'

'Oh no, you're my favourite.'

'Ah, you say that to all the girls.'

'You bet I do.'

We smiled at one another, as if we had suddenly agreed about something. I suppose in a way we had. I remember I felt quite cheerful as I locked up the drug trolley, but then I often did at dawn.

Sometimes if it was quiet I'd open up the big glass doors in bay two and step out on to the balcony for a few minutes, just to breathe in some morning air. Once I stood there just before it began to rain, and thought that the air had a fresh tint of green to it. I saw a pigeon that day too, from above. I remember its pretty, muted back feathers, its clopping wings and small still head, all in flight through the clear greenish air, so far below me that for an instant I could pretend that I was flying too.

I went back into bay two but the telephone rang before I could get the first set of bolts undone. I checked my watch: 5.30. She was early.

'Rebecca Ward, Staff Nurse.'

'Ah, hallo dear, this is Mrs Brownlow, you know, Johnny's mother –'

'Hallo, yes, he's had a really good night, I've just been talking to him, he's fine.'

'Oh good, oh, thank you dear, is it Susan?'

'Chris.'

'Oh, hallo, Chris, I'm sorry to have disturbed you dear, I know how busy you are –'

'No, that's all right. Really.'

'Well, I'll be in later, all right dear?'

'Of course, all right, bye now.'

'Bye-bye dear.'

I hung up and sat for a moment with my hand on the receiver. We were really quiet that morning. I had two good students, Sally and Jan, and an auxiliary, a surly sort who'd kept her name to herself but worked well enough. West Indian, she was. She was lumbering around now with the urinal trolley and twanging up the blinds. Sally was doing the six o'clock signs and turning off the dim red night-lights, and Jan was doing the teas. The infusions were all on time. No one was dying. The CVP lines were all patent. So I had a few unaccustomed minutes to myself, to sit about sighing.

'Was that her again?'

It was Sally, leaning against the desk. She looked a bit wild, her mascara all smudged in black rings round her eyes and her hair falling down.

'Yes.'

Sally lowered her voice. 'Does she know?'

'Of course.'

She glanced back at Johnny's side of the bay.

'But he doesn't?'

'Bet he does. Bet he's guessed.'

'Why? What'd he say?' She glinted.

'Nothing. I just think he knows, that's all. You finished all the signs, then?'

'Nearly. Give us a chance. Has the Gestapo been?'

'Not yet. Push off. I'm busy.'

'Jawohl,' said Sally, clicking her heels. She swung round and goosestepped jerkily away into bay two and presently I heard her giggling by Mr Dooley's bed.

I found the kardex under a pile of computer printouts and checked through my report. I was on indefinite nights, eight nights on, six nights off, and sometimes I felt I might forget my own name. But I knew all my patients well enough. Twenty-seven patients in all. Three single rooms, two bays, and the far end.

In the far end and the singles lay the least ill men. By day they limped about in dressing-gowns, read *Tidbits*, volunteered to give out the teas, took naps, idled. By night they snored, or wanted cups of tea, or aspirins. In the bays, nearer the nurses' desk to be under my qualified eye, lay the grots and sickies. The grots, the incontinent geriatrics, lay strapped into their beds in bay one, cot-sides up, waiting to pop off. The sickies lay in bay two. That was where the real action was, as Sally would say.

Bed 10, Harold Fletcher, 54, for Mr Haldane, colonic reanasto-mosis, fourth day post-op.; and

Bed 11, Brian Dooley, 63, for Mr Harrison, oesophageal varices (watch out, could blow at any minute); and

Bed 12, Joseph Miller, 72, for Mr Haldane, carcinomatosis, not for resus., does not know; and

Bed 13, John Brownlow, 22, for Mr Haldane, carcinomatosis, on cytotoxics, not for resus., does not know; and

Bed 14, empty tonight and

Bed 15, Henry Goldbloom, 58, for Mr Haldane, query carcinoma query stomach.

I shut the kardex up and checked the time again. Only 5.40. I thought about a cigarette. There was still Mr Colonic Washout to be seen to, down in the far end, but he was all Sally's this morning, I'd only have to oversee. I ferreted around under the desk for my handbag, and the double doors at the end of the corridor bashed open. She always opened them like that, smacking at them with her two broad raised palms.

'Achtung,' murmured Sally, passing me.

Footsteps clumped.

'Good morning, Sister.'

She rolled up, nodded.

'Staff.' She was a nasty sort, that Night Sister, a happy blackleg during the last NUPE strike, manning the dinner trolleys with a glad Dunkirk-spirit smile. She picked up my report and slouched sourly round the ward without speaking.

'Untidy ward, nurse,' she said to me, back at the desk. 'Locker tops. Do something about it.'

'Right, Sister. Good morning.'

'See you tonight.' She stumped off. I went to find Sally in the sluice. She had the trolley all set.

'Talk to him all the time, okay? He's embarrassed to death and scared as well, he natters all the time. So talk back, all right?'

'Right.'

'And hold the out-end against the side of the bucket so's it makes less noise, see, no splashing noises.'

'Right.'

'You're all right?'

'Look, just go and have your smoke, okay?'

'You mind your manners,' I said, and went.

That day while I slept Mr Colonic Washout had his gas-trectomy and came back from theatre more dead than alive, and was put into bay two next to Johnny; and Mr Dooley, 63, for Mr Harrison, burst his oesophageal varices during a ward round ('Went off with a real bang,' said the Late Staff at report) and shot fountains of blood over half-a-dozen terrified medical students and, as it happened, Mr Harrison himself.

'All over his Savile Row,' added the Late Staff reminiscently. There was a fleck of dried blood over one of her eyebrows, I noticed.

'Bed 12, Mr Miller, you know him don't you, he had a good day . . .'

Johnny had had a good day too. Two of the day students, when they'd washed their arms and faces and turned their aprons inside out, had sat on his bed and explained what oesophageal varices were, and how Johnny personally was not to worry about them, or about Mr Dooley or in fact about anything at all, ever.

So Johnny told me anyway.

'Hallo, Chrissy.'

'How you doing?'

'Wonderful. It's all go round here. A real show.'

He talked about Mr Dooley for a while.

'Blood always looks worse than it is,' I said. 'It always sort of spreads around and looks like pints and pints – '

'It *was* pints and pints.'

'I'm sorry. I wish you hadn't seen it.'

'He's going to be all right though.'

'He's doing really well.' I touched Johnny's hand. There was another beaded bruise on his forearm where one of the infusions had slid through the vein and pushed 5% dextrose into his flesh. Both his slender arms were covered in bruises and scars, as if he were a junkie. Which of course, at the time, he was.

'I due a shot?'

'Not yet. An hour's time.'

'Good-oh. See you then.'

I checked his infusions, timed them. They were running well. He had four of them, two in each arm, and a nasogastric tube strapped to his cheek, so that anything inside him could come straight out without causing him too much trouble. Fluid drained from it, slowly, constantly, a pale brackish liquid with a mysterious admix of dark flecks.

'Mint sauce,' said Johnny, seeing me eying it. I pulled a face at him and passed on to Mr Colonic Washout, newly incarnated now as Mr Geoffrey Chester, 57, for Mr Haldane, Ca stomach and complete gastrectomy, knows.

'Hallo.'

'Hallo, nurse.'

'Got any pain?'

'No. I'm fine, thank you.'

He lay there afraid to move. Only his eyes moved. He had a tube down too, connected to a suction machine beside the bed. I bent down to look at it. It was a small machine, with rather a fetching action, clean little wheels busily revolving.

'All hooked up,' said Mr Chester, his eyes straining down at me. I straightened up.

'It's sort of to give your insides a rest. To keep you all empty inside, to give the stitches a chance. Are you thirsty?'

'Bit.'

I gave him a quick mouthwash.

'Put your tongue out, right out, that's right – '

I gently swabbed his cracked old tongue with glycerine and lemon. He kept on staring up at me, and I saw that the pale grey irises of his eyes were ringed with cream. Arcus senilis, I thought, that's interesting, I must remember to tell Sally and Jan to have a look . . .

'You're an angel, you are,' said Mr Chester suddenly, as I cleared the swabs away. I gave him a little smile and shook my head, but still I felt my insides all relax with pleasure. I felt smooth all over. Well, who wouldn't? It had been an impulse of love that had made him speak.

Touch the sick tenderly and they will be grateful; not grudgingly, as if you had lent them something or done them a kindness, but purely, physically grateful, with a gratitude indistinguishable from love. A limited and temporary love, of course, but vehement, perceptible even when undeclared. It doesn't happen all the time. But it happens often enough. It's love-without-strings, the basis, perhaps, of all our calling: love-without-strings, the nurses' perk.

'Right now. Ring the bell if you need anything. If you get any pain. You let me know. All right?'

'Thank you, nurse. Thank you.'

'Anything at all. Just ring the bell.'

Love-without-strings.

No time for such tender scenes the following night. Night six, that was. A night to remember.

Report was twenty minutes late.

'Sorry about this,' said the Late Staff. She had been crying. 'It's like World War Three in there,' she said, gesturing over the desk at the bays. There had been a death. One of the grots lay limp and yellow behind his curtains.

'He was gasping all afternoon,' said the Late Staff, knuckling at the mascara under her eyes. 'He's only just gone, we haven't had a chance to do him. Oh, and Jan Geeson called, she's not coming in, she's off sick.'

'Oh Christ,' I said.

'I tried to get you someone else, but no joy yet.'

'Aux?'

'Irma.'

'Oh bloody hell.'

'I know. Sat down the far end with the *Daily Mirror*. I'm sorry. Look, I'll just get on with it, try Night Sister, you've got to get someone.'

I began to tremble. Report was twenty minutes late, even

with three student nurses, two staff nurses, and the aux; I was being left with the aux, and Sally. And it was drug night.

'It's bloody drug night,' I said out loud, interrupting.

The Late Staff shook her head, and went on. I wondered if I was going to cry too. There were infusions running in two of the single rooms, and three blood drips – that meant observations every fifteen minutes – in bay two, where Mr Chester was brewing a cardiac arrest and bedsores and everyone else had multiple infusions or CVP lines. Two colonic washouts and an enema in the far end, and five incontinent grots and a stiff; and it was bloody drug night.

'So good luck, that's all I can say,' ended the Late Staff. 'See you in the morning.'

'If I last so long,' I said.

I sent Sally to check the far end and went to run round bay two, where two of the infusions had already stopped and Johnny was 500 mls behind on one of his, the yellow one with the vitamins in it, but that was Day's fault, not mine.

'Hallo, Chrissy.'

'Hallo, can't stop tonight, sorry,' and I whipped the bandages off Mr Chester's forearm and stroked his blocked vein until oh thank you Lord the spasm relaxed and the drips started again but no such luck with Mr Goldbloom's stalled juices next door, and now everyone on blood was due signs again, and it took me four minutes, fast as I was, and that meant four minutes taken out of every fifteen until the bloods were through and two of them ran all night and the other didn't end till 4 am.

Sally came in.

'Far end?'

'Quiet mostly. Coupla drugs at midnight.'

'Single room's calling. Check the drips too.'

'Right.' She tore off.

I felt a great lifting wave of affection for her and ran with it into bay one thinking that if I could just get through the first hour everything would be all right, but then I saw the drawn curtains and remembered again that it was drug night: I must go all through the drug cupboard, the stock cupboards, and the refrigerator, opening all the little bottles and packets, counting everything, pills, ampoules, powders, bandages, elastoplasts, rubber gloves, and re-order the shortfalls in triplicate, or all the following week nurses would be running out of essentials, and cursing, and chasing all over the hospital to forage; and someone like Johnny would be kept waiting for pain relief, for attention, for comfort.

I held on to someone's bed-table and said to myself, Now, don't panic, don't panic. Keep calm, call Night Sister, beg and plead, get someone. Call Night Sister, call Dr Whatsit for Mr Goldbloom's drip. Don't panic, don't panic.

I ran back to the telephone – don't believe all that old stuff about nurses never running, I'd have used roller skates if I could've got away with it, in fact on busy nights I often fantasized about it, shooting down to the far end with an enema bag and my trusty wheels – and called Dr Whatsit, who said she'd come round when she could but probably not for an hour, by which time, I knew, Mr Goldbloom's drip would be hopelessly out of kilter but Baldy Haldy'd just have to lump it, and then I tried Night Sister.

'You called me.'

'Yes, oh Sister, I'm so short-staffed, I've got so many ill patients and we've had a death, please Sister, I need someone.'

There was a pause. I could hear her breathing.

'Well,' she said at last, 'there's no one to send. I'm sure you can cope.'

'Sister, I can't Sister, please.'

'Look, I'm sorry, it's impossible.' She sounded huffy already.

'Well then Sister, can I leave the drugs out, could I do them tomorrow?'

'Of course you can't. Out of the question.'

'But it's dangerous, we can't see to them all, there's only me and a student – '

'Nonsense. We can't all have perfect staffing levels, nurse. Just do your best, I'm sure you can do that. You've got an aux, haven't you?'

'Yes, but – '

'Or I can report that you are unable to efficiently manage your ward.'

Silence. My heart's going to burst.

'Nurse?'

'I'll do what I can, Sister.'

'I'll be along presently. Do buck yourself up, nurse.'

Buck up, I mouthed at the receiver as I crashed it down. Buck up, fuck off!

And I'd wasted time. I ran back to bay two, where someone was wailing: Mr Goldbloom had wet the bed and was close to tears. So was I. I ran and called Sally and charged back with the linen trolley and we changed the bed in record time but we were out of clean pyjamas so Sally had to pound down a floor to male ortho so that Mr Goldbloom's shame could be covered.

'I'm so sorry, nurse.'

'Please. Don't worry about it.'

'You're so busy.'

'It's not your fault.'

He went on apologizing and glooming until I could've slapped him and said, For God's sake shut up and go to sleep! And then there were drugs to give out. I ran around with the trolley, Oh, why not roller skates, I could arabesque along the corridors, my arms stretched out in front, the tray with two red-and-black bombers and a mouthful of water held out before me like a crown on a cushion.

Old buffer down the far end: 'I can't get these pink things down, lovey, they're that big.'

'Take some more water then, Mr Bulford.'

The next lot of blood signs were due two minutes ago. I motion Sally to go and do them, which means I can't give any more drugs out until she gets back to check them. My hands are shaking. Old buffer tilts his head back, waggles his cheeks from side to side.

'Gone?'

'No, dear, sorry.'

'Never mind, just take your time,' I say between clenched teeth. 'That's all right.'

It was about then that I realized I could manage everything, just about and skimpily, if I didn't take any breaks and cut Sally's down to fifteen minutes, just time for her to throw her egg-and-chips down and maybe buy me a sandwich to eat while I did the drugs. I began to feel a bit better and even managed a smile, I remember, when the old buffer forced his last horse-pill down.

'That's the ticket, Mr Bulford, sleep tight!'

That was night six. I was running on air by dawn, high as a kite on not eating and coping against the odds: drugs as potent as any. Sally and I got the giggles over the early teas and sang 'Morning Has Broken Like the First Morning' in quavery soprano voices as we shot up the blinds, and when Mr Fletcher opened his gummy eyes and said, 'Where's me morning kiss?' Sally pranced over and gave him one.

Of course the drips were all hopelessly out and one of the colonic washouts had been more of an enema really – 'Just relax, Mr Pointer!' for Christ's sake – but the drugs were all done and everyone was more or less clean and dry and if some of the urine bags were close to bursting well all that bloody troop of day staff could cope. So I told Sally anyway.

I remember I felt like hugging her goodbye when we finally got off duty, and I know she felt the same way about me. You see it often enough in war films, that simple comrades-in-arms love between soldiers who've shared a close look at chaos. That was how Sally and I felt, and if we never worked together again we'd still greet one another with real affection in twenty years' time, should we meet.

Perhaps it's the love that old soldiers meet to commemorate, rather than the battle? But old nurses don't have reunions. Though Sally and I could: not the Waterloo Dinner but the

Rebecca Night Six Banquet, with food served in kidney dishes on mouth-care sets, and the champagne flowing like blood-drips.

That was night six.

Night seven wasn't much fun either, though things were quite a bit calmer. After report I went straight to bay two to check the drips and say hallo, but Baldy Haldy was there before me, glaring at the fluid charts at the end of Mr Miller's bed. Mr Chester, I saw, was on a waterbed, a very squashy affair. He lifted a feeble hand to wave at me and the movement bounced him gently up and down like a little boat at sea. He held his hand up, palm towards me, and bounced, his face grave.

'Mr Haldane.'

'Just what have you all been up to, these charts are ridiculous. I don't know why you bother to keep them, why we bother to write them, look at this!'

I looked. 1000 mls behind schedule.

'I'm sorry, Doctor. We were short-staffed.' It sounded more like an excuse than a fact. 'I'm sorry,' I said again.

Baldy snorted, slammed the chart shut, dropped it on the bed-table and stalked off. I picked it up and hung it up properly and ran after him.

'Please Doctor!' I caught up with him in the corridor. He was a big man, waxy and pale-eyed.

'Well?'

'Oh, ah, Mr Chester. That waterbed.'

'*If* you nurses turned him every two hours as they did in the old days, *nurse*, he wouldn't need a waterbed!'

'I meant, it's just that it's so squashy, is he for resus.?'

'Of course he's for resus.'

'I mean, if he arrests, we can't do him on that bed, we'd have to lift him out – '

'Look, what's the matter with you lot, it saves you work, doesn't it, you turn him less, the CVP lines don't come to bits, what's the problem, nurse?'

I should've kept quiet. I should have realized I'd hardly have been the first to point all this out to him. But I went on: 'If he arrests, we'd have to lift him on to the floor, I don't know if – '

'Look!' Mr Haldane hissed. 'What d'you want, eh? It's my decision, is that what you want? My decision, he stays in the waterbed, all right?'

'Right.'

'Good. Goodnight. Nurse.'

And off he stomped. Well, I'd had a bad day too. I'd been too high to sleep for a long time. When I'd finally slept I'd dreamt about Johnny, that I was standing by his bed trying to get one of his infusions, the yellow one with the vitamins, to run on time. I was counting the drips and timing them as I so often did in reality, one . . . two . . . three, watching each arc of gold become the bead, each bead become, slowly, the heavy tear-shaped drop. One . . . two . . . three . . . and Johnny lying shadowy and slender in his bed, so close beside me I could've reached out and laid my hand upon his breast.

The dream had woken me up, and I hadn't slept again after it. Three hours sleep that day. My eyes were sticky, my legs ached.

'Achtung,' said Sally, passing me with the linen trolley. The corridor doors bashed open.

'Nurse.'

'Sister.'

She slouched around as usual. At the desk she said, 'That waterbed. Won't do. Too squashy.'

'Really, Sister?'

'I'll mention it to Mr Haldane.'

'Oh. Thank you, Sister.'

'Night.'

I gave her my nicest smile. 'Goodnight, Sister.'

Jan was back and the aux was good, so I spent most of the night in bay two, sweating over Mr Chester. His bed was surrounded by get-well cards. One of them was hand-drawn, a child's picture of Mr Chester in bed, a matchstick man all wired up, with his CVP lines, drains, drips, whirring pump, and catheter bag. Bandy triangular nurses stood about the bed holding trays, and GET WELL GRANDAD was written in tilted multi-coloured capitals across the top.

'We're losing him,' said Dr Whatsit, sighing by the desk.

'I'm scared stiff,' I told her. 'We pull him off the bed – if we can – and all his wires'll cross. It'll be a hell of a mess.'

She nodded. 'I know. Still. Maybe it won't happen.'

We looked at one another and knew that it would. A question of time, that was all.

He kept going, though, all that night. I washed his face a lot. He was nearly unconscious most of the time. Someone's grandad, sweating with death.

Johnny had a paperback. He was pretty lively, they'd upped his dosage, and he was still awake at one o'clock. I went over to him. He smiled at me. There was a little gap, I noticed, between his two front teeth.

'Listen to this, Chrissy.'

It was a poetry book. I recognized the cover, we'd used it at school. I wondered what fool had given it to him.

> 'Every Morn and every Night
> Some are Born to sweet delight.
> Some are Born to sweet delight,
> Some are Born to Endless Night.'

I looked at him anxiously, but he was grinning.

'That's you,' he said.

'What?'

'Says here.' He turned back to the book, frowned, appeared to read.

> 'Some are Born to sweet delights,
> Some are on Indefinite Nights.'

I laughed outright.

'You idiot!'

Johnny laughed too. 'Not bad for one o'clock in the morning.' In the light from the bedside lamp I saw how jaundiced his eyes had grown, how bronze his skin.

'You should be asleep.'

'I can sleep any time.' He turned to put the book away and I saw that his hair was beginning to fall out. There was a big pale bald patch at the back of his head. The pillow was littered with dark, shed hairs.

'D'you ever read poetry, Chris?'

'Can't understand it.'

'Oh, you don't have to understand it, I don't always understand it, I just – '

'Nurse, oh nurse!' It was Mr Goldbloom, poor leaky Mr Goldbloom.

'Oh, nurse, I'm so sorry, oh dear, oh dear – '

In the canteen that night a nurse I'd never seen before sat down beside me and said, 'You on Rebecca?'

'Yes.'

'How's Johnny Brownlow?'

I gave her a look. She had a fair fat face, with triangles of brilliant blusher on her cheekbones, and her hat was pinned low on her forehead in a saucy Edwardian tilt, sure sign, in that hospital, that she was a bit of a tart.

'Not so good,' I said.

'I can hardly believe he's still alive,' says this tarty sort, screwing her eyes up against her cigarette smoke. She wore lots of crumbly blue mascara. 'I was there,' she went on, 'when he come in. Appendix, they thought. Opened him up, had a look, and bam it's last rites and telling his mum he won't last the night. How long you been there?'

'About five weeks,' I said.

'So what they doing for him?' This was a new voice, someone across the table. I knew her vaguely, we'd both done a stint as students on the same ophthalmic ward.

'You've never worked on Rebecca,' I said to her.

'No, but everyone knows Johnny.' There was a murmuring round the whole table as she spoke, and I looked up and saw that, for once, everyone there was in on the same conversation.

'He's just so lovely,' said the student on my left. I knew her, she was a friend of Sally's. I looked at her, at her silly smile, and pushed away my plate.

'It's such a crying shame,' said the tarty one. 'I mean, he's so *nice* as well, he got to know my name, I never told him, he just got to know it somehow. I used to talk to him a fair bit.' She sighed.

'Does his girlfriend still come in?' Another new voice: staff nurse on Pettit ward.

'I don't know,' I said, 'I've only done nights.' I found my cigarettes. I was trembling a little.

'Every day she'd come in. Ever so pretty. A model.'

'No, she was an art student,' said the tarty one.

'It's just so sad,' sighed Sally's friend.

'What they doing for him anyway?'

'Cytotoxics,' I said. 'Then some sort of new-fangled radiation, I don't understand what, you know they don't tell you much on nights.'

'How's he taking it?'

'Jaundiced. His hair's coming out.'

'Oh no . . .' more murmurs, commiseration.

'Why don't they let him go?'

'They never know when to give in.'

'It's such a shame.'

I stood up, swung my bag on to my shoulder.

'Got to get back early,' I said, stubbing out my cigarette. The table was littered, dirty plates, cellophane, spilt water, flecks of ash.

'Tell him I was asking after him,' said the tarty one. 'Tell him Janet, bet he'll remember.'

I didn't go straight back to work, instead I locked myself in the staff toilet to try to think. I could not at first name the emotion that had made me tremble so in the canteen. It seemed to have too many strands to have just the one name, and I was not sure how far I really wanted to investigate them. I lit another cigarette: think.

I had been angry. Because they had talked about him, because I had joined in. We had tossed his name to and fro across that soiled table as if tragedy made him public property. We had used luxurious sentimental voices, the voices we might use to discuss any ersatz celluloid tear-jerker.

I had been surprised, too, simply surprised that he was remembered so vividly by nurses who hardly knew him, or who had nursed him months before.

Anger, surprise; I didn't mind admitting to them.

I balanced my cigarette on the china toilet-paper holder and stood up. There was a square of mirror over the sink and I looked into it at my scrawny white face and red-rimmed eyes. Third strand: jealousy.

Jealous professionally, jealous privately. Jealous, because his life was my responsibility, not theirs. Mine. My carelessness could kill him, not theirs. It was me that soothed him, not them. He was mine to talk about, not theirs.

And privately. Tell him Janet, bet he remembers —

I picked my cigarette up again.

And why, *why* did they all know him? The reply to that one was the most uncomfortable of all. Because he was young, and beautiful, and dying, he fulfilled all our most romantic notions of what nursing might mean. Only wartime fills hospital beds with beautiful damaged young men, and there was no war. Johnny was all we had: a lovely young man, unattainable, weaker than a child. Not just love-without-strings: romantic love-without-strings. Passion-without-strings.

There's something wrong about bloody nursing, I thought, throwing my cigarette stub into the toilet bowl. Or about nurses? Or about me?

I pinned my hat on very straight on the top of my head, and went back to work.

*

Night eight followed. My last night. My last night, as it happened, on Rebecca. I was moved the following week to a pediatric ward. No explanation was given. I didn't expect one. The Night Sister gave me a fulsome report; that didn't surprise me either.

The last night on Rebecca was the quietest I ever had there.

While I'd slept Mr Chester had arrested. It was 3.30 pm, they told us at report: visiting time. There were visitors everywhere. Mr Chester had three.

He was still on the waterbed. They tried to pull him up and over the bed-sides and he weighed so much it was like a tug-of-war with a corpse as rope; his latest blood transfusion unhooked and swung round, spraying Mr Goldbloom, who screamed, and the CVP line fell apart and tangled up one of the student nurses as she heaved at Mr Chester from one side, and tripped her so that she fell forwards on to him in the waterbed, and they couldn't hold him once they'd lifted him, but dropped him heavily on to the floor with a crash of falling drip-stands and bedside waterjugs and mouth-care trays . . .

He died anyway. They had the fire brigade up – the cardiac arrest team I mean – running round in circles and braying orders and shooting drugs into all parts and (so it always seems) all comers. But he died anyway.

That was at 3.30 pm.

I came on at ten and Lord the place was quiet. As if the fright of Mr Chester's going had put everyone on their best behaviour. Or that, the Reaper having struck so wildly elsewhere, everyone else felt immune, if not exactly in good spirits.

So, come 4 am, Sally, Jan, and I sat at the desk with a pot of tea. The aux had her own tray down in the far end. It was the first time we'd managed this illicit treat all week. We talked about night six and Jan groaned and apologized. We ate buttered toast. It was so quiet. The far end slumbered, snoring in tune. The singles slept. The grots were all out cold. The sickies dripped in good time.

'It's the last night,' said Sally. 'We're leaving it nice for them.'

'Hush!' I said, but too late. Almost as I spoke there was a crash and a ripple of spattering noises from bay two.

'No, I'll go,' I said. I got up and went into the bay. At first all I could hear there was breathing. Mr Chester's waterbed had gone, replaced by an ordinary empty bed. His cards and flowers were all gone too. No one spoke to me. I crept about in the dim red light, checking. Not Mr Goldbloom, for a wonder. Not Mr Dooley, shrunken alcoholic Mr Dooley, paying for past whiskies with his own present blood. Not Mr Miller, no trouble, Mr Miller. Not Mr Fletcher, lonely Mr Fletcher.

Johnny was crying. I drew the curtain partly round him and turned the bright day-lamp against the wall so that it would give just a little light, and switched it on. He held one yellow skeletal hand over his eyes. He hardly looked human. Monday was barber-day, and Johnny had had his head shaved. It had given me quite a shock when I first came on duty. I sat down on the bed.

'Hey, hari krishna.'

He smiled at that. 'Hari hari,' he said back. 'Don't you like it?'

'I'm not sure,' I said.

'The barber came. It was all falling out, I reckoned it'd look better all off, see.'

'I'll get used to it. What did you drop?' The bed was soaked on the other side.

He gave a sob at that, and eventually said, 'Orange juice.'

'They're never letting you drink?'

'Just the taste,' he said. His yellow eyes filled again. 'I'm all sticky.'

'You're a daftie,' I said. 'I'll get some water. Just a sec.'

I went and filled a bowl, giving Sally and Jan a dismissive little wave as I passed the desk. 'Nothing serious.'

'You're lucky being next to the window,' I said to Johnny, as I cleared the locker top and put the bowl down. I'd change the bed afterwards, with Sally. I covered him up with the fleecy bath-blanket and slid the wet sheet off him from beneath it.

'Not really. I mean, I asked. I was over by the door, I asked to be moved so that I could see out.'

I took his flannel, wetted it, squeezed it out, gave it to him. 'Face,' I said.

'I can see the stars sometimes,' said Johnny, his voice muffled as he scrubbed away weakly at his eyes. 'Just before dawn, when the city's lights are, you know, lower. Mostly they're too bright though.' He passed the flannel back to me and I gave him the towel.

He dried himself and said, 'I wonder how far away you can see London. Miles into space, I reckon. Or those American cities. Las Vegas. New York. I bet you can see New York from the moon.'

I soaped the flannel and picked up his left hand and washed it for him, carefully so as not to disturb the new drip in the back of it.

'I saw Orion once, out of the window. The stars, you know, Orion.'

'I know him,' I said. Johnny's palm was sticky with orange juice. 'He looks like Elvis Presley.'

Johnny laughed. 'What you mean?'

'The way he's standing there. Hips all slanted.'

'That's his sword-belt.'

'Nah, it's Elvis the Pelvis. A real star, see. Up there with all the rest.' I rinsed his hand, dried it.

'Like a neon sign,' said Johnny dreamily. 'A neon sign, like in Las Vegas. Orion in Las Vegas.'

I picked up his other hand.

'Ow.'

'Sorry. Nasty bruise.'

'Yeah, they were practising.'

'Well, they've got to learn somehow, you know.'

'You're rotten to me, you are.'

I started on his arms: long and very slender, like those of a slim girl, with long tender muscles just defined beneath the skin.

'Look at my needle tracks.'

'That one must've hurt.'

'It did. Here, Chrissy.'

'What?' I patted his arms with the towel.

'That Mr Chester.'

'Yes.' I tried not to sound guarded.

'I was thinking. My turn next.'

'Who says so?' I was smooth: you'd never have guessed how my heart turned over with fright.

'I say so.'

I folded the bath-blanket back and soaped the flannel again. I did everything slowly and carefully, trying to stay calm. If he asked me outright, what should I say?

'Why's that?' I asked. I began to wash his chest. There was no hair there, because of the cytotoxics; or perhaps he was just too young anyway. His skin was a deep clear bronze. He could've been a bronze image lying there, or an alien creature from another world, with his golden eyes and smooth skull and graven yellow arms. An alien creature. Only his weakness showed that he was human.

'I just know,' he said. I dried him and spread powder on his chest, as silky as a child's under my hand. I remembered my dream. I stopped where I was, my hand on his breast, my palm over the little dark nipple.

'They're going to irradiate me,' said Johnny lightly. 'I'm gonna glow in the dark.'

He grinned, and I took my hand away, and the crisis, if it had been a crisis, was over. I didn't really understand what had happened. I wasn't even sure that anything had.

I didn't think about it too hard either. There were no conclusions I wanted to reach.

I could've ended this story here: left it as an account of what a certain job was like. For me, I mean. I'm not claiming to speak for anyone else.

But there's a coda.

It happened six months afterwards: a Saturday in high summer. I'd left the hospital in the April, and hadn't taken another permanent job yet. I was doing agency work to keep going. I was really low that day. My boyfriend had just thrown me over. He was a medical student, in fact he was one of those sprayed with Mr Dooley's life-blood all those months before. We didn't talk about Rebecca though. We didn't talk about anything very much. Perhaps that's why we didn't last so long.

Anyway, it was a bright Saturday in July and I was at the library, too low to look smart. My hair had needed washing two days before, as well. Lord, I was depressed.

I was wandering up and down looking along the shelves and swinging my empty plastic bag when I saw a skinny God-squad type freak over by reference. I felt a bit scornful, all those shaven heads and rattling money boxes turn me right off. Then, as I got closer, I saw who it was.

For a moment I felt dizzy with sheer surprise. It was Johnny, of course. Jeans and a T-shirt. Thin as before, but upright, walking, no drips, no drains, no needle tracks. Johnny, his head still shaved, one skinny wrist out, leaning against the books, reading.

I felt no pleasure that I can remember, just shock. I backed quickly behind the thrillers and peered out, my heart pounding. He turned a page, intent. For six months I had hardly thought of him. I watched him, remembering: You can see New York from the moon. Orion in Las Vegas. Some are born to Sweet Delights, some are on Indefinite Nights.

I could've walked up to him, spoken his name: 'Johnny, for God's sake! This is wonderful!'

I remembered my last night on Rebecca, the lascivious tenderness of the blanket bath.

If I spoke to him, what would he say, what would he do? I

had no doubt he would remember me. He would remember my name.

What would he say, what would he do?

He would look down at me, and smile, and judge me. He would notice me. I would no longer be extended womanhood, beyond judgement if not beyond love. He was a man again, able, if he so wanted, to ask of me everything I knew I would never give him, not him, not anyone. Indefinite Nights, that's me.

I honestly can't say whether I'd have behaved differently if I'd been happier or better-dressed. As it was I didn't hesitate. My heart was beating very fast. I backed some more, very quietly, and hid behind the great wall of engineering textbooks at the back of the hall, and stayed there until I was quite sure that he had gone.

ANGELA HUTH

*

The Weighing Up

The last time I weighed myself, yesterday morning to be precise, the scales registered twelve stone and one ounce. That is not a record. I have been several pounds heavier. On rare occasions, these last five years, and quite by chance, I've also been a pound or so lighter.

You may be surprised by my saying this, and possibly not believe me, but I am not depressed by my weight. Passing shop windows, or the occasional glance in a mirror, confirm that all hope of ever retrieving my old, slight shape, has quite gone. And I don't mind.

The funny thing is, nor does Jeremy. We married twenty-three years ago when I was a mere slip of a thing – an old joke was that he referred to me as a *slipover* rather than a pushover. Food, then, did not concern me much. I cooked because I had to: meals for the children, dinner for Jeremy on the rare occasions he was home. But I did make quite an effort, for years, with Sunday lunch. There were constant disputes about whether it should be chocolate pudding or Brown Betty (as a family, we all love apples) each week. I made whatever they finally decided upon, and enjoyed their appreciation.

It was after Sam and Kathy left for university and only Laura, our youngest, was left at home, that I became unstuck. The trouble was, used to making enough for five healthy appetites, I miscalculated when cooking for two. I always made too much, to be on the safe side. There was always things left over. Remembering the post-war economy of my own childhood, and not liking to see things go to waste, I found it hard to leave them in the fridge or larder to await reheating. It became impossible to throw them away. Finishing them off myself – cold rice pudding for elevenses, cold chicken curry for tea, time doesn't matter to an anarchistic eater – became my habit.

By the time Laura finally left, too, to go to Durham, I had noticed the conspicuous change in my figure. I should have taken some strong hold – gone on a diet, changed my eating habits, whatever. But no. One of the pleasures I came to look forward to was a proper three-course dinner alone in front of the television. Plus half a bottle of Jeremy's nice white wine. He always said, 'Help yourself from the cellar whenever you want to,' and I would take him at his word. Another pleasure was breakfast: all those fried glistening things I had cooked for years for the children and never eaten myself, I now found immensely enjoyable. They gave a good start to the morning. They would keep me going till the chocolate biscuits and coffee at eleven, later followed by homemade bread and soup for lunch.

The children, when they came home, teased me mildly about my middle-aged spread. They found it odd I had put on so much weight considering I seemed to be eating no more than usual. For, out of habit, or perhaps secret shame, in front of them I remained quite abstemious, piling their plates with second and third helpings but toying with just one small helping myself. I contemplated confessing to them my secret vice, but then couldn't face it. Besides, they didn't go on about it, accepted me lovingly as always. As for Jeremy – home less than ever despite retirement being only four years off – he made no comment at all.

Jeremy is in shipping. It has always been his job, ever since he came down from Balliol. I'm ashamed to say after twenty-three years of marriage I still don't know *precisely* what it is he does in shipping. Sales, I think. 'Do you have to sell a liner like a man who sells double glazing?' I once asked, but he was concentrating on something else, or perhaps considered it a question not worth answering, though he would never have been so rude as to say so.

For Jeremy is a very kind man. In matters of consideration, you could not fault him. That is not to say he is a man of declarations. His appreciation is expressed in other ways. Compliments have never sprung readily from his lips, and indeed I'm sometimes unsure he even observes things that might inspire other men to words of praise: Laura's new short hair, or one of my better soufflés, for instance. And yet he plainly cares deeply for his family. When he *is* home – and his business takes him all over the world, sometimes for weeks on end, for most of the year – he gives us his full attention. He asks questions, goes for walks with Sam, talks about Renaissance poets to Kathy and the history of politics to Laura, and takes an interest in my herbaceous border and the state of my old-fashioned roses. 'Sorry I've got to go again,' he says, when his time is up. And I know he means it. He looks full of regret.

Away from us, he sends postcards, calls occasionally at inconvenient hours – though, heavens, the sound of his voice is never inconvenient – from Australia or wherever. I always get a decent warning of his homecoming. Mrs Manns, his secretary, gives a ring saying what time he is due at Heathrow, so there is no chance of my letting him down. A company chauffeur meets him at the airport these days, but I can be sure of having ready his favourite shrimp vol-au-vents, or risotto, or, best of all, baked red mullet. Plus, of course, a bottle of wine in the fridge.

He always seems to be pleased to be home. Lately, he's taken to bringing me chocolates. He apologizes they have come from the airport, time being very scarce – but they're invariably very expensive and elaborately beribboned. Particularly good, of course, when he returns from Brussels or Zurich. We have established a funny little routine after our first reunion dinner: I offer him one of the heavenly chocolates: he refuses. 'You have them all for yourself,' he says with his generous smile. And once he's gone away again – I don't open them till then – that's just what I do.

I'm sitting now by the study fire, the latest box — a fine assortment of soft centres — by my side. I've watched the nine o'clock news, and *Panorama*, and am quite content. I choose my third — fourth? fifth perhaps? — and last for the evening: a walnut cluster. The hand that plucks it, I notice, is a plump, puffed-up thing compared with what it used to be. The nails are still a pretty shape, but my wedding ring sits deep beside two banks of flesh. I could never get it off, now: it will have to be buried with me. The ankles and feet, stretched out, match the hands in puffiness. No longer can I wear the pretty shoes that I used to love to find, and which caused people to pay many a compliment. The arms are large and heavy. Once delicate wrist and elbow bones now quite obliterated by fat, and the stomach is swollen to the same size as when I was six months pregnant. None of these things worries me dreadfully, but I do observe them. Thank God we are designed so as not to see our own faces — that was an almighty piece of tact on the Lord's part. For on the occasions I'm forced to study the face, I admit to a certain desolation. Simply because it doesn't look like the one I remember best. 'If you'd just lose a stone or two, Mam,' Laura said a week or so ago, 'you'd be exceptionally good-looking. I mean, you've got the features. It's just that they're becoming obscured.'

It's true. (Laura has always been the most loving and most honest of the children. She's the one who minds most about this metamorphosis.) I did have fine eyes: but as the cheeks have swollen their size has diminished. And the once pointed chin is now indeterminate, mingling with underchins that ripple down to a doughy chest. My hair still shines from time to time, I think. But I'm not attractive any more. I'm fat, fat, fat.

Perhaps if Jeremy were to complain, I would make a serious effort to do something about it. This I reflect on sometimes: I am so much less busy now and have time for introspection. (A dangerous pastime, I always think. I don't indulge too often.) But as Jeremy does not complain, and remains as considerate to me and appreciative of home life as he is able in the brief times he is here, why make the effort? As it is, I am peaceful, lazier these days, and happy. And it's time to go to bed.

It's a windy night. Draughts slightly move the curtains. The weather forecast warned of tempestuous autumn days ahead. Well, if it rains tomorrow I shall stay at home with bean soup for lunch, and make a list of ingredients for the Christmas cake. Some people might be daunted by my solitary days of trivial pursuits. I like them. Besides, it's not a barren life. There is always Jeremy's next return to look forward to.

Yesterday he rang from Tokyo to say he doubted if he could get home by the weekend. He would ring again if plans changed. I stir, meaning to get up. The telephone on the table beside me rings. It can only mean that plans *have* changed.

'Hello?' says a woman. I do not know her voice. 'Is that Ada Mullins?'

'Avril,' I say.

'Sorry. I knew it was something beginning with A. Couldn't for the life of me remember what.' She gave a small laugh, but not a friendly one.

'Who are you?' I ask.

'I'm Richenda Gosforth.'

Silence.

'Richenda . . .?'

I do not know a Richenda, I'm almost sure. Perhaps she's a friend of one of the children.

'Gosforth.' Silence for a moment or two. 'I'm the mother of Jeremy's baby. Your husband Jeremy.'

'Yes, yes. I know Jeremy's my husband,' I say. My fingers fiddle with the velvet ribbon twisted into a multi-looped bow on the lid of the chocolate box. I feel very calm.

'Look, Av – Mrs Mullins,' says Richenda Gosforth. 'Jeremy wanted to keep all this from you. He'll probably be livid with me when he finds out I've rung you. But I think you should know the truth.'

'Really?' I say, but it isn't really a question as I'm not sure what she's talking about.

'Well, the truth is, Jeremy and I have been together for nearly two years now. I've been like a second wife to him in a way. I suppose you could say I've had all the glamour but none of the real advantages.'

'None of the real advantages?' I echo.

'Absolutely not. I mean, yes, I've had the trips abroad, the first-class flights, the champagne, the hanging about in hotel suites while he's in his conferences. But what I've never had with Jeremy is a *base*. That's been your privilege. You've got the base with Jeremy.'

'That's true,' I say. 'Jeremy and I have certainly had a solid base for a good many years now. Man and wife.'

'Exactly. And you hold the trump card, *being* his wife.'

'I am his wife, yes.' Another pause.

'You're being very nice,' continues Richenda Gosforth. 'I thought you'd be screaming mad at me. I had to have three whiskeys before making this call. Anyhow, about the baby. I thought you should know about the baby. When I first told Jeremy, heavens, was he put out! Wanted to whizz me off to an abortionist straight away. He didn't want anything to *rock the boat*, as he put it.'

'That's always been a concern of his, not to rock the boat,' I reflect. We give a small, clashing laugh. When the laughter dies, Richenda Gosforth goes on with her story.

'But I said: no way, Jeremy. I'm not going to be pushed about for your convenience. My baby's not going to be murdered just to suit you. I'm going to have it.'

'Quite right,' I say, being anti-abortion myself, and to end another silence.

'Jason was born three weeks ago,' says Richenda, 'and when Jeremy saw I had no intention of changing my mind, I must say he was very decent about it all. He set me up in this flat near Richmond Park, and he's paying for a part-time nanny so I'll be able to go back to work. He was in Canada for the actual birth, but he comes to see us as often as he can. I'm expecting him for the weekend when, I've told him, we've finally got to thrash things out.'

'He'll be with *you*, this weekend?' I say. 'To thrash things out?'

'Exactly. Unless, that is, his plans change, and he can't make it.'

I feel the merest smile twitch the corners of my mouth. 'His plans do change,' I say.

'I'm sorry if all this is coming as an awful shock to you,' says Richenda. 'But I thought if I could tell Jeremy I'd spoken to you, although he might be angry, it would make things easier.'

'I hope so,' I said.

It might not make things *much* easier, I think, Jeremy not being a man who thrives on confrontation.

'The thing is *this*. In a word, Mrs Mullins, Jeremy is the love of my life. I want to marry him. I think, to be honest, he feels the same.'

She is silent again. I feel I should help her out.

'And I'm the stumbling block,' I say.

'Exactly. You're the stumbling block. Jeremy's told me a million times he can't leave you, break up the family. *Yet*, anyway. *Some time*, he says, perhaps. But he says he can't bring himself to leave you at the moment, whatever he feels for me and Jason, for reasons he can't explain. You're a taboo subject, actually. So I don't know anything about you. I don't know if you're old or young or middle-aged, fat or thin, whether you work or not, whether you're a good wife and mother. I don't know *anything* about you. Jeremy goes all blank if I ask any questions. He simply won't talk about you —' She breaks off with a sob in her voice. I wait for her to recover. 'Mrs Mullins, forgive me for saying this, but although he keeps his silence I get the impression that *there's not much going on between you and Jeremy*. Would you mind if he left you?'

I see my dimpled fingers twirl faster through the pretty loops of the velvet bow. Would I mind if he left me? It is a question I have never asked myself.

'It's a question I've never asked myself,' I tell Richenda

Gosforth, 'and a question I trust I shall never have the need to ask myself.'

I glance down at my feet, slumped inwards upon themselves, conveying the weariness that seemed to be congealing my veins, making me hungry. I lift the lid from the chocolate box and rustle through the crisp, empty, pleated brown-paper cases that once held the delicious collection of soft centres.

'Oh,' says Richenda Gosforth, eventually. 'Really?'

She does not sound deflated. She's obviously a determined young woman (I presume young, anyway) out to get her own way.

'Well, I think you should think about it all, if you would. I mean, after all, nothing's ever going to be quite the same again, now, is it? Knowing Jeremy has a mistress and baby tucked away somewhere. As you can imagine, Mrs Mullins, I shall be insisting on no less for Jason than your children had – private education, holidays with Jeremy, all that sort of thing –'

'Quite,' I hear myself interrupting. I am still thinking calmly. The impertinence of the girl. The weariness turns into a heavy physical thing that clouds my whole body.

'So you think it over and I'll ring you back,' she suggests in a bossy voice.

'Oh no, don't ring me back, if you don't mind,' I say, wanting this insane conversation to end, now. I put down the receiver.

The wind still shuffles the curtains. The silence is broken only by the small cracking sounds of the empty chocolate papers as my hand despairs through them in hope of a last one: but no, there are none left. But Jeremy, when he comes early next week, I must now suppose, will not let me down. Jeremy is a loving man. He will bring me new chocolates, lovingly chosen by himself. He is not the sort of man to hurt his wife and family. If there is a complicated side of his life, he will protect us from it. Perhaps he has always done this. Perhaps there have been other . . . complications over the years.

This whole daft matter is, in fact, scarcely worth thinking

about, because nothing can ever affect us. The solid base
Richenda Gosforth seemed so to envy cannot be disturbed by
an outside force. When Jeremy comes, I shall welcome him. He
will be pleased to be back, as always. I shall offer him the
chocolates he has brought me. He will refuse. We will laugh,
exchange news. Naturally, I shall not mention the silly business
of Richenda Gosforth's telephone call. I would never dream of
intruding in that way. Where there is trust, there is no place
for intrusion. I would rather not have known about this
squalid girl, of course, but Jeremy will deal with her. He is
very competent at sorting out all manner of things. Never will
he know, from me, that I know about his son. That is the least
a wife can do, keep her silence, if she is to practise her real love
for her husband.

I shall lash out on Monday evening: I shall lash out on
turbot and a mousseline sauce, and he'll chide me a little for
my extravagance, but really be pleased at the effort I've made.
We will have one of our quiet and peaceful evenings together –
happy, easy with each other as is our custom. As usual, he will
be suffering from jet lag – funny how after flying so many
thousands of miles it still affects him – and fall asleep instantly
his head touches the pillow. Sometimes I watch his sleeping
face for hours. Good, kind, searingly familiar. Oh Jeremy. I
think I know you well. I *do* know you well.

Somehow it is nearly midnight. Long past my normal
bedtime. In the circumstances, I think I shall treat myself to a
mug of hot chocolate and a piece of toast and dripping, the
stuff of midnight feasts as a child. Now, standing, in anticipation of such pleasure the weariness has quite fled. I am large
and strong and Jeremy's wife. I am warm with trust.

After a while, I go to the kitchen, pour boiling milk into
the mug of chocolate powder, and stir the creamy bubbles.
I choose a pretty tray for the drink and toast and dripping,
and make my way, quite sure of our unchanging love,
to bed.

*

A Love Match

It was Mr Pilkington who brought the Tizards to Hallowby. He met them, a quiet couple, at Carnac, where he had gone for a school-masterly Easter holiday to look at the monoliths. After two or three meetings at a café, they invited him to their rented chalet. It was a cold, wet afternoon and a fire of pine cones crackled on the hearth. 'We collect them on our walks,' said Miss Tizard. 'It's an economy. And it gives us an object.' The words, and the formal composure of her manner, made her seem like a Frenchwoman. Afterwards, he learned that the Tizards were a Channel Island family and had spent their childhood in Jersey. The ancestry that surfaced in Miss Tizard's brisk gait and erect carriage, brown skin and compact sentences, did not show in her brother. His fair hair, his red face, his indecisive remarks, his diffident movements – as though with the rest of his body he were apologizing for his stiff leg – were entirely English. He ought not, thought Mr Pilkington, to be hanging about in France. He'd done more than enough for France already. For this was in 1923 and Mr Pilkington, with every intention of preserving a historian's impartiality, was nevertheless infected by the current mood of disliking the French.

The weather continued cold and wet; there was a sameness about the granite avenues. Mr Pilkington's mind became increasingly engaged with the possibility, the desirability, the positive duty of saving that nice fellow Tizard from wasting his days in exile. He plied him with hints, with suggestions, with tactful inquiries. Beyond discovering that money was not the obstacle to return, he got no further. Tizard, poor fellow, must be under his sister's thumb. Yet it was from the sister that he got his first plain answer. 'Justin would mope if he had nothing to do.' Mr Pilkington stopped himself from commenting on the collection of pine cones as an adequate lifework. As though she had read his thought, she went on, 'There is a difference between idling in a foreign country and being an idler in your own.' At that moment Tizard limped into the room with crayfish bristling from his shopping basket. 'It's begun,' he said ruefully. '*La Jeune France* has arrived. I've just seen two young men in pink trousers with daisy chains round their necks, riding through the town on donkeys.' Mr Pilkington asked if this was a circus. Miss Tizard explained that it was the new generation, and would make Carnac a bedlam till the summer's end. 'Of course, there's a certain amount of that sort of thing in England, too,' observed Mr Pilkington. 'But only in the South. It doesn't trouble us at Hallowby.' As he spoke, he was conscious of playing a good card; then the immensity of the trump he held broke upon him. He was too excited to speak. Inviting them to dine at his hotel on the following night, he went away.

By next evening, more of *La Jeune France* had arrived, and was mustered outside the hotel extemporizing a bullfight ballet in honour of St Cornély, patron saint of cattle and of the parish church. Watching Tizard's look of stoically endured embarrassment Mr Pilkington announced that he had had a blow; the man who had almost promised to become curator of the Beelby Military Museum had written to say he couldn't take up the post. 'He didn't say why. But I know why. Hallowby is too quiet for him.'

'But I thought Hallowby had blast furnaces and strikes and all that sort of thing,' said Tizard.

'That is Hallowby juxta Mare,' replied Mr Pilkington. 'We are Old Hallowby. Very quiet; quite old, too. The school was founded in 1623. We shall be having our modest tercentenary this summer. That is why I am so put out by Dalsover's not taking up the curatorship. I hoped to have the museum all in order. It would have been something to visit, if it rains during the Celebrations.' He allowed a pause.

Tizard, staring at the toothpicks, inquired, 'Is it a wet climate?'

But Mr Pilkington was the headmaster of a minor public school, a position of command. As if the pause had not taken place, raising his voice above the bullfight he told how fifty years earlier Davenport Beelby, a rich man's sickly son, during a lesson on the Battle of Minden awoke to military glory and began to collect regimental buttons. Buttons, badges, pikes, muskets and bayonets, shakos and helmets, dispatches, newspaper cuttings, stones from European battlefields, sand from desert campaigns – his foolish collection grew into the lifework of a devoted eccentric and, as such collections sometimes do, became valuable and authoritative, though never properly catalogued. Two years ago he had died, bequeathing the collection to his old school, with a fund sufficient for upkeep and the salary of a curator.

'I wish you'd consider coming as our curator,' said Mr Pilkington. 'I'm sure you would find it congenial. Beelby wanted an Army man. Three mornings a week would be quite enough.'

Tizard shifted his gaze from the toothpicks to the mustard jar. 'I am not an Army man,' he said. 'I just fought. Not the same thing, you know.'

Miss Tizard exclaimed, 'No! Not at all,' and changed the subject.

But later that evening she said to her brother, 'Once we were there, we shouldn't see much of him. It's a possibility.'

'Do you want to go home, Celia?'

'I think it's time we did. We were both of us born for a sober, conventional, taxpaying life, and if – '

'*Voici Noël!*' sang the passing voices. '*Voici Noël! Voici Noël, petits enfants!*'

She composed her twitching hands and folded them on her lap. 'We were young rowdies once,' he said placatingly.

A fortnight later, they were Mr Pilkington's guests at Hallowby. A list of empty houses had been compiled by Miss Robson, the secretary. All were variously suitable; each in turn was inspected by Miss Tizard and rejected. Mr Pilkington felt piqued that his offer of a post should dance attendance on the aspect of a larder or the presence of decorative tiles. Miss Tizard was a disappointment to him; he had relied on her support. Now it was the half-hearted Tizard who seemed inclined to root, while she flitted from one eligible residence to another, appearing, as he remarked to the secretary, to expect impossibilities. Yet when she settled as categorically as a queen bee the house she chose had really nothing to be said for it. A square, squat mid-Victorian box, Newton Lodge was one of the ugliest houses in Hallowby; though a high surrounding wall with a green door in it hid the totality of its ugliness from passers-by, its hulking chimneys proclaimed what was below. It was not even well situated. It stood in a deteriorating part of the town, and was at some distance from the school buildings and the former gymnasium – Victorian also – which had been assigned to the Beelby Collection. But the house having been chosen, the curatorship was bestowed and the move made. Justin Tizard, rescued from wasting his days in exile – though too late for the tercentenary celebrations – began his duties as curator by destroying a quantity of cobwebs and sending for a window-cleaner.

All through the summer holidays he worked on, sorting things into heaps, subdividing the heaps into lesser heaps. Beelby's executors must have given carte-blanche to the packers, who had acted on the principle of filling up with anything that came handy, and the unpackers had done little more than tumble things out and scatter them with notices saying 'DO NOT DISTURB'. The largest heap consisted of objects he could not account for, but unaccountably it lessened, till the day came when he could look round on tidiness. Ambition seized him. Tidiness is not enough; no one looks twice at tidiness. There must also be parade and ostentation. He bought stands, display cases, dummies for the best uniforms. Noticing a decayed wooden horse in the saddler's shop, he bought that, too; trapped, with its worser side to the wall and with a cavalry dummy astride, it made a splendid appearance. He combed plumes, shook out bearskins, polished holsters and gunstocks, oiled the demi-culverin, sieved the desert sand. At this stage, his sister came and polished with him, mended, refurbished, sewed on loose buttons. Of the two, she had more feeling for the exhibits themselves, for the discolouring glory and bloodshed they represented. It was the housewife's side that appealed to him. Sometimes, hearing him break into the whistle of a contented mind, she would look up from her work and stare at him with the unbelief of thankfulness.

Early in the autumn term, Mr Pilkington made time to visit the museum. He did not expect much and came prepared with speeches of congratulation and encouragement. They died on his lips when he saw the transformation. Instead, he asked how much the display cases had cost, and the dummies, and the horse, and how much of the upkeep fund remained after all this expenditure. He could not find fault; there was no reason to do so. He was pleased to see Tizard so well established as master in his own house. Perhaps he was also pleased that there was no reason to find fault. Though outwardly unchanged, the Tizard of Carnac appeared to have been charged with new contents – with something obstinately reckless beneath the easy-going manner, with watchfulness beneath the diffidence. But this, reflected Mr Pilkington, might well be accounted for by the startling innovations in the museum. He stayed longer than he meant, and only after leaving remembered that he had omitted to say how glad he was that Tizard had accepted the curatorship. This must be put right; he did not want to discourage the young man who had worked so hard and so efficiently, and also he must get into the way of remembering that Tizard was in fact a young man – under thirty. Somehow, one did not think of him as a young man.

*

Justin Tizard, newly a captain in an infantry regiment, came on leave after the battle of the Somme. His sister met the train at Victoria. There were some pigeons strutting on the platform and he was watching them when a strange woman in black came up to him, touched his shoulder, and said 'Justin!' It was as though Celia were claiming a piece of lost luggage, he thought. She had a taxi waiting, and they drove to her flat. She asked about his health, about his journey; then she congratulated him on his captaincy. 'Practical reasons,' he said. 'My habit of not getting killed. They were bound to notice it sooner or later.' After this, they fell silent. He looked out of the window at the streets so clean and the people so busy with their own affairs. 'That's a new Bovril poster, isn't it?' he inquired. Her answer was so slow in coming that he didn't really take in whether it was yes or no.

Her flat was new, anyway. She had only been in it since their mother's remarriage. It was up a great many flights of stairs, and she spoke of moving to somewhere with a lift, now that Tim's legacy had made a rich woman of her. The room smelled of polish and flowers. There was a light-coloured rug on the floor and above this was the blackness of Celia's skirts. She was wearing black for her fiancé. The news of his death had come to her in this same room, while she was sorting books and hanging pictures. Looking round the room, still not looking at Celia, he saw Tim's photograph on her desk. She saw his glance, and hers followed it. 'Poor Tim!' they said, both speaking at once, the timbre of their voices relating them. 'They say he was killed instantaneously,' she went on. 'I hope it's true – though I suppose they always say that.'

'I'm sure it is,' he replied. He knew that Tim had been blown to pieces. Compassion made it possible to look at her. Dressed in black, possessing these new surroundings, she seemed mature and dignified beyond her actual three years' seniority. For the first time in his life he saw her not as a sister but as an individual. But he could not see her steadily for long. There was a blur on his sight, a broth of mud and flame and frantic unknown faces and writhing entrails. When she showed him to his bedroom she stepped over mud that heaved with the bodies of men submerged in it. She had drawn the curtains. There was a bed with sheets turned back, and a bedside lamp shed a serene, unblinking light on the pillows. 'Bed!' he exclaimed, and heard the spontaneity die in his voice. 'Wonderful to see a bed!'

'And this is the bathroom. I've got everything planned. First of all, you must have a bath, lie and soak in it. And then put on these pyjamas and the dressing-gown, and we will have supper.'

Left to himself he was violently sick. Shaking with fatigue, he sat in a hot scented bath and cleaned his knees with scrupulous care, like a child. Outside was the noise of London.

The pyjamas were silk, the dressing-gown was quilted and wrapped him round like a caress. In the sitting room was Celia, still a stranger, though now a stranger without a hat. There was a table sparkling with silver and crystal, smoked salmon, a bottle of champagne. It was all as she had planned it for Tim — Oh, poor Celia!

They discussed their mother's remarriage. It had been decided on with great suddenness, and appeared inexplicable. Though they refrained from saying much, their comments implied that her only reason for marrying a meat king from the Argentine was to get away from England and the war. 'There he was, at eleven in the morning, with a carnation — a foot shorter than she,' said Celia, describing the return from the registry office.

'In that case, he must be four foot three.'

'He is exactly four foot three. I stole up and measured him.'

Spoken in her imperturbable voice, this declaration struck him as immensely funny, as funny as a nursery joke. They laughed hilariously, and after this their evening went almost naturally.

Turning back after his unadorned, brotherly 'Good night, Celia,' he exclaimed, 'But where are you sleeping?'

'In here.' Before he could demur she went on, 'The sofa fits me. It would be far too short for you.'

He told her how balmily he had slept, one night behind the lines, with his head on a bag of nails.

'Exactly! That is why tonight you are going to sleep properly. In a bed.'

She heard him get into bed, heard the lamp switched off. Almost immediately she heard his breathing lengthen into slumber. Then, a few minutes later, he began to talk in his sleep.

Perhaps a scruple – the dishonourableness of being an eavesdropper, a Peeping Tom – perhaps mere craven terror, made her try not to listen. She began to read, and when she found that impossible she repeated poems she had learned at school, and when that failed she polished the silver cigarette box. But Justin's voice was raised, and the partition wall was thin, and the ghastly confidences went on and on. She could not escape them. She was dragged, a raw recruit, into battle.

In the morning she thought she would not be able to look him in the face. But he was cheerful, and so was she. She had got off from the canteen, she explained, while he was on leave; they had nothing to do but enjoy themselves. They decided to have some new experiences, so they went up the Monument. If he wants to throw himself off, she thought, I won't stop him. They looked down on London; on the curve of the Thames, the shipping, the busy lighters. They essayed how many City churches they could identify by their spires. They talked about Pepys. She would be surprised, Justin said, how many chaps carried a copy of the *Diary*, and she asked if bullets also glanced off Pepys carried in a breast pocket. So they made conversation quite successfully. And afterwards, when they had decided to go for a walk down Whitechapel High Street and lunch off winkles at a stall, many people glanced at them with kindness and sentimentality, and an old woman patted Celia's back, saying, 'God bless you, dearie! Isn't it lovely to have him home?'

Whitechapel was a good idea. The throng of people carried some of the weight of self-consciousness for them; the wind blowing up-river and the hooting of ships' sirens made them feel they were in some foreign port of call, taking a stroll till it was time to re-embark. He was less aware that she had grown strange to him, and she was momentarily able to forget the appalling stranger who raved in her bed all night.

They dined at a restaurant, and went on to a music hall. That night he took longer to fall asleep. She had allowed herself a thread of hope, when he began to talk again. Three Justins competed, thrusting each other aside: a cold, attentive observer, a debased child, a devil bragging in hell. At intervals they were banished by a recognizable Justin interminably muttering to himself, 'Here's a sword for Toad, here's a sword for Rat, here's a sword for Mole, here's a sword for Badger.' The reiteration from that bible of their childhood would stick on the word 'rat'. 'Got you!' And he was off again.

The next day they went to the Zoo. The Zoo was not so efficacious as Whitechapel. It was feeling the pinch, the animals looked shabby and dejected, many cages were empty. Two sleepless nights had made Celia's feet swell. It was pain to walk, pain to stand. She wondered how much longer she could keep it up, this 'God bless you, dearie' pretence of a lovely leave. The day accumulated its hours like a windlass. The load grew heavier; the windlass baulked under it, but wound on. He went to bed with the usual 'Good night, Celia'. As usual she undressed and put on that derision of a nightdress, and wrapped herself in an eiderdown and lay down to wait under the smiling gaze of Tim's photograph. She felt herself growing icy cold, couldn't remember if she had wound her watch, couldn't remember what diversion she had planned for the morrow, was walking over Richmond Bridge in a snowstorm, when she noticed he had begun again. *She noticed*. It had come to that. Two nights of a vicarious endurance of what was being endured, had been endured, would continue to be endured by a cancelled generation, had so exhausted her that now she felt neither horror nor despair, merely a bitter acquiescence. Justin went on with his Hail Devil Rosary, and in France the guns went on and on, and the mud dried into dust and slumped back into mud again. People went down to Kent to listen to the noise of the guns: the people in Kent said that they had grown used to it, didn't hear it any longer. The icy cold sensation bored into her midriff, nailed her down in sleep.

Some outcry, some exclamation (she could not afterwards remember what it was), woke her. Before she knew what she was doing she was in the next room, trying to waken the man who lay so rigidly in her bed, who, if she could awaken him, would be Justin, her brother Justin. 'Oh, poor Justin, my poor Justin!' Throwing herself on the bed, she clasped him in her arms, lifted his head to lie against her breast, kissed his chattering lips. 'There, there!' She felt him relax, waken, drag her towards him. They rushed into the escape of love like winter-starved cattle rushing into a spring pasture.

When light came into the room, they drew a little apart and looked at each other.

'Now we've done it,' he said; and hearing the new note in his voice she replied, 'A good thing, don't you think?'

Their release left them no option. After a few hours they were not even astonished. They were mated for life, that was all – for a matter of days, so they made the most of it. At the end of his leave they parted in exaltation, he convinced that he was going off to be killed, she that she would bear his child, to which she would devote the remainder of her existence.

A little later she knew she was not pregnant.

Early in the new year Justin, still panoplied in this legendary and by now rather ludicrous charmed life, was made a major. In April he was wounded in the leg. 'Nothing to worry about,' he wrote; 'just a few splinters. I am in bed, as peaceful as a pincushion.' Later, she heard that he had been moved to a hospital on the outskirts of London. One of the splinters had escaped notice, and gas gangrene had developed in the wound.

I shall be a peg leg, he thought. It's not decent for a peg leg to make love; even to his sister. He was ravaged with fret and behaving with perfect decorum when Celia was shown in – dressed all in leaf green, walking like an empress, smelling delicious. for a moment the leaf-green Celia was almost as much of a stranger as the Celia all in black had been. When she kissed him, he discovered that she was shaking from head to foot. 'There, there,' he said, patting her. Still holding his hand, she addressed herself to charming Nurse Painter. Nurse Painter was in favour of sisters. They weren't so much trouble, didn't upset a patient, as sweethearts or wives did – and you didn't have to be hanging around all the time, ready to shoo them off. When Celia came next day, Nurse Painter congratulated her on having done the Major no end of good. There had been a lot of pus; she liked to see a lot of pus.

They continued to give satisfaction; when Justin left hospital with a knee that would always be stiff and from time to time cause him pain, Nurse Painter's approval went with them. A sister was just what he wanted – there would be no silly excitement; and as Miss Tizard was a trifle older than the Major, there would be a restraining hand if called for. If Nurse Painter had known what lay beneath this satisfactory arrangement, it is probable that her approval would not have been seriously withdrawn. The war looked like going on for ever; the best you could hope for was a stalemate. Potatoes were unobtainable, honesty was no more, it was hate and muddle wherever you looked. If a gentleman and lady could pluck up heart enough to love and be happy – well, good luck to them!

Justin and Celia went to Oxfordshire, where they compared the dragonflies on the Windrush with the dragonflies on the Evenlode. Later, they went to France.

Beauty cannot be suborned. Never again did Justin see Celia quivering with beauty as she had done on the day she came to him in hospital. But he went on thinking she had a charming face and the most entertaining eyebrows in the world. Loving each other criminally and sincerely, they took pains to live

together happily and to safeguard their happiness from injuries
of their own infliction or from outside. It would have been
difficult for them to have been anything but inconspicuous, or
to be taken for anything but a brother and sister – the kind of
brother and sister of whom one says, 'It will be rather hard for
her when he marries'. Their relationship, so conveniently
obvious to the public eye, was equally convenient in private
life, for it made them unusually intuitive about each other's
feelings. Brought up to the same standard of behaviour, using
the same vocabulary, they felt no need to impress each other
and were not likely to be taken aback by each other's likes and
dislikes. Even the fact of remembering the same foxed copy of
The Swiss Family Robinson with the tear across the picture of the
boa constrictor was a reassuring bond. During the first years in
France they felt they would like to have a child – or for the
sake of the other's happiness ought to have a child – and
discussed the possibilities of a child put out to nurse, learning
French as its native speech, and then being adopted as a
postwar orphan, since it was now too late to be a war orphan.
But however the child was dated, it would be almost certain to
declare its inheritance of Grandfather Tizard's nose, and as a
fruitful incest is thought even worse of than a barren one, they
sensibly gave up the idea; though regretting it.

Oddly enough, after settling in Hallowby they regretted it
no longer. They had a home in England, a standing and things
to do. Justin had the Beelby Museum; Celia had a household.
In Hallowby it was not possible to stroll out to a restaurant or
to bring home puddings from the pastry cook, fillets of veal
netted into bolsters by the butcher. Celia had to cook seriously,
and soon found that if she was to cook meals worth eating she
must go shopping too. This was just what was needed for their
peace and quiet, since to be seen daily shopping saved a great
deal of repetitious explanation that she and Justin could not
afford to keep a servant in the house but must be content with
Mrs Mugthwaite coming in three afternoons a week, and a
jobbing gardener on Fridays. True, it exposed her to a certain

amount of condolence and amazement from the school wives, but as they, like Mrs Mugthwaite, came only in the afternoons, she could bear with it. Soon they came more sparingly; for, as Justin pointed out, poverty is the sturdiest of all shelters, since people feel it to be rather sad and soon don't think about it, whereas her first intention of explaining that ever since Aunt Dinah had wakened in the middle of the night to see an angered cook standing over her with a meat hatchet she had been nervous of servants sleeping under the same roof would only provoke gossip, surmise and insistent recommendations of cooks without passions. Justin was more long-sighted than Celia. She always knew what to do or say at the moment. He could look ahead, foresee dangers, and take steps to dodge them.

They did not see as much of Mr Pilkington as they had apprehended, and members of the staff were in no hurry to take up with another of Pilkington's Pets. Celia grew alarmed; if you make no friends, you become odd. She decided that they must occasionally go to church, though not too often or too enthusiastically, as it would then become odd that they did not take the Sacrament. No doubt a great many vicious church attenders took the Sacrament, and the rubric only forbids it to 'open and notorious evil-livers', which they had every intention of not being; but she could see a scruple of honour at work in Justin, so she did not labour this argument. There was a nice, stuffy pitch-pine St Cuthbert's near by, and at judicious intervals they went there for evensong – thereby renewing another bond of childhood: the pleasure of hurrying home on a cold evening to eat baked potatoes hot from the oven. How old Mr Gillespie divined from Justin's church demeanour that he was a whist player was a mystery never solved. But he divined it. He had barely saved Celia's umbrella from being blown inside out, remarking, 'You're newcomers, aren't you? You don't know the east wind at this corner,' before he was saying to Justin, 'You don't play whist, by any chance?' But probably he would have asked this of anyone not demonstrably a raving maniac, for since Colin Colbeck's death he, Miss Colbeck and Canon Pendarves were desperate for a fourth player. Canon Pendarves gave dinner parties, with a little music afterwards. Celia, driven into performance and remembering how Becky Sharp had wooed Lady Steyne by singing the religious songs of Mozart, sat down at the piano and played 'The Carmen's Whistle', one of the few things she reliably knew by heart. This audacious antiquarianism delighted the Canon, who kept her at his side for the rest of the evening, relating how he had once tried to get up a performance of Tallis's forty-part motet.

The Tizards were no longer odd. Their new friends were all considerably older than they; the middle-aged had more conscience about the war and were readier to make friends with a disabled major and his devoted maiden sister. In time, members of the staff overlooked their prejudice against Pilkington Pets and found the Tizard couple agreeable, if slightly boring.

Returning from their sober junketings Justin and Celia, safe within their brick wall, cast off their weeds of middle age, laughed, chattered and kissed with an intensified delight in their scandalous immunity from blame. They were a model couple, the most respectable couple in Hallowby, treading hand in hand the thornless path to fogydom. They began to give small dinner parties themselves. They set up a pug and a white cat. During their fifth summer in Hallowby they gave an evening party in the Beelby Museum. This dashing event almost carried them too far. It was such a success that they were begged to make an annual thing of it; and Celia was so gay, and her dress so fashionable, that she was within an inch of being thought a dangerous woman. Another party being expected of them, another had to be given. But this was a very different set-out: a children-and-parents party with a puppet show, held in St Cuthbert's Church Room, with Canon Pendarves speaking on behalf of the Save the Children Fund and a collection taken at the door. The collection was a master stroke. It put the Tizards back in their place as junior fogies – where Justin, for his part, was thankful to be. He had got there a trifle prematurely, perhaps, being in his mid-thirties, but it was where he intended to end his days.

He was fond of gardening, and had taken to gardening seriously, having an analysis made of the Newton Lodge soil – too acid, as he suspected – buying phosphates and potash and lime and kainite, treating different plots with different mixtures and noting the results in a book. He could not dig, but he limpingly mowed and rolled the lawn, trained climbing roses and staked delphiniums. Within the shelter of the wall, delphiniums did magnificently. Every year he added new varieties and when the original border could be lengthened no further a parallel bed was dug, with a grass walk in between. Every summer evening he walked there, watching the various blues file off, some to darkness, some to pallor, as the growing dusk took possession of them, while the white cat flitted about his steps like a moth. Because one must not be wholly selfish, from time to time he would invite a pair of chosen children to tea, cut each of them a long delphinium lance (cutting only those which were going over, however) and set them to play jousting matches on the lawn. Most of them did no more than thwack, but the two little Semples, the children of the school chaplain, fought with system, husbanding their strokes and aiming at each other's faces. Even when they had outgrown jousting they still came to Newton Lodge, hunting snails, borrowing books, helping him weigh out basic slag, addressing him as 'Justin'.

'Mary is just the age our child would have been,' remarked Celia after one of these visits. Seeing him start at the words, she went on, 'When you went back to be killed, and I was quite sure I would have a baby.'

'I wouldn't stand being called Justin – if she were.'

'You might have to. They're Bright Young Things from the cradle on, nowadays.'

By now the vogue for being a Bright Young Thing had reached even to Hallowby, its ankles growing rather muddied and muscular on the way. It was not like Celia to prefer an inferior article, and Justin wondered to see her tolerance of the

anglicization of the *Jeune France* when the original movement
had so exasperated her. He hoped she wasn't mellowing;
mellowness is not the food of love. A quite contrary process,
however, was at work in Celia. At Carnac, even when accepting
Pilkington as a way out of it, the exaltation of living in defiance
of social prohibitions and the absorbing manoeuvres of seeming
to live in compliance with them had been stimulus enough; she
had had no mercy for less serious rebels. But during the last
few years the sense of sinking month by month into the
acquiescence of Hallowby, eating its wholesome lotus like
cabbage, conforming with the inattentiveness of habit – and
aware that if she overlooked a conformity the omission would
be redressed by the general conviction that Justin Tizard,
though in no way exciting, was always so nice and had a sister
who devoted her life to him, so nice for them both, etc. etc. –
had begun to pall, and the sight of any rebellion, however
puerile, however clumsy, roused up her partisanship. Since she
could not shock Hallowby to its foundations, she liked to see
these young creatures trying to, and wished them luck. From
time to time she even made approaches to them, solicited their
trust, indicated that she was ranged on their side. They
accepted, confided, condescended – and dropped her.

When one is thus put back in one's place, one finds one has
grown out of it, and is a misfit. Celia became conscious how
greatly she disliked Hallowby society. The school people
nauseated her with their cautious culture and breezy heartiness.
The indigenous inhabitants were more bearable, because they
were less pretentious; but they bored her. The Church, from
visiting bishops down to Salvation Army cornet players, she
loathed for its hypocrisy. Only in Hallowby's shabbiest quarter
– in Edna Road, Gladstone Terrace and Gas Lane – could she
find anyone to love. Mr Newby the fishmonger in his malodor-
ous den; old Mrs Foe among her sallowing cabbages and
bruised apples; Mr Raby, the grocer, who couldn't afford to
buy new stock because he hadn't the heart to call in the money
his poorer customers owed him, and so had none but the

poorest customers — these people were good. Probably it was only by their goodness that they survived and had not cut their throats in despair long ago. Celia began to shop in Gas Lane. It was not a success. Much as she might love Mr Newby she loved Justin better, and when a dried haddock gave him food poisoning she had to remove her custom — since the cat wouldn't touch Newby's fish anyhow. These disheartening experiences made her dislike respectable Hallowby even more. She wanted to cast it off, as someone tossing in fever wants to cast off a blanket.

The depression began. The increase of Mr Raby's customers drove him out of business: he went bankrupt and closed the shop. Groups of unemployed men from Hallowby juxta Mare appeared in Gas Lane and Edna Road and sang at street corners — for misfortune always resorts to poor neighbourhoods for succour. People began to worry about their investments and to cut down subscriptions to such examples of conspicuous waste as the Chamber Music Society. Experts on nutrition wrote to the daily papers, pointing out the wastefulness of frying, and explaining how, by buying cheaper cuts of meat and cooking them much longer, the mothers of families on the dole would be able to provide wholesome adequate meals. Celia's uneasy goodwill and smouldering resentment found their outlet. As impetuously as she had flung herself into Justin's bed, she flung herself into relief work at Hallowby juxta Mare. Being totally inexperienced in relief work she exploded there like a nova. Her schemes were so outrageous that people in authority didn't think them worth contesting even; she was left to learn by experience, and made the most of this valuable permission. One of her early outrages was to put on a revue composed and performed by local talent. Local talent ran to the impromptu, and when it became known what scarification of local reputations could be expected, everyone wanted to hear what might be said of everyone else and Celia was able to raise the price of admission, which had been sixpence, to as much as half a guinea for the best seats. Her doings became a joke; you never knew what that woman wouldn't be up to next. Hadn't she persuaded Wilson & Beck to take on men they had turned off, because now, when half the factory stood idle, was the moment to give it a spring cleaning? Celia worked herself to the bone, and probably did a considerable amount of good, but her great service to Hallowby juxta Mare was that she made the unemployed interested in their plight instead of dulled by it, so that helpers came to her from the unemployed themselves. If she was not so deeply impressed by their goodness as she had been by the idealized goodness of Mr Newby and Mrs Foe, she was impressed by their arguments; she became political, and by 1936 she was marching in Communist demonstrations, singing:

> Twenty-five years of hunger and war
> And they call it a glorious Jubilee.

Inland Hallowby was also looking forward to the Jubilee. The school was rehearsing a curtailed version of Purcell's *King Arthur*, with Mary Semple, now home from her finishing school, coming on in a chariot to sing 'Fairest Isle'. There was to be folk dancing by Scouts and Guides, a tea for the old people, a fancy-dress procession; and to mark the occasion Mr Harvey, J.P., one of the school governors, had presented the Beelby Museum with a pair of buckskin breeches worn by the Duke of Wellington on the field of Talavera. 'I shall be expected to make a speech about them,' groaned Justin. 'I think I shall hire a deputy and go away for the day.'

Celia jumped at this. 'We'll both go away. Not just for the day but for a fortnight. We'll go to Jersey, because you must attend the Jubilee celebrations on your native island – a family obligation. Representative of one of the oldest families. And if we find the same sort of fuss going on there, we can nip over to France in the Escudiers' boat and be quit of the whole thing. It's foolproof, it's perfect. The only thing needed to make it perfectly perfect is to make it a month. Justin, it's the answer.'

She felt indeed that it was the answer. For some time now, Justin had seemed distrait and out of humour. Afraid he was unwell, she told herself he was stale and knew that he had been neglected. An escapade would put all right. Talavera had not been fought in vain. But she couldn't get him to consent. She was still persuading when the first letter arrived. It was typed and had been posted in Hallowby. It was unsigned, and began, 'Hag.'

Reading what followed, Celia tried to hold on to her first impression that the writer was some person in Hallowby juxta Mare. 'You think you're sitting pretty, don't you? You think no one has found you out.' She had made many enemies there; this must come from one of them. Several times she had been accused of misappropriating funds. Yes, that was it: '. . . and keep such a tight hold on him.' But why *him*? It was as though two letters lay on the flimsy page – the letter she was bent on reading and the letter that lay beneath and glared through it. It was a letter about her relations with Justin that she tore into bits and dropped in the wastepaper basket as he came down to breakfast.

She could hardly contain her impatience to get the bits out again, stick them on a backing sheet, make sure. Nothing is ever quite what it first was; the letter was viler, but it was also feebler. It struck her as amateurish.

The letter that came two days later was equally vile but better composed; the writer must be getting his or her hand in. A third was positively elegant. Vexatiously, there was no hint of a demand for hush money. Had there been, Celia could have called in the police, who would have set those ritual springes into which blackmailers – at any rate, blackmailers one reads of in newspapers – walk so artlessly. But the letters did not blackmail, did not even threaten. They stated that what the writer knew was common knowledge. After two letters, one on the heels of the other, which taunted Celia with being ugly, ageing and sexually ridiculous – letters that ripped through her self-control and made her cry with mortification –

the writer returned to the theme of common knowledge and concluded with an 'It may interest you to hear that the following know all about your loathsome performances' and a list of half a dozen Hallowby names. Further letters laconically listed more names. From the outset, Celia had decided to keep all this to herself, and still held to the decision; but she hoped she wouldn't begin to talk in her sleep. There was less chance of this, as by now she was sleeping scarcely at all.

It was a Sunday morning and she and Justin were spraying roses for greenfly when Justin said, 'Puss, what are you concealing?' She syringed Mme Alfred Carrière so violently that the jet bowed the rose, went beyond it and deluged a robin. Justin took the syringe out of her hand and repeated the question.

Looking at him, she saw his face was drawn with woe. 'No, no, it's nothing like that,' she exclaimed. 'I'm perfectly well. It's just that some poison-pen imbecile . . .'

When he had read through the letters, he said thoughtfully, 'I'd like to wring that little bitch's neck.'

'Yes, it is some woman or other, isn't it? I felt sure of that.'

'Some woman or other? It's Mary Semple.'

'That pretty little Mary Semple?'

'That pretty little Mary Semple. Give me the letters. I'll soon settle her.' He looked at his watch. 'No, I can't settle her yet. She'll still be in church.'

'But I don't understand why.'

'You do, really.'

'Justin! Have you been carrying on with Mary Semple?'

'No, I wouldn't say that. She's got white eyelashes. But ever since she came home Mary Semple has been doing all she can to carry on with me. There I was in the Beelby, you see, like a bull at the stake. No one comes near the place now; I was at her mercy. And in she tripped, and talked about the old days, telling me her little troubles, showing me poems, pitying me for my hard lot. I tried to cool her down, I tried to taper it off. But she was bent on rape, and one morning I lost all patience, told her she bored me and that if she came again I'd empty the fire bucket over her. She wept and wailed, and I paid no attention, and when there was silence I looked cautiously round and she was gone. And a day or so after' – he looked at the mended letter – 'yes, a couple of days after, she sat her down to take it out of you.'

'But, Justin – how did she know about us?'

'No fire without smoke, I suppose. I daresay she heard her parents cheering each other along the way with Christian surmises. Anyhow, children nowadays are brought up on that sort of useful knowledge.'

'No fire without smoke,' she repeated. 'And what about those lists?'

'Put in to make your flesh creep, most likely. Even if they do know, they weren't informed at a public meeting. Respectable individuals are too wary about libel and slander to raise their respectable voices individually. It's like that motet Pendarves used to talk about, when he could never manage to get them all there at once. Extraordinary ambitions people have! Fancy wanting to hear forty singers simultaneously yelling different tunes.'

'It can be done. There was a performance at Newcastle – he was dead by then. But, Justin – '

'That will do, Celia. I am now going off to settle Mary Semple.'

'How will you manage to see her alone?'

'I shall enter her father's dwelling. Mary will manage the rest.'

The savagery of these last words frightened her. She had not heard that note in his voice since he cried out in his sleep. She watched him limp from the room as though she were watching an incalculable stranger. A moment later, he reappeared, took her hand, and kissed it. 'Don't worry, Puss. If need be, we'll fly the country.'

Whatever danger might lie ahead, it was the thought of the danger escaped that made her tremble. If she had gone on concealing those letters – and she had considered it her right and duty to do so – a wedge would have been driven between her and Justin, bruising the tissue of their love, invisibly fissuring them, as a wedge of ice does in the living tree. And thus a scandal about their incest would have found them without any spontaneity of reaction and distracted by the discovery of how long she had been arrogating to herself a thing that concerned them both. 'Here and now,' she exclaimed, 'I give up being an elder sister who knows best.' Justin, on his way to the Semples', was muttering to himself, 'Damn and blast it, why couldn't she have told me sooner? If she had it would all be over by now.' It did not occur to him to blame himself for a lack of openness. This did not occur to Celia, either. It was Justin's constancy that mattered, not his fidelity – which was his own business.

When he reappeared, washed and brushed and ready for lunch, and told her there would be no more billets-doux from Mary, it was with merely tactical curiosity that she asked, 'Did you have to bribe her?' And as he did not answer at once, she went on to ask, 'Would you like potted shrimps or mulligatawny? There's both.'

They did not have to fly the country. Mary Semple disposed of the rest of her feelings by quarrelling with everyone in the cast of *King Arthur* and singing 'Fairest Isle' with such venom that her hearers felt their blood run cold, and afterwards remarked that stage fright had made her sing out of tune. The people listed by Mary as cognizant showed no more interest in the Tizards than before. The tradesmen continued to deliver. Not a cold shoulder was turned. But on that Sunday morning the balance between Justin and Celia had shifted, and never returned to its former adjustment. Both of them were aware of this, so neither of them referred to it, though at first Celia's abdication made her rather insistent that Justin should know best, make decisions, assert his authority. Justin asserted his authority by knowing what decisions could be postponed till the moment when there was no need to make them at all. Though he did not dislike responsibility, he was not going to be a slave to it. Celia's abdication also released elements in her character which till then had been penned by her habit of common sense and efficiency. She became slightly frivolous, forgetful and timid. She read novels before lunch, abandoned all social conscience about bores, mislaid bills, took second helpings of *risotto* and mashed potatoes and began to put on weight. She lost her aplomb as a driver and had one or two small accidents. She discovered the delights of needing to be taken away for pick-me-up holidays. Mrs Mugthwaite, observing all this, knew it was the Change, and felt sorry for poor Mr Tizard; the Change wasn't a thing that a brother should be expected to deal with. From time to time, Justin and Celia discussed leaving Hallowby and going to live somewhere away from the east-coast climate and the east wind at the corner by St Cuthbert's, but they put off moving, because the two animals had grown old, were set in their ways, and would be happier dying in their own home. The pug died just before the Munich crisis, the cat lived on into the war.

So did Mr Pilkington, who died from overwork two months before the first air raid on Hallowby juxta Mare justified his insistence on constructing an air-raid shelter under the school playing fields. This first raid was concentrated on the iron-works, and did considerable damage. All next day, inland Hallowby heard the growl of demolition explosives. In the second raid, the defences were better organized. The enemy bombers were driven off their target before they could finish their mission. Two were brought down out to sea. A third, twisting inland, jettisoned its remaining bombs on and around Hallowby. One dropped in Gas Lane, another just across the road from Newton Lodge. The blast brought down the roof and dislodged a chimney stack. The rescue workers, turning the light of their torches here and there, noting the usual disparities between the havocked and the unharmed, the fire-place blown out, the portrait smiling above it, followed the trail of bricks and rubble upstairs and into a bedroom whose door slanted from its hinges. A cold air met them; looking up, they saw the sky. The floor was deep in bits of rubble; bits of broken masonry, clots of brickwork, stood up from it like rocks on a beach. A dark bulk crouched on the hearth, and was part of the chimney stack, and a torrent of slates had fallen on the bed, crushing the two bodies that lay there.

The wavering torchlights wandered over the spectacle. There was a silence. Then young Foe spoke out. 'He must have come in to comfort her. That's my opinion.' The others concurred. Silently, they disentangled Justin and Celia, and wrapped them in separate tarpaulin sheets. No word of what they had found got out. Foe's hypothesis was accepted by the coroner and became truth.

*

Savages

Mabel's family lived in a cottage at the end of our avenue and we were forever going back and forth, helping, borrowing tea or sugar or the paper, or liniment, agog for each other's news. We knew of Mabel's homecoming for weeks, but what we did not know was whether she would come by bus or car, and whether she would arrive in daylight or dusk. She was coming from Australia, making most of the journey by ship, and then crossing on the sailboat to Dublin, and then by train to our station, which was indeed rustic and where a passenger seldom got off. She would be tired. She would be excited. She would be full of strange stories and strange impressions. How long would she stay? What would she look like? Would her hair be permed? What presents, or what knick-knacks would she bring? Would she have an accent? Oh, what novelty. These and a thousand other questions assailed us, and as the time got nearer, her name and her arrival were on everyone's lips. I was allowed to help her mother on the Saturday and in my eagerness I set out at cockcrow, having brought six fresh eggs and the loan of our egg beater. First task was to clear out the upstairs room. It smelled musty. Mice scrambled there, because her family kept their oats in it. It was an attic room with a skylight window and a slanting ceiling. In fact, it was only half a room, because of the way one kept bumping one's head on the low, distempered ceiling. My job was to scoop oats with a trowel and pour it into a sack. So buoyed up was I with anticipation that now and then I became absentminded and the oats slid out of the sack once again. From time to time her mother would say, 'I hope she hasn't an accident,' or 'I hope she hasn't broken her pledge,' but these things were said to disguise or temper her joy. The thing is, Mabel's coming had brought hope and renewal into her life.

Mabel had been gone for ten years, and the only communications in between had been her monthly letter and some photographs. The photos were very dim and they were always with other girls, smirking, so that one didn't see what she was like in repose. Also, she always wore a hat, so that her features were disguised. Mabel worked as a lady's companion, and her letters told of this lady, her wrath, the sunflowers in her garden, and the beauty of her German piano which was made of cherrywood.

'I expect she'll stay for the summer,' her mother said, and I thought that a bit optimistic. Who would want to stay three or four months in our godforsaken townland? Nothing happened except the land was ploughed, the crops were put down, there was a harvest, a threshing, then geese were sent to feast on the stubble, and soon the land was bare again. None of the women wore cosmetics, and in the local chemist shop the jars of cold cream and vanishing cream used to go dry because of no demand. Of course, we read about fashions in a magazine and we knew, my sisters and I knew, that ladies wore tweed costumes the colour of mulberries, and that they sometimes had silk handkerchiefs steeped in perfume which they wore underneath their bodices for effect. Not for a second did I think Mabel would stay long, but had I said anything her mother would have sent me home. We carried a trestle bed up, put the clean sheets on and the blankets, and then hung a ribbon of adhesive paper for the flies to stick to. The place still smelled musty, but her mother said that was to be expected and that if Mabel was ashamed of her origins, she had another guess coming.

We went downstairs to get on with the baking. Her mother cracked the six fresh eggs into the bowl and beat them to a frothlike consistency. Then she got out the halves of orange peel and lemon peel, and in the valleys were crusts of sugar that were like ice. I longed for a piece. I was put sieving the flour and I did it so energetically that the flour swirled in the air, making the atmosphere snow-white. At that moment her husband came in and demanded his dinner. She said couldn't he see she was making a cake. She referred him to the little meat safe that was attached to a tree outside in the garden, whereupon he growled and wielded his ash plant. It seems there was nothing in the meat safe, only buttermilk.

'Don't addle me,' she said.

'Is it grass you would have me eat?' he said, and I saw that he was in imminent danger of picking up the whisked eggs and pitching them out in the yard, where we would never be able to retrieve them because hens, ducks and pigs paddled in the muck out there.

'Can't you give me a chance,' she said, but seeing that he was about to explode, she stooped, avoiding a possible blow, and then from under a dish she hauled out an ox tongue that she had boiled that morning. It was of course meant for Mabel, but she realized that she had better be expedient. As she cut the tongue he watched, barely containing his rage. As I saw her put the knife to it, I thought, Poor oxen had not much of a life either living or dead. She cut it thinly as she was trying to economize. In the silence we heard a mouse as it got caught in the trap that we had just put down in Mabel's room. Its screech was both sudden and beseeching. Her husband picked up a slice of the tongue with his hand, being too impatient to wait for it to be handed on the plate. I too wanted to taste it, but not by itself. I would have loved it with a piece of pickle, so that the taste was not like oxen but like something artificial, something out of a jar. He ate by the fire, munching loudly, asking me for another cut of bread, and quick. He drank his tea from an enamel mug, and I could hear it going glug-glug down his gullet. He had never addressed a civil word to me in his life.

The baked cake was the most beautiful sight. It was dark

gold in colour, it had risen beautifully, and there were small cracks on the top into which she secretly poured a drop of whiskey to give it, as she said, an aroma. I asked if she was going to ice it, but she seemed to resent that question. For some absurd reason I began to wonder who Mabel would marry, because of course she was not yet married and she must not be left on the shelf, as that was a most mortifying role.

'You can go home now,' her mother said to me.

I looked at her. If looks can talk, then these should have. My look was an invocation. It was saying 'Let me come for Mabel's arrival.' I lingered, thinking she would say it, but she didn't. I praised the cake. I was lavish in my praise of it, of the clean windows, of the floor polish, the three mice caught and consigned to the fire, of everything. It was all in vain. She did not invite me.

The next day was agony. Would I be let go? It was still not broached and I tried a thousand ruses and just as many imprecations. I would pick up the clock that was lying face down, and if I had guessed the time to within minutes, then I would surely go. A butterfly had got caught between the two panes of opened window and I thought, If it finds its way out unaided, then I shall go. In there it struggled and beat its wings, it kept going around in circles to no purpose, yet miraculously shot up and sailed out into the air, a vision of soft, fluttering orange-brown. Not to go would be torture. But worse than that would be if my sisters were let go and I was told to mind the house. It sometimes happened. Why mind a house than was solid and vaster than oneself? Extreme diligence took possession of me and such a spurt of tidiness that my mother said it was to our house Mabel should be arriving. If only that were so!

After the tea, when I had washed up the dishes, I could no longer contain myself and I began to snivel. My mother pretended not to notice. She was changing her clothes in the kitchen. She often changed there and held the good clothes in front of the fire to air them. The rooms upstairs were damp, the wardrobes were damp, and when you put on your good clothes you could feel the damp seeping into your bones. She was brusque. She said why ringlets and why one's best cardigan. I cried more. She said to put it out of one's head and announced that none of the children was going, as the McCann kitchen was far too small for hordes. She said to cut out the sobs and do one's homework instead. While my father shaved I went under the table to pray. It was evident he was in a bad mood because of the way he scraped the stubble off his chin. He said that not even a day like this could be enjoyed. He said why did he have to fodder cattle and my mother said because there was no one else to do it.

After they had gone, my sisters and I decided to make pancakes. As it happened, my older sister nearly set fire to the house because of the amount of paraffin she threw on to the stove. I shall never forget it. It was like the last day, with flames rising out of the stove, panels of orange flame going up the walls, and my other sister and I screaming at her to quench it, quench it. The first thing to hand was a can of milk, which we threw on it in terror. Luckily we conquered it, and all that remained was a smell of paraffin and a terrible smell of burned milk. The pancake project was abandoned and we spent the next hour trying to air the place and clean the stove. Docility had certainly taken hold of us by the time my mother and father returned. It was dark and we could hear the hasp of the gate and then the dogs bounding toward the door and then the latch lifting. My mother was first. She always came first so as to be able to put on the kettle for him and so as to get on with her tasks. First thing we noticed was the parcel under her arm. It was in tissue paper and it had been opened at one end. My sister grabbed it as my mother wrinkled up her nose and said there was something burning. We denied that and harried her to tell, tell. Mabel had come, was tired from her journey, spoke in a funny accent, and said that in Australia wattles meant mimosa trees and not mere sticks or stones.

By then my father had arrived and said that he was a better-

looking man than Mabel himself and then did an impersonation
of her accent. It was like no accent I had ever heard. My father
said that the only interesting thing about her was that she
backed horses and had been to race meetings in Sydney. My
mother said that she had been marooned out on some sheep
station and had met very few people, only the shearers and the
lady she worked for. My mother pronounced on her as being
haggard and with a skin tough and wizened from the heat. The
present turned out to be pale-blue silk pyjamas. I could see my
mother's reaction – immense disappointment that was border-
ing on disgust. She had hoped for a dress or a blouse, she had
certainly hoped for a wearable. For another thing, pyjamas
were shameful, sinful. Men wore pyjamas, women wore night-
gowns. Shame and disgrace. My mother folded them up quickly
so as not to let my father see them, in case it gave him ideas.
She bundled them into a cupboard and it was plain to see that
she was nettled. She would have even liked a remnant so as to
be able to make dresses for us. It seemed that the homecoming
was something of an anticlimax and that even Mabel's father
couldn't understand a word that she had said. It seems that the
men who had come to vet her agreed that she wasn't worth
tuppence and the women were most disappointed by her
attire. They had expected her to be wearing high-heeled court
shoes, preferably suede, and it seems she was wearing leather
shoes that were almost, but not quite, flat. To make matters
worse, they were tan and her stockings were tan and her skin
was slightly tan, and along with all that, she was in a bright-
red suit. My mother said she looked like a scarecrow and she
was very loud.

Next day it rained. So fiercely the hailstones beat against
the window frames, pelting them like bullets. The sky was
ink-black, and even when a cloud broke, the silver inside was
dark and oppressive, presaging a storm. I was sent around the
house to close the windows and put cloths on the sills in case
the rain soaked through. I saw a figure coming up the avenue
and thought it might be a begging woman with a coat over her

head. When we heard the knocking on the back door, my
mother opened it sharply, poised as she was for hostilities.

'Mabel,' my mother said, surprised, and I ran to see her. She
was a small woman with black bobbed hair, a very long nose,
and eyes which were like raisins and darting. She wore rubber
overshoes, which she began to remove, and as she held on
to the side of the sink, I stood in front of her. She asked me
was I me and said that the last time she had seen me I
was screaming my head off in a hammock, in the garden.
Somehow she expected me to be pleased by this news, or
at least to be amused.

What struck me about her was her abruptness. In no time
she was complaining about those two old fogies, her mother
and father, and telling us that she was not going to sit by a fire
with them all day long and discuss rheumatism. Also, she
complained about the house, said it wasn't big enough.

My mother calmed her with tea and cake, and my father
asked her what kind of horses they bred in Australia. He
wagered a bet that they were not as thoroughbred as the Irish
horses. To that my mother gave a grunt, since our horses
brought us nothing but disappointment and debt. When
pressed for other news, Mabel said that she had seen a thing or
two, her eyes had been opened, but she would not say in what
way. She hinted at having undergone some terrible shock and I
thought that possibly she had been jilted. She described a tea
they drank out of glasses, sitting on the verandah at sundown.
My mother said it was a wonder the hot tea didn't crack the
glasses. Mabel said she should never have come home and that
when she woke up that morning and heard the rain on the
skylight she had yearned to go back. Yet in no time she was
contradicting herself and said it was all 'outback' in Australia
and who wanted to live in an outback. My father said he'd
make a match for her, and gradually she cheered up as she sat
at the side of the stove and from time to time popped one or
the other foot in the lower oven for warmth. Her stockings
were lisle and a very unfortunate colour, rather like the colour

of the stirabout that we gave to the hens and the chickens. She
had an accent at certain moments, but she lost it whenever she
talked about her own people. She said their house was nothing
but a cabin, a thatched cabin. When she said indiscreet things,
she laughed and persisted until she got someone to join in.

'Mabel, you're a scream,' my mother said, while also pretending to be shocked at the indiscretions.

Very reluctantly my father had gone out to fodder, and
Mabel was drinking blackberry wine from a beautiful stemmed
glass. When she held the glass up, colours danced on her cheek
and then ran down her throat, just as the wine was running
down inside. Presently her face got flushed and her eyes teary,
and she confessed that she had thought of Ireland night and
day for ten years, had saved to come home, and now realized
that she had made a frightful mistake. She sniffled and then
took out a spotted handkerchief.

'Faraway hills look green,' my mother said, and the two of
them sighed as if a wealth of meaning had been exchanged. My
mother proposed a few visits they could make on Sundays, and
buoyed up by the wine and these promises, Mabel said that
she had a second present for my mother but that in the
commotion the previous evening she had been unable to find
it. She said it must be somewhere in the bottom of her trunk.
It was to be a brush and comb set, with matching bone tray.
We never saw it.

It took several months before Mabel paid me any attention.
She had favoured my sisters because they were older and
because they had ideas about how to set hair, how to paint
toenails, and how to use an emery board or a nail buffer. It was
either of them she took on her Sunday excursion, and it was
either of them she summoned on the way home from school so
as to sit with her in the garden and chat. It proved to be a
scorching summer and Mabel had put two deck chairs in their
front garden and had planted lupins. She never let anyone pass
without hollering, as she was avid for company. In the autumn

my sisters went away to school, and suddenly Mabel was in need of a walking companion. My mother had long since ceased to go with her, because Mabel was mad for gallivanting and had worn out her welcome in every house up the town, and in many houses up the country.

One Sunday she chose me. It was the very same as if she had just arrived home, because to me she was still a mysterious stranger. We were calling on a family who lived in the White House. It had been given that name because the money for it had come from relatives in America. It was a yellow, two-storey, pebble-dash house set in its own grounds with a heart-shaped lawn in front. At the edge of the lawn there was a flower bed in which there had been dark-red tulips, and at the far end was a little house with an electricity plant. They were the only people in the neighbourhood to have electricity, and that plus the tulips, plus the candlework bedspreads, plus the legacies from America, made theirs the most enticing house in the county. As we went up their drive, my white canvas shoes adhered to the tarmac, which was fresh and melting. The house with its lace-edged fawn blinds was quiet and suggested luxury and harmony. Needless to say, they had cross dogs, and at the first sound of a yelp Mabel lagged behind, while telling me to stand my ground and not give off an adrenalin smell. A boy who was clipping the privet hedge saved us by calling the dogs and holding them by their tawny manes. They snarled like lions.

Since we were not expected, a certain coolness ensued. The mistress of the house was lying down, her husband was in bed sick, and the little serving girl, Annie, didn't ask us to cross the threshold. All of a sudden the dummies appeared. They were brother and sister, and though I had often heard of them, and even seen them at Mass devoutly fingering their rosary beads, I had no idea that they would be so effusive. They descended on us. They mauled us. They strove with tongue and lips and every other feature to talk to us, to communicate. The movements of their hands were fluent and wizard. They pulled us into the kitchen where the female dummy put me up on a chair so she could look at the pleats in my coat, and then the buttons. She herself was dressed in a terrible hempen dress that was almost to her ankles. Her brother was in an ill-fitting coarse suit. They were in-laws of the mistress of the house and it was rumoured that she did not like them. She was trying to say something urgent when the mistress, who had risen from her nap, came in and greeted us somewhat reservedly. Soon we were seated around the kitchen table, and while Mabel and the mistress discussed who had been at Mass, and who had taken Holy Communion, and who had new style, the dummies were pestering me and trying to get me to go outside. They would puff their cheeks out in an encouragement to make me puff mine.

Mabel and the mistress of the house began to talk about her husband. They moved closer together. They were like two people conspiring. A terrible word was said. I heard it. It was the word haemorrhage. He was haemorrhaging. Only women did that. I began to go dizzy with dread. I gripped the chair by its sides, then put one hand on the table for further security and began to hum. My face must have been burning, because soon the dummies realized there was something wrong, and thinking only one thing, they pulled me toward a door and down a passage to a lavatory. It was a cold spot and there was a canister of scouring powder left on a ledge, as if Annie had been cleaning and had gone off in a hurry or a sulk. They kept knocking on the door and when I came out inspected me carefully to see that my coat was pulled down. The lady dummy, whose pet name was Babs, drew me into the kitchen, and as we stood in front of the fire, she did a little caper. She had a tea cloth in one hand and held it out as if she were keeping a bull at bay. She was told by the mistress of the house to put it down or she would be sent to the dairy. Her twin brother affected the most terrible huff by letting out moans that were nearly animal, and by moving his eyes hither and thither and at such a speed I thought they would drop out. He, too, was threatened with a sojourn in the dairy. At length so chastised were they that they each took a chair and sat with their backs to us and refused when asked to turn around.

The mistress said they needed a good smacking.

After an age the mistress offered us a tour of the house. When she opened the drawing-room door, what one first saw was the sun streaming in through the long panes of glass and bouncing on the polished furniture. She muttered something about having forgotten to draw the blinds. Pictures of cows and ripening corn hung on either side of the marble mantelpiece, and in the tiled fireplace there was an arrangement of artificial flowers – tea roses, yellow, apricot and gold. Not only that, but the flowers in a round thick rug matched. To look at it you felt certain that no one had stepped on that rug, that it was pristine like a wall hanging. Its pile and its softness made one long to kneel or bask in it. Mabel of course commented on the various things, on the curtains, for instance, which were sumptuous; on the pelmet that matched; on the long plaited cord by which the curtains could be folded or parted. Pulling it, I had a fancy that I was opening the curtains of a theatre and that presently through the window would come a troupe of performers. The mistress of the house was pleased at our excitement and as a reward she took something from the china cabinet and let me hold it. It was a miniature cabin made of blackthorn wood. It had a tiny door that opened the merest chink.

Next we saw the breakfast room and then the dining room, which by contrast was dark and sombre, save for the gleam of the silver salver on the sideboard. Next we saw the bathroom, with its green bath, matching basin, and candlewick bath mat. But we were not brought up that last flight of stairs, which led to the bedrooms, lest our footsteps waken her husband and make him want to get up. He was craving to get up and go out in the fields. Up there, the darkness was extreme because of a stained-glass window. The hallway seemed a bit sepulchral and quite different from the downstairs room. I could hear the crows cawing ceaselessly, and it occurred to me that before long there would be a death in the house, as I believe it occurred to them, because they looked at one another and shook their heads in silent commiseration.

The kitchen clock chimed five and still we sat in hope of something to eat. Mabel rubbed her stomach to indicate that she was hungry, while the mistress put on her apron and said that soon it would be milking time and time to feed calves and do a million things. Halfheartedly she offered us a cup of tea. There was nothing festive about it, it was just a cup of tea off a tray, four scones, and a slab of strong-smelling yellow country butter. It was not fashioned into little burr balls as I had expected. Mabel kicked me under the table, knowing my disappointment. There was no cake and no cold meat. Mabel judged people's hospitality by whether they gave her cold meat or not.

On the way home she lamented that there was not a bit of lamb, no chicken, no beetroot or freshly made potato salad with scallions.

It was a warm evening and the ripe corn in the fields was a sight to behold. Here and there it had lodged, but for the most part it was high and victorious, ready for the thresher. She said, 'I wonder what they're doing in Australia now,' and ventured to say that they missed her. She asked did I like those flowers my mother fashioned by putting twirls of silver and gold paper over the ears of corn. When I said no, she hurrahed. It meant that she and I were now friends, allies. Of course, I knew that I had betrayed my mother and would pay for it either by being punished or by having bouts of remorse. She took out her flapjack to apply some powder. It was a tiny gold flapjack and the powder puff was in shreds.

Mabel made a face at herself and then asked if I had a boy yet. The word 'boy', like the word 'haemorrhage', threatened to make me faint. She said soon I would have a boy and to be careful not to let him lay a finger on me, because it was a well-known fact that one could get a craze for it and end up ruined, imprisoned in the Magdalen Laundry, until you had a baby. She might have launched into some more graphic tales but a car came around the corner and she jumped up and waved so as to summon a lift.

In the town we called on a woman to whom Mabel had given a crocheted tea cosy, and our reward was two long glasses of lemonade and a plate of currant-topped biscuits. Mabel was prodigal with her promises. She volunteered to crochet a bedcover and asked the woman if there were any favourite colours, or more important, if there were any colours she could not abide. She burped as we walked down the hill and over the bridge toward home. It was getting dark and the birds were busy with both song and chatter. Every bird in every tree had something to say. As we passed the houses we could hear people banging buckets and dishes, and by the light of a lantern we saw one woman feeding calves at her doorstep. As each calf finished its quota, its head was pulled out to give the next calf a chance. Those whose heads were outside the bucket kept butting and kicking and were in no way satisfied. We knew the woman but we did not linger, as Mabel whispered that it would be dull old blather about new milk and sucking calves. Mabel did not like the country and had no interest in tillage, sunsets, or landscape. She objected to pools of water in the roadside, pools of water in the meadows, the corncrake in the evening, and the cocks crowing at dawn. As we walked along she took my hand and said that henceforth I was to be her walking companion. It was a thrill to feel her gloved hand awkwardly pressing on mine. Untold adventures lay ahead.

Sometimes on our travels we met with a shut door or we were not asked to cross the threshold. But these rebuffs meant nothing to her and she merely designated the people as being ignorant and countrified. As luck would have it, our third Sunday we struck on a most welcoming house. It was a remote house, first along a tarred road, then a dirt road, and then across a stream. Our hosts were two young girls who were home from England, and great was their pleasure in receiving company. They were home for a month but were already aching to go back. The older one, Betty, was a nurse, and Moira, her sister, was a buyer in a shop and consequently they dressed like fashion plates. We went every Sunday, knowing that they would be waiting for us and that they had got their father and mother out of the house visiting cousins. It was such a thrill as we got to the stream and took off our shoes and stockings, then let out raucous sounds about the temperature of the water, but really to alert them. It was clean silvery water with stones beneath, some round and smooth, some pointed. They would hear us and run down the slope to welcome us, while also asking in exaggerated accents if the water was like ice. To hear our names called was the zenith of welcome.

We would be brought through the kitchen into the parlour, while they told Nora, their young sister, to put the kettle on and to be smart about it. The parlour was dark, with red embossed wallpaper, and we all sat very upright on hard horsehair sofas. It so happened that I had begun to do impersonations of the dummies, and immediately they requested them. As a reward I was given a slice of coconut cake that they had brought back from England and that was kept in a tin with a harlequin figure on the lid. It was a bit dry but much more exotic than their homemade cake. Mabel would let her tongue roll over her top and bottom teeth, then ask if there was any meat left, whereupon Moira would lift a plate that exactly adhered to another plate and reveal that she had kept Mabel a lunch.

'You sport, you,' Mabel said. Her accent would suddenly sound Australian.

'Don't mention it,' Moira would say airily.

Our visits sustained them. With us they could discuss fashion and fit on their finery, then later do the Lambeth Walk in the big flagged kitchen. Doing this led to howls of laughter. Always, one of us got the step wrong and the whole thing had to be recommenced. Even their sheepdog thought it was hilarious and moved about in a clumsy way to the strains of the music from the crackling wind-up gramophone. We alternated at being ladies or gents, and we had conversations that ladies and gents have.

'Do you come here often?' or 'Next dance, please,' or 'Care for a mineral?' was what our partners said. Afterward we lounged in the chairs breathless, and then we set out for a walk, or, as they called it, 'a ramble'. It was on one of these rambles that we met Matt. An auspicious meeting it proved to be. He had the reputation of being a queer fellow, a recluse. He had gone to Canada, made some money, and had come back to marry his childhood sweetheart, but was jilted on the eve of the wedding. Some said that the marriage was broken off because the two families couldn't agree about land, others said she thought his manners too gruff; at any rate, she fled to England. Matt was a tall man with a thin face, a wart, and longish hair. He looked educated, as if he spent time poring over books and almanacs. It seems he had newfangled ideas about planting trees, whereas most of the farmers just felled them for firewood. There was something original about him. It may have been his gravity or his silence. He could go into a public house and drink a pint of porter without passing a word to anyone, even the publican. He never visited any of his neighbours and had his Christmas dinner at home, with his brother, who was supposed to be a bit missing in the head. Matt met us down by the river. He had a stick in his hand and his hat was pushed back on his head. He must have been driving cattle, because he was perspiring a bit, but he still looked dignified. Moira had picked some sorrel and was eating it, saying it was like lemon juice and very good for one's skin. He stood apart from us, but at the same time he was taking stock. At least that's what one read from his smile. There was mockery in his smile, but there was also scrutiny. Betty and Moira knew him, knew his moods, and pretended not to notice that he was there.

'Wouldn't you all fancy sugar plums?' he said to no one in particular. Mabel was the first to respond.

'Are they ripe?' she asked.

'They're ripe,' he said, but in such an insolent way we were not sure if he was telling the truth or just tantalizing us.

'I much prefer damsons,' Moira said.

'Damsons are too tart,' Mabel said; 'damsons are only fit for jam.'

'Please yourselves,' he said, and sauntered off, letting a whistle escape from his lips. Mabel called out, were we invited or not.

'As you wish,' he said, and nodding to each other, we followed. I thought we were like cows ambling across a field, not quite a herd, and not herded but all heading in the same direction and feeling aimless. It was a beautiful autumn evening, with the sun a vivid orb and in the sky around it rivers of red and pink and washed gold. His was a two-storey stone house and the front door was closed. It looked very dead and secretive. There was a hand pump in the yard, and as he passed it, he worked the handle a few times to replenish the trough underneath. We could hear the calves lowing, and suddenly the cock started to crow as if disapproving. Hens ran in all directions and there were two small bonhams wallowing in some mud. It was anything but cheerful. He did not invite us in.

In contrast, the orchard was a great tangle of trees and fruit bushes all smothered in convolvulus and the grass needed to be scythed. The apples looked so tempting, blood-red and polished, while the plums were like dusky globes ready to drop off. He put one to his lips. It was the first time anything approaching pleasure touched his countenance.

'Help yourselves,' he said, and I thought, Perhaps he is a generous man, perhaps he is kind inside and only needs four or five girls giggling and gorging to draw him out. Mabel was intrepid as she picked three plums and debated which to sample first. The two girls, having been to England, were much more polite and did not rhapsodize over the taste and did not drip juice on to their chins. Mabel declared that there would be no stopping her now, that she would come Sunday after Sunday while the fruits lasted. He picked up a lid of a tin can that had been lying in the grass, lined it with a few wide leaves, and handed it to me with the instruction that we were to bring some home. It was obvious that he took great pleasure in the fact that we were all so excited.

'No one ever eats them . . . they just rot,' he said.

'That's a shame,' Mabel said, and she winked at him, and he winked back. It is an odd thing how a face can suddenly alter. It was not that she appeared beautiful, but she had a kind of lustre and her glances were knowing and piquant.

'We'll raid you every autumn,' she said, and I thought of life as being charmed, a series of autumns just like then, the sun going down, the beautiful globes of fruit like lamps, waiting to be plucked, our happiness undimmed. In my hand I felt the softness of a plum, yet knew the hardness of the stone deep within it, and I knew that my optimism was unwise.

'How long are you home for?' he asked Moira.

'Long enough,' she said, and shrugged. Her reply both shocked and dazzled me. I thought, What a wonderful way to talk to a man, to be at once polite and distant, to be scornful without being downright rude, to parry. Then he broached the subject of the carnival. The carnival was to take place at the end of the month. Mabel asked if he'd take her for a ride on the swing-boats or the bumper cars, and he smiled at each one of us and said he hoped he would have the pleasure.

'We'll be gone back,' Betty said.

'You ought to stay for the carnival,' Mabel said, but I knew she did not mean it and was looking forward to a time when she would see Matt without the competition of two younger, comelier girls. God knows what fancies were stirred in her then. Perhaps she thought – a bachelor, a two-storey house, a man she could cook for, prosperity, a wedding. She clung to his coat sleeve by way of thanking him, but he did not like that.

He left abruptly and said to help ourselves to the black plums as well. On our way home the others made fun of him, made fun of his wart and the unmatching buttons on his coat.

'And what about his anatomy?' Mabel said, and we all burst out laughing, though we did not know why.

He appeared the last night of the carnival, danced with the two elderly Protestant girls, excelled himself at the rifle range, and won a jug, which he gave to Mabel. She had been trailing around after him the whole evening and asked him up for the Ladies' Choice. No one knows for sure if they went behind the tent, but they were missing for a while, and the following day Mabel was trembling with excitement. She told everyone that Matt 'had what it takes'. She had a home perm, which did not suit her, and also she wrote to the woollen mills to ask if they had remnants sufficient to make two-pieces or three-pieces, and in anticipation she reserved the dressmaker. The money for these fripperies came from the few remaining bonds that she cashed. Her mother did not know. Her father did not know. I thought how courageous in a way was her recklessness. She was younger, giddier, and in good spirits with everybody. One morning she met me on my way to school. There was a light frost and the plumes of grass looked like ostrich feathers. Feeling my bare hands, she said that she would knit me gloves before the winter. I wondered why she was so affectionate. Then came the command. I was to get away early from school and I was to tell the teacher that we were expecting visitors, hence I had to help my mother with sausage rolls and dainties. I dreaded telling a lie, but she had a hold over me because of my impersonation of the dummies. She told me where to meet her and what time. There was a downpour after lunch, and when I came upon her she was cursing the rain, cursing the fates, and putting her hands up to protect her frizzled hair. Her hair hung in absurd wet ringlets over her forehead and made her look like a crabbed doll.

'What the hell kept you,' she said, and started to walk.

Before long I learned that I was to take a letter to Matt. She conveyed me some of the way and then crouched against a wall to wait. There was a roaring wind, and she looked pathetic as she huddled there in suspense.

'Take the shortcut through the woods,' she said. It was an old wood and dark as an underworld. In the wind the branches swayed and even the boughs seemed to waver. Every time a bird chirped or every time a branch snapped, I thought it was some monster come to tackle me. I talked out loud to keep things at bay, I shouted, I ran, and at moments doubted if I would ever get there. The thought of her huddled beneath a wall in her good coat, reeking of perfume, drove me on. The perfume was called Californian Poppy and it had a smell of carnations. I could barely distinguish the path through the wood so obscure was it, and briars barred the way. My heart gave a leap of joy when I saw the three chimney pots and realized that I was almost there. The house seemed even lonelier than on the first day. Everything – the hall door, the stone itself, the window frames – everything was green and sodden from rain. It looked a picture of desolation, a house with no other houses to buffet or befriend it and no woman to hang curtains or put pots of geraniums on the sill. It would have been ghostly except for the fowl and the snorting of the pigs. I reckoned they would kill the pigs for Christmas. Matt was not at home. His brother gaped through the window, then drew the bolt back and peered out and said without being asked, 'He's gone to Gort and won't be back.' I feared now some worse incident, so I thrust the note into his hand, bolted down the yard, did not wait to close the iron gate, and hurried into the woods, which by comparison were safe.

Mabel was livid. She called me every name under the sun. An eejit, a fool, a dunce, an imbecile. She wanted me to go back for the letter, but I said the brother would have read it by now and going back would only show that we were culpable.

'You little poltroon,' she said, and I thought she would brain me with the point of a stick which she brandished and prodded in the air. The rain had stopped, but the drops came in sudden bursts from the trees, and each time she ducked to protect her hair. Our walk home was wretched. Not a word passed between us. The only thing I heard was an occasional smack as she clacked her tongue against the roof of her mouth to verify her rage. We parted company as we got to the town, and she said that was the last time we would be seen walking together. I did not plead with her, knowing that it was in vain. Poor Mabel. It was pitiful to think of how she had dressed up and had worn uncomfortable court shoes under her galoshes and had been lavish with the perfume, all to no avail. But I could not tell her I pitied her, as she would have exploded. I don't know what she did then, whether she went back to search for him or went into the chapel to give outlet to her grief. She might even have called on her friend the lady publican for a few glasses of port. All I know is that she stopped speaking to me, and when we met on the road she would give a toss of her head and look in the opposite direction. Sundays reverted to being long dull days when one waited fruitlessly for a caller.

After Christmas there was a ghastly rumour and it was that Mabel was having a baby. It resounded throughout the parish. It was at first hotly denied by Mabel's mother, who was told it in the strictest confidence by my mother. Mabel had grown a bit stout, her mother conceded, but that was because she ate too much griddle bread. The denial and the excuse pacified people, but not for long. Within a month Mabel had swelled, and one day a few of the women set a terrible trap for her. Polly, the ex-midwife and her nearest neighbour, who had fainted upon hearing of Mabel's downfall, enlisted Rita, a young girl, to help in their ruse.

The plan was that they would invite Mabel to tea, flatter her by telling her how thin she looked, and then, having put her off guard, Rita was to steal up on her from behind and put a measuring tape around her waist. It turned out that Mabel was gross, and by nightfall the conclusion was that Mabel was indeed having a baby. After that she was shunned at Mass, shunned on her way down from Mass, and avoided when she went into the shops. People were weird in the punishments they thought should be meted out to her. Throughout all this Mabel did nothing but grin and smile and say what marvellous weather it was. If people were too snooty, she went up to them and said, 'Go on, tell me what you're thinking of me.' She would dare them to give an opinion. My mother said that it would be a mercy if someone were to take a stick to Mabel, and her mother said that when Mabel's father got to hear of it he would kick her arse through the town. Mabel had few friends – the lady publican, the postman, who himself had once got a girl into trouble, and the dummies, who mauled her as she came out of Mass, not knowing that she was to be ostracized. She went to the town at all hours and cadged cigarettes off the men once they were drunk.

'Whose is it, Mabel?' she was asked by one of these drunkards.

'Your guess is as good as mine,' she said, manifesting no shame at all. She did not go to see Matt and she did not even mention him. He kept to himself and was not seen at Mass. Strange that a posse of men led by her father did not go either. It may have been because Matt was superior, having been to Canada, and also, he kept a shotgun and might fire as they came through the yard. The priest promised her mother that he would go when the weather got finer, but he kept putting it off and instead made a most lurid sermon about impurity. The women in the congregation coughed, blushed and were deeply affected by it all. All Mabel did was smirk and cross her legs, which was a disrespectful thing to do in a holy place. It was decided that she was losing her reason, hence her outrageous behaviour. She alternated between being very talkative and being gloomy. She sat in the hen house for hours, smoking and brooding. Getting cigarettes was at that time one of her biggest problems, because she had extended her credit in all the shops. She asked me if ever I got a shilling or found money to get her a packet of fags. Then she made me listen at the wall of her stomach and said wasn't it full of mischief.

My parents were enlisted to help. A stranger was to come to our house and I was not sure what he was to do for Mabel, but he was crucial. A man in a long brown leather coat and matching gauntlet gloves arrived in his motor just before dark. He was shown into the front room, where my parents and Mabel's mother spoke to him. Mabel was with me in the kitchen where she did nothing but make faces. She had discovered the satisfaction of making faces. She scrunched up her nose, stuck out her tongue, and rolled her eyes in all directions.

'I can paddle my own canoe,' she said, as she paced back and forth. Watching her I kept imagining the most terrible metamorphosis going on inside her and tried to calculate how old the thing was. She asked if the people up the street ever spoke about her and I lied by saying no. She said a lot of people had a lot of bees in their bonnet, yet when they reproached her she quailed. She went in with bowed head and bowed back. Presently my mother came out and said to lay a tray quickly. She was surprisingly cheerful, as if he had promised to perform a miracle. She bustled about the kitchen and said what a mercy it was that we did not have such a cross to bear. Then she asked me to put a doily on the cake plate and to make sure the cake knife had no mould or rust.

To this day I do not know whether the stranger was a faith healer or a quack, or perhaps a bachelor in search of a wife. At any rate, after he left, spirits sagged. There was another consortium and it was decided that they would tell Mabel's father that night. His shock upon hearing it was such that he could be heard roaring half a mile away, and it seems it took three people to hold him down as he threatened to go to Mabel's room in order to kill her. Gradually he was mollified with hot whiskey and the assurance that the event had happened in the most untoward and unfortunate way, in short, that Mabel had been molested by a stranger. Thus, rage was transferred to a brute who had come and gone, and now Mabel was told to come down and eat her supper. It seems she sat hunched over the fire snivelling and fiddling with the tongs while her father ranted. He had somehow got it into his head that it was a tinker who had done the deed, and he cursed every member of that fraternity, both male and female. He was made to swear that he would not strike her, and when my parents left, the family was as happy as might be expected under such woeful circumstances.

The next day Mabel's mother went to town to buy wool, and in her spare time she began to knit vests, matinee coats and little boots. But it could not be said that she and Mabel became reconciled. Her mother would sit out in the yard scraping the ground with a stone or a stick making V's and circles, and asking her Maker to take pity on her. Not a word passed between the two women, only growls. When the mother came into the kitchen Mabel went out to the hen house. No one knew where the birth would take place and no one knew when. No arrangements were made. Mabel got highly strung when asked and burst into tears and said that no one in the whole wide world loved or understood her. She was a sight, in a brown tweed coat and knitted cap. Being large did not become her, and in contrast her face looked minute. She went to the chapel every afternoon as if to atone, and as it got nearer her time, people were less vicious about her.

It was a summer's day and the men were in the hayfield when Mabel's labour commenced. The Angelus had just struck. When her mother heard the first howl, she ran with the tongs still in her hand on to the road for help. She hailed a passing cyclist and told him to get the doctor quick. The doctor, who was a locum, was bound to be in the dispensary at that hour. I was nearby playing shop with two of my friends and we were sent to fetch my mother. Soon pots of water were boiled,

Mabel was crying and begging for ether. My friends and I were both drawn to the house and repelled by it. At every sound Mabel's mother asked was it coming, yet she avoided going into the room. She merely called in through the open door. Mabel was becoming delirious as the pains got worse, but mercifully we saw the doctor arrive. He was brusque, asked what the trouble was, and said, 'Tch ... tch ... tch,' when told.

'Why haven't I seen her sooner?' he said, and then frowned as if he decided that everyone in the neighbourhood was wanting. Mabel was howling as he entered, but soon after, a calm descended, and we remained in the kitchen, full of suspense and muttering a prayer. It was not long until he came out.

'You can put that stuff away,' he said, referring to the swaddling clothes and the aluminium bath that was filled with water. Mabel's mother concluded that the infant was dead and said, 'Lord have mercy on its soul.'

'There is no *it*,' he said. 'She's no more pregnant than I am.'

My mother and Mabel's mother were aghast. It was as if some terrible trick had been played on them. Naturally they were incredulous.

'There's nothing there, I've examined her.'

'But, Doctor, is that possible?' my mother asked accusingly.

'It's all hogwash,' he said. He did not know the circumstances and nobody bothered to tell him. He simply said that it was a pity he had not been consulted sooner and then announced that his fee would be two pounds and he'd like it there and then. From the room the crying had stopped and no one took the slightest trouble to go in. No one went near her. It was as if she had taken on the marks of a leper. Her mother glared in that direction and said that her only daughter had brought them nothing but disaster. To have to tell this to the parish was the last straw. The waves in her white hair bristled, and she reminded me of nothing so much as a weasel, poised to spit. Her withheld temper was worse than all her husband's exclaiming.

'Let her break it to him herself,' she said, pointing a fist toward the closed door. If one can curse in silence, she did it then, so resolute and so full of hatred was her expression. By way of consolation my mother said that surely Mabel could not be right in her head. Her words were hardly a solace.

From the room now there was a low keen. No doubt Mabel was still lying down, bunched up as she had been in labour and perhaps waiting for a kind word. No one ventured in. Her mother emptied the tea leaves into the front garden and with a swish told my two friends, who had been waiting outside, to vamoose. Back in the kitchen she began to list Mabel's faults and lament the money she had cost them since she came home. Money on tonics, money on style, money on faddish food when she got those cravings at night.

'Tinned salmon, no less,' she said sourly, and told my mother that her pension each week had gone toward Mabel's fancies. Then for no reason she recalled a large beautiful hand-painted urn that Mabel had broken when young. It seems that from the confines of her pram Mabel had reached up to embrace it and toppled it instead. This announcement seemed to confirm that Mabel was, from birth, a rotten egg. Mabel's attraction to the opposite sex had been in the nature of a disease.

It would be funny to see her thin, having just seen her that morning large and cumbersome. The rush crib was still on the kitchen table and the sight of it an affront. I wanted to bring her a slice of cake, or tea in her favourite china cup, but I was afraid to disobey them. I felt that this now would be as much a quality of mine as my eyes or my hair, this paralysis in my character, this wanting to step in but not daring to, this dreadful hesitancy. I would, I wouldn't. Thus I wrestled, but the weight of their opprobrium won and I did not go in, nor did they, and the whimpering went on, the chant of a hopeless creature.

We did not lay eyes on Mabel again. Just as the shame of pregnancy had made her brazen and untoward, so now the

shame of non-pregnancy had made her withdrawn. She refused
to see anyone and barely broke her fast. One evening, after
dark, she left as she had once arrived, in a hackney car, and
from that moment her memory was banished. The only reminder was that next day on the clothesline were her blankets,
her patchwork quilt, and some baby clothes. Her parents had a
Mass said in the house, and in time it was as if she had never
come home, as if she were still in Australia.

Some said that she was in Dublin working for nuns, others
said that she worked in a nursing home, and still others that
she was a charwoman. These were just stories. No one ever
knew the truth, but it is certain that Mabel withered and
finally died without ever having been reinstated with family or
friends, and that she is buried in some strange and unmarked
place.

*

The New People

Millicent Graves is leaving.

Today, with her friend and companion, Alison Prout, she has been for her last walk to the village and back. She has sat for a while on a wooden seat under the war memorial. The ice-cream van, playing four bars of a tune she thought was called 'The Happy Wanderer', drew up by the war memorial and obscured her view of the village green, the pub, the bank and the co-op. A few kids queued at the van's window. Millicent Graves, who had heard on Radio 4 that some ice-cream men were also drug traders, stared at the children. They were pale and obese. Millicent Graves imagined that inside their skulls was confusion and darkness.

Upstairs now Alison Prout is packing clothes. The clothes are Millicent's. There are hats and furs, unworn for thirty years but preserved in boxes with mothballs and tissue paper. There is a black lace ballgown and a black velvet 'theatre dress'. There are white kid gloves and oyster-coloured stockings. Millicent can remember the feel of these ancient clothes against her skin. She has told Alison to pack them all – even the black lace gown and a hat with ostrich plumes – because she wants to believe that in her new life there will be the time and the climate for a little eccentricity. She can see herself in the old feathered hat, perfect for keeping the hot sun off her head. She might, she has decided, go shopping in it and enjoy watching the shopkeepers' faces as out from its ridiculous shade comes her order for half a kilo of parmesan. Or it might become a gardening hat, in which case it will be the nuns who spy her on the other side of their wall – a small but striking figure in her new landscape, going round with the watering can, placing cool stones on the clematis root. Alison Prout has had a bitter argument with Millicent on the subject of clothes, certain as she is that Millicent's motive for taking them is detestable vanity. Millicent was, long ago, beautiful. Now, she is, simply, old. But the clothes, the foolish, expensive clothes, are a reminder – another among many reminders – of her power. And that power, Alison admits to herself as she folds and sorts her friend's possessions, is not yet completely spent.

In a week's time, Millicent and Alison, who have lived together in the cottage for nineteen years, will have left it for ever and The New People will have moved in.

It is a summer afternoon and the light on the garden is beguiling, Alison thinks, as she passes and re-passes the small bedroom window, carrying Millicent's things. Millicent is downstairs, dusting the weasel. She has promised Alison that she will 'make a start on the books'. There are more than two thousand of these. When The New People first arrived to look round the cottage they appeared genuinely afraid at the sight of them. They'd imagined thick walls, perhaps, but not this extra insulation of literature. Then, as Millicent led them on into the sitting room and they noticed the stuffed weasel under its glass cloche, their fear palpably increased, as if the long-dead animal was going to dart at their ankle veins. And yet they didn't retreat. They knew the weasel would be leaving with the women; their glances said, 'We can take down all these book shelves'. As they left, they muttered, 'We shall be instructing the agents . . .'

After they'd gone, Alison had started to cry. 'They'll change it all,' she sobbed, 'I always imagined people like us would buy it.' Millicent reprimanded her. 'Change is good,' she said fiercely, 'and anyway, dear, there are no more people like us.'

But later that evening, Millicent found that she too was looking at the shape and detail of rooms and wondering how they would be altered. After supper, she'd gone out into the garden and stared at the summer night and thought, they will never see it as I see it, those New People, because even if their hands don't change it, their minds will. 'We've got ghosts now!' she announced to Alison as she went in. 'Ghosts who come before instead of after.'

Now, polishing the weasel, Millicent senses that the ghosts are with her in the sitting room. She turns round. 'What we don't understand,' they say, 'is why you're going.'

'Ah,' says Millicent.

Then she notices that Alison has crept down from sorting the old clothes and is sitting in an armchair, saying nothing.

'Is it a long story?'

'No,' says Millicent. 'I'm going because I've been replaced. I look around, in very many places where I once was and now I not only do not see myself there, I see no one who ever resembled me. It's as if I have been obliterated. And I can't, at the age of sixty-nine, accept my obliteration, so I am simply going somewhere where I shall be visible again, at least to myself.'

The New People look utterly perplexed. They want to say, 'We knew you literary folk were a bit mad, a bit touched, but we thought you tried to make sense to ordinary people. We thought this was common courtesy.'

'No,' snaps Millicent, reading their minds, 'it is not common courtesy, yet what I am saying is tediously simple.'

'Well, I'm afraid we don't understand it.'

'Of course you don't. Of course you don't . . . ' Millicent mumbles.

'What you still haven't told us,' say The New People, trying to drag the conversation on to a solid foundation, 'is where you're actually going.'

Millicent looks at Alison. Alison turns her face towards the window and the afternoon sun shines on her hair, which is still reddish and only dulled a little with grey.

'Umbria,' says Millicent.

'Sorry?' say The New People.

'Yes. The house we're buying is by a convent wall. It belonged to the nuns for centuries. It was a place where important guests were put. Now, we shall be the "guests".'

At this point, The New People get up. They say they have to leave. They say they have a great friend who's mad on Italian food and who is starting a local Foodie Society. 'Tonight,' they laugh, 'is the inaugural nosebag!'

Millicent turns away from them and goes back to her polishing. When she looks round again, she finds they've gone.

'They've gone!' she calls to Alison, who is after all upstairs and not sitting silently in a chair.

'What, Millie? Who've gone?'

'Those people,' says Millicent, 'those ghosts. For the time being.'

At supper in the kitchen, Alison says: 'I think I'm going to try not to think about The New People, and if I was you, I'd try not to think about them either.'

'What a very complicated construction that is, Alison,' says Millicent, helping herself to the raspberries she picked a few moments ago in the dusk.

'Particularly tomorrow evening,' says Alison.

'Why particularly tomorrow evening?'

'While I'm out.'

'Out? Where are you going?'

'To say goodbye to Diana.'

'I see,' says Millicent. 'Well, it is going to be extremely difficult *not* to think about them, because they will be here.'

'They're only here in your mind, Millie.'

'I mean, they will actually *be here*. They're bringing a builder.'

'Tomorrow evening?'

'Yes. They're driving down from London.'

'Oh. Then I won't go out.'

'That would be considerate.'

'On the other hand, I promised Diana . . .'

'I marvel that you feel an emotional goodbye to be necessary.'

'Not "emotional".'

'In fact, why not, when we get to Italy, just send a postcard?'

'As if we were on holiday, I suppose you mean.'

Millicent sniffs. Another thing she hopes of her future life is that Alison, fifty next year, will have no more love affairs. She's never expressed this hope, except in her recent poetry, which, as once-praising, now-contemptuous critics have noted, is all about betrayal. She hadn't realized that betrayal was so unfashionable a subject nor indeed that her poems were 'all about' it. Perhaps, she decides capriciously, she will ask The New People about these things and watch their moons of faces closely to see whether or not they understand the words.

They arrive at seven. Alison has promised to be back by seven-thirty. On entering the cottage, they say, God, they're sorry, but since their last visit someone has told them that she, Millicent Graves, is quite a famous poetess and it's awful to say they'd never heard of her.

'Oh, I see,' says Millicent. 'Then why did you say you thought literary people were mad?'

'I beg your pardon?' they say.

'You said you knew that literary folk were a bit touched . . .'

'We said that?'

'Or did I imagine it?'

'You imagined it. You must have done.'

They introduce the builder. He doesn't look, to Millicent Graves, like a builder, but more like a town councillor, wearing a brown suit and brogues. 'Perhaps you're a New Builder?' she asks. The man frowns and tugs out a pipe. He says he's been in the construction business half a lifetime. 'I think,' says Millicent, as she pictures Alison arriving at Diana's house and being greeted with a kiss, 'that everything's become very different and confusing.'

She leads them in. As they reach the sitting room, and the builder starts to look up at the bowed ceiling beams and to prod the springy, flaking plaster of the walls Millicent finds she can't remember the name of The New People and wonders in fact whether she's ever known it.

'Oh, Prue and Simon,' they tell her.

Yes, she wants to say, but the surname? What was that? Something like Haydock-Park, wasn't it, or is that a Grand Prix circuit or a racecourse? She asks the New Builder his name. 'Jack Silverstone,' he announces impatiently.

'Lord!' exclaims Millicent. 'Everybody's careering about.'

The New People glance at each other. We must obliterate every trace of her, says this fearful look. And Jack Silverstone nods, as if in reassurance: It can all be changed. You won't know it's the same house. It's going to cost a bit, that's all.

'Where do you want to start?' asks Millicent.

'Oh . . . ' says Prue.

'Well . . .' says Simon.

'Upstairs,' says Jack Silverstone.

So now, as Millicent gets out the sherry bottle from Alison's tidy kitchen cupboard, they're up above her head in the bathroom. Conversations, in timber-framed houses, escape as easily as heat through the floors and Millicent can hear Prue say to Jack Silverstone: 'This is the one drawback, Jack.' And it appears that Prue wants two bathrooms. Though they will only use the cottage at weekends, she feels, 'It simply isn't viable with one.'

'What about downstairs?' asks Jack Silverstone.

'Downstairs?'

'The little room next to the kitchen.'

'Her study? Convert that into a second bathroom?'

'Why not? Got no use for a study, have you?'

'Simon?'

'Good God, no. Don't plan to bring work here. Need a phone, that's all.'

They start to clatter towards the stairs. Now they'll come

down and go into the study, where nothing has ever been disturbed but only moved about gently to accommodate the hoover, and start a conversation about piping.

Millicent leaves the sherry unpoured and marches quickly to the desk where all the unfashionable words on the subject of dereliction have been set down and picks up the telephone. By the time The New People have opened her door and exclaimed with barely concealed annoyance at finding her there, she has dialled Diana's number and has begun to wonder whereabouts in Diana's very beautiful house Alison may be standing or sitting or even lying down, because although it is now 7.25 by the silent study clock, Millicent is certain that Alison is still there and that unless summoned immediately she will come home very late, long after The New People have gone, leaving Millicent alone with the darkness and the ghosts.

The telephone rings and isn't answered. The New People have retreated to the kitchen where impatiently in their minds they are tearing Millicent's old cupboards off the walls.

'So tell us why you're going. Won't you?' say The New People, sipping sherry.

'Well,' says Millicent, 'I'll tell you a story, if you like.'

'A story?'

'Yes. And it's this. Men have never been particularly important to me, but one man was and that was my father. He was a scientist. All his early work was in immunology. But then he became very interested in behaviours, animal behaviour and then human behaviours. And from this time, our family life was quite changed, because he started bringing to his laboratory and then into the house all kinds of strangers. They would mostly be very unhappy people and their unhappiness and noise made it impossible for us to live as we'd once lived and everything we valued – silence, for instance, and little jokes that only we as a family understood – had disappeared for ever. And then my youngest sister, Christina, whom I loved very very much, committed suicide. So you see. Sometimes one has to act.'

Three faces, turned in expectation towards Millicent, turn away.

'Dreadful story,' mumbles Prue.

'Can we have a look at the study now?' says Jack Silverstone.

'Yes,' says Millicent. 'My study in Italy overlooks the nuns' vegetable garden. They told me they hoe in silence, but I expect from time to time one might hear them murmuring, don't you think?'

They don't know how to reply. In the study, they whisper. They've understood now how their plans can be overheard.

Millicent pours herself more sherry and notices that, as she predicted, Alison is not home and that the sun has gone down behind the laurels.

The New People emerge, beaming. Clearly, they have decided where the lavatory can go and where the bath. Millicent fills their glasses. 'The convent is, of course, crumbling,' she tells them, 'that's why the nuns have been forced to sell off the guest house – to try to repair the fabric. The Church in Italy used to hold people in their blood. Prayer was food. But it isn't like that any more. It's in decay, and all over the place there are empty churches and the old plaster saints have been replaced by plastic things.'

'There's a lot of shoddy muck about,' says Jack Silverstone, 'take my trade . . . '

'One imagines that perhaps certain African or South American Indian tribes are held to certain ways and certain places in their blood, but I think no one else is, do you? Certainly not in this country, unless it's an individual held to another individual by love. What do you think?'

'Well,' says Prue.

'Time,' says Simon.

'Time?' says Millicent.

'Yes. If you're in something like Commodities, as I am, you don't have the time for any other commitments.'

'And as for the Church,' says Jack Silverstone, 'all that ever was was bloodthirsty.'

At this moment, Millicent hears the sound of Alison's car. It's eight thirty-five. The New People get up and thank Millicent for the sherry and tell her they've seen everything they needed to see.

Alison looks white. Her straight, small mouth is set into an even straighter, smaller line. Millicent decides to ignore – at least for the time being – the set of Alison's mouth and tells her friend with a smile: 'They're called the Haydock-Parks!'

'No, they are *not*, Millicent,' snaps Alison. 'Why do you always have to get names wrong?'

'What are they called, then?'

'The Hammond-Clarks.'

'Oh well, the builder is called Silverstone.'

'I very much doubt it.'

'You always doubted a great deal that was true, dear. He is called Silverstone, and I shall from now on refer to these people as the Haydock-Parks because it suits them extremely well.'

Alison goes angrily up the stairs and into her room. The door closes. Her anger, Millicent notices, has made the house throb. She wonders how many times and in what degree the timbers and lathes have shifted, over all the years, to the violent commotions of their friendship. She ponders the origin of the phrase 'brought the house down' and wonders if it was originally applied to anger and not to laughter. How splendid if, as their removal van drove away, the house gave one final shudder of release and collapsed in a pile of sticks at The New People's feet.

She waits for a while for Alison to come down. She's hungry, but she refuses to eat supper alone.

She goes out into the garden and folds up the two deck chairs. 'Order before night' was a favourite saying of her father's, and before he started imposing a more or less perpetual state of disorder on their previously calm and prospering household, he would, each evening, observe his own strict ritual of collecting every toy scattered around the house and garden and returning it to its place in the nursery, before checking that all the downstairs windows were shut, the curtains drawn, the silver cupboard locked, the backgammon board closed, the lights extinguished and the eiderdowns in place over the bodies of his sleeping daughters. Millicent remembers that Christina once admitted to her that she would often let her eiderdown slip on to the floor on purpose and lie awake waiting for this infinitely comforting moment when it would be lifted gently from the floor and placed over her. When the strangers kept arriving, there was not time in her father's life for 'order before night'; there was, as Millicent remembers it, simply night. It descended swiftly. Patiently, the family waited for dawn, but it never came. Christina died. Millicent retreated from death by starting to write poetry.

She hadn't expected fame. It had come as suddenly and as unexpectedly as the arrival of the strangers. And it had changed her, made her bold, excited and free. Other people complained about it; Millicent Graves always found it an absorbing companion. Now, she misses it. Her frail hope is that in Italy she will miss it less. It still astonishes her that work once so highly valued can now be so utterly forgotten.

She props up the deck chairs in the porch. In the distance, she hears the church clock chime the three-quarter hour. The evening is warm. She wonders how often and for how long the convent tolls its massive bells and whether these summonses will help to structure a future which she knows she hasn't imagined fully enough. Alison has expressed anxiety about the bells, complaining that the days will seem long enough without being woken at dawn.

Resigned to an evening alone, Millicent makes a salad and eats it. She supposes Alison is sleeping, but then when the telephone rings, it's answered upstairs. Tiptoeing to the sitting room, Millicent can hear Alison talking in halting sentences, as if she's trying not to cry. Millicent sniffs. 'I'm much too old for all this!' she says aloud.

In the night, the ghosts of The New People come into

Millicent's room and tear off her wallpaper and replace her old velvet curtains with something called a festoon blind, that draws upwards into big bunches of fabric, like pairs of knickers.

'I see,' says Millicent.

They don't say anything. They're standing back and admiring the window.

'We used to wear cotton knickers like that,' Millicent tells them. 'I never saw my own, not from any provocative angle, but I used to see Elizabeth's and Christina's when we were invited to parties and they would bend down to do up their shoes, and I used to think that the backs of girls' legs looked very strong and lovely.'

The New People are utterly silent and satisfied and fulfilled by the curtains and have drifted off into a contented sleep with the festoons falling caressingly about their heads.

'Night in this cottage,' Millicent whispers, knowing that nothing she says will wake them, 'is usually kind because it's quiet. I've found that in this quiet I've often started to understand things which may not have been plain to me during the day.

'It was during one particular night, very, very cold, with that bitter feeling of snow to come, that I decided that I couldn't endure it, the unloveliness of England, I just couldn't stand it any more, its comatose people, its ravaged landscape. Because we're in a dark age, that's what I think. But no one listens to what I think any more. Millicent Graves is out of fashion, passé, past, part of what once was, a voice we no longer hear.

'So I decided I would go. It seemed, from that night, inevitable. And you see where I've put myself? Slap up against a convent wall! But do you know why I'm able to do that? Because the wall itself, which I believed was so strong, so much more substantial than anything we have left in this brutal-minded country, the wall itself is crumbling! The money I've paid for my little house will prop it up for a bit, but I don't think it will rebuild it, and the best I can hope for is that it doesn't collapse on my head – not till I'm buried, at least.'

At this mention of burial, Millicent sees The New People open their eyes and listen and she thinks she knows why they look so startled: the thought has popped into their minds that despite all the expensive re-planning and re-decorating they're going to do, traces of Millicent's habitation may still remain in the house to disturb them. They imagine how they might be made aware of her. They're giving a dinner party, say. Friends of Simon's from the City will have driven down with their wives, and suddenly Prue or Simon will remember that even the walls of the dining-room used to be lined with books, and the flow of conversation, which is as easy for them as the flow of money, will be halted – just for a moment – because one of them, searching for a word or phrase, understands for a second that there are thousands of words they will never use or even know and remembers that access to these words was once here, in the very room, and is now lost. The moment passes. It's all right. But Simon and Prue both separately wonder, why is it not possible never to think of her?

'Good!' says Millicent aloud. 'That's something, at least, their little discomfort.'

She has gone to sleep and is dreaming of Italy when she's woken by Alison's gentle tap on her door. This knocking on each other's doors is a courtesy neither would want to break; it allows them to share their life without any fear of trespass.

Millicent puts on her light and Alison comes in and sits down on the end of her bed. 'I couldn't sleep, Millie,' she says, 'I think we have to talk.'

'Yes, dear,' says Millicent.

Millicent decides to put on her glasses, so that she can see Alison clearly. Dishonesty must not be allowed to slip past her because dishonesty she can never forgive. She watches Alison's breasts rise as she takes a big breath and says with great sadness: 'I'm not certain that I can go to Italy with you. I think that, for the moment, it's not possible for me to go.'

Millicent blinks. Her eyes were always like a bird's eyes, hooded above and beneath.

'Diana, I suppose.'

'Partly so.'

'And the other part?'

Alison's eyes have been turned away from Millicent until now, but as she speaks, she looks up into her face.

'I can't,' she says, 'feel all the pessimism you feel. Don't think I'm being harsh, Millie, when I say that I feel that some of it comes not from the way our world has changed, but from the way *you've* changed – from being very beautiful and praised, to being . . .'

'Old and despised.'

'That's how you choose to see it. I don't think anyone despises you. They've just learned over the years to disagree with you sometimes and not praise everything you write.'

'They don't praise any of it, Alison. They want me to be quiet.'

'Well, again, that's how you've decided to see it.'

'No. They do. But that's not what you've come to discuss. I suppose it's Diana's beauty, is it? You're infatuated.'

'I may be. What I find I can't believe when I'm with her is that this country has lost all the good things it had. I know it's lost some of them, but I don't believe it's "finished", as you say it is. I just can't believe that, Millie. I can't. And I know that if I go to Italy, I'm going to miss it. I'm going to be homesick for England.'

'What for?' says Millicent indignantly. 'For riots? For waste? For greed? For turkeyburgers?'

'Of course not.'

'Then for what? For this garden, maybe. Or Diana's garden. But what are English gardens, dear? They're fragile oases, preserved by one thing and one thing only: money. And when the economy falters, as falter it undoubtedly will, all your peace of mind – that keeps you in the garden and other people outside it, suffering in those concrete estates – will vanish. Then what joy or satisfaction will you get from the garden?'

'I can't believe it will come to that.'

'It's coming, Alison. Do you know what the Haydock-Parks are going to put in before anything else? A burglar alarm.'

'I know all that. But there are so very many decent people, Millie, who want the country to survive, who want to make things better . . . '

'Decent people? Who? Name one decent person.'

'The kind of people we've always known . . . '

'Our friends? I don't think they're "decent", Alison. I think they're infinitely corruptible and infinitely weak, and when it comes to saving England, the task simply isn't going to fall to them, it's going to fall to people like the Haydock-Parks, The New People, and what kind of "salvation" do you ever imagine that's going to be?'

Alison is silent. When she thinks about it, she is perfectly happy to let Millicent win the argument. What she will not let her do is change her mind.

The silence endures. Alison picks at the fringe of her dressing-gown cord. Millicent takes off her glasses and rubs her eyes.

'I have never,' says Millicent after a while, 'been at all good at being quite and utterly alone. How in the world do you think I'm going to get on in that Italian house without you?'

'I really don't know, Millie,' says Alison sadly, 'I expect I shall worry about you a great deal.'

Refusing to think about Alison after she has gone back to her own room, Millicent snaps out the light and lies on her back and sees the dawn starting to frame the curtains. Just outside her window is a clump of tall hazel bushes. Pigeons have roosted in these trees for as long as Millicent can remember and she thinks now that if she's going to miss one thing, it will be the murmuring of these birds.

They lull her to sleep. She dreams her dead sister, Christina, comes and stands by her bed and puts her child's hand on Millicent's grey head. 'I am wearing,' Christina announces solemnly, 'the Haydock-Parks' curtains, just to mess them up, and in a few moments I'm going to drink this little phial of White Arsenic I've stolen from father's lab, and it will make me die.'

'Don't die, Christina,' Millicent begs, 'dear Christina . . . '

'Oh no, I'm definitely going to die,' says Christina, 'because I think loss is the saddest thing anyone could possibly imagine. Don't you, Millie? I think losing something you once had is the most unbearable thing of all. Don't you?'

'What have you lost, Christina? I'll find it again for you. I'll get it back, whatever it was. Just as long as you don't die . . . '

'No. You can't get it back. Thank you for offering, Millie, but I know that what we once had in this house went away when the strangers arrived and even if mother pleaded and begged and *made* father send them away, I know that they damaged us, damaged our love, and however hard we tried to get it for ourselves again, we never ever could.'

This dream is so sad that Millicent has to wake herself up, even though she knows that her old head which her fifteen-year-old sister was touching is very tired and in need of sleep.

Thoughts of Christina and of death linger with her. She feels, as she has never felt before, afraid not so much of death, but, in dying, of yielding territory to others who may desecrate and destroy the few things which have seemed precious to her and which, in the absence of any belief in God, have been part of a code by which she's tried to live.

In Italy, she promises her new hosts, the nuns, she will alter nothing in their house, nothing fundamental, and to the land around it she will behave kindly. But when she dies, what will happen to it? Who will come next? Which strangers?

'Probably,' she says aloud to the pigeons, 'it's wiser to own no territory at all and just be like that man in my Samuel Palmer print, who lies down alone in the landscape with his book.'

Next door, she hears Alison get up.

'Daybreak,' announces Millicent.

ROSE MACAULAY

*

Miss Anstruther's Letters

Miss Anstruther, whose life had been cut in two on the night of 10 May 1941, so that she now felt herself a ghost, without attachments or habitation, neither of which she any longer desired, sat alone in the bed-sitting-room she had taken, a small room, littered with the grimy, broken and useless objects which she had salvaged from the burnt-out ruin round the corner. It was one of the many burnt-out ruins of that wild night when high explosives and incendiaries had rained on London and the water had run short: it was now a gaunt and roofless tomb, a pile of ashes and rubble and burnt, smashed beams. Where the floors of twelve flats had been, there was empty space. Miss Anstruther had for the first few days climbed up to what had been her flat, on what had been the third floor, swarming up pendent fragments of beams and broken girders, searching and scrabbling among ashes and rubble, but not finding what she sought, only here a pot, there a pan, sheltered from destruction by an overhanging slant of ceiling. Her marmalade for May had been there, and a little sugar and tea; the demolition men got the sugar and tea, but did not care for marmalade, so Miss Anstruther got that. She did not know what else went into those bulging dungaree pockets, and did not really care, for she knew it would not be the thing she sought, for which even demolition men would have no use; the flames, which take anything, useless or not, had taken these, taken them and destroyed them like a ravaging mouse or an idiot child.

After a few days the police had stopped Miss Anstruther

from climbing up to her flat any more, since the building was scheduled as dangerous. She did not much mind; she knew by then that what she looked for was gone for good. It was not among the massed debris on the basement floor, where piles of burnt, soaked and blackened fragments had fallen through four floors to lie in indistinguishable anonymity together. The tenant of the basement flat spent her days there, sorting and burrowing among the chaotic mass that had invaded her home from the dwellings of her co-tenants above. There were masses of paper, charred and black and damp, which had been books. Sometimes the basement tenant would call out to Miss Anstruther, 'Here's a book. That'll be yours, Miss Anstruther'; for it was believed in Mortimer House that most of the books contained in it were Miss Anstruther's, Miss Anstruther being something of a bookworm. But none of the books were any use now, merely drifts of burnt pages. Most of the pages were loose and scattered about the rubbish-heaps; Miss Anstruther picked up one here and there and made out some words. 'Yes,' she would agree. 'Yes, that was one of mine.' The basement tenant, digging bravely away for her motoring trophies, said, 'Is it one you wrote?' 'I don't think so,' said Miss Anstruther. 'I don't think I can have . . .' She did not really know what she might not have written, in that burnt-out past when she had sat and written this and that on the third floor, looking out on green gardens; but she did not think it could have been this, which was a page from Urquhart's translation of Rabelais. 'Have you lost *all* your own?' the basement tenant asked, thinking about her motoring cups, and how she must get at them before the demolition men did, for they were silver. 'Everything,' Miss Anstruther answered. 'Everything. They don't matter.' 'I hope you had no precious manuscripts,' said the kind tenant. 'Books you were writing, and that.' 'Yes,' said Miss Anstruther, digging about among the rubble heaps. 'Oh yes. They're gone. They don't matter . . .'

She went on digging till twilight came. She was grimed from head to foot; her only clothes were ruined; she stood knee-deep in drifts of burnt rubbish that had been carpets, beds, curtains, furniture, pictures, and books; the smoke that smouldered up from them made her cry and cough. What she looked for was not there; it was ashes, it was no more. She had not rescued it while she could, she had forgotten it, and now it was ashes. All but one torn, burnt corner of note-paper, which she picked up out of a battered saucepan belonging to the basement tenant. It was niggled over with close small writing, the only words left of the thousands of words in that hand that she looked for. She put it in her note-case and went on looking till dark; then she went back to her bed-sitting-room, which she filled each night with dirt and sorrow and a few blackened cups.

She knew at last that it was no use to look any more, so she went to bed and lay open-eyed through the short summer nights. She hoped each night that there would be another raid, which should save her the trouble of going on living. But it seemed that the Luftwaffe had, for the moment, done; each morning came, the day broke, and, like a revenant, Miss Anstruther still haunted her ruins, where now the demolition men were at work, digging and sorting and pocketing as they worked.

'I watch them close,' said a policeman standing by. 'I always hope I'll catch them at it. But they sneak into dark corners and stuff their pockets before you can look round.'

'They didn't ought,' said the widow of the publican who had kept the little smashed pub on the corner, 'they didn't ought to let them have those big pockets, it's not right. Poor people like us, who've lost all we had, to have what's left taken off of us by *them* . . . it's not right.'

The policeman agreed that it was not right, but they were that crafty, he couldn't catch them at it.

Each night, as Miss Anstruther lay awake in her strange, littered, unhomely room, she lived again the blazing night that had cut her life in two. It had begun like other nights, with the wailing siren followed by the crashing guns, the rushing hiss of incendiaries over London, and the whining, howling pitching of bombs out of the sky on to the fire-lit city. A wild, blazing hell of a night. Miss Anstruther, whom bombs made restless, had gone down once or twice to the street door to look at the glowing furnace of London and exchange comments with the caretaker on the ground floor and with the two basement tenants, then she had sat on the stairs, listening to the demon noise. Crashes shook Mortimer House, which was tall and slim and Edwardian, and swayed like a reed in the wind to near bombing. Miss Anstruther understood that this was a good sign, a sign that Mortimer House, unlike the characters ascribed to clients by fortune-tellers, would bend but not break. So she was quite surprised and shocked when, after a series of three close-at-hand screams and crashes, the fourth exploded, a giant earthquake, against Mortimer House, and sent its whole front crashing down. Miss Anstruther, dazed and bruised from the hurtle of bricks and plaster flung at her head, and choked with dust, hurried down the stairs, which were still there. The wall on the street was a pile of smoking, rumbling rubble, the Gothic respectability of Mortimer House one with Nineveh and Tyre and with the little public across the street. The ground-floor flats, the hall and the street outside, were scrambled and beaten into a common devastation of smashed masonry and dust. The little caretaker was tugging at his large wife, who was struck unconscious and jammed to the knees in bricks. The basement tenant, who had rushed up with her stirrup pump, began to tug too, so did Miss Anstruther. Policemen pushed in through the mess, rescue men and a warden followed, all was in train for rescue, as Miss Anstruther had so often seen it in her ambulance-driving.

'What about the flats above?' they called. 'Anyone in them?'

Only two of the flats above had been occupied, Miss Anstruther's at the back. Mrs Cavendish's at the front. The rescuers rushed upstairs to investigate the fate of Mrs Cavendish.

'Why the devil,' enquired the police, 'wasn't everyone downstairs?' But the caretaker's wife, who had been downstairs, was unconscious and jammed, while Miss Anstruther, who had been upstairs, was neither.

They hauled out the caretaker's wife, and carried her to a waiting ambulance.

'Everyone out of the building!' shouted the police. 'Everyone out!'

Miss Anstruther asked why.

The police said there were to be no bloody whys, everyone out, the bloody gas pipe's burst and they're throwing down fire, the whole thing may go up in a bonfire before you can turn round.

A bonfire! Miss Anstruther thought, if that's so I must go up and save some things. She rushed up the stairs, while the rescue men were in Mrs Cavendish's flat. Inside her own blasted and twisted door, her flat lay waiting for death. God, muttered Miss Anstruther, what shall I save? She caught up a suitcase, and furiously piled books into it – Herodotus, *Mathematical Magick*, some of the twenty volumes of *Purchas his Pilgrimes*, the eight little volumes of Walpole's letters, *Trivia*, *Curiosities of Literature*, the six volumes of Boswell, then, as the suitcase would not shut, she turned out Boswell and substituted a china cow, a tiny walnut shell with tiny Mexicans behind glass, a box with a mechanical bird that jumped out and sang, and a fountain pen. No use bothering with the big books or the pictures. Slinging the suitcase across her back, she caught up her portable wireless set and her typewriter, loped downstairs, placed her salvage on the piled wreckage at what had been the street door, and started up the stairs again. As she reached the first floor, there was a burst and a hissing, a huge *pst-pst*, and a rush of flame leaped over Mortimer House as the burst gas caught and sprang to heaven, another fiery rose bursting into bloom to join that pandemonic red garden of night. Two rescue men, carrying Mrs Cavendish downstairs, met Miss Anstruther and pushed her back.

'Clear out. Can't get up there again, it'll go up any minute.'

It was at this moment that Miss Anstruther remembered

the thing she wanted most, the thing she had forgotten while she gathered up things she wanted less.

She cried, 'I must go up again. I must get something out. There's time.'

'Not a bloody second,' one of them shouted at her, and pushed her back.

She fought him. 'Let me go, oh let me go. I tell you I'm going up once more.'

On the landing above, a wall of flame leaped crackling to the ceiling.

'Go up be damned. Want to go through that?'

They pulled her down with them to the ground floor. She ran out into the street, shouting for a ladder. Oh God, where are the fire engines? A hundred fires, the water given out in some places, engines helpless. Everywhere buildings burning, museums, churches, hospitals, great shops, houses, blocks of flats, north, south, east, west and centre. Such a raid never was. Miss Anstruther heeded none of it; with hell blazing and crashing round her, all she thought was, I must get my letters. Oh dear God, my letters. She pushed again into the inferno, but again she was dragged back. 'No one to go in there,' said the police, for all human life was by now extricated. No one to go in, and Miss Anstruther's flat left to be consumed in the spreading storm of fire, which was to leave no wrack behind. Everything was doomed – furniture, books, pictures, china, clothes, manuscripts, silver, everything: all she thought of was the desk crammed with letters that should have been the first thing she saved. What had she saved instead? Her wireless, her typewriter, a suitcase full of books; looking round, she saw that all three had gone from where she had put them down. Perhaps they were in the safe keeping of the police, more likely in the wholly unsafe keeping of some rescue-squad man or private looter. Miss Anstruther cared little. She sat down on the wreckage of the road, sick and shaking, wholly bereft.

The bombers departed, their job well done. Dawn came, dim and ashy, in a pall of smoke. The little burial garden was

like a garden in a Vesuvian village, grey in its ash coat. The air
choked with fine drifts of cinders. Mortimer House still burned,
for no one had put it out. A grimy warden with a note-book
asked Miss Anstruther, have you anywhere to go?

'No,' she said, 'I shall stay here.'

'Better go to a rest centre,' said the warden, wearily doing
his job, not caring where anyone went, wondering what had
happened in North Ealing, where he lived.

Miss Anstruther stayed, watching the red ruin smouldering
low. Sometime, she thought, it will be cool enough to go into.

There followed the haunted, desperate days of search which
found nothing. Since silver and furniture had been wholly
consumed, what hope for letters? There was no charred sliver
of the old locked rosewood desk which had held them. The
burning words were burnt, the lines, running small and close
and neat down the page, difficult to decipher, with the o's and
a's never closed at the top, had run into a flaming void and
would never be deciphered more. Miss Anstruther tried to
recall them, as she sat in the alien room; shutting her eyes, she
tried to see again the phrases that, once you had made them
out, lit the page like stars. There had been many hundreds of
letters, spread over twenty-two years. Last year their writer
had died; the letters were all that Miss Anstruther had left of
him; she had not yet re-read them; she had been waiting till
she could do so without the devastation of unendurable weeping. They had lain there, a solace waiting for her when she
could take it. Had she taken it, she could have recalled them
better now. As it was, her memory held disjointed phrases,
could not piece them together. Light of my eyes. You are the
sun and the moon and the stars to me. When I think of you life
becomes music, poetry, beauty, and I am more than myself. It
is what lovers have found in all the ages, and no one has ever
found before. The sun flickering through the beeches on your
hair. And so on. As each phrase came back to her, it jabbed at
her heart like a twisting bayonet. He would run over a list of
places they had seen together, in the secret stolen travels of

twenty years. The balcony where they dined at the Foix inn, leaning over the green river, eating trout just caught in it. The little wild strawberries at Andorra la Vieja, the mountain pass that ran down to it from Ax, the winding road down into Seo d'Urgel and Spain. Lerida, Zaragoza, little mountain-towns in the Pyrenees, Jaca, Saint Jean Pied-du-Port, the little harbour of Collioure, with its painted boats, morning coffee out of red cups at Villefranche, tramping about France in a hot July; truffles in the *place* at Perigueux, the stream that rushed steeply down the village street at Florac, the frogs croaking in the hills about it, the gorges of the Tarn, Rodez with its spacious *place* and plane trees, the little walled town of Cordes with the inn courtyard a jumble of sculptures, altar-pieces from churches, and ornaments from châteaux; Lisieux, with ancient crazy-floored inn, huge four-poster, and preposterous little saint (before the grandiose white temple in her honour had arisen on the hill outside the town), villages in the Haute-Savoie, jumbled among mountain rocks over brawling streams, the motor bus over the Alps down into Susa and Italy. Walking over the Amberley downs, along the Dorset coast from Corfe to Lyme on two hot May days, with a night at Chideock between, sauntering in Buckinghamshire beech-woods, boating off Bucklers Hard, climbing Dunkery Beacon to Porlock, driving on a June afternoon over Kirkdale pass . . . Baedeker starred places because we ought to see them, he wrote, I star them because we saw them together, and those stars light them up for ever . . . Of this kind had been many of the letters that had been for the last year all Miss Anstruther had left, except memory, of two-and-twenty years. There had been other letters about books, books he was reading, books she was writing; others about plans, politics, health, the weather, himself, herself, anything. I could have saved them, she kept thinking; I had the chance; but I saved a typewriter and a wireless set and some books and a walnut shell and a china cow, and even they are gone. So she would cry and cry, till tears blunted at last for the time the sharp edge of grief, leaving only a dull lassitude, an end of being. Sometimes she would take out and look at the charred corner of paper which was now all she had of her lover; all that was legible of it was a line and a half of close small writing, the o's and a's open at the top. It had been written twenty-one years ago, and it said, 'Leave it at that. I know now that you don't care twopence; if you did you would' . . . The words, each time she looked at them, seemed to darken and obliterate a little more of the twenty years that had followed them, the years of the letters and the starred places and all they had had together. You don't care twopence, he seemed to say still; if you had cared twopence, you would have saved my letters, not your wireless and your typewriter and your china cow, least of all those little walnut Mexicans, which you know I never liked. Leave it at that.

Oh, if instead of these words she had found light of my eyes, or I think of the balcony at Foix, she thought she could have gone on living. As it is, thought Miss Anstruther, as it is I can't. Oh my darling, I did care twopence, I did.

So each night she cried herself to sleep, and woke to drag through another empty summer's day.

Later, she took another flat. Life assembled itself about her again; kind friends gave her books; she bought another typewriter, another wireless set, and ruined herself with getting necessary furniture, for which she would get no financial help until after the war. She noticed little of all this that she did, and saw no real reason for doing any of it. She was alone with a past devoured by fire and a charred scrap of paper which said you don't care twopence, and then a blank, a great interruption, an end. She had failed in caring once, twenty years ago, and failed again now, and the twenty years between were a drift of grey ashes that once were fire, and she a drifting ghost too. She had to leave it at that.

*

The Man Who Kept the Sweet Shop
at the Bus Station

The man who kept the sweet shop at the bus station was disappointing, years afterwards. He had been the one excitement of the repetitive journeys home, when the country girls bought cheese and onion crisps and sherbet for the 269 to Whittenden and Coxstaple and the city girls loitered in the car park, feeling in some unexpressed way deprived of the country girls' extra half hour of gossip (and also, they suspected, shared homework), and spat emerald saliva on to the tarmac. The man who kept the sweet shop, if you thought about it, which they didn't, was almost the only man in their schoolgirls' lives. There was the chaplain, but he wasn't a man, not completely, and there was sticky-eyed Bert, the gardener, but he didn't count; already separated from them by an unbridgeable social gulf, servilely mowing the lawns in full view of a history lesson. Only the sweet shop man rolled his sly eyes at them, when they bought toffee walnut whips and seemed to caress the palm of their hands with the coins ('urgh, urgh') when he gave them their change.

His was the only sweet shop at the bus station, but, even if there had been another, they would most likely not have gone there. Years later, when they came down for weekends on the London coach, they saw the grand new coffee shop called 'Beans' in the arcade and imagined they envied today's High School girls, sophisticatedly nibbling wholemeal parkin and health bars in the bus shelter. But they didn't really. Their own schooldays had been lifted out of the ordinary by the mystique of their sweet shop man.

His shop didn't have a name. It wasn't even a proper building, but something white and oblong, that had been delivered on a lorry and dumped beside the car park like a maimed car. Inside, the walls were stacked with bars and chews. With more than four of them in there, you couldn't open the door. The man had a private room at the back, where God knows what he did. He was always in it when they came in at four twenty (or four twenty-five, if it had been games last period) and there would be a tingling moment of expectation before his shadow fell across the doorway and they heard his critical cough.

'More sweeties?' he said, or sometimes nothing. He just arched one eyebrow and seemed to bore into their blazers with his glassy blue eyes.

Mary Hunniwell, top in English, said he leered. But 'leer' was an odd, ugly word and the feeling his crumpling cheeks gave them was not ugly in the least. Mary Hunniwell had a word for everything: 'sordid' for the sweet shop, 'puerile' for the sweets. Some of them wished obscurely that Mary Hunniwell would stay outside in the car park. But she bought more sweets than anyone, chewing on their yielding, puerile gooeyness in a particularly brutal way. She sometimes cheeked the sweet shop man too. 'When are you going to give us a discount then? You know it's cheaper in the Post Office.'

It was on one of those occasions that the man held on to her inky fingers with the silver and whispered, 'What would you give me in return, dearie?' White spit came into the corners of his mouth when he spoke.

'Urgh,' cried Mary Hunniwell, snatching back her hand, and they all jostled out into the car park, gasping and exclaiming, and half of them blamed Mary Hunniwell and half of them blamed the sweet shop man.

They decided he was probably a pervert, after that. He had

an ordinary, thin face, he wore normal clothes. But there was something definitely suspicious about his cramped shop, with the drowsy smell of cachous and the crackling paper, that made them need to go in there every day of term.

There was a skylight in the ceiling, which let down a little grey light. On wet days, the rain made a noise overhead like lavatories. And the cardboard boxes were packed so tightly on the shelves that it often took them ages to make up their minds.

It was a nine-mile ride to Whittenden, eleven to Coxstaple. The country girls had plenty of time to discuss the sweet shop man. They hinted to the city girls that there was something a bit funny about their bus driver too; slimy Pete with the slicked-back hair. But, because they couldn't all watch him, he never took in quite the same way. He wasn't old enough, in any case.

They led a rich conversational life on the long back seat. The cigarette smoke, the bodies and the shopping baskets made a solid wall between them and propriety. They talked openly about their teachers' oddities and the fluffy privacies of other girls' desks. Sometimes they reached desperate intimacies just before Whittenden Bus Garage followed by promises, shouted down the bus, to forget them. But, somehow, the information was never discussed elsewhere. So no one ever pointed out at school how the girls who went home on the 269 did consistently better homework and often had similar ideas for compositions. Perhaps, in the staff room, it was attributed to a better breakfast and country air.

They gradually took over the sweet shop man. They had longer to wait for tea; they bought more sweets. In senior years, when the city girls were first to have boyfriends, because they had the cinema and 'Bumps' discotheque at weekends, the country girls compensated with a richer fantasy life.

They used that aching journey home, through pole-axed villages and wet fields, to transform their emptiness into enigma. There was something nearly frenzied about the way they piled on to the back seats (the ones in front hanging over the high seatbacks), and tore the paper off their chocolate bars with dexterous teeth. They didn't mind touching one another, which they absolutely loathed at school. They liked (unconsciously) the steamed-up windows and the bouncing, the cramped, red chenille and the body smell. Awash with conspiracy, they created interest.

He had a past life; of that they were sure. But how and where he had acquired his funny look, his strange character, was at their discretion. There was always a strong voice in favour of crime, sex crime. But they had other, equally reasonable explanations; he was hiding from someone strong, who bore him a grudge, he was 'on drugs', he was a secret agent. What did he do all day, before they came? Alone in his little cabin with his radio? There were few customers at the bus station. They imagined him groping in the twilight for mugs of tea and pastel-coloured biscuits.

Uneven comments can be remembered:

'It's his eyes which get me. I think they're icy and piercing.' (Anathea Judd.)

'I'd never buy anything unwrapped in there.' (Sarah Whittaker.)

'Have you noticed the way he twitches his neck?' (Mary Hunniwell.) 'It's a neurotic obsession.'

'I can't bear the way his Adam's apple jumps under his skin.'

'His nails – '

'His teeth – '

Because the rest of the sweet shop man was cut off by the counter.

One afternoon, the shop was closed, for sickness it said on the door. It stayed closed for three weeks. The man came back a funny colour, bluey under his natural red. They hoped the Public Health had fumigated his shop before it was re-opened.

After the summer holidays, the shop was always a little

more down-at-heel. They didn't talk about it, but sometimes they remembered it during the last period of the first day of term and felt unreasonable excitement as they watched the classroom clock inch towards four p.m. The loud bell would screech hysterically in the hall and send a sickly tremor through their necks.

Of course the bus journeys came to a natural end. One by one, they moved off to share seats further forward with St Aloysius boys. Only a few were left, uncompensated, at the back. They began the Sixth Form and dieting. Nobody would be seen dead coming out of the sweet shop, cheeks bulging. Their drives were diverted towards courses, college, a future, pass marks, all of which they wanted, passionately. They discovered their submerged hatred for the glum, provincial town; scuffed their resentful heels along its pavements and lounged sulkily against its walls. They worked themselves into a fever for the terrible climax of the exams, chewed pens, didn't sleep and privately admired their hollowed cheeks. The results fell like Biblical judgements into a torpid summer; secretarial college, the Poly, speech and drama, University. They met in coffee bars to exchange fates. Someone said sneeringly that Mary Hunniwell would stay on to try Cambridge. In the autumn, everyone else fled, ramming their big cases through train doors with a sweating sense of moment. After that, they never came back at all, not for years and years.

For months at a time, they even forgot where they came from, absorbed in being original or sullen or beautiful. The luckier ones changed beyond recognition. And the endless, flat years of their school life sank swiftly under the accumulation of interesting months.

The full, grimy tedium of the bus station struck them on winter afternoons, when they rushed from the London coach, drove by in cars. And the fate of Anathea Judd, who had actually stayed there and got married, who worked, it was rumoured, in W. H. Smith, seemed terrible beyond words.

In the thick, wet light, black corrugated shelters pockmarked the small concrete plain. Pools of spilt oil reflected the green council lamps. Around three sides of the plain, red, municipal buildings blocked off a view. On the fourth, traffic lights and impermanent poles made a shoddy entrance. The small alterations of the years (the new café, the muddy coats of paint) only stressed the hopeless boredom of the place. It had nothing interesting for them on their busy journeys to London, nothing at all. They clambered aboard the coach and didn't look out. They fixed their minds on flats in Bayswater and handbags. What a place to spend one's life.

They didn't see the sweet shop. It was at the opposite end of the bus station and they none of them now ate sweets. They had no mental picture of the shop's inside. Only sometimes, rarely, they forgot their cigarettes, or their newspaper. And trotting, swearing, across the concrete five minutes before their coach was due to go, they would remember the sweet shop.

When the High School girls came back, they always pretended not to remember him. He could see the pretence in their averted eyes and their casual gestures. He remembered them in their little blue blazers, all smudgy-nosed and sticky at his counter. He remembered how they all came belting over the car park after school and he heard their shoes clattering on the tarmac. He always waited till they were inside and panting to come out of his cubicle; it was a daily game he played. But they'd been stand-offish, even then, too special to talk to ordinary people. He liked to talk to people. About the racing to the bus drivers, about the weather to everyone else. It annoyed him that those little misses wouldn't join in, with their uppity voices and their uniform. He teased them gently in revenge.

The schoolgirls' faces came back hidden in new shapes, bought grown-up magazines, snapped 'Twenty Marlborough'. It made him angry to see how unapproachable they had become.

They were always shocked to see the same man working there. Had he gone on making jokes about walnut whips during the exhilarating years while they were changing? It quite disturbed them. It was as if he denied all progress, stuck bleakly in his hut, twitching his scrawny neck and smiling.

*

Addy

Mrs Burton was in a taxi on her way to a dinner when she realized with horror that Addy, her old dog, was dying.

For some time she'd noticed that Addy was behaving strangely. It was as if she had become senile. When Mrs Burton took her out into the street for her evening walk, she now felt obliged to put her on a lead. Addy had once been traffic-trained. Mrs Burton used to be able to open the front door of her building and wait while the dog sniffed at the lamp-post and the railings and then stepped into the gutter to do what Mrs Burton called 'her business'. Addy never would have dreamt of defiling the pavement. She did her 'business' with such grace and her movements were so feminine and delicate she looked as if she was dropping a discreet curtsey. Having accomplished what was expected of her, she used to come trotting back obediently into the house.

Recently Addy's behaviour had become very peculiar whenever she was let out into the street. If any strangers passed her, she started to follow them. It upset Mrs Burton to see the way she would go limping after their shoes as if she was devoted to them. She had always been a very loving dog, but now when she trailed the heels of strangers her lovingness seemed undiscriminating and deranged.

Mrs Burton would call her name, but Addy seemed unable to recognize it. Mrs Burton had to run after the old dog and carry her back to the house otherwise she'd have followed the feet of strangers wherever they happened to take her.

Mrs Burton no longer trusted Addy's traffic-sense. She

feared she might suddenly see a stranger on the other side of the street and decide she wanted to follow him. There was a danger she might step into the road without looking to the left or right and go under the wheel of a car.

Three days ago when Mrs Burton got back from work she noticed that Addy did not come bouncing and wagging to the door of her flat to greet her. She barked a welcome, but she remained sitting on her favourite sofa. Addy had very beautiful gold-brown eyes and when Mrs Burton went over and patted her, she noticed they had an imploring expression. It was as if she wished to apologize for a discourtesy.

Addy's head still looked young and it no longer matched her body. She was a border sheep-dog and she still had an aquiline aristocratic head, but with age she had lost her figure and it spread over the sofa like a fat cushion of brown fur.

Mrs Burton had decided she ought to take the old dog out for a walk. 'Come on,' she clicked her fingers at Addy whose portly body gave a helpless shudder. She seemed unable to move from the sofa.

Mrs Burton picked her up and carried her downstairs and took her into the street. When she was put down, Addy's hind-legs collapsed under her. She struggled bravely, but she was unable to take a step. If she wanted to follow strangers, she was no longer able to do so.

Mrs Burton became alarmed. What could have happened to Addy? She picked her up and carried her to the gutter and supported her and she managed to do her 'business'. She hated the look in the dog's eyes. It was too like the expression Mrs Burton's mother used to have when she had to be lifted on to the bedpan. Addy's eyes were yellow with humiliation. Once she'd carried her back up into her flat, Mrs Burton put her down on her favourite sofa. It was then that Addy had started panting.

Mrs Burton had wondered if she ought to get the vet. But she couldn't see what he could do for Addy. The dog was really now very ancient and her old age had caught up with her. From now on Addy would have to be treated like a crippled invalid. Mrs Burton brought her some water which she accepted. She offered her some dog meat which she refused. Mrs Burton felt it was all right to leave her and she went out to see a play with a woman friend. There seemed to be nothing very wrong with Addy except that she kept on panting.

When Mrs Burton returned around midnight, Addy was asleep. She looked quite peaceful. Mrs Burton went to bed, but she suffered from insomnia. She tossed around, restless and anxious. It was as if she was waiting for something unpleasant to happen and yet she wasn't quite certain what it was.

It was around three o'clock in the morning when Mrs Burton heard an odd sound from the living room. It was the noise of violent scratching. She got up and went next door to investigate and she saw that Addy was no longer on the sofa. She had somehow managed to get down on to the floor and she had dragged herself into a corner behind an armchair.

Addy was squatting there on her collapsed haunches and with her front paws she was digging the thick wall-to-wall carpet of the living-room. She didn't stop when Mrs Burton found her doing this. Her claws continued to tear at the carpet as if she was a rabbit digging a burrow.

'Addy! What on earth are you doing!' Mrs Burton found herself speaking very sharply as if she expected an answer. Addy went on with her digging and there was a desperation in the way that her claws ripped the fluffy pile from the carpet. 'Stop it!' Mrs Burton shouted at her. 'Stop it at once, Addy! You are ruining the carpet!'

She stopped immediately. She had always been very obedient. Mrs Burton picked her up and gave her a soft little smack of disapproval. She saw the look of reproach in Addy's eyes. Mrs Burton was very aware of the softness and the vulnerability of her fat old body as she carried her back to the sofa. Once Mrs Burton had made Addy comfortable, she kissed her nose to show she had forgiven her. She noticed that it felt very dry. Addy was still panting and suddenly she gave such a loud pant it sounded like an agonized sigh. Mrs Burton patted her soothingly and left her to go back to bed.

The next day Addy seemed neither better nor worse. Mrs Burton took her out before she went to work and went through the same routine of lifting the weak old animal while she urinated.

When Mrs Burton returned in the evening, Addy was still sitting on the sofa. There seemed nothing very much the matter with her except that she still kept on quietly panting. Mrs Burton was tired and she felt a certain resentment when she had to carry her outside. Once Addy had drunk some water and refused some food, Mrs Burton put on an evening dress and went off to a dinner party. As she closed the front door behind her and left her on her own, she decided that if the dog still refused to eat in the morning, she would ask the vet to come and look at her.

It was not until she was in a taxi that Mrs Burton wondered if Addy had been trying to tell her something important. Had she refused to understand the poor animal's message because she didn't want to accept it? Could Addy be dying? Did she want Mrs Burton to know it? When she was digging the living-room carpet, had she been trying to dig her own grave? She had been trained not to cause an inconvenience or mess.

When Addy had followed strangers, had it been an act of despair? She couldn't tell Mrs Burton that she was dying. Even when she made signals that tried to convey this fact, Mrs Burton remained deaf to them. Maybe Addy had hoped that strangers could recognize that she was dying and treat her accordingly. Had she followed their heels with this blind devoted hope?

Mrs Burton knew that she ought to tell the cab-driver to turn round and take her straight back to her house. If Addy was dying, it was extremely cruel to let her die all on her own. She had always been so loving and obedient, first to Mrs Burton's daughter, Mavina, and then to Mrs Burton. One of them should hold the poor old creature in her arms and give her some affection and comfort as she died. Addy was only a dog, but she deserved this human tribute.

Mrs Burton felt like a criminal, but she did not tell the driver to turn back. Mrs Fitz-James, the woman who had invited her to dine, had once been a pupil at the same school. They had once been great friends as little girls but the years had passed and their lives had gone in different directions and they had not kept in touch. Recently they'd met at a cocktail party, and Mrs Burton had been intimidated by the self-assurance with which Mrs Fitz-James met the world. She had turned into a very striking and elegant woman, but Mrs Burton disliked the way she had become both snobbish and brittle. Mrs Fitz-James was married to a wealthy London banker and she boasted about her husband as if she'd won him like a trophy. Mrs Burton remembered that Mrs Fitz-James had once won the high-jump on sports day. When she'd been handed a gold cup, she seemed unable to let go of it, but had stood there hugging it to her chest with cheeks that were pink with triumph.

When the two women met again, Mrs Fitz-James asked Mrs Burton a few condescending questions and soon made it apparent that she pitied her old school-friend for having made a mess of her life and wasted her opportunities. Her arched eyebrows had risen with sarcastic sympathy when she heard that Mrs Burton had ended up as a divorcee without sufficient alimony. She looked appalled when she heard that Mrs Burton had been forced to get a job in London in order to support herself.

Hoping to wriggle out of the uncomfortable spotlight of her old friend's condescension, Mrs Burton reminded her of a silly episode that had taken place when they were both at school. Did Mrs Fitz-James remember how they had made paper pellets and flicked them at the behind of the geography teacher, Miss Ball? Mrs Fitz-James remembered and she gave a tinkle of affected pleasure.

Miss Ball was most probably dead by now, but she had once been important to Mrs Fitz-James and Mrs Burton, and her

voluminous behind was still vivid to them and they were each
glad to find another human being who recalled it. It was on the
strength of this frail bond that for a moment, they both drew
closer to each other, and it was then that Mrs Fitz-James had
asked Mrs Burton to come and dine.

The moment Mrs Burton accepted the invitation she regretted it. She suspected it had been issued out of competitiveness
rather than affection. Mrs Fitz-James very probably wanted
her less fortunate school-friend to be allowed a tantalizing peep
at the desirable life she felt she now led. Exactly as if they were
still at school, Mrs Fitz-James wanted to show-off.

Now, as Mrs Burton rode on in the taxi, she realized that if
she had found Mrs Fitz-James a little more congenial, she
would have telephoned her and explained that she could not
come to her dinner party. She knew it would be very rude if
she cancelled at such short notice. If she defected, even if she
explained that her dog was dying, she doubted Mrs Fitz-James
would consider it an adequate excuse. The numbers at the
dinner party would be made uneven. Men would have to sit
next to men. Her hostess was a woman who obviously cared
very much about such matters. If Mrs Burton suddenly refused
the invitation, Mrs Fitz-James would be extremely annoyed.
Women like Mrs Fitz-James frightened Mrs Burton. Their self-
confidence and elegance and their patronizing attitudes made
her feel inadequate and uncouth. Mrs Burton despised herself
for her cowardice, but she knew she was not going to turn
back to look after Addy. She tried to persuade herself the dog
was not really dying. Addy had become weak and wheezing,
but she could probably go on for years in the same condition.

When Mrs Burton walked into Mrs Fitz-James's drawing
room, her hostess came swaying gracefully to greet her, holding
out a beautifully manicured hand that gleamed with valuable
rings. Mrs Fitz-James was looking even more handsome than
when her old friend had last seen her, and her honey-coloured
hair was looped around her ears and held in place by diamond
clips. She was wearing a tight-fitting satin gown which showed

off her supple and well-exercised figure. The very sight of her made Mrs Burton feel dumpy, middle-aged and badly dressed.

Mrs Fitz-James kissed her and was very gushing and friendly. She made a joke about Miss Ball, the geography teacher. She was trying to put Mrs Burton at her ease. But they had exhausted that subject and neither found it all that funny. Mrs Fitz-James then admired Mrs Burton's evening sandals and asked her where she had been clever enough to find them. Mrs Burton had owned them for years, but never before had she felt her shoes were quite so shabby, old-fashioned and down-at-heel.

'I'm really thrilled you could come.' Mrs Burton disliked the way Mrs Fitz-James was like an actress, word-perfect in her social lines.

A group of guests were standing round the ornate marble mantelpiece in the drawing room. The men looked prosperous and upper-class, and they were wearing dinner-jackets.

Mrs Fitz-James introduced her to her banker husband. He looked much like all the other men in the room, but his mouth seemed just a little more cruel than theirs, and he had a slightly more supercilious and world-weary eye. When he was told that Mrs Burton had been at school with his wife, he looked surprised. 'How amusing!' he said.

There were also several women in long, glamorous dresses, but Mrs Burton hardly dared to look at them when she had to shake their hands. She was too frightened that their beauty and stylishness would make her feel even more unattractive and dreary than she'd felt when speaking to Mrs Fitz-James.

A butler brought Mrs Burton a glass of champagne. Out of nerves she drank it in one gulp and then wished she'd had the poise and the good sense to sip it.

A scarlet-faced man started to make conversation with her. He had blue, sentimental eyes and snowy-white hair with a fluffy texture as if it had been blow-dried. He told her that he was a race-horse owner and asked if she was interested in horses. She murmured that she liked horses very much, but unfortunately, she had never had much to do with them. He said that racing was a drug, but unlike most drugs it often made you quite a lot of money! Mrs Burton smiled with fake amusement. She suspected he had made this remark many times before, and like an old comedian, he believed that well-tried jokes always worked the best.

The butler refilled Mrs Burton's glass and she took care not to drink her champagne quite so quickly as before. She told the race-horse owner that she worked in a firm which published educational books. 'That must be very interesting.' His white head nodded knowingly. Mrs Burton felt the conversation was swaying in the wind like a rope-bridge that connected different terrains.

Mrs Burton took a third glass of champagne. She wished to God she had never come. She kept thinking of Addy. Mrs Fitz-James was describing a house she was having built in Sardinia. She complained of the problems she was having getting the plumbing installed and the laziness of the local work-men.

'Have you ever been to Sardinia?' the florid race-horse owner asked her. He was valiant with his good manners. He kept trying to find the perfect topic that would stimulate her.

'No, I've never been to Sardinia.'

'I hear it is very beautiful.'

'That's what they say.'

The butler announced that dinner was ready. The table gleamed with perfectly polished silver and its mahogany shimmered in the candlelight. Mrs Burton knew from the look of Mrs Fitz-James's table that the food was going to be delicious. This made her feel unhungry.

Mrs Fitz-James placed Mrs Burton between the race-horse owner and another depressed-looking man with grey hair. When the butler filled Mrs Burton's glass with white wine, she once again gulped it down as if it was water. By now, she was feeling too drunk to care if the other guests at the table looked at her with horror, fearing she was an alcoholic.

'I'm feeling very upset tonight,' she suddenly announced to

the race-horse owner. She wanted to prevent him from embarking on any meaningless general conversation. He seemed to be
a boring and mindless man, but at least he could be her
listener. She was angry that she had come to this deadly dinner
party and she felt quite unable to find the strength to weave
any more threads of social chit-chat. She would speak only
about the subject that haunted her.

Her neighbour looked concerned. 'I'm very sorry to hear
you are upset. What has happened?' She had already noticed he
seemed to have a sentimental streak and now his watery blue
eyes had become sympathetic and avuncular.

'I'm worried about my old dog. This evening I had the
awful feeling that she is dying.'

'How old is your dog?' he asked her.

'In human terms she must be about eighty-eight, maybe
eighty-nine.'

'So she's really a very ancient lady.' Her neighbour nodded
gravely.

'Yes, I'm afraid that's true. And recently she hasn't seemed
at all well.'

'It's funny how attached one gets to the old things,' he said.
'I remember I was very cut up when my old Labrador died.'

The butler served Mrs Burton some creamy white soup
which she looked at with a feeling of nausea. The race-horse
owner leant towards her as if he was confiding a secret.

'If your dog is very old, I'm afraid she is bound to die quite
soon. You will just have to accept it. When she passes on you
must look on it philosophically. I'm sure your dog has had a
very happy life with you. When she goes – you must comfort
yourself with that.'

Mrs Burton looked at her soup and it seemed to have turned
a hideous grey. She kept thinking of Addy digging the carpet.
Her neighbour kept repeating that she had to be philosophical.
He seemed to get a relish from saying that word, just as he was
relishing the soup she couldn't eat.

Addy's life had not been as pleasant as the race-horse owner assumed. There had been a few years when she had been well-treated. That was when Mavina loved her and they had lived in the country. At that time Mavina was always kissing Addy. She played with her all day long and she had exercised her properly and let her run hunting rabbits in the fields.

It was as if Mavina's love for Addy had been a childish disease like measles. She had caught a violent dose of it and then when she went off to boarding school, she got rid of it. Mavina had once carried snapshots of Addy in her purse. Now she carried love letters from her boyfriend. Mavina was glad to see Addy on the occasions that she visited Mrs Burton. But her gladness was luke-warm. Addy no longer had any real magic for Mavina. She would be sad to hear that the old dog had died. Something that had been important to her in her childhood would have perished. But Mavina was at university now and all her other interests would soon smother the news of Addy's death.

After Mrs Burton was divorced, she had moved to London and got a job. She had taken Addy with her, but she had never felt she was her dog. Often she had been quite a nuisance to Mrs Burton because she needed to be let out and fed. But having known how Mavina had once doted on the dog, she had thought it disloyal to get rid of her.

Mrs Burton had never been a dog-lover and she'd not been prepared to allow her life to be ruled by Addy's needs. When she went off to work, Addy had been left alone in the house all day. Mrs Burton could never muster any excitement when she was greeted by the dog when she got back home, although she knew that Addy had been moping and pining, and waiting in a frenzy of anticipation for her return. Addy's rapturous delight when she saw her come through the door irritated rather than gratified Mrs Burton. She disliked all her barking and squirming, and when she jumped up and put her front paws on her skirt, Mrs Burton had always pushed her down.

Addy's relationship with Mavina had been one of mutual passion. After Mavina's father left Mrs Burton, the little girl had needed to stifle her feelings of hurt and betrayal by pouring her love on to an object she saw as perfect because it was not human. Everything about the dog had delighted Mavina in that period. She loved the smell inside her ears and she claimed it was like the smell of car-seats. She refused to sleep unless Addy was tucked beside her under the bedclothes. Sometimes Mavina made her lie on her back with her head propped up on pillows in a position so undog-like, Mrs Burton found it almost unkind. But Addy had seemed perfectly happy so she had not protested. Mrs Burton only made a fuss whenever she found Mavina licking the dog's pink tongue because she was terrified her daughter would get some dangerous disease.

Mavina used to believe that Addy could understand anything that was said to her. And when Mavina spoke to her, it almost seemed to be true, for she instantly obeyed the child's peculiar commands. Mavina would give her a lump of sugar and order the dog not to swallow it. Addy then kept it in her mouth gazing up at Mavina with an expression of slavish adoration. When the little girl told her to spit it out she immediately obeyed. After that Mavina allowed her to eat the sugar lump and she squealed with delight because Addy had been so clever and abstemious. She then over-fed her with sweet biscuits to let her know how much the trick had pleased her. She would hug her and pat her until Addy got so over-excited she often seemed like a mad dog jumping around and barking as if she had been driven demented by such intense approval.

In those years, whenever anything upset Mavina, her first instinct had been to run to find Addy. She clasped the dog in her arms as if she was a teddy bear and when Mavina cried, she liked to bury her face in Addy's thick, reassuring fur.

Sitting at this formal and inane dinner party, Mrs Burton felt that she suddenly wanted to cry. She battled to prevent herself from doing so because her tears would be hypocritical. Very likely they would be treated with sympathy and that would make her feel all the more corrupt. If she was to cry, her neighbour would explain to the rest of the table that she was distressed because her beloved old dog was dying. It would be disgusting if she allowed all these strangers in expensive clothes to condole with her.

Addy had been used and violated by Mavina and Mrs Burton. Mavina had once needed Addy's love and loyalty as therapy and then she had betrayed her, for she had lost all interest in the dog once her adoration ceased to have any value for her. Addy had been too dumb to comprehend that human beings were fickle. When she was moved to the cold foster-home of Mrs Burton's ownership, she had always hopelessly tried to recreate the idyllic relationship that she had been falsely taught to accept as her due.

She had guarded Mrs Burton's flat as she should have been allowed to guard sheep. She seemed only to let herself half-sleep for, if there was any noise outside the door, she always sprang up with ears pricked in order to bark a warning. Mrs Burton suddenly remembered that she'd insisted that Addy be spayed. That was one more area where Addy had been cheated.

Although Mrs Burton had seen that she was kept alive, she now felt convinced her indifference towards the dog had been vicious. Once she'd moved from the country, she had made her lead the life of an urban prisoner. Addy had such a gregarious and friendly nature that Mrs Burton hated to think of all the hours that the poor animal had spent alone in the flat.

'Have some croutons,' her expansive neighbour said. He was holding out some kind of china terrine. He started spooning some crisp brown squares of bread into her soup. Mrs Burton was suddenly feeling dizzy, but she looked down at them floating. They became soggy in front of her eyes, but for a while they kept bobbing on the surface and they all seemed like desperate, drowning creatures.

Her soup no longer seemed like soup. As if she was hallucinating, she saw it as a dangerous lake and she felt she ought to dive in and try to save the drowning croutons. But somehow something stopped her and she could only stare at them in panic and watch them as they perished.

'Are you feeling all right?' the race-horse owner asked her. He was not very sensitive, but he noticed she was looking peculiar.

Mrs Burton found she couldn't answer him. She couldn't say she felt all right. By now only one of her croutons retained any distinct shape. The rest had sunk into the liquid. It was this last lonely crouton that Mrs Burton found the most disturbing, for at moments it seemed to be her mother, at other moments it seemed to be Addy.

Before she had died, Mrs Burton's mother had been very brave and angry sitting in her wheel-chair in the home for arthritics. She had watched television most of the day until the arthritis had gone into her lids and crippled their muscles so that she was unable to keep her eyes open. After that she had just sat in her wheel-chair, so immobile she'd seemed like a statue.

Mrs Burton had gone to read to her once a week. But her visits had never been much of a success. Invariably her mother had told her she was reading too fast or complained that she was mumbling. It had never been very long before her mother irritably ordered her to stop reading because she didn't like the book that Mrs Burton had chosen.

The food in the home for arthritics had been ill-cooked and unappetizing. Mrs Burton continually sent her mother various delicacies so that the old lady could have some relief from the dreariness of the diet of the institution. When she visited, she brought smoked salmon and jars of taramasalata and pâté. But her mother always left them untouched on the table beside her wheel-chair. On one occasion she had screamed at Mrs Burton like a child. Tears started pouring down her cheeks. She had reminded her that if you couldn't take any exercise, it was impossible to work up any appetite. She had also been very annoyed by some hot-house grapes that Mrs Burton had once brought her. Her mother had refused to taste one single grape. She complained that the pips would get stuck in her teeth.

Yet Mrs Burton had always felt guilty that she had not invited her mother to come and live with her. Once her mother had become a total invalid, she still insisted she couldn't bear to be a burden on the family. If this claim had been a lie, Mrs Burton had taken it literally. She knew she could never have tolerated the presence of that critical old lady who would have sat all day long like some huge accusing statue in her household.

If she'd agreed to nurse her mother, the old woman would have become magnified by Mrs Burton until she seemed colossal. Her mother's fury at her own paralysis would have paralysed Mrs Burton. It would have prevented her from giving any love and attention to Mavina, for her confidence would have shrivelled like a prune, totally withered by her inability to make any reparation for the cruel disease that had stricken the old lady.

Even when her mother was in perfect health, she had always had an intensely dissatisfied nature. Her mother's bitterness had once been diffused, but her arthritis had brought all its disparate strands together, and it had found a perfect focus. Imprisoned by her pain-ridden and crippled body, she had felt she could give full vent to all her ancient indignation, seeing it as finally justified.

Mrs Burton knew she could never have allowed her home to be dominated by someone who sat in her wheel-chair sometimes expressing her rage by stoical silences, sometimes releasing it in distressing little displays of demonic petulance. Even in her very best periods of bravery, Mrs Burton's mother would have sat with eyes closed in her daughter's household like some disturbing and vast grey monument that had been erected to commemorate the destruction of every human hope.

At the dinner party, Mrs Burton picked up her spoon and mashed her last lonely crouton until it became invisible. She was aware that her neighbour was staring at her in horror. She had squashed it with much too much violence. He was obviously shocked by her table manners. He thought, that like an infant, she was playing with her food.

The crouton had completely disappeared, but Mrs Burton felt freezing cold. Her neighbour found her weird, but he could not guess how restrained she was being. She would have liked to have screamed and jumped up from the table and run out of this loathsome house where ghosts had appeared in her soup and accused her of deserting them at the very moment when they'd most needed her. Mrs Burton controlled herself and she found her own control a little despicable. She felt deranged by guilts from the past and the present, but she disguised it and her need to do so seemed craven. She thought it shameful she was so frightened to arouse the disapproval of people for whom she had only scorn.

The dinner continued. More and more food was served. The courses seemed endless. Mrs Burton sat there and quietly endured this dreadful meal, imprisoned by her good manners. She picked at some duck and she dabbed her lips with her napkin in the most lady-like fashion. She did nothing further that could disturb her bovine neighbour. He chatted on to her and she kept nodding and giving him no indication that when she helped herself to a tiny portion of summer pudding she found it an agonizing struggle to force herself to take even the tiniest mouthful. That evening it sickened her to taste anything that was the colour of blood.

When Mrs Fitz-James finally got up from the table after the coffee and the brandy she was followed by all the other women and she started leading them up the stairs to some bathroom where she wanted them 'to powder their noses'. The men remained in the dining-room and they continued drinking port and brandy.

And then Mrs Burton suddenly rebelled. She felt it would be unsufferable to join the little feminine and perfumed cortège of Mrs Fitz-James. She refused to go up to her hostess's luxurious bedroom and sit around with all these ladies who would make her feel like a used tea-bag while they prinked and gushed and admired each other's dresses, shoes and hair-styles.

No one noticed Mrs Burton as she slipped into the hall and got her coat. She opened the front door very quickly and went out into the street. She was glad it was rude to leave without saying goodbye. She was relieved that at last she had done something impolite.

She was fortunate for she saw a taxi and hailed it. On the way back to her flat, she wondered if she had a fever. Once she got back to her building, her legs were shaking as she went upstairs. There was not a sound when she turned her key in the flat door. As she came in, she saw with horror that Addy was not on the sofa. It took Mrs Burton only a few seconds to find her. Addy had dragged herself into the corner behind the armchair very near where she'd done her digging. She was lying with her face to the wall.

Mrs Burton went over and picked her up. Addy felt heavy and rigid. Her amber eyes had gone dark. They had the sightless stare of glass eyes. There was no life in Addy's plump body and yet her fur still seemed to continue to have a life of its own. It felt soft and comforting and warm.

Mrs Burton stood very still in the centre of her flat cradling Addy. She noticed how quiet it was. She realized it would always be unpleasantly quiet in the flat now that she would be living completely on her own. She felt much less distraught than she'd felt at the dinner party. She had allowed Addy to die all alone, but it seemed futile and self-deceiving to torment herself with self-recriminations. If she had missed Mrs Fitz-James's dinner party and stayed in the flat with Addy, those few hours would have been unable to make reparation for all the days that Addy had spent locked up like a convict condemned to solitary.

Addy was released now. Addy had been too simple. She had seemed to believe that if she behaved as humans taught her, they would start to treat her as an equal, whereas they were only capable of endowing her with certain human characteristics. According to their varying self-indulgent whims they could turn her into a figure which embodied their shifting guilts and fantasies. But Addy had never managed to have any ultimate reality for the people she had been attached to. Once the veneer of their projections was stripped away, they could only see her as a dog.

Mrs Burton tightened her grip on Addy's motionless body. Through the years Addy had been a witness to so many painful moments in Mrs Burton's life. She had also been the speechless witness to many moments of happiness. Addy's relationship with Mrs Burton had lasted much longer than the latter's marriage.

Addy felt like a stuffed toy. Mrs Burton wished she could feel more regret for her death. All the wriggling life and bark had gone from Addy, but she was no longer threatened by decrepitude and pain and loneliness. Mrs Burton felt exhausted and frightened of the future. She envied Addy her stillness.

She suddenly wanted to make the dog a little gesture, and she couldn't tell whether her behaviour sprang from remorse or affection. As if she was hoping that her animal victim could help comfort her sense of desolation, she bent over and buried her face in the woolly thicket of Addy's brown fur.

JESSIE KESSON

*

Stormy Weather

'You lot gone deaf! First bell's gone!'

Bertha stood at the dormitory door. Cocooned within a subtle 'insolence of office', recently acquired when she had been promoted from being 'one of the orphanage girls' to 'orphanage servant'.

'Lying steaming there!'

'Steaming', uttered in Bertha's voice, sounded an obscenity. Nobody, Chris remembered from her vigil at the window, had 'steamed' more than Bertha herself, when she had occupied a bed in the dormitory.

Fat! Oozing! Pimply! The remembered image flashed through Chris's mind – a dirk unsheathed . . .

'And *you!*' Bertha said, directing her attention to Chris.

'I'm up and dressed,' Chris pointed out, cool, logically, without turning her face from the window.

'ANYHOW!' Bertha withdrew herself on a word which, although bereft of meaning, she could always infuse with threat.

'Little children love ye one another . . .'

Despite long acquaintance with the command on the large text on the wall, signed by St Paul, the girls in the dormitory had never truly 'loved one another'. Self-preservation was their first priority. Urgent, yet fragile and easily shattered.

'First bell's gone,' Chris felt in honour bound to remind her still recumbent colleagues. But without emphasis. Without insistence. Reluctant to let go of the rare moments of privacy that only early morning could bring. Desired always, but essential on Fridays. Band of Hope night.

Hope was indeed the operative word. It had taken the minister time and patience to persuade Matron to let the older girls 'out' on Friday evenings on a two-mile walk to the church hall for the weekly temperance meeting.

Matron was no doubt aware that whatever fate the future held for the girls, none of them, at least in this period of their lives, was in any danger of 'drinking themselves to death'. A realist, Matron sensed that there was more danger in a two-mile unchaperoned evening 'outing'.

On top of which, she was a strategist of the first order; with a dash of the subtle, delaying tactics of the first Elizabeth.

Since the minister was also a trustee of the orphanage, his requests were almost impossible to deny. Matron had conceded, 'allowing' the girls to attend the Band of Hope. But with one proviso – depending on the weather!

It was this proviso that kept Chris glued to her position in front of the window, searching for signs in the morning sky. For it didn't need rain itself to cancel the weekly outing. The 'threat' of rain was enough for Matron to defy the minister, and the whole United Free Kirk of Scotland.

Oh! Never had a small girl of fourteen been up against such a powerful adversary. And never was an autumn and winter so full of Fridays which 'threatened rain'! Nor even more the runes of childhood so fervently invoked could diminish the threat:

> Rainie, rainie rattlestanes
> dinna rain on me
> rain on Johnnie Groat's hoose
> far across the sea . . .

Second bell clanging through the dormitory stirred the sleepers into disgruntled wakefulness, and filled the room with complaint. Alice, unaware at last of Chris keeping vigil, and of the reason for such a vigil, shuffled towards the window.

'It's going to rain,' she prophesied. 'It's going to pour! We won't get to the Band of Hope tonight.'

'It could clear up before night,' Chris said, ignoring the gloat that had sounded in Alice's voice. 'It sometimes does,' she reflected, taking a last lingering look at the skyline, before making her way out of the dormitory.

'And,' she reminded Alice, in an attempt to get a little of her own back, 'it's *your* turn to empty all the chamber-pots – except the boys'. I emptied them all yesterday.'

'I always get the dirty jobs,' Alice protested, 'always me!'

'Not always,' Chris pointed out, reaching for the door, anxious to escape the 'my-turn-your-turn' arguments that began each day – '*I* get landed with *most* of the dirty jobs.'

She did too! A fact confirmed when she reached the boys' dormitory for her first task of the morning – stripping their beds, examining the mattresses of the incontinent boys.

No Hamlet was ever forced into reaching a decision such as the one that confronted Chris. To report or not to report that large, damp stain that spread itself across James Dobie's mattress? No thought of nobility troubled her mind. It was the pact that caused her dilemma. Formed between herself and James Dobie in their early years in the orphanage.

'I can't find no bottom to your hunger,' Matron had said of them, anxious, puzzled as if the fault was her own. 'There never seems to be enough for you.'

'Table manners' which they had to memorize in their first weeks in the orphanage had no 'small print' as warning!

> In silence I must take my seat
> and say my Grace before I eat
> Must for my food with patience wait
> Till I am asked to hand my plate
> Must turn my head to cough or sneeze
> And when I ask, say 'if you please'.
>
> I must not speak a useless word
> For children should be seen not heard

I must not talk about my food
Nor fret if I don't think it good.
My mouth with food I must not crowd
Nor while I'm eating speak aloud.

When told to rise then I must put
My chair away with noiseless foot
and lift my heart to God above
In praise for all His wondrous love

It never mentioned porridge! Nor the fact that if you didn't eat your porridge you got no tea and bread and butter to follow.

Orphanage porridge, made the night before, so that by morning you could cut it up into thick, lukewarm slices, sent even Chris's voracious, indiscriminate stomach rising up in revolt. James Dobie became her eager and willing receptacle. Thus, the pact was formed. Wolfing down his own portion, while Chris picked warily round the edge of her plate. The transference of plates, with years of practice behind it, was a miracle of dexterity and timing!

All such subterfuges, Chris reflected, never escaped the gimlet eyes of her fellow-orphans, and had to be paid for – help with their home lessons, the coin in demand.

Engulfed in a passing moment of self-pity, assailed by the long-lost, but still remembered freedom of home, Chris struggled towards a decision.

Had James been less incontinent this morning, she would simply have turned his mattress, concealed the 'evidence' and sent up a prayer. 'Don't let Matron be in her examining mood.'

The risk was too great. On Friday, of *all* days, when good behaviour was an unspoken, but important, proviso for attendance at the Band of Hope.

'James Dobie has wet his bed, Matron.'

Nobody in the whole wide world could twist a situation with the dexterity of Matron. Chris suddenly found herself the target of Matron's displeasure.

'Did you waken James Dobie last night?'

'Yes, Matron'.

'Are you sure?'

'Yes, Matron.'

'Did he use his chamber pot?'

'Yes, Matron.'

'How do you know he used it?'

'I heard him!'

'Oh traitor untrue,' said the king 'now thou has betrayed me thrice, who would have thought that thou . . .'

James Dobie had not yet learned *Morte D'Arthur* at school, but complete comprehension of it was held within his eyes, accusing Chris from the opposite side of the breakfast table.

The flourish with which he scraped his porridge plate clean, before clasping it firmly to his chest and settling down and back in his chair to concentrate on Chris, dithering around the mess of congealed porridge which now confronted her – no tea, no bread – a dark beginning to an already cloud-threatened day.

'Christina Forbes!'

Bertha's voice broke through the argumentative 'whose-turn-to-do-what' claims that always preceded washing-up, and halted Chris in her assertions. For full titles were used amongst themselves only on formal – or foreboding – occasions.

'Matron wants to see you in her sitting-room – at once!'

'It's for something bad?' Her question, tentatively put, was purely rhetorical since it would not be answered by Bertha in her official capacity.

'I *know* it's for something bad.'

Chris flicked swiftly through her memory for recent, but so far undiscovered sins of omission and/or commission. 'I know. By the sound of your voice.'

'So this,' Matron stood guardian over Chris's opened school-bag on her desk, waving aloft a small, oft-creased bundle of jotter pages, '*this* is why you are always so keen on the Band of

Hope. I might have suspected it. Who is the boy who writes that he "can't wait for Friday night"?'

'Till I see you again' – silently Chris completed the sentence for Matron, and, in the doing, recollected every word written on the pages. The lines of 'X's' for kisses, the P.S. of regret 'wish they were not on paper, but were real . . .', embarrassment negated by the inner certainty.

'At least there's not *one* dirty thing in the letters . . .'

'A boy at school, Matron – he lives with his grandfather, he's *nearly* an orphan!' Chris volunteered the information in the hope that such a common cause might influence Matron. 'He's got navy stockings with yellow tops . . .' Suddenly she heard herself sharing with Matron the few facts she herself knew about the boy. '. . . He's got a bike. He can freewheel down Barclay's Brae without once touching his handlebars – you'd like him if you knew him. I know you would!'

Evincing no sign of a shared 'liking', Matron set the pages down on her desk.

'The thing is,' she concluded, after long consideration, 'you're getting too old for the Band of Hope. It's time we were thinking of your *future*. Getting ready for it, when you go into service. There's the old sewing-machine – we could make a start on Friday nights, teaching you to use it – underwear, night-dresses, petticoats, things you'll need when you start your job . . .'

'What punishment?'

Her colleagues clustered around her in the scullery, avid for her downfall.

'None.'

'*No* punishment?' The disbelief in Bertha's voice atoned for much.

'None,' Chris confirmed, thrusting up her sleeves to attack the washing-up. 'I can't be bothered going to the Band of Hope tonight,' she informed them casually. 'I'm getting too old for it, it's for children, Matron says. She's going to teach me to use her *new* sewing-machine.'

'*Her* new sewing-machine?' Bertha asked aghast.

'Her new sewing-machine. To sew my frocks for leaving.'

'Frocks!' Bertha grumbled, 'all *I* had to make was night-gowns and petticoats!'

'You're not *me*,' Chris reminded her, plunging her hands into the sink, '*are* you now?'

> It's raining
> It's pouring
> The old man is snoring.

ANNE DEVLIN

*

Passages

I have a strange story to tell. Even now it is not easy for me to
remember how much I actually did hear or see, and how much
I imagined. The journey between the shore of memory and the
landfall of imagination is an unknown distance, because for
each voyager it is a passage through a different domain. This
story has a little to do with mapping that passage, but only a
little: it is also a confession.

In the summer of '72 I was travelling in Ireland, calling on
friends in Dublin, seeing relatives in the West, putting minor
touches to my book on dreams, looking for more folk-tales, and
eavesdropping on people's dreams without drawing too much
attention to the fact that it was my profession. I have been
involved in analysis for several years. I'm not popular with
colleagues because they see me as a kind of 'pop' analyst − a
collector of stories. And in a way that is what I am. On this
occasion, while I was staying in Dublin at Sandycove in a
house belonging to some friends who had gone abroad for a few
months, a girl came to see me.

She had heard I was in Dublin, indeed she knew that I was
expected to give a public lecture at Trinity that evening on the
subject of my book and so she came to see me because she had
a dream to tell me. This is not so strange as it sounds. I had
asked several of my colleagues at the university if any of the
undergraduates they taught would be prepared to volunteer
unusual or disturbing dreams which might help in my research.
I was not interested in individual analysis, or the concept of
'cure' − I made that perfectly clear: I was interested merely in

the content of dream stories as a source for fiction. My earlier publication had been on 'History and the Imagination: a study of Nordic, Greek and Celtic Mythology'. My next inevitable step was to turn my attention to dream territory. I had advertised and asked for people with particularly unusual, disturbing or prophetic dreams to come forward; I had promised privacy in that I did not wish to know the identity of the people concerned.

An old college friend of mine who was teaching history at Trinity rang me on the morning the girl came to see me. He explained that one of his students had a dream to tell which she did not wish to write down but which she thought might be of interest to me. I agreed to see her at his insistence. This was the girl who came. I was more aware of the dangers of exposing dreams than most others; dreams are very confessional; they offer a power relationship to the hearer in that they ask for absolution. They are a freeing device for the speaker, but the sin has to rest with someone: the priest absolves the sin he also carries with him; like the Christ figure he carries the cross that others may be free. This was not a role I cherished or viewed with any great pleasure. I was very wary of people who did invite others to unburden themselves – the result could only be masochism or sadism: the wilful acceptance of suffering or the inflicting of pain: there was no other way. I would either be hurt or hurt in my turn: being human I could not remain neutral. I met the girl with extreme reluctance; and wondered at her motives for wishing to confront me with her story.

Her appearance did nothing to allay my fears; in fact, it increased what I already felt would be a momentous and disturbing meeting. I remember her now as looking very child-like: she had the sort of paedophilic look of a small elf – which some men find appealing. She was tense and anxious, as though at some point she had taken the decision to hold back. I did not like her much. I find that sort of woman manipulative; full of little betrayals, because of all the insecurity of her knowing that she did not rank among the women. Fear was written all over her face.

She looked as if she were on the run from something. And I knew, because I had seen such cases before, that she was haunted. During our opening small talk her utterances came out in jagged phrases, exclamations, sentences begun then abandoned, then taken up with a different subject: she made so many promising beginnings yet never knew quite how to complete them. But in relation to one thing she was utterly articulate: the story she told.

This, then, was how she began:

'When I was thirteen I was invited to spend the long summer vacation at the home of a friend who lived in Dublin. Sheelagh Burke was at school with me, we both attended the Dominican Convent in Portstewart. I was a day-girl; my father owned a newspaper shop in the Diamond in Portstewart. Sheelagh was a boarder; her parents lived in Dublin, where her father had something to do with property investment. I was never very clear. The thing about the upper middle classes even in Ireland is that the source of their income is never very precisely located; it is only a petty bourgeois mentality like mine which would seek to pin people to their incomes.'

The girl had a disconcerting habit of standing back and analysing her statements – placing them in a social context thereby dismissing her own assumptions. Her tutor said she was a natural historian, if only she had the confidence to follow it through. I understood too that there had been some disturbance in her studies of a few years, but was not clear about the nature of this, and had not asked. These thoughts were going through my mind as she continued.

'My parents were delighted at the invitation: this was precisely why they had wanted me to go to grammar school – to make friends like Sheelagh Burke. The Burke house at Sandycove

was not far from here, and it was remarkable. It was at the far
end of that long stretch of coast road which runs away from
Trinity corner in the direction of the Dun Laoghaire ferry
terminal, beyond the Martello Tower and still further. I
remember arriving there so well. The house formed part of a
terrace set back from the main road. There was a small green
in front and a gravel path or drive separated the green from the
four double-fronted Georgian houses which stood there; the
house belonging to the Burkes was the last of the four – that is,
the one furthest from Dublin city. Like the other houses it was
three storeys high and had a basement, with a separate entrance
by the railings outside the front door. The basement was
something new in the way of houses to me. In a seaside town
like Portstewart there is only the unrelenting parade of low-
lying bungalows in wide bare salt-stripped gardens, occasionally
relieved by some modern two-storey houses, a row or two of
Victorian terraces and of course the Convent itself, a castle of
Gothic proportions perched on the cliff face. I had never been
in a house with a basement before, and absolutely nothing of
the neighbourhood I grew up in equalled the elegance of this
fine wide-roomed house, with its brass handles and porticoes,
wooden stairways and cornices. A further treat was still to
come with that house – the waves of the Irish Sea broke upon
the back wall. The garden literally ran away to the sea. From
the music-room windows we had uninterrupted views of the
sea and the day marked out for us by the comings and goings
of the Holyhead ferry.

I was given a room at the top of the house on the same floor
as Sheelagh and Peggy – who lived in – and the view from my
window was of Howth Head. I even remember the colour of
the room: it was a strong bold rose colour and the walls were
full of prints of flowers and birds. The curtains matched the
cover on the bed. I recorded every detail of this house,
committed it to memory like I did my Latin grammar. I never
questioned that this too was part of my general education.
After a time it became clear to me why I had been asked to

spend the summer with Sheelagh; she was lonely, there wasn't anyone else around. Her parents were remarkable by their absence. Her father, whom we saw fleetingly, flew in and out of Dublin airport with such regularity it made my head spin. Places like Zurich, Munich and New York crept in the conversation by way of explaining these disappearances. I think I met her mother as she was passing through the music room one day on her way to lunch. And even though she lived in the house and was not flying in and out of the country, we saw even less of her. I recall that she said something like: 'Hello, you're Sheelagh's little friend aren't you. How nice of you to come.' The only other inhabitants of the house appeared to be a brother who was a student at UCD, reading medicine or some suitably middle-class professional subject. Peggy, whom I have already mentioned, was a sort of housekeeper cum Nanny; her role was never very clearly defined. And as Peggy was slow on her feet and found the stairs too much from time to time, there was a young girl living in also to help. She lived in the basement and was called Moraig. I said that Sheelagh's brother was an inhabitant, that was not strictly true; he had a flat somewhere in the city, and only came home at weekends to eat Peggy's Sunday lunch.

You can imagine from this that we spent a good deal of time on our own, Sheelagh and I. We played tennis, or went swimming off the rocks at the bottom of the garden; occasionally we took long bus rides into the city and ended up having tea and cakes at Bewleys. I had never had tea in a café before, and certainly not without an adult present. It seemed to me, because of the absence of adults in our lives that summer, that we had in fact grown up; the world was unmoved by our innocence. When we ordered tea in Bewleys it appeared. No one said, as they might have done in a tea shop at home, 'What are you two children up to?' They took us seriously in Dublin. I felt I had entered a newly sophisticated world. In a few short weeks of being at that house, my confidence grew. I discovered that beds left unmade were magically made up. Clothes, even socks, could be hurled around the room with no fear of losing them; they would reappear fresh and clean a few days later. The best china and glass was used without restraint; and, even if broken, was always replaced or renewed without fuss. It put all my mother's restraints and little fussy ways in perspective: 'If you don't pick that up you will lose it; if you don't tidy that away it won't last; we can't use the best china we might break it.' For the first time I felt I had an answer to her. What did it matter when life could be lived like this? I knew then that something was ruined for me. I have dwelt rather long on this beginning because I wanted to remember what it was like up to the point when everything changed, and not try to suppress any of the details. Perhaps, though, I have romanticized it a little, but I don't think so. The important thing is this is how it impressed me.

The music room, as it was called, was a long rectangle running from front to back of the house on the ground floor. It was a very grand room with a wide marble fireplace, two squashy sofas and a couple of battered armchairs; it had a sanded pine floor and a large indestructible and rather tatty rug – which Sheelagh said was Indian. This was considered the children's room. It had been abandoned to the Burke children several years before; the smarter apartments and drawing room, which was out of bounds to us, were on the floor above. I never knew why it earned the name of the music room, except perhaps it might have referred to the volume of noise emanating from it; because the only concession to a musical instrument that I could see was an upright piano which nobody appeared to play or knew how to, standing against the same wall as the fireplace. On the opposite wall to the piano and the fireplace ran row upon row of silent books, and I believe there was a record player somewhere. But I can't quite remember where it was situated. Long small-paned windows filled the short walls at either end of the room so that the light ran right through. From the Sandycove road to the Irish Sea the view was uninterrupted.

In the evenings when the wind coming off the sea rattled the windows, it was often quite noisy and indeed airy in the music room, even after the curtains were drawn. And it was on one such occasion while sitting in front of the fire with the wind fanning the flames, when Moraig had retreated to her basement, and Peggy was in bed with a cold, that we conceived of the idea of whiling away the evening by telling ghost stories. That is, I would. Sheelagh never told stories. In fact, she could never remember the important details, and she would often have to turn to me and say: 'What comes next? I forget.'

I began with a favourite of both of us. I was not very original. I often told the same story twice, but usually with embellishments or twists. And Sheelagh was such a good listener and such an awful rememberer that every time she heard the story she said it sounded different. This encouraged me tremendously. I began with a story of Le Fanu's about the expected visitors who never arrive: at one point in the evening the family who are waiting for the visitors hear the sound of carriage wheels roll on the gravel, they all rush outside and find no one. What I had not allowed for when I was telling this favourite tale of ours, was the fact that right outside the music room was a gravel drive. And, at precisely the part in the story when I started to explain that at the time the family heard the wheels of the carriage on the gravel, the expected visitor had died, at precisely that moment a car drew up very slowly on the gravel drive outside the music-room window. Sheelagh took one leap off the carpet where we were sitting in front of the fire and fled out of the room, saying that she didn't want to hear any more. I was left in the music room, still sitting in front of the fire, amazed at her alacrity. Normally, I would have been laughing myself sick at my ability to scare her, as I had often done in the past, but the trouble was this time I had scared myself. The massive coincidence necessary to tell an effective ghost story had just occurred. At precisely the time when I was explaining the significance of ghostly wheels on gravel as a portent of death – a car drew up. In all my years of telling ghost stories at school, and arranging for bells to ring or doors to open at crucial moments, I had never stage-managed anything so effective as that car drawing up when it did.

I found myself sitting in the dark of the room with only the light from the fire throwing grotesque shadows on to the walls and the groans of the wind whistling around me as company. I knew then that I could not bring myself to move through the darkness towards the door or beyond into the dark hall and then up three flights of stairs past all those closed doorways and little landings to my bed. I was riveted. So I stayed sitting still with my back to the fire, watching the silent occupants of the darkness, until I calmed down. Once or twice I imagined I saw the handle of the door turning, so I tried to think of something pleasant. But when I looked away to the window all the elements of stories I had told in broad daylight on the beach, or in the gym or the second-form common room, began to reassemble around me. And I wished I hadn't had such a fertile imagination. Then, just when I managed to convince myself of my silliness and was beginning to work out how I could make another story out of this incident, something happened which arrested me so completely that I thought my heart would stop. From behind me in the fire I heard a little cry; not a groan, like the wind made, of that I am absolutely clear. It began like a short gasp and became a rising crescendo of 'hah' sounds; each one was following the one before, and getting louder each time. I experienced a moment of such pure terror that I felt my heart would burst with the strain as I waited for the gasps to reach their topmost note. Suddenly, just when the sounds had come to a peak, I felt myself propelled from the room and ran screaming upstairs. I take no responsibility for that action; a voice simply broke from my throat which corresponded to screams.

In this state, I ran up three flights and straight into the arms of the warm, white-clad and still smelling of sleep Peggy. She had been under sedation all day because of her cold when the screams brought her to the banisters. Sheelagh was standing

behind her, clutching Peggy's nightgown and howling like a
lost dog. Peggy was furious rather than consoling I seem to
remember. She smacked both of us to make me stop screeching
and Sheelagh stop howling, and then asked us what we thought
we were up to. 'Bringing the house down like that' was how
she put it. Characteristically Sheelagh blamed me for scaring
her by telling the story; I blamed her for leaving me downstairs.
Peggy resorted to her usual threats of 'Right Madam. You go
straight back to Portstewart in the morning. Do ye hear?' And
for the first time in the six weeks I had been there I wished she
meant it. I had had enough of the freedom of the place; inside,
a small voice that I thought I had grown out of was saying: 'Oh
Mammy, I want to go home.' Eventually, she got us both back
to bed. Calmed, and much scolded, and therefore reassured, I
went to sleep.

I am always afraid to go to sleep. I have been ever since that
time, and still have lingering doubts about it. It has something
to do with going to sleep with one reality and waking up with
another. It was like this on that particular morning. It was late
when I woke; the morning boat to Holyhead leaving Dun
Laoghaire was already filling the space in the horizon between
the shore and Howth Head at the half-way point. I did not
wake up myself as I normally do, but was wakened instead by
the arrival of Peggy carrying breakfast. She told me to eat up
and get dressed and come downstairs when I was ready. There
were two men who wished to talk to me. Sheelagh, she
explained, was already awake and I could see her after I spoke
to the men. She busied herself picking up my clothes and
laying things out while I ate breakfast. What surprised me was
that she stayed until I had finished and then supervised my
washing. I had reached the stage where I was bashful about
dressing and wished she would go. But she didn't. When I was
ready we went downstairs. I was absolutely convinced now
that something momentous had occurred. 'How come Moraig
didn't bring breakfast this morning?' I asked, as I reached the
foot of the stairs with the tray. Looking back, I am amazed at

the ease with which I had become accustomed to being waited upon. Peggy did not answer but said: 'Come and meet the gentlemen who would like to talk to you.' We went into the music room and I have to admit to experiencing a momentary shudder as we passed through the door.

My suspicions were further confirmed at finding Sheelagh's father there, along with two men. The room looked different in the morning light; below, the boat was still slipping past Howth and out to the open sea. On the other side of me I caught sight of a number of cars parked on the green verge; there were some people moving up and down the basement steps. One of the men in the room moved between me and this view from the window. He shook hands and called himself Mr Maguire. He then introduced the other stranger, his friend Mr O'Rourke. I can't recall much of what they looked like except that they were both tall and Mr Maguire was heavier than Mr O'Rourke. But I guessed that they were policemen.

'We want you tell us now,' said Maguire, 'what it was that made you scream last night.'

I couldn't believe it; I turned to Peggy in alarm. Had she called the police because I had screamed? Before I could reply, Sheelagh's father uttered the first words he had ever spoken to me.

'Now don't worry, just tell Mr Maguire what happened. No one is going to hurt you.'

Peggy squeezed my arm to encourage me I expect, but immediately I decided that this was precisely what they would do – hurt me – and burst into loud sobs. When I stopped crying, they persisted with the questions and so I explained how the ghost story had frightened us. I explained about the wheels on the gravel drive; how Sheelagh had fled from the room leaving me; how I sat on until I thought I heard sounds coming from the fire behind me.

'Voices from the flame?' Mr O'Rourke said, looking meaningfully. 'You heard a voice talking to you from the fire?'

'Now that's enough Jack!' Maguire said.

'Well not exactly a voice talking, more calling out,' I explained. I am quite convinced that O'Rourke felt himself in the presence of a mystic who was in touch with speaking flames. But the other policeman wasn't so sure about the presence of the Holy Ghost in the proceedings, he kept bringing me back to what I actually did hear.

'Can you repeat the sounds you thought you heard?' he asked.

'I'm not sure,' I said, 'but I'll try.'

I began to call in the way I thought I had heard the voice call out the evening before. To make the sound I had to take short gasps, and eventually when I was quite breathless I stopped.

'Why did you stop?' Maguire asked.

'Because I didn't hear the rest,' I explained.

'Why?'

'Because I was screaming so loudly at the time.'

And that was all. The interview was over and so was the holiday. Sheelagh and her father drove me to the station later and I did return to Portstewart on that day after all. I would have been glad enough about it except that I felt I was going home in some disgrace, and I was not exactly sure why. Sheelagh spoke very little to me, she seemed very downcast, and told me that she was being sent to an aunt in the West of Ireland for the rest of the summer. 'I hate it there. I'll go mad with boredom,' she said. The last time I saw her she was waving goodbye from the platform at Connelly Station. She did not return to school in September, and she did not write to me as she promised. My parents never questioned my early return as I was sure they would. I gave up telling stories after that.'

'But what happened?' I asked. I found myself growing impatient. 'And what has all this to do with dreams?'

'You're rushing me,' she said. 'And I have to unfold it slowly. They never told me and I didn't ask because somewhere deep down I already knew that it was something profoundly disturbing. Then, one day, when seven years had passed, the truth surfaced to confront me, and this is what happened. I went to Queen's as a first-year history student in '68; the first year of the disturbances in the city. But I wasn't really interested in politics and knew little about what was happening, except that there were mass meetings in the union, the McMordie Hall and in the streets. It was the beginning of the civil rights movement, when educated Catholics had awakened to political consciousness. Coming from Portstewart I never had any sense of the discrimination that Catholics in the city seemed to feel. It never occurred to me that there were official and unofficial histories. Or that Protestants could go through school never having heard of Parnell or the Land League. I always thought that history was simply a matter of scholarship. In the seminars during my first year at university the students were fighting and hacking and forging out of the whole mass of historical detail a theory which made it right for them to march through the streets of Belfast to demand equal rights for Catholics. It was the most exciting year of my life; inevitably I fell in love.

He was a counterpoint to everything my father with his little shop and cautious peace-keeping ways stood for. He was outspoken and clever and courageous; he didn't care who he offended, and he held back for nothing and no one. Until that time I had spent my whole life living on the edge of the kind of respectability that people who run a corner shop find necessary in order to secure a trade and therefore their livelihood. I had heard my father humour the diverse opinions of so many of the customers that I grew to believe opinions were something one expressed but did not necessarily believe in, or indeed act upon. As we ran a newsagent's it became the venue for discussion of current events, particularly on a Sunday morning, when the locals would stroll in to collect the 'sundies' and debate the week's news at leisure.

'It's about time O'Neill got the finger out over this free-trade business. Why should Lemass do all the running?'

'Ah, now, Mr O'Neill's a good man,' I can hear my father interrupt. 'He sends his girl to the convent. Did you know that?'

'No, it's not the same O'Neill. You're thinking of the brother.'

'It's not a brother; he's the man's uncle.'

'That's just the trouble, the government's full of O'Neills; it's very confusing.'

My father always had a good word to say about everyone. If any politician was criticized he was quick to find some redeeming feature. With the result that I too became something of an apologist when it came to historical circumstances. That is, until I found myself walking en route from the university to the City Hall beside a provoking and thoroughly objectionable undergraduate: John Mulhern. I remember going home for the weekend following some of the first civil rights marches Belfast had witnessed, and finding my father fuming over the early dispatches of the Sunday papers.

'Fools and trouble-makers that's all they are! We have a fine, peaceful little country here. What do they have to go making trouble for?'

I kept my involvement a secret and refused to be drawn into any of the discussions in the shop which ranged during the eleven o'clock Mass. It was a feature of most Sunday mornings that the women went to Mass while the men stayed in the papershop. Then I heard my father say, 'I can't afford a political viewpoint!' as someone tried to draw him out. 'That is a political viewpoint – pure petty bourgeoisie self-interest' was my unexpected reply. It came straight out of the mouth of John Mulhern. I knew I should not have said it (a) because I couldn't justify it, and (b) because I had as good as betrayed my father by taking sides against him in the shop. There was a deafening silence, so much so that you could actually hear the waves crashing along the wall of the promenade some distance down the hill.

'That's the stuff! You young ones with your education will

tell them boys at Stormont where to get off!' said the man who had provoked the row in the first place. My father, whose anger was all in his face until that point, burst out, 'If that's all the good a university education has done for you, I rue the day you ever went to that place.'

The conversation was over. I fled into the back of the shop and he followed me. 'Your mother and I broke our backs scraping and saving to give you a chance. If this is how you repay us you can take yourself out of here back to your friends in Belfast with their clever remarks and smart ways; but don't ever come here again, shaming me in front of my friends.'

We never talked about anything important after that; I withdrew and so did they. I was thrown almost completely on to my friends in the city until I ceased to come home at all. My parents had ceased to expect me to. Occasionally I suppose they would read about this march or that and would guess I was there.

This is peripheral I know, but I am coming to the point. I said that the truth about that summer all those years before reappeared at a particular moment. I have given you all this detail because I am a historian and a materialist and somewhere in all these factors an answer may emerge as to why at this particular period in my life the truth, or a perception, should become clear to me.

It was the sixth of January when we returned to Belfast from Derry after the civil rights march which had taken four days to reach Derry had been attacked at Burntollet Bridge. I remember we, John and I, and two other students who lived in his house, were all feeling very fragile, very tired, and yet strangely elated. Something had been brought to the surface in the façade of political life – the cracks were throwing all sorts of horrors out into the sunlight. I had never slept with John before until that night.

We had begun to make love and I was lying back in the dark looking at him. I closed my eyes and suddenly I found myself crying out in a way which was strangely familiar: I uttered or heard myself utter a series of small gasps until at the point when the note rose to its highest point I opened my eyes. Then I screamed and screamed and screamed. I imagined that John would strangle me and screamed out in terror. After that the room was full of lights and voices. As soon as the lights came on of course I was no longer afraid of him. The other students in the house thought I ought to have a sedative so a doctor was called. He tried to get me to take a sleeping pill, but I only wanted to rid myself of what I knew. 'She was murdered. Moraig was murdered. He strangled her.' I was rambling on incoherently, as it must have appeared to the onlookers, trying to piece together parts of the story of seven years before. I felt bombarded by signs and images and the meaning of events. They persisted in making me take the sleeping pill and so I gave in. Afterwards I resented having done so, because when I did reawaken I knew that I had passed from that state for ever, and would never arrive at a perception so intensely felt again. With the morning and the new awareness my parents came, and with them a chill. As though they had brought with them the bleak wind which blows in off the Atlantic along the prom and leaves small deposits of sea-salt in the corners of their mouths. I felt the ice kisses on my damp cheek and tasted the bitterness of those salt-years. Before them lay the wreck of a daughter in whom they have invested everything.

The last communication I had with my parents prior to that day was a letter from my mother on the first of January wishing me well for the New Year and informing me of the death of Sheelagh Burke. She had driven off a cliff at Westpoint – near her aunt's house in Galway a few days before. There is a faint irony in that; her banishment was from Dublin to Westpoint seven years before. It was as though everything had come full circle; some strange mystery had unravelled – wound down. I seem to remember that the tone of my mother's letter was half-reproachful as though in Sheelagh's death was some responsibility of mine. I put the letter in my bag and took it with me on the march; but I lost it somewhere on the road to Derry. I explain this detail again because it may also have been a factor prompting the truth of that evening when Moraig was murdered to the surface of my mind. You see, I too had come to feel that the whole event was the result of some strange invocation of mine. I had called up, or dreamed up, the death just as surely as if I had murdered Moraig.'

'But you didn't dream it; you say it happened!' I said, reminding her.

'I haven't told you the rest of the story.'

'So far you haven't told me anything original: this is either Sleeping Beauty or Alice in Wonderland!' I said irritably. 'But please go on.'

'Haven't you realized yet that at precisely the moment in my story when I was explaining the significance of wheels on the gravel drive as a sign of death, the car carrying the murderer drew up? I created the event. What is more I later heard a woman making love up to the point of strangulation when I began screaming for her. It was no mystical experience: I heard her cries coming up through the chimney passage. Apparently her bed was right next to the boxed-in fireplace in the basement. When I sat with my back to the fireplace I heard everything. Seven years later when I made love for the first time I re-experienced the earlier memory and found the truth.'

'The truth?'

'Yes. When I was making love and I opened my eyes one split second before I screamed out, I saw something. The face I was looking at was not the face of my lover.'

'Whose face did you see?'

'I saw Sheelagh's brother. I saw John Burke's face.'

We regarded each other openly for the first time, in the way two human beings do when the mask has slipped – stripped away by either love or fear – and familiar traces of another remembering show through.

'At what point in the story did you recognize me?' she asked.

'Very early on; but I wanted to hear you out. At one point you almost had me believing you were someone else. I found myself thinking that I was listening to another coincidental story. You changed the names and the house location; that was imaginative. But you rather over-dramatized my sister's death. She did not drive off the cliff at Westpoint. She died of a heroin overdose in a basement flat in Islington. She had become a drop-out a few years before and we lost touch with her. So you see reality is more ignominious. Still she would have liked your version better − it romanticized her. But then I seem to remember you have a panache for that. Why did you come here with this memory? I find it all very painful.'

'Why did I come?'

She had no sympathy for my pain; I had not stopped her but made her angry instead.

'You can ask me that? I have spent three years of my life in a hospital. Did you know?'

I shook my head.

'I can't sleep with the light out; I can't lie in the dark in case I see your face. For three years I took their drugs and their treatments but I kept my secret because I knew that the one thing which would cure me was that one day I would be able to confront you with the truth.'

'The truth? What is the truth?'

'You killed Moraig.'

'Your hallucination of one face on to another isn't proof of a person being a murderer.'

'Not proof − truth!' she said emphatically. 'The imagination presents or dramatizes as well as intuiting a reality which is nearer the truth than any perception we arrive at through understanding, that is what I believe. And that is what I came here to find out. If I haven't awoken to reality after all this time, then I have awoken to madness. If I'm not through to truth then I'm through to madness. I believe you murdered Moraig because I saw your face.'

'Have you told anyone else?'

'No one – not until now,' she said. 'I need an admission from you – not a denial. I am either sane or mad.'

'It's metaphysics. Sanity or insanity,' I said.

'It's not metaphysics. It's the difference between truth and lies.'

'Let me give you a better explanation of what happened – one you can live with. The car drawing up was a coincidence; it may or may not have had something to do with the murderer's arrival. But two half-hysterical little girls managed to convince themselves that they heard it and so it must be like that. A servant girl, Moraig, was murdered by her lover; and you heard her cries as you said, through the chimney passage. Now there is another factor which you haven't mentioned. One of those little girls had a massive crush on her friend's brother. She also knew that he was friendly with Moraig. She knew because she sometimes watched him; and perhaps she saw them exchanging glances. Isn't it possible that you saw his face when your lover – also called John – was making love to you for the first time because that was the face you wanted to see? You fused the murder of Moraig and the desire to see me into one single incident. And you went to great lengths to say how much you loved this other John – I found it a total diversion, an unconvincing obsession with that part of the story. Was it in case I guessed that you chose him for the resemblance between the names? John's name and mine are the same in reality and in the story. Why?'

'Because I wanted you to remember,' she said. 'I wanted to see your fear, as you have seen mine. Nothing you have said convinces me that you did not kill Moraig.'

'Don't persist with this,' I warned her. 'I've offered you a way out. You have a strong healthy young mind now – don't pursue this fantasy path any further.'

'That is exactly why I came to see you. To find my way back to a path I once knew. I don't want an explanation or a denial but I need an admission of your guilt before I can break out of this . . .' She paused as though she knew the word but could not use it; it came out eventually '. . . nightmare!'

At that point she began to cry.

I watched her very closely and realized for the first time that she was wrong; she did not need an admission; she was already free. In the telling of her story she had changed. She had lost the haunted look: she had confessed. After a while when she was quieter, I asked: 'What became of John Mulhern – your lover? You didn't say.'

'After that night it wasn't the same between us. He was afraid of me, and I think I was of him. I was taken home for a while to Portstewart and nursed by my mother. A short time after that I was admitted to a sanatorium, as I have already told you. I came to Dublin only this year, to resume my studies. They thought I was better out of the North. He became something in the paramilitary, and is very well known. I heard that he married someone recently, but I don't recall the details.'

'He didn't wait for you to heal?'

'No. He didn't wait.'

It was that time of day when the Holyhead ferry has passed the tip of Howth on its journey out to open sea; the sun shone on the rocks at Sandycove, and a woman, young, but a woman none the less – faint lines around the mouth marked her out – standing by a window, traced its slow passage forth. There would be many comings and goings to and from the shore, and many more passages to make as time went by; but at that moment, all her attention was with this one.

I looked away from the window; and found myself alone in the room.

*

Mannequin

Twelve o'clock. Dèjeuner chez Jeanne Veron, Place Vendôme.

Anna, dressed in the black cotton, chemise-like garment of the mannequin off duty was trying to find her way along dark passages and down complicated flights of stairs to the underground from where lunch was served.

She was shivering, for she had forgotten her coat, and the garment that she wore was very short, sleeveless, displaying her rose-coloured stockings to the knee. Her hair was flamingly and honestly red; her eyes, which were very gentle in expression, brown and heavily shadowed with kohl; her face small and pale under its professional rouge. She was fragile, like a delicate child, her arms pathetically thin. It was to her legs that she owed this dazzling, this incredible opportunity.

Madame Veron, white-haired with black eyes, incredibly distinguished, who had given them one sweeping glance, the glance of the connoisseur, smiled imperiously and engaged her at an exceedingly small salary. As a beginner, Madame explained, Anna could not expect more. She was to wear the jeune fille dresses. Another smile, another sharp glance.

Anna was conducted from the Presence by an underling who helped her to take off the frock she had worn temporarily for the interview. Aspirants for an engagement are always dressed in a model of the house.

She had spent yesterday afternoon in a delirium tempered by a feeling of exaggerated reality, and in buying the necessary make up. It had been such a forlorn hope, answering the advertisement.

The morning had been dreamlike. At the back of the wonderful decorated salons she had found an unexpected sombreness; the place, empty, would have been dingy and melancholy, countless puzzling corridors and staircases, a rabbit warren and a labyrinth. She despaired of ever finding her way.

In the mannequins' dressing-room she spent a shy hour making up her face — in an extraordinary and distinctive atmosphere of slimness and beauty; white arms and faces vivid with rouge; raucous voices and the smell of cosmetics; silken lingerie. Coldly critical glances were bestowed upon Anna's reflection in the glass. None of them looked at her directly . . . A depressing room, taken by itself, bare and cold, a very inadequate conservatory for these human flowers. Saleswomen in black rushed in and out, talking in sharp voices; a very old woman hovered, helpful and shapeless, showing Anna where to hang her clothes, presenting to her the black garment that Anna was wearing, going to lunch. She smiled with professional motherliness, her little, sharp, black eyes travelling rapidly from la nouvelle's hair to her ankles and back again.

She was Madame Pecard, the dresser.

Before Anna had spoken a word she was called away by a small boy in buttons to her destination in one of the salons: there, under the eye of a vendeuse, she had to learn the way to wear the innocent and springlike air and garb of the jeune fille. Behind a yellow, silken screen she was hustled into a leather coat and paraded under the cold eyes of an American buyer. This was the week when the spring models are shown to important people from big shops all over Europe and America: the most critical week of the season . . . The American buyer said that he would have that, but with an inch on to the collar and larger cuffs. In vain the saleswoman, in her best English with its odd Chicago accent, protested that that would completely ruin the chic of the model. The American buyer knew what he wanted and saw that he got it.

The vendeuse sighed, but there was a note of admiration in her voice. She respected Americans: they were not like the

English, who, under a surface of annoying moroseness of manner, were notoriously timid and easy to turn round your finger.

'Was that all right?' Behind the screen one of the saleswomen smiled encouragingly and nodded. The other shrugged her shoulders. She had small, close-set eyes, a long thin nose and tight lips of the regulation puce colour. Behind her silken screen Anna sat on a high white stool. She felt that she appeared charming and troubled. The white and gold of the salon suited her red hair.

A short morning. For the mannequin's day begins at ten and the process of making up lasts an hour. The friendly saleswoman volunteered the information that her name was Jeannine, that she was in the lingerie, that she considered Anna rudement jolie, that noon was Anna's lunch hour. She must go down the corridor and up those stairs, through the big salon then . . . Anyone would tell her. But Anna, lost in the labyrinth, was too shy to ask her way. Besides, she was not sorry to have time to brace herself for the ordeal. She had reached the regions of utility and oilcloth: the decorative salons were far overhead. Then the smell of food – almost visible, it was so cloudlike and heavy – came to her nostrils, and high-noted, and sibilant, a buzz of conversation made her draw a deep breath. She pushed a door open.

She was in a big, very low-ceilinged room, all the floor space occupied by long wooden tables with no cloths . . . She was sitting at the mannequins' table, gazing at a thick and hideous white china plate, a twisted tin fork, a wooden-handled stained knife, a tumbler so thick it seemed unbreakable.

There were twelve mannequins at Jeanne Veron's: six of them were lunching, the others still paraded, goddesslike, till their turn came for rest and refreshment. Each of the twelve was a distinct and separate type: each of the twelve knew her type and kept to it, practising rigidly in clothing, manner, voice and conversation.

Round the austere table were now seated Babette, the gamine, the traditional blonde enfant: Mona, tall and darkly beautiful, the femme fatale, the wearer of sumptuous evening gowns. Georgette was the garçonne: Simone with green eyes

Anna knew instantly for a cat whom men would and did adore, a sleek, white, purring, long-lashed creature . . . Eliane was the star of the collection.

Eliane was frankly ugly and it did not matter: no doubt Lilith, from whom she was obviously descended, had been ugly too. Her hair was henna-tinted, her eyes small and black, her complexion bad under her thick make-up. Her hips were extraordinarily slim, her hands and feet exquisite, every movement she made was as graceful as a flower's in the wind. Her walk . . . But it was her walk which made her the star there and earned her a salary quite fabulous for Madame Veron's, where large salaries were not the rule . . . Her walk and her 'chic of the devil' which lit an expression of admiration in even the cold eyes of American buyers.

Eliane was a quiet girl, pleasant-mannered. She wore a ring with a beautiful emerald on one long, slim finger, and in her small eyes were both intelligence and mystery.

Madame Pecard, the dresser, was seated at the head of the mannequins' table, talking loudly, unlistened to, and gazing benevolently at her flock.

At other tables sat the sewing girls, pale-faced, black-frocked – the workers heroically gay, but with the stamp of labour on them: and the saleswomen. The mannequins, with their sensual, blatant charms and their painted faces were watched covertly, envied and apart.

Babette the blonde enfant was next to Anna, and having started the conversation with a few good, round oaths at the quality of the sardines, announced proudly that she could speak English and knew London very well. She began to tell Anna the history of her adventures in the city of coldness, dark and fogs . . . She had gone to a job as a mannequin in Bond Street and the villainous proprietor of the shop having tried to make love to her and she being rigidly virtuous, she had left. And another job, Anna must figure to herself, had been impossible to get, for she, Babette, was too small and slim for the Anglo-Saxon idea of a mannequin.

She stopped to shout in a loud voice to the woman who was serving: 'Hé, my old one, don't forget your little Babette . . .'

Opposite, Simone the cat and the sportive Georgette were having a low-voiced conversation about the tristeness of a monsieur of their acquaintance. 'I said to him,' Georgette finished decisively, 'nothing to be done, my rabbit. You have not looked at me well, little one. In my place would you not have done the same?'

She broke off when she realized that the others were listening, and smiled in a friendly way at Anna.

She too, it appeared, had ambitions to go to London because the salaries were so much better there. Was it difficult? Did they really like French girls? Parisiennes?

The conservation became general.

'The English boys are nice,' said Babette, winking one divinely candid eye. 'I had a chic type who used to take me to dinner at the Empire Palace. Oh, a pretty boy . . .'

'It is the most chic restaurant in London,' she added importantly.

The meal reached the stage of dessert. The other tables were gradually emptying; the mannequins all ordered very strong coffee, several liqueur. Only Mona and Eliane remained silent; Eliane, because she was thinking of something else; Mona, because it was her type, her genre to be haughty.

Her hair swept away from her white, narrow forehead and her small ears: her long earrings nearly touching her shoulders, she sipped her coffee with a disdainful air. Only once, when the blonde enfant, having engaged in a passage of arms with the waitress and got the worst of it was momentarily discomfited and silent, Mona narrowed her eyes and smiled an astonishingly cruel smile.

As soon as her coffee was drunk she got up and went out.

Anna produced a cigarette, and Georgette, perceiving instantly that here was the sportive touch, her genre, asked for one and lit it with a devil-may-care air. Anna eagerly passed her cigarettes round, but the Mère Pecard interfered weightily. It was against the rules of the house for the mannequins to smoke, she wheezed. The girls all lit their cigarettes and smoked. The Mère Pecard rumbled on: 'A caprice, my children. All the world knows that mannequins are capricious. Is it not so?' She appealed to the rest of the room.

As they went out Babette put her arm round Anna's waist and whispered: 'Don't answer Madame Pecard. We don't like her. We never talk to her. She spies on us. She is a camel.'

That afternoon Anna stood for an hour to have a dress draped on her. She showed this dress to a stout Dutch lady buying for the Hague, to a beautiful South American with pearls, to a silver-haired American gentleman who wanted an evening cape for his daughter of seventeen, and to a hook-nosed, odd English lady of title who had a loud voice and dressed, under her furs, in a grey jersey and stout boots.

The American gentleman approved of Anna, and said so, and Anna gave him a passionately grateful glance. For, if the vendeuse Jeannine had been uniformly kind and encouraging, the other, Madame Tienne, had been as uniformly disapproving and had once even pinched her arm hard.

About five o'clock Anna became exhausted. The four white and gold walls seemed to close in on her. She sat on her high white stool staring at a marvellous nightgown and fighting an intense desire to rush away. Anywhere! Just to dress and rush away anywhere, from the raking eyes of the customers and the pinching fingers of Irene.

'I will one day. I can't stick it,' she said to herself. 'I won't be able to stick it.' She had an absurd wish to gasp for air.

Jeannine came and found her like that.

'It is hard at first, hein? . . . One asks oneself: Why? For what good? It is all idiot. We are all so. But we go on. Do not worry about Irene.' She whispered: 'Madame Veron likes you very much. I heard her say so.'

★

At six o'clock Anna was out in the rue de la Paix; her fatigue forgotten, the feeling that now she really belonged to the great, maddening city possessed her and she was happy in her beautifully cut tailor-made and beret.

Georgette passed her and smiled; Babette was in a fur coat.

All up the street the mannequins were coming out of the shops, pausing on the pavements a moment, making them as gay and as beautiful as beds of flowers before they walked swiftly away and the Paris night swallowed them up.

*

Another Survivor

He's fifty now, but the day his mother and father took him to the railway station with the one permitted suitcase, clutching a satchel crammed with entomological collecting equipment he refused to leave behind, that chilly, too-harshly-bright day of a windy, reluctant spring, was in 1938, and he was twelve years old. With the other children lucky enough to be included in this refugee group going to England, and their agitated and mournful parents, they moved to the far end of the platform in an attempt to make themselves less conspicuous. Rudi recognized two of the boys from last year at school. Since the holidays he had been kept at home: Jewish students were no longer acceptable; nor were they safe. A few children had begun to cry, unable not to respond to the tears their parents tried so hard to repress. The entire group emanated a terrible collective desolation, unaffected by any individual attempt to put a good face on matters, or hopeful talk of a future reunion. For all of them, it was their last sight of each other, their last goodbye. Sharing a stridently upholstered couch with three men as withdrawn into their separate worlds as he is, staring unseeingly at other patients moving restlessly around the crowded day-ward, Rudi's face is still marked by the same appalled expression which had settled on it that morning so many years ago.

His parents belonged to families who had lived in the city for generations. Though Rudi was an only child, there had been many houses and apartments where he was welcome and at home, many celebrations to attend and cousins to play with.

The family ramified through the professions: doctors, lawyers, academics, architects: one of those cultivated, free-thinking manifestations of Jewish emancipation whose crucial importance to the European spirit only became apparent after its destruction. His father had been a biologist, his mother a talented amateur pianist. At night, in the dormitory of the school he was put into by the same kindly people who had organized his rescue, he tried to make himself sleep by seeing how many themes he could bring back to mind from the music she had played. He remembered their apartment full of the sound of her piano, and himself creeping up behind her, steps deadened by the soft Persian rugs whose silk nap glinted like water in the mote-laden beams of afternoon sunlight coming through creamy net curtains, hoping to reach the piano stool and put his hands over her eyes before she even realized he was home from school.

That was the picture he had kept on the iconstasis of his mind during the years when there was no news of them at all. That, and another one – walking in the country one Sunday with his father. Even now, through the distractions of hospital life, he distinctly remembers the surge of pride and intellectual excitement when he suddenly understood what his father was explaining about the particular structure and composition of the hills around them – a lesson in geography and geology; and he remembers, also, how he called upon that memory to sustain him through every boyhood crisis.

Though he mastered English quickly and did his schoolwork well, the only thing that really interested him was the prospect of taking part in the war and adding his energy to the battle against Nazism. But he never managed to see any fighting or even get on to the continent of Europe before it ended. And then, after seven years of suspense, of great swoops between optimism and an absolute conviction that he would never see his parents alive again, the camps were opened up and the first reports and pictures began to appear. The effort he makes, even now, is to shut off parts of his mind, to push all that

information away. Nightmares, day-mares – black, white, bleeding, disembowelled, flayed: Goya-esque mares with staring,
maddened eyes had been galloping across the wincing terrain of
his brain ever since. But he was not able to stop collecting
facts; nor stop imagining how every atrocity he heard or read
about might have been suffered by his parents.

Then he calmed down, came through it – another survivor.
So much time passed that he could even acknowledge how
privileged and fortunate he was, weighed in the balance of the
global misery. Every morning over breakfast he could read in
the newspapers stories of war, famine, torture, and injustice,
and be no more affected by them than the newspaper readers of
that time were by the catastrophe which engulfed him and his
family. He was healthy, prosperous, successful. His wife had
not left him. His children were growing up. His work presented
no real problems. It was just that now, after more than thirty
years, he was overcome with a most intense yearning for his
mother. He felt as though he were still a boy of twelve, gone
away from home for the first time: the adoring son of a proud,
doting mother (that identity which in truth had been his,
which had been waiting all this time for him to admit to and
assume) who cannot be diverted by promises of even the most
fabulous pleasures if they will keep him away from her one
moment longer. And the strength of this feeling made him
aware of how much he had repressed when it had really
happened.

For the first time he was able to remember what his mother
had been like before the war. During the intervening years,
memory had been blotted out by imagination, which is always
stronger. He had only been able to imagine her as a victim, not
as a woman at the height of her vigour and self-confidence.
This release of memory from the prison of fear had brought
about her resurrection.

Twenty years ago when Rudi and Barbara found their
house, the streets between Camden Town and Primrose Hill

were neither fashionable nor expensive. They had lived there ever since, while houses around them changed hands for ten and twenty times what they paid. It had been fixed up and periodically redecorated but basically retained the style of the era when they moved in: austere and utilitarian, student-like; with white-walled, charcoal-grey and neutral coloured rooms intended as the background for rational living. He had been attracted to Barbara because she seemed so rational. Nothing about their house reminded him of where he had lived until the age of twelve. The two interiors were entirely different.

Barbara had never been interested in how the house looked. Since the last of the three children started school she had trained and qualified as a social worker, and was out for most of the day and quite a few evenings. Rudi, who had become an accountant after the war, found he was bringing more work home, and often spent whole days at his desk in the big open all-purpose room on the ground floor. There was nothing wrong with his corner – it had been especially planned so that everything necessary was within reach; but sitting there one early winter afternoon he looked around and wondered how he had lived for so long in this bleak, characterless environment. At home, he thought – and became aware that home was not this house at all – everything had been so much prettier and more comfortable; more comforting, too; gratifying to the eye and the spirit in a way the room he now sat in gave no indication of understanding or allowing for. He had a strong, momentary hallucination of his mother as she must have been in 1933 or 1934, perfumed and elegantly dressed to go out for the evening, walking a few steps through the door and glancing around. He had become inured to and then unaware of the frayed, stained upholstery they'd never bothered to replace after the children had outgrown their destructive phase. Through her slightly slanting pale blue eyes, he saw the muddy, formless paintings friends had given them years ago which remained the only decorations, and watched them narrow with distaste and incomprehension before she disappeared without having noticed him.

Walking home from the tube station next day, Rudi was surprised by how many antique shops had opened in the district. A lamp on display reminded him of one in the dining-room of his childhood home. It had stood on the right-hand side of a large, ornately carved sideboard, and he had loved the winter evenings when its opalescent glass shade glowed like a magic flower. Antique shops had always made him feel ignorant and gullible, but he forced himself to go inside. The lamp was more expensive than any comparable object he had ever bought, and as he wrote a cheque he was sweating as though engaged in the commission of a fearful, dangerous crime. Standing and lit on his desk, the lamp made everything in the room seem even more nondescript. He could not stop looking at it.

'Oh, that's new, isn't it?' Barbara remarked as she hurried through the house between work and a meeting, tying a headscarf over her short blonde hair. 'I forgot some papers,' she explained, 'or I wouldn't have come back. I've left something for supper for you and the children.'

'That's really beautiful. I'd like to do a drawing of it,' Faith said. She was the elder of the two girls, and had just become an art student. Though circumstances had made him an account-ant, Rudi often wondered if he had betrayed his potential. He thought of himself as an artist manqué. Faith was the only one of the children who took after him. It would be hard to tell that Mavis and Tony had a Jewish father. They were much more like Barbara's side of the family.

Most fathers he knew would be more likely to spend time at the weekend with sons rather than daughters. But Tony had never given him an opportunity to develop that sort of special relationship. When not at school the boy was always out somewhere with friends – an eminently social being. Mavis, the baby of the family, had been her mother's girl from the start, and so Rudi and Faith had been left to make their own Saturday excursions. Visiting museums and galleries with her, combined pleasure and anguish. He was grateful for the op-portunity to view paintings or statues which had excited and drawn him back to them over and over again as a young man, but which he had not seen for years. It was wonderful to watch Faith's knowledge and appreciation increase, to witness the development of this lovely, perceptive creature. The anguish came when he remembered visiting museums with his mother; when he recognized the inherent sensitivity of Faith's responses, so similar to what his mother's had been; when his pleasure at her responses made him aware of what his mother must have felt about him.

Often they would set out with no particular destination, call in at bookshops or wander around street markets. Now, Rudi had an aim, and they would search for pictures, rugs, china, bits of furniture – anything that reminded him of the comfortable bourgeois home he had grown up in. Faith thought it perfectly natural to buy so much – while he found it much easier to spend money in the company of his pretty, auburn-haired seventeen-year-old daughter than when he was alone. He had loved her from the first sight of her hour-old face. What had touched his heart so profoundly, though he had not known it at the time, was an unmistakable and strongly marked resemblance to his mother. The echoes and parallels and actual duplications between his daughter and mother incremented like compound interest once he began to look for them. Because of this, he felt he had to do whatever he could to help her, as though the years torn from his mother's life could be made good somehow if Faith were happy and fulfilled.

The difference between his recent acquisitions and the rest of the furnishings gave the house a hybrid quality and disturbed them all. Rudi began to be irritable and dissatisfied, suspecting that he would never manage to achieve a convincing reproduction of his parental home. It was becoming harder to summon up his mother's image with the same marvellous tangibility. The lamps and rugs and little tables were useless magic. And yet even the memory of her first, vivid return as the person she really had been instead of only the dehumanized victim which was all he had been able to imagine since the war, was enough to change his relationship to everything.

He found it difficult to believe that he and Barbara were actually husband and wife. She was so calm, so settled and busy and mature; like a kindly, abstracted nurse. He'd had a nursemaid rather like Barbara, when he was about six years old. Apart from commenting on the amount of money he must be spending, she seemed benignly indifferent to the transformation of the house. In bed, though, when the light was out and he took her warm, silent, acquiescent body into his arms, he could not stop himself from imagining that she was his mother. Frequently, he felt about to burst into tears. The sight of his glaring eyes and pale, tense, puffy face in need of a shave, repelled him when he caught sight of it in the bathroom mirror.

Rudi had avoided talking to the children about the war, the camps, and how his parents died. He had never even managed to give them any explanation about their connection to Judaism. Now he felt it was too late to begin, and was bitterly ashamed of his cowardice. Of course his mother would have wanted her grandchildren to know everything. Perhaps that was why she had come back, and, because he was not fulfilling his duty, the reason for her withdrawal. This thought put him into a deep depression for several days. But that Saturday afternoon on the Portobello Road with Faith, he saw a dress very like one his mother used to wear, dangling from the rail of an old-clothes stall. It gave him an idea. If his mother would not appear of her own free will, dressing Faith in similar clothes might force her back.

Faith was delighted with the dress and hurried him home so she could try it on. The others were out and the house was empty. When Faith came down the stairs Rudi was astounded by the uncanny resemblance. This was not a fantasy or hallucination, but a solid, breathing figure of flesh – a revenant: his mother even before he had known her, before his birth, when she had been a young girl. He was awestruck and terrified.

Unaware that she was being used for conjuration, his daughter had innocently assumed the identity of a dead woman.

He had succeeded beyond his imaginings. His mother was in the room – but how many of her? There was the young girl incarnated in his once more recognizable daughter (recreated in any case by the natural laws of genetic inheritance): the two of them fused into this touching being for whom he had been trying to make the appropriate setting with every object purchased: and another – the one he had not wanted to meet again ever.

It was the victim who had haunted him for years. Perhaps those lamps and rugs had not been bought to lure back the girl and untroubled woman, after all – but to ward off this one. Gaunt, dirty, cowed, huddled defensively near the foot of the staircase and wearing the threadbare clothes of a camp inmate, she glared with sick, unrecognizing eyes towards him. The sight made him want to die. He could see them both at the same time, they were only a few feet apart, though inhabiting separate universe.

'Take off that dress!' he commanded. 'Go upstairs and take it off right now!'

Faith stared with amazement. 'I don't want to take it off.' The concentration camp woman vanished at the sound of her voice. 'I like it. I want to wear it all the time. It's lovely. The girls at school will all want to have dresses like this.'

'You look stupid in it,' he said desperately. 'You look ridiculous.'

'I don't think I do.' Her expression was defiant and challenging.

The only way to control his fear of breaking down was to stiffen his spirit with anger. Faith could not understand what was happening. 'Take that dress off immediately or I'll tear it off.' She knew he would, yet refused to obey and stood her ground.

He had crossed the empty space between them in less than a moment. The cloth was soft and old and gave easily. She screamed with shock and fear. The turmoil of his emotions was sickening. He thought he would lose consciousness. She was in his power and he was tormenting her like a camp guard who could not resist exercising that power; as though she were his specially chosen victim. There must have been someone who singled out his mother in the same way.

She pulled away from him, clutching the torn dress together, and ran up the stairs. 'Fascist!' she shouted, her voice thick with tears. He opened the front door and walked out of the house.

It's dark and cold, but he walks rapidly ahead, with no plan or choice of direction, completely indifferent to where he is going, his mind quite empty. After a time, the emptiness on all sides makes him realize that he must have crossed the road and climbed Primrose Hill. He tries sitting down on a bench, but the moment he stops moving, he is swamped by such self-contempt that he cannot bear it, so he starts walking again. He knows that if he goes back he will break into Faith's room and probably beat her to death. His stride lengthens. He is walking down Park Road now, down Baker Street, crossing Piccadilly, crossing the river; a tall, thick-bodied man unable to stop walking. He is going to keep walking until a car knocks him down or someone fells him with a blow, until he reaches the end of his endurance and drops in his tracks.

*

Nothing Missing But the Samovar

It was July when he went to Morswick, early autumn when he left it; in retrospect it was to seem always summer, those heavy, static days of high summer, of dingy weather and outbursts of sunshine, of blue sky and heaped clouds. Of straw and horseflies. Blackberries; jam for tea; church on Sunday. The Landers.

Dieter Helpmann was twenty-four, a tall, fair young man, serious-looking but with a smile of great sweetness; among his contemporaries he seemed older than he was, sober, reserved, the quiet member of a group, the listener. He had come from Germany to do his post-graduate degree – a thesis on nineteenth-century Anglo-Prussian relations. His father was a distinguished German journalist. Dieter intended to go into journalism himself; he was English correspondent, now, for a socio-political weekly, contributing periodic articles on aspects of contemporary Britain. His English was perfect: idiomatic, lightly accented. His manners were attractive; he held doors open for women, rose to his feet for them, was deferential to his elders. All this made him seem slightly old-fashioned, as did his worried liberalism, which looked not shrewd nor edgy enough for a journalist. His gentle, concerned pieces about education, industrial unrest, the housing problem, read more like a sympathetic academic analysis of the ills of some other time than energetic journalism.

It was 1957, and he had spent eighteen months in England. The year before – the year of Suez and Hungary – he had seen his friends send telegrams to the Prime Minister fiercely dis-

sociating themselves from British intervention; he had agonized
alongside them outraged both with and for them; he had
written an article on 'the alienation of the British intellectual'
that was emotional and partisan. His father commented that
he seemed deeply committed – 'The climate appears to suit
you, in more ways than one.' And Dieter had written back,
'You are right – and it is its variety I think that appeals the
most. It is a place that so much defies analysis – just as you
think you have the measure of it, you stumble across yet
another confusing way in which the different layers of British
life overlap, another curious anachronism. I have to admit that
I have caught Anglophilia, for better or for worse.'

He had. He loved the place. He loved the sobriety of the
academic world in which he mostly moved. He loved all those
derided qualities of reserve and restraint, he loved the landscape. He liked English girls, while remaining faithful to his
German fiancée, Erika (also engaged on post-graduate work,
but in Bonn). He liked and respected what he took to be a
basic cultural stability; here was a place where things changed,
but changed with dignity. To note, to understand, became his
deep concern.

All that, though, took second place to the thesis. That was
what mattered at the moment, the patient quarrying into a
small slice of time, a small area of activity. He worked hard.
Most of his waking hours were spent in the agreeable hush of
great libraries, or alone in his room with his card index and his
notebooks.

He had been about to start writing the first draft when it
happened. 'I have had the most remarkable piece of luck,' he
wrote to Erika. 'Peter Sutton – he is the friend who is working
on John Stuart Mill, you remember – is married to a girl who
comes from Dorset and knows a family whose forebear was
ambassador in Berlin in the 1840s and apparently they still
have all his papers. In trunks in the attic! They are an
aristocratic family – Sir Philip Lander is the present holder of
the title, a baronetcy. Anyway, Felicity Sutton has known

them all her life (she is rather upper-class too, but intelligent, and married Peter at Cambridge, where they both were – this is something of a feature of the young English intelligentsia, these inter-class marriages, Peter of course is of a working-class background), and mentioned that I would be interested in the papers and they said at once apparently that I would be welcome to go down there and have a look. It certainly is a stroke of luck – Felicity says she got the impression there is a vast amount of stuff, all his personal correspondence and official papers too. I go next week, I imagine it will all be rather grand . . .'

There was no car to meet him, as promised. At least, he stood at the entrance to the small country station and the only waiting cars were a taxi and a small pick-up van with open back full of agriculture sacks. He checked Sir Philip Lander's letter: date and time were right. Apprehensively he turned to go to the telephone kiosk – and at the moment the occupant of the van, who had been reading a newspaper, looked up, opened the door and stepped out, smiling.

Or rather, unfolded himself. He was immensely tall, well over six foot. He towered above Dieter, holding out a hand, saying my dear fellow, I'm so sorry, had you been there long – I didn't realize the train was in – I say, is that all the luggage you've got, let me shove it in the back . . .

Bemused, Dieter climbed into the van beside him. It smelled of petrol and, more restrainedly, of horse.

They wound through lanes and over hills. Sir Philip boomed, above the unhealthy sound of the van's engine, of topography, of recollections of Germany before the war, of the harvest. He wore corduroy trousers laced with wisps of hay, gum-boots, a tweed jacket. He was utterly affable, totally without affectation, impregnable in his confidence. Dieter, looking out of the window, saw a countryside that seemed dormant, the trees' dark drooping shapes, the cattle huddled in tranquil groups, their tails lazily twitching. The phrase of some historian about 'the long deep sleep of the English people' swam into his head; he listened to Sir Philip and talked and had the impression of travelling miles, of being swallowed up by this billowing, drowsy landscape.

Once, Sir Philip stopped at a village shop and came out with a cardboard carton of groceries; the van, after this, refused to start and Dieter got out to push. As he got back in, Sir Philip said, 'Thanks so much. Very old, I'm afraid. Needs servicing, too – awful price, nowadays, a service. Oh, well . . .' They passed a pub called the Lander Arms, beetle-browed cottages, an unkempt village green, a Victorian school, turned in at iron gates that shed curls of rusting paint, and jolted up a long, weedy, rutted drive.

It could never have been a beautiful house, Morswick: early seventeenth century, satisfactory in its proportions, with a moderately ambitious flight of steps (now cracked and crumbling) to the front door, but without the gilding of any famous architectural hand. The immediate impression was of a combination of resilience and decay: the pockmarked stone, the window frames unpainted for many years, the pedestal-less urns with planting of woody geraniums, the weeds fringing the steps, the rusted guttering.

They went in, Dieter had a muddled impression of welcoming hands and faces, a big cool hallway, a wide oak staircase, perplexing passages and doors culminating in a room with a window looking out on to a field in which a girl jumped a large horse to and fro over an obstacle made from old oil-drums. He changed his shirt, watching her.

Only later, over tea, did he sort them all out. And that took time and effort, so thunderstruck was he by the room in which it was eaten, that bizarre – preposterous – backdrop to brown bread and butter, Marmite, fish paste and gooseberry jam.

It was huge, stone-flagged, its exterior wall taken up with one great high window, as elaborate with stone tracery as that of a church transept. There were family portraits all round the room – a jumble of artistic good and bad – and above them jutted banners so airy with age as to be completely colourless. The table at which they sat must have been twelve feet long; the wood had the rock-hard feel of immense age; there was nothing in sight that was new except the electric kettle with which Lady Lander made the tea. ('The kitchen is such miles away, we do as much as we can in here . . .')

He stared incredulously at the banners, the pictures, at pieces of furniture such as he had only ever seen before in museums. These, though, were scarred with use, faded by sun, their upholstery in ribbons: Empire chairs and sofas, eighteenth-century cabinets, pedestal tables, writing desks, bureaux. Bemused, he smiled and thanked and spread jam on brown bread and was handed a cup of tea by his hostess.

She was French, but seemed, he thought, poles removed from any Frenchwoman he had ever known – there was nothing left but the faintest accent, the occasional misuse of a word. And then there was the mother-in-law, old Lady Lander, a small pastel figure in her special chair (so fragile-looking, how could she have perpetrated that enormous man?) and Madame Heurgon, Lady Lander's mother, and the two boys, Philip and James, and Sophie, the old French nurse, and Sally, who was sixteen (she it was who had been jumping that horse, beyond the window).

He ate his tea, and smiled and listened. Later, he wrote to his father (and forgot to post the letter): 'This is the most extraordinary family, I hardly know what to make of them as yet. The French mother-in-law has been here twenty years but speaks the most dreadful English, and yet she never stirs from the place, it seems – I asked her if she went back to France often and she said, "Oh, but of course not, it is so impossibly expensive to go abroad nowadays." The boys go away to boarding school, but the girl, Sally, went to some local school and is really barely educated at all, daughters are expendable, I suppose. And they are all there, all the time, for every meal, the old nurse too, and in the evenings they all sit in the drawing-room, listening to the wireless – comedy shows that bewilder them all, except the children, who try to explain the jokes and references, all at once, so no one can hear a word anyway. The old ladies, and the nurse, are in there all day, knitting and sewing and looking out of the window and saying how hot it is, or how cold, and how early the fruit is, or how late, day after day, just the same, there is nothing missing but the samovar . . . Sir Philip is out most of the time, in the fields, he is nothing if not a working farmer, tomorrow I shall help him with some young bullocks they have up on the hill.

'I have not yet looked at the papers.'

That first day there had been no mention of the papers at all; and he had not, he realized, as he got into bed, given them so much as a thought himself. After tea he had been shown round the place by Sally and the boys: the weedy gardens where couch grass and bindweed quenched the outline of tennis court, kitchen garden, and what had once been a formal rose garden with box hedges and a goldfish pond. From time to time they met Lady Lander, hoeing a vegetable bed or snipping the dead heads from flowers; she worked with a slow deliberation that seemed appropriate to the hopeless task of controlling that large area. To go any faster would have been pointless – the forces of nature were winning hands down in any case – to give up altogether would be craven. There was no gardener, Sally said – 'The only men are Daniels and Jim, and Jim's only half really because he's on day release at the Tech and of course Daddy needs them on the farm all the time.'

They toured the stables (a graceful eighteenth-century courtyard, more architecturally distinguished than the house) and admired the Guernsey cows grazing in a paddock nearby. Sir Philip came down the drive on a tractor, and dismounted to join them and explain the finer points of raising calves to Dieter: this was a small breeding herd. 'Of course,' he said, 'it doesn't really make sense, economic sense, one never gets enough for them, but it's something I've always enjoyed doing.'

Sally broke in, 'And they *look* so nice.'

He beamed at the cows, and his daughter. 'Of course. That's half the point.'

A car was approaching slowly, taking the ruts and bumps with caution, a new model. Sir Philip said, 'Ah, here's George Nethercott, we're going to have a chat about those top fields'. He moved away from them as the car stopped, saying, 'Good evening, George, very good of you to come up – how's your hay going, I'm afraid we're making a very poor showing this year, I'm about three hundred bales short so far. I say, that's a very smart car . . .'

His voice carried in the stillness of the early evening; it seemed the only forceful element in all that peace of pigeons cooing, cows cropping the grass, hypnotically shifting trees.

Sally said, 'Mr Nethercott's land joins our farm on two sides. Daddy may be going to sell him the three hill fields because we've got to have a new tractor next year, it's a pity, you oughtn't to sell land . . .' Her voice trailed away vaguely, and then she went on with sudden enthusiasm, 'I say, do you like riding? Would you like to try Polly?'

'You will never believe it, I have been horse-riding,' he wrote to Erika. 'Not for long, I hasten to say – I fell off with much humiliation, and was made a great fuss of. They are such a charming family, and have a way of drawing you into everything they do, without ever really bothering about whether it is the kind of thing you are fitted for, or would like . . . So that I find myself leading the most extraordinary – for me – life, mending fences, herding cattle, picking fruit, hay-making.

'Next week I must get down to the papers.'

Sir Philip had taken him up to the attics. 'I really don't know what we shall find,' he said. 'Things get shoved away for years, you know, and one has very little idea . . . I've not been up here for ages.'

There were pieces of furniture, grey with dust, and suitcases, and heaps of mouldering curtains and blankets; a sewing-machine that looked like the prototype of all sewing-machines; gilt-framed pictures stacked against a wall; a jumble of withered saddlery that Sir Philip picked up and examined. 'I wonder if Sally mightn't be able to make use of some of this.'

Dieter, looking at an eighteenth-century chest of drawers pushed away beneath a dormer window, and thinking also of the furniture with which the rest of the house was filled, said, 'You have some nice antique pieces.' Sir Philip, still trying to unravel a harness, said, 'Oh no, Dieter, not really, it's all just things that have always been here, you know.' He put the harness down and moved away into another, inner attic room with a single small window overlooking the stable-yard. 'I have a feeling the stuff we're looking for is in these boxes here.'

Later, Dieter sat at a small folding green baize card table he had found in a corner, and began to open the bundles of letters and papers. It was much as Felicity Sutton had predicted: there were family letters all mixed up with official correspondence both from and to the Sir Philip Lander of the 1840s. It was a research worker's gold-mine. He glanced through a few documents at random, and then began to try to sort things out into some kind of order, thinking that eventually, before he left, he must suggest tactfully that all this should be deposited in the Public Record Office or some other appropriate place. In the meantime it was just his own good luck . . .

Curiously, he could not feel as excited or interested as he should. He read, and made a few notes, and yawned, and beyond the fly-blown window small puffy clouds coasted in a sky of duck-egg blue, the garden trees sighed and heaved, and if he lifted himself slightly in his chair he could see down into the stable-yard where Sally was in attendance on that enormous horse of hers, circling its huge complacent rump with brush and comb. Presently Sir Philip drove the tractor into the yard, and, with one of the boys, began to unload bales of hay. Dieter put his pen down, tidied his notes into a pile, and went down to help.

★

He had never known time pass so slowly – and so fast. The days were thirty-six hours long, and yet fled by so quickly that suddenly he had been there for two and a half weeks. Much embarrassed, he went one morning to find Lady Lander in the kitchen and insist that he should pay for his keep.

She was making jam. The room was filled with the sweet fruity smell; flies buzzed drunkenly against the windows. Astonished, she said, 'Oh, but of course not, we couldn't hear of such a thing, you are a guest.'

'But I am staying so long, originally Sir Philip suggested a few days, and with one thing and another it has got longer and longer. Please, really I should prefer . . .'

She would have none of it.

He hardly knew himself how it was that his departure was always postponed. Of course, he had done no work at all, as yet, on the papers, but he could get down to that any time. And always there was something that loomed – 'You must be sure to be here for the County Show next week,' Sir Philip would say. 'You'll find it amusing if you've not seen that kind of thing before – do you have the equivalent in Germany, I wonder?' Or Sally would remember suddenly that the first cubbing meet was in ten days' time. 'You'll still be here, won't you, Dieter? Oh, you must be – honestly, if you've never seen a meet . . .'

He protested to Lady Lander – 'Please, I would be happier . . .', but could see that there was no point in going on. 'In any case,' she said, turning back to the pink-frothing pan on the stove, 'you have been most helpful to my husband, he is always short-handed at this time of year, I am afraid only that we drive you into things you would never normally dream of doing. You must say, you know, if it bores you – we tend to forget, down here, that not everyone lives this kind of life.'

And she, he wondered, had she not once been someone quite different? On Sundays, both she and her mother appeared for church in quite unfashionable but recognizably expensive clothes – silk dresses and citified hats of pre-war style. In these incongruous outfits, they walked down the lane to the village church. The family filled the whole of the front pew; Sir Philip's confident tenor led the sparse congregation; afterwards they would all stand, every week, for the same amount of time, chatting to the vicar. Then back to Morswick, stopping again from time to time to talk with village people.

He had thought, when he first came, that it was feudal, and had been amused. Now, his perceptions heightened, he saw otherwise. 'It is not that they are not respected,' he wrote to his father. 'Far from it – people are deferential to them – a title still means something, and they have always been the big family in these parts. But it is as though they are runners in a race who are being outstripped without even realizing it. I think they hardly notice that their farming neighbours have new gadgets they have not – washing machines, televisions – that theirs is the shabbiest car for miles around, that the Morswick tractor is so out-of-date Nethercott (the neighbour) declined the loan of it when his broke down. And why? you will be saying, after all they have land, a house, possessions. But the land is not good, a lot of it is rough hill-grazing, I suppose that is at the root of the problem – and a mansion and a family past are not very realizable assets. I certainly can't imagine them selling the furniture. But when you come down to it – it is as though there is also some kind of perverse lack of will, as though they both didn't know, and didn't want to know.'

The children were where it most showed. Beside their contemporaries – the sons and daughters of the local farming families (many of them at private schools, their country accents fast fading), they seemed quaint, too young for their ages, innocent. Sally, talking to other adolescent girls at an agricultural show, was the only one without lipstick, a hair-do, the quick glancing self-consciousness of young womanhood. She seemed a child beside them.

At the cubbing meet – held outside the village pub – he found it almost unbearable. Standing beside Lady Lander, he watched her. Lady Lander said, 'She's not well mounted, I'm afraid, poor darling – we've only got old Polly these days.'

It was a huge horse, with a hefty muscularity that suggested carthorse ancestry. Seated on it, Sally towered above the dapper ponies of the other children. Beaming, unconscious of the vaguely comic figure she cut, she yanked the horse's head away from a tray of glasses that was being carried around, and waved at Dieter. She wore her school mack over grubby breeches and a pair of battered hunting-boots. The other girls were crisp in pale jodhpurs, tweed jackets and little velvet caps.

Dieter was wrenched by pity, and love.

He adored her. With horror he had recognized his own feelings, which smacked, it seemed to him, of paedophilia. She was sixteen; her rounded features, her plump awkward body, were raw with childishness. He was obsessed by her. He forced himself to contemplate her ignorance, her near-illiteracy. He thought of Erika, of her sharp clever face, the long hours of serious discussion, the shared concerns, and it did no good at all.

And Sally had not the lightest inkling, nor ever would, of how he felt. She jostled him in puppyish horse-play; she worked beside him in the harvest field, her breasts straining at her aertex shirt, her brown legs as shiny with health and vigour as the rump of that incongruous horse she rode; he could hardly take his eyes off her, and was appalled at himself.

In the evenings, he played board games with the two boys, held skeins of knitting wool for old Lady Lander as she wound the balls. Sometimes, he took a book from the great high cases that lined the walls of the drawing-room. They held an odd assortment: bound volumes of *Punch*, row upon row, Edwardian books about hunting and fishing, the classic Victorian novelists, books of humorous verse, Henty and Buchan and Rider Haggard. He read with perplexity novels like *The Constant Nymph*, *Precious Bane* and *Beau Geste* that seemed to fit not at all with the concept of English twentieth-century literature that he had formed after two years' carefully selective leisure reading.

Scanning the titles on the shelves, he had a confusing impression of being presented with a whole shadow culture of which he had been unaware. Yet again he felt his own judgements and perceptions to be hopelessly inadequate. Sir Philip, standing beside him at the book case one evening, said, 'Glad to see you're making use of the library, Dieter – I'm afraid none of us get much time for reading.' There was hardly a single recent addition, not an untattered dust-cover to be seen.

On a day of sullen rain clouds, when the whole landscape seemed sunk in apathy, the old tractor broke down with more than usual finality. For hour after hour, Sir Philip and Daniels crawled around it, oiling and adjusting; Dieter, on edge with vicarious anxiety (it was needed for several urgent jobs), watched in frustration, cursing his lack of mechanical know-how. The worry on Sir Philip's face distressed him greatly; he longed to help. Eventually, the tractor sputtered into fitful life, and everybody stood back smiling. Sir Philip said, 'Well Daniels, we shan't have any of these crises next year, when we've got the new one, I hope.' And Daniels said, 'That's right, sir, we'll be in clover then', and added, looking down the drive, 'Here's Mr Nethercott now.'

Nethercott had come, though, to talk not about fields but to look at the bull Sir Philip proposed selling. It was a young bull, whose performance was proving unreliable. Daniels was in favour of going over to artificial insemination. Sir Philip had reluctantly concurred, as they stood side by side at the gate, a few days before, watching the bull at work among the cows in a steeply sloping field opposite. Sir Philip said, 'You're right, Daniels, I'm not too happy about him either.'

'Silly bugger don't realize he got to do it downhill.'

Sir Philip turned away. 'Oh well, there's nothing to be done – he'll have to go. Now, George Nethercott's wanting a bull, I know – I'll give him a ring tonight.'

And now Nethercott too stood at the field gate, studying the bull. Other matters were talked of for a while, then he said, 'How much were you thinking of asking for him?'

Sir Philip named a price.

Nethercott nodded. There was a brief silence and then he said with a trace of embarrassment, 'He might well work out more satisfactory than he looks just now – but the fact is, what I'm looking for's going to cost a fair bit more than that. Thanks for letting me have a look at him, though.'

A week or so later, they heard through the postman that Nethercott had paid five hundred pounds for a bull at the Royal Show. Sir Philip said, 'Well, good heavens! Lucky fellow.' He was standing with Dieter in the front drive, the two or three brown envelopes that the postman had brought in his hand. 'I really don't know how people manage it, these days. He's a good chap, Nethercott – they're a nice family. His grandfather used to work here, you know, for mine – stable-lad he was, I think. Well, I suppose we might get on with that fencing today, eh?'

Up in the attic, the sun striking through the window had browned Dieter's single page of notes; there was a faint paler stripe where the pencil lay.

At the beginning of September, the boys went back to boarding school. The corn was down, the blackberries ripening, the green of the trees spiced here and there with the first touch of autumn colour. Since he had come here, Dieter realized, the landscape had changed, working through its cycle so unobtrusively that only with an effort did one remember the brimming cornfields of July, the hedgerows still bright with wild flowers, the long light evenings. Now, the fields were bleached and shaven, the hedges lined with the skeletal heads of dried cow-parsley and docks, the grass white with dew in the mornings. It came as a faint shock to realize that the place was not static at all, that that impression of deep slumber was quite false, that change was continuous, that nothing stood still. That he could not stay here for ever.

There was a dance, in the local market town, in connection

with some equestrian activity, to which he went with Sally and her parents. It was the first time, he realized, that he had ever been anywhere with them when the whole family had not come, grandmothers and all. Sally wore an old dress of her mother's that had been cut down for her; it did not fit and was unbecoming, but she shone with excitement and anticipation. In the hotel where the dance took place, the other young girls were waiting about in the foyer in sharp-eyed groups and he was stricken again at Sally's frumpish looks in contrast to their fashionable dresses, their knowingness. But she was quite happy – laughing, greeting acquaintances.

He danced with her once at the beginning, and then left her with a group of her contemporaries. But later, the evening under way, whenever he saw her she was dancing with friends of her parents, or sitting alone on one of a row of gilt chairs at the edge of the room, holding a glass of lemonade, but still radiant, tapping her foot in time to the music. After a while he went over and sat beside her.

'Are you having a good time, Sally?'

'Marvellous!'

'Let's dance, shall we?'

She was clumsy; he had to steer her round the room. She said, 'Sorry, I'm hopeless. We did have dancing lessons at school but it's quite different when it's a real man, and anyway I always had to take man because of being tall, so I'm no good at being the woman. I say, Mummy says perhaps I can go to the hunt ball this year – will you still be here?'

He said, 'I'm afraid not. I have to go back before the term begins in October.'

'Oh, what a pity.' They danced in silence for a minute or two and then she said suddenly, 'What are you going to do after you've finished your – your what's-it, the thing you're writing?'

'I shall go back to Germany and get a job. I expect I shall get married,' he added after a fractional pause. He had never spoken of Erika at Morswick.

'Will you?' She looked amazed. 'Gosh – how exciting. Do write and tell us won't you, so that we can send a present.'

She beamed up at him; she smelled of toothpaste and, very faintly, of a cheap scent that she must have acquired in secrecy and tentatively used. He had seen, once, into her room; there had been a balding toy dog on the pillow, photographs of horses pinned to the walls, glass animals on the windowsill. She said, 'Do you know, they want me to go to a sort of finishing school place in Grenoble next year.'

'I should think you would like that.'

She said, 'Oh no, I couldn't possibly go. I couldn't bear to leave Morswick. No, I can't possibly.'

Dieter said, 'Sally, I think you should, I really do.'

She shook her head.

Later, back at Morswick, he sat with Sir Philip in the drawing-room; Sally and her mother had gone to bed. Sir Philip had taken a bottle of whisky from the cupboard and poured them both a glass: it was almost the first time Dieter had ever seen alcohol produced at Morswick, except for the glass of sherry offered to their rare visitors. Sir Philip said, 'Quite a successful evening, I thought. Of course, you get a rather a different kind of person at this sort of do now – it's not really like before the war. I daresay my father would be a bit taken aback if he was still alive.'

He began to talk about his war-time experiences in Italy and France: he had been with the Sicily landings, and then in Normandy shortly after D-day, advancing through France and into Germany. Remembering suddenly the delicacy of the subject, he looked across at Dieter and said, 'I hope you don't . . . of course, one realized at the time how many people like yourself, like your father . . . What a wretched business it all was, so much worse in many ways for you than for us.'

Dieter said, 'I think you would be interested to see Germany now. I wish you would come to visit us – my father would be so delighted to make arrangements, if all of you could come, or perhaps at least the boys and Sally.'

'How awfully kind. We really must try to — you know, I can't think when we last had a holiday of any sort. Yes, we really must.' He swilled the whisky in his glass, peering down into it. 'Yes. Of course, one is so awfully tied up here, being pretty short-handed nowadays. I daresay things will pick up in time, though. I must admit, it is getting a bit hard to manage just at the moment — still, we keep our heads above water. Anyway, I really mustn't burden you with our problems. By the way, I hope you didn't mean what you said earlier about leaving us next week — I'd imgined we'd have you with us for some time to come. There's the harvest festival on Sunday week — I'm sure Jeanne was intending to rope you in for one thing and another.'

'I have to get back — the term begins soon, you see. My supervisor — well, they must wonder what on earth has become of me. And in any case, you've been far too kind already, too hospitable. I don't know how to thank you enough.'

'I'm afraid what with one thing and another you've not had all that much time to put in on those papers. They've been of some interest, I hope?'

Dieter said, 'Oh yes, extremely interesting.'

The day before he was to leave he went to the attic to clear up the green baize table. His note-pad, with its single page of notes, was curled at the edges now, and dusty. Insects had died on the opened bundles of letters. Beyond the window, the landscape had slipped a notch further into autumn: there was a mist smoking up from the fields, and long curtains of old man's beard hanging down the wall beside the stable-yard. He tied up the letters again and put them away in the trunk, folded the card table, gathered up his things. He opened the window for a moment, with some vague notion of airing the place, and heard, faintly, Sally whistling as she did something out of sight in one of the loose boxes.

His departure for the station was delayed for a few minutes by the arrival of Nethercott. Sir Philip stood with him at the field gate nodding and listening. When at last he finished, and Nethercott, apologizing for turning up at what was obviously an inappropriate moment, had driven away, the whole family was gathered on the steps to say goodbye to Dieter. He had shaken hands with them all, several times; everyone was smiling and interrupting. Sir Philip came across the drive to them and said, 'Sorry about that – had to have a word or two since he'd taken the trouble to come up.'

Lady Lander said, 'What was it about?'

'Oh, just the fields – you know, the hill fields. He'd like to make an offer for them but I'd got things a bit wrong. I'm afraid – they're worth rather less than I'd imagined, on the current market. Rather a lot less, I'm afraid. George was awfully apologetic – you'd have thought it was his fault. He's a good chap.'

'Oh dear, does that mean no new tractor?'

'I suppose it does. I don't know how I'm going to break that to poor Daniels. Well, anyway,' he went on cheerfully, 'we'll be able to send the old one for a thorough overhaul, we'll have to make do with that. Now, Dieter, we'd better be on our way, hadn't we, where's your case . . .'

He saw them like that, in his mind's eye, for long after – the women – standing on the front steps waving and smiling. 'It's au revoir, anyway,' Lady Lander had said, 'because we shall see you again, next time you're in our part of the world, shan't we?' And her mother-in law, that frail old lady in her pale floppy clothes and regimental brooches, had piped up, 'Oh yes, we're always here, you know, you'll always find us here', and Sally was calling out not to forget to let them know about the wedding. She had given him a hug and a kiss; the feel of her arms, her warm soft face, the smell of her, stayed with him all the way to the station, and beyond. And the sight of them, and of the house behind, frozen in the furry yellow light of the September morning, like an old photograph – the figures grouped around the steps, the house with its backdrop of fields and hills and trees.

At the station, Sir Philip shook him by the hand. 'We've enjoyed having you, Dieter. You must get down to us again sometime. You'll find everything goes on much as ever at Morswick. And the best of luck with your doctorate.'

In the train, Dieter began a letter to Erika, and then sat staring out of the window at that placid landscape (the landscape of Constable, he told himself, of Richard Wilson, of the English novelists) and saw only the irresistible manifestations of change: the mottled trees, the tangle of spent growth in the hedgerows.

JANE GARDAM

*

Stone Trees

So now that he is dead so now that he is dead I am to spend
the day with them. The Robertsons.

On the Isle of Wight. Train journey train journey from
London. There and back in a day.

So now that he is dead –

They were at the funeral. Not their children. Too little. So
good so good they were to me. She – Anna – she cried a lot.
Tom held my arm tight. Strong. I liked it. In the place even
the place where your coffin was, I liked it, his strong arm.
Never having liked Tom that much, I liked his strong arm.

And they stayed over. Slept at the house a night or two.
Did the telephone. Some gran or someone was with their
children. Thank God we had no children. Think of Tom/Anna
dying and those two children left –

So now that you are dead –

It's nice of them isn't it now that you are dead? Well, you'd
have expected it. You aren't surprised by it. I'm not surprised
by it. After all there has to be somewhere to go. All clean all
clean at home. Back work soon someday. Very soon now for
it's a week. They broke their two week holiday for the funeral.
Holiday Isle of Wight where you/I went once. There was a dip,
a big-dipper dip, a wavy line of cliffs along the shore, and in
this dip of the cliffs a hotel – a long beach and the waves
moving in shallow.

Over stone trees.

But it was long ago and what can stone trees have been?
Fantasy.

So now that you are dead so now —

Sweetie love so now that you are dead I am to spend the day with the Robertsons alone and we shall talk you/I later. So now —

The boat crosses. Has crossed. Already. Criss-cross deck. Criss-cross water. Splashy sea and look —! Lovely clouds flying (now that you are dead) and here's the pier. A long, long pier into the sea and gulls shouting and children yelling here and there and here's my ticket and there they stand. All in a row — Tom, Anna, the two children solemn. And smiles now — Tom and Anna. Tom and Anna look too large to be quite true. Too good. Anna who never did anything wrong. Arms stretch too far forward for a simple day.

They stretch because they want. They would not stretch to me if you were obvious and not just dead. Then it would have been, hullo, easy crossing? Good. Wonderful day. Let's get back and down on the beach. Great to see you both.

So now that you are dead —

We paced last week. Three.

Tom. Anna. I.

And other black figures wood-faced outside the crematorium in blazing sun, examining shiny black-edged tickets on blazing bouquets. 'How good of Marjorie — fancy old Marjorie. I didn't even know she —' There was that woman who ran out of the so-called service with handkerchief at her eyes. But who was there except you my darling and I and the Robertsons and the shiny cards and did they do it then? Were they doing it then as we read the flowers? Do they do it at once or stack it up with other coffins and was it still inside waiting as I paced with portly Tom? Christian Tom — Tom we laughed at so often and oh my darling now that you are dead —

Cambridge. You can't say that Tom has precisely changed since Cambridge. Thickened. More solid. Unshaken still, quite unshaken and — well, wonderful of course. Anna hasn't changed. Small, specs, curly hair, straight-laced. Dear Anna how we sat and worked out all. Analysed. Girton. We talked about how many men it was decent to do it with without being wild and when you should decide to start and Anna said none and never. Not before marriage you said. Anna always in that church where Tom preached and Tom never looking Anna's way, and how she ached. So now that −

Sweet I miss you so. Now that you are −. My darling oh my God!

In the train two young women. (Yes thanks Anna, I'm fine. Nice journey. First time out. It's doing me good. Isn't it a lovely day?) There were these two women talking about their rights. They were reading about all that was due to them. In a magazine.

'Well, it's only right isn't it?'

'What?'

'Having your own life. Doing your thing.'

'Well−'

'Not − you know. Men and that. Not letting them have all the freedom and that. You have to stand up for yourself and get free of men.'

We come to the hotel and of course it is the one. The one in the dip of the cliffs almost on the beach, and how were they to know? It's typical though, somehow. We didn't like them my darling did we, after Cambridge very much? We didn't see them − dropped them in some way. We didn't see them for nearly two years. And we wondered, sometimes, whatever it was we had thought we had had in common − do-good, earnest Tom, healthy face and shorts, striding out over mountains singing snatches of Berlioz and stopping now and then to pray. And you were you and always unexpected − alert, alive, mocking and forever young and now that you are −

But they were there again. In California. You at the university and I at the university, teaching a term; and there − behold the Robertsons, holding out their arms to save America. Little house full of the shiny-faced, the chinless − marriage counsellors, marriage-enrichment classes oh my God! And one child in Anna and one just learning to walk. We were taken to them by somebody just for a lark not knowing who they'd turn out to be and we said – 'Hey! Tom and Anna.'

And in Sacramento in a house with lacy balconies and little red Italian brick walls and all their old Cambridge books about and photographs we half-remembered, we opened wine and were very happy; and over the old white-washed fireplace there was Tom's old crucifix and his Cambridge oar. And I sat in the rocking chair she'd had at Girton and it felt familiar and we loved the Robertsons that day in sweaty, wheezing Sacramento because they were there again. This is no reason. But it is true.

We talked about how we'd all met each other first. Terrible party. Jesus College. Anna met Tom and I met you my darling and it was something or other – Feminism, Neo-Platonism, Third World – and there you were with bright, ridiculous, marvellous, mocking eyes and long hard hands and I loved you as everyone else clearly loved you. And the Robertsons talked sagely to one another. They were not the Robertsons then but Tom and Anna. We never became the anythings, thank God. There was no need because we were whatever the appearance might be one person and had no need of a plural term and now that –

Sweetie, do you remember the *smell* of that house? In Cambridge? And again in Sacramento? She liked it you know. She left dishes for a week and food bits and old knickers and tights in rolls on the mantelpiece and said, 'There are things more important.' Under the burning ethic there was you know something very desperate about Anna. Tom didn't notice her. Day after day and I'd guess night after night. He sat in the rocking chair and glared at God. And meeting them again just the same, in Sacramento, you looked at the crucifix and the oar and at me, your eyes like the first time we met because there we both remembered the first time, long ago. Remembering that was a short return to each other because by then, by America, I knew that you were one I'd never have to myself because wherever you were or went folk turned and smiled at you and loved you. Well, I'd known always. I didn't face it at first, that one woman would never be enough for you and that if I moved in with you you would soon move on.

Everyone wanted you. When we got married there was a general sense of comedy and the sense of my extraordinary and very temporary luck.

It is not right or dignified to love so much. To let a man rule so much. It is obsession and not love, a mental illness not a life. And of course, with marriage came the quarrelling and pain because I knew there were so many others, and you not coming home, and teasing when you did and saying that there was only me but of course I knew it was not so because of – cheap and trite things like – the smell of scent. It was worst just before the Robertsons went away.

But then – after California – we came here to this beach once and it was September like now, and a still, gold peace. And the hotel in the dip, and the sand white and wide and rock pools. And only I with you. You were quieter. You brought no work. You lay on the beach with a novel flapping pages and the sand gathering in them. We held hands and it was not as so often. It was not as when I looked at you and saw your eyes looking at someone else invisible. God, love – the killing sickness. Maybe never let it start – just mock and talk of Rights. Don't let it near. Sex without sentiment. Manage one's life with dignity. But now that you are dead –

And one day on that year's peaceful holiday we walked out to the stone trees which now I remember. They told us, at the hotel, that in the sea, lying on their stone sides, on their stone bark and broken stone branches, were great prehistoric trees, petrified and huge and broken into sections by the millennia and chopped here and there as by an infernal knife, like rhubarb chunks or blocks of Edinburgh candy, sand coloured, ancient among the young stones.

Trees so old that no one ever saw them living. Trees become stone. I said, 'I love stone,' and you said, 'I love trees,' and kicked them. You said, 'Who wants stone trees?' And we walked about on them, a stone stick forest, quite out to sea, and sat and put our feet in pools where green grasses swayed and starfish shone. And you said – despising the stone trees – there is only ever you – you know – and I knew that the last one was gone and the pain of her and you and I were one again. It was quite right that you loved so much being so much loved and I am glad, for now that you are dead –

I shall never see you any more.

I shall never feel your hand over my hand.

I shall never lean my head against you any more.

I shall never see your eyes which now that you are –

'The sandwiches are egg, love, and cheese, and there's chocolate. We didn't bring a feast. It's too hot.'

'It's lovely.'

'Drink?'

'I don't like Ribena, thanks.'

'It's not. It's wine. In tumblers. Today we're having a lot of wine in very big tumblers.'

(Anna Robertson of evangelical persuasion, who never acts extremely, is offering me wine in tumblers. Now that you are dead.)

'It's nice wine. I'll be drunk.'

The children say, 'You can have some of our cake. D'you want a biscuit?' They've been told to be nice. The little girl pats sand, absorbed, solemn, straight-haired, grave like Tom. The older one, the boy, eats cake and lies on his stomach aware of me and that my husband has died and gone to God.

And you have gone to God?

You were with God and you were my god and now that you –

The boy has long legs. Seven-year-old long legs. The boy is a little like you and not at all like Tom. He rolls over and gives me a biscuit. I'm so glad we had no children. I could not have shared you with children. We needed nobody else except you needed other girls to love a bit and leave – nothing important. You moved on and never mind. I didn't. I did not mind. The pain passed and I don't mind and I shall not mind now that you are dead.

The boy is really – or am I going mad altogether – very like you.

The boy is Peter.

Says, 'Are you coming out on the rocks?'

'I'm fine thanks, Peter. I'm drinking my wine.'

'Drink it later and come out on the rocks. Come on over the rocks.'

See Anna, Tom, proud of Peter being kind to me and only seven. They pretend not to see, fiddling with coffee flask, sun-tan oil. 'Wonderful summer,' says Anna.

'Wonderful.'

'Come on the rocks.'

'Peter – don't boss,' says Anna.

'Leave your wine and come,' says Peter, 'I'll show you the rocks.'

So I go with this boy over the rocks my darling now that you are dead and I have no child and I will never see you any more.

Not any more.

Ever again.

Now that you are –

It is ridiculous how this boy walks.

How Anna wept.

'Look, hold my hand,' says Peter, 'and take care. We're on old trees. What d'you think of that? They were so old they turned to stone. It's something in the atmosphere. They're awful, aren't they? I like trees all leafy and sparkly.'

'*Sparkly* trees?'

'Well, there'd be no pollution. No people. Now just rotten stone.'

'I like stone.'

He kicks them, 'I like trees.'

And I sit down my love because I will not see you any more or hold your hand or put my face on yours and this will pass of course. They've told me that this sort of grief will pass.

But I don't want the grief to change. I want not to forget the feel and look of you and the look of your live eyes and the physical life of you and I do not want to cease to grieve.

'Look, hey, look,' says Peter and stops balancing. 'The tide is coming in.' The water slaps. The dead stone which was once covered with breathing holes for life takes life again, and where it looked like burned out ashy stone there are colours, and little movements, and frondy things responding to water, which laps and laps.

'Look,' says Peter, 'there's a star-fish. Pink as pink. Hey – take my hand. Mind out. You mustn't slip.' (This boy has long hard hands.) 'The tide is coming in.'

How Anna cried.

The tide is coming in and it will cover the stone trees and then it will ebb back again and the stone trees will remain, and already the water is showing more growing things that are there all the time, though only now and then seen.

And Peter takes my hand in yours and I will never see you any more – How Anna cried. And things are growing in the cracks in the stones. The boy laughs and looks at me with your known eyes. Now that you are.

FAY WELDON

*

Weekend

By seven-thirty they were ready to go. Martha had everything packed into the car and the three children appropriately dressed and in the back seat, complete with educational games and wholewheat biscuits. When everything was ready in the car Martin would switch off the television, come downstairs, lock up the house, front and back, and take the wheel.

Weekend! Only two hours' drive down to the cottage on Friday evenings, three hours' drive back on Sunday nights. The pleasures of greenery and guests in between. They reckoned themselves fortunate, how fortunate!

On Fridays Martha would get home on the bus at six-twelve and prepare tea and sandwiches for the family: then she would strip four beds and put the sheets and quilt covers in the washing machine for Monday: take the country bedding from the airing basket, plus the books and games, plus the weekend food – acquired at intervals throughout the week, to lessen the load – plus her own folder of work from the office, plus Martin's drawing materials (she was a market researcher in an advertising agency, he a freelance designer) plus hairbrushes, jeans, spare T-shirts, Jolyon's antibiotics (he suffered from sore throats), Jenny's recorder, Jasper's cassette player and so on – ah, the so on! – and would pack them all, skilfully and quickly, into the boot. Very little could be left in the cottage during the week. ('An open invitation to burglars': Martin.) Then Martha would run round the house tidying and wiping, doing this and that, finding the cat at one neighbour's and delivering it to another, while the others ate their tea; and would usually, proudly, have everything finished by the time they had eaten their fill. Martin would just catch the BBC2 news, while Martha cleared away the tea table, and the children tossed up for the best positions in the car. 'Martha,' said Martin, tonight, 'you ought to get Mrs Hodder to do more. She takes advantage of you.'

Mrs Hodder came in twice a week to clean. She was over seventy. She charged two pounds an hour. Martha paid her out of her own wages: well, the running of the house was Martha's concern. If Martha chose to go out to work – as was her perfect right, Martin allowed, even though it wasn't the best thing for the children, but that must be Martha's moral responsibility – Martha must surely pay her domestic stand-in. An evident truth, heard loud and clear and frequent in Martin's mouth and Martha's heart.

'I expect you're right,' said Martha. She did not want to argue. Martin had had a long hard week, and now had to drive. Martha couldn't. Martha's licence had been suspended four months back for drunken driving. Everyone agreed that the suspension was unfair: Martha seldom drank to excess: she was for one thing usually too busy pouring drinks for other people or washing other people's glasses to get much inside herself. But Martin had taken her out to dinner on her birthday, as was his custom, and exhaustion and excitement mixed had made her imprudent, and before she knew where she was, why there she was, in the dock, with a distorted lamp-post to pay for and a new bonnet for the car and six months' suspension.

So now Martin had to drive her car down to the cottage, and he was always tired on Fridays, and hot and sleepy on Sundays and every rattle and clank and bump in the engine she felt to be somehow her fault.

*

Martin had a little sports car for London and work: it could nip in and out of the traffic nicely: Martha's was an old estate car, with room for the children, picnic baskets, bedding, food, games, plants, drink, portable television and all the things required by the middle classes for weekends in the country. It lumbered rather than zipped and made Martin angry. He seldom spoke a harsh word, but Martha, after the fashion of wives, could detect his mood from what he did not say rather than what he did, and from the tilt of his head, and the way his crinkly, merry eyes seemed crinklier and merrier still – and of course from the way he addressed Martha's car.

'Come along, you old banger you! Can't you do better than that? You're too old, that's your trouble. Stop complaining. Always complaining, it's only a hill. You're too wide about the hips. You'll never get through there.'

Martha worried about her age, her tendency to complain, and the width of her hips. She took the remarks personally. Was she right to do so? The children noticed nothing: it was just funny lively laughing Daddy being witty about Mummy's car. Mummy, done for drunken driving. Mummy, with the roots of melancholy somewhere deep beneath the bustling, busy, every-day self. Busy: ah so busy!

Martin would only laugh if she said anything about the way he spoke to her car and warn her against paranoia. 'Don't get like your mother, darling.' Martha's mother had, towards the end, thought that people were plotting against her. Martha's mother had led a secluded, suspicious life, and made Martha's childhood a chilly and a lonely time. Life now, by comparison, was wonderful for Martha. People, children, houses, conversations, food, drink, theatres – even, now, a career. Martin standing between her and the hostility of the world – popular, easy, funny Martin, beckoning the rest of the world into earshot.

★

Ah, she was grateful: little earnest Martha, with her shy ways and her penchant for passing boring exams – how her life had blossomed out! Three children too – Jasper, Jenny and Jolyon – all with Martin's broad brow and open looks, and the confidence born of her love and care, and the work she had put into them since the dawning of their days.

Martin drives. Martha, for once, drowses.

The right food, the right words, the right play. Doctors for the tonsils: dentists for the molars. Confiscate guns: censor television: encourage creativity. Paints and paper to hand: books on the shelves: meetings with teachers. Music teachers. Dancing lessons. Parties. Friends to tea. School plays. Open days. Junior orchestra.

Martha is jolted awake. Traffic lights. Martin doesn't like Martha to sleep while he drives.

Clothes. Oh, clothes! Can't wear this: must wear that. Dress shops. Piles of clothes in corners: duly washed, but waiting to be ironed, waiting to be put away.

Get the piles off the floor, into the laundry baskets. Martin doesn't like a mess.

Creativity arises out of order, not chaos. Five years off work while the children were small: back to work with seniority lost. What, did you think something was for nothing? If you have children, mother, that is your reward. It lies not in the world.

Have you taken enough food? Always hard to judge.

Food, Oh, food! Shop in the lunch-hour. Lug it all home. Cook for the freezer on Wednesday evenings while Martin is at his car-maintenance evening class, and isn't there to notice you being unrestful. Martin likes you to sit down in the evenings. Fruit, meat, vegetables, flour for home-made bread. Well, shop bread is full of pollutants. Frozen food, even your own, loses flavour. Martin often remarks on it. Condiments. Everyone loves mango chutney. But the expense!

London Airport to the left. Look, look, children! Concorde? No, idiot, of course it isn't Concorde.

Ah, to be all things to all people: children, husband, employer, friends! It can be done: yes, it can: super woman.

Drink. Home-made wine. Why not? Elderberries grown thick and rich in London: and at least you know what's in it. Store it in high cupboards: lots of room: up and down the step-ladder. Careful! Don't slip. Don't break anything.

No such thing as an accident. Accidents are Freudian slips: they are wilful, bad-tempered things.

Martin can't bear bad temper. Martin likes slim ladies. Diet. Martin rather likes his secretary. Diet. Martin admires slim legs and big bosoms. How to achieve them both? Impossible. But try, oh try, to be what you ought to be, not what you are. Inside and out.

Martin brings back flowers and chocolates: whisks Martha off for holiday weekends. Wonderful! The best husband in the world: look into his crinkly, merry, gentle eyes; see it there. So the mouth slopes away into something of a pout. Never mind. Gaze into the eyes. Love. It must be love. You married him. *You*. Surely *you* deserve true love?

Salisbury Plain. Stonehenge. Look, children, look! Mother, we've seen Stonehenge a hundred times. Go back to sleep.

Cook! Ah cook. People love to come to Martin and Martha's dinners. Work it out in your head in the lunch-hour. If you get in at six-twelve, you can seal the meat while you beat the egg white while you feed the cat while you lay the table while you string the beans while you set out the cheeses, goat's cheese, Martin loves goat's cheese, Martha tries to like goat's cheese — oh, bed, sleep, peace, quiet.

Sex! Ah sex. Orgasm, please. Martin requires it. Well, so do you. And you don't want his secretary providing a passion you neglected to develop. Do you? Quick, quick, the cosmic bond. Love. Married love.

Secretary! Probably a vulgar suspicion: nothing more. Probably a fit of paranoics, à la mother, now dead and gone.
At peace.
R.I.P.
Chilly, lonely mother, following her suspicions where they led.

Nearly there, children. Nearly in paradise, nearly at the cottage. Have another biscuit.

Real roses round the door.

Roses. Prune, weed, spray, feed, pick. Avoid thorns. One of Martin's few harsh words.

'Martha, you can't not want roses! What kind of person am I married to? An anti-rose personality?'

Green grass. Oh, God, grass. Grass must be mown. Restful lawns, daisies bobbing, buttercups glowing. Roses and grass and books. Books.

Please, Martin, do we have to have the two hundred books, mostly twenties' first editions, bought at Christie's book sale on one of your afternoons off? Books need dusting.

Roars of laughter from Martin, Jasper, Jenny and Jolyon. Mummy says we shouldn't have the books: books need dusting!

Roses, green grass, books and peace.

Martha woke up with a start when they got to the cottage, and gave a little shriek which made them all laugh. Mummy's waking shriek, they called it.

Then there was the car to unpack and the beds to make up, and the electricity to connect, and the supper to make, and the cobwebs to remove, while Martin made the fire. Then supper – pork chops in sweet and sour sauce ('Pork is such a *dull* meat if you don't cook it properly': Martin), green salad from the garden, or such green salad as the rabbits had left. ('Martha, did you really net them properly? Be honest, now!': Martin) and sauté potatoes. Mash is so stodgy and ordinary, and instant mash unthinkable. The children studied the night sky with the aid of their star map. Wonderful, rewarding children!

Then clear up the supper: set the dough to prove for the bread: Martin already in bed: exhausted by the drive and lighting the fire. ('Martha, we really ought to get the logs stacked properly. Get the children to do it, will you?': Martin) Sweep and tidy: get the TV aerial right. Turn up Jasper's jeans where he has trodden the hem undone. ('He can't go around like *that*, Martha. Not even Jasper': Martin)

Midnight. Good night. Weekend guests arriving in the morning. Seven for lunch and dinner on Saturday. Seven for Sunday breakfast, nine for Sunday lunch. (Don't fuss, darling. You always make such a fuss': Martin) Oh, God, forgotten the garlic squeezer. That means ten minutes with the back of a spoon and salt. Well, who wants *lumps* of garlic? No one. Not Martin's guests. Martin said so. Sleep.

Colin and Katie. Colin is Martin's oldest friend. Katie is his
new young wife. Janet, Colin's other, earlier wife, was Martha's
friend. Janet was rather like Martha, quieter and duller than
her husband. A nag and a drag, Martin rather thought, and
said, and of course she'd let herself go, everyone agreed. No
one exactly excused Colin for walking out, but you could see
the temptation.

Katie versus Janet.

Katie was languid, beautiful and elegant. She drawled when she
spoke. Her hands were expressive: her feet were little and
female. She had no children.

Janet plodded round on very flat, rather large feet. There was
something wrong with them. They turned out slightly when
she walked. She had two children. She was, frankly, boring.
But Martha liked her: when Janet came down to the cottage
she would wash up. Not in the way that most guests washed
up — washing dutifully and setting everything out on the
draining board, but actually drying and putting away too. And
Janet would wash the bath and get the children all sat down,
with chairs for everyone, even the littlest, and keep them quiet
and satisfied so the grown-ups — well, the men — could get on
with their conversation and their jokes and their love of
country weekends, while Janet stared into space, as if grateful
for the rest, quite happy.

Janet would garden, too. Weed the strawberries, while the men
went for their walk; her great feet standing firm and square
and sometimes crushing a plant or so, but never mind, oh
never mind. Lovely Janet; who understood.

Now Janet was gone and here was Katie.

Katie talked with the men and went for walks for the men, and moved her ashtray rather impatiently when Martha tried to clear the drinks round it.

Dishes were boring, Katie implied by her manner, and domesticity was boring, and anyone who bothered with that kind of thing was a fool. Like Martha. Ash should be allowed to stay where it was, even if it was in the butter, and conversations should never be interrupted.

Knock, knock. Katie and Colin arrived at one-fifteen on Saturday morning, just after Martha had got to bed. 'You don't mind? It was the moonlight. We couldn't resist it. You should have seen Stonehenge! We didn't disturb you? Such early birds!'

Martha rustled up a quick meal of omelettes. Saturday nights' eggs ('Martha makes a lovely omelette': Martin) ('Honey, make one of your mushroom omelettes: cook the mushrooms, separately, remember, with lemon. Otherwise the water from the mushrooms gets into the eggs, and spoils everything.') Sunday supper mushrooms. But ungracious to say anything.

Martin had revived wonderfully at the sight of Colin and Katie. He brought out the whisky bottle. Glasses. Ice. Jug for water. Wait. Wash up another sinkful, when they're finished. 2 a.m.

'Don't do it tonight, darling.'
It'll only take a sec.' Bright smile, not a hint of self-pity. Self-pity can spoil everyone's weekend.
Martha knows that if breakfast for seven is to be manageable the sink must be cleared of dishes. A tricky meal, breakfast. Especially if bacon, eggs and tomatoes must all be cooked in separate pans. ('Separate pans means separate flavours!': Martin)

*

She is running around in her nightie. Now if that had been Katie — but there's something so *practical* about Martha. Reassuring, mind; but the skimpy nightie and the broad rump and the thirty-eight years are all rather embarrassing. Martha can see it in Colin and Katie's eyes. Martin's too. Martha wishes she did not see so much in other people's eyes. Her mother did, too. Dear, dead mother. Did I misjudge you?

This was the second weekend Katie had been down with Colin but without Janet. Colin was a photographer: Katie had been his accessorizer. First Colin and Janet: then Colin, Janet and Katie: now Colin and Katie!

Katie weeded with rubber gloves on and pulled out pansies in mistake for weeds and laughed and laughed along with everyone when her mistake was pointed out to her, but the pansies died. Well, Colin had become with the years fairly rich and fairly famous, and what does a fairly rich and famous man want with a wife like Janet when Katie is at hand?

On the first day of the Colin/Janet/Katie weekends Katie had appeared out of the bathroom. 'I say,' said Katie, holding out a damp towel with evident distaste. 'I can only find this. No hope of a dry one?' and Martha had run to fetch a dry towel and amazingly found one, and handed it to Katie who flashed her a brilliant smile and said, 'I can't bear damp towels. Anything in the world but damp towels,' as if speaking to a servant in a time of shortage of staff, and took all the water so there was none left for Martha to wash up.

The trouble, of course, was drying anything at all in the cottage. There were no facilities for doing so, and Martin had a horror of clothes lines which might spoil the view. He toiled and moiled all week in the city simply to get a country view at the weekend. Ridiculous to spoil it by draping it with wet towels! But now Martha had bought more towels, so perhaps everyone could be satisfied. She would take nine damp towels back on Sunday evenings in a plastic bag and see to them in London.

On this Saturday morning, straight after breakfast, Katie went out to the car – she and Colin had a new Lamborghini, hard to imagine Katie in anything duller – and came back waving a new Yves St Laurent towel. 'See! I brought my own, darlings.'

They'd brought nothing else. No fruit, no meat, no vegetables, not even bread, certainly not a box of chocolates. They'd gone off to bed with alacrity, the night before, and the spare room rocked and heaved: well, who'd want to do washing-up when you could do that, but what about the children? Would they get confused? First Colin and Janet, now Colin and Katie?

Martha murmured something of her thoughts to Martin, who looked quite shocked. 'Colin's my best friend. I don't expect him to bring anything,' and Martha felt mean. 'And good heavens, you can't protect the kids from sex for ever; don't be so prudish,' so that Martha felt stupid as well. Mean, complaining and stupid.

Janet had rung Martha during the week. The house had been sold over her head, and she and the children had been moved into a small flat. Katie was trying to persuade Colin to cut down on her allowance, Janet said.

'It does one no good to be materialistic,' Katie confided. 'I have nothing. No home, no family, no ties, no possessions. Look at me! Only me and a suitcase of clothes.' But Katie seemed highly satisfied with the me, and the clothes were stupendous. Katie drank a great deal and became funny. Everyone laughed, including Martha. Katie had been married twice. Martha marvelled at how someone could arrive in their mid-thirties with nothing at all to their name, neither husband, nor children, nor property and not mind.

Mind you, Martha could see the power of such helplessness. If Colin was all Katie had in the world, how could Colin abandon her? And to what? Where would she go? How would she live? Oh, clever Katie.

'My teacup's dirty,' said Katie, and Martha ran to clean it, apologizing, and Martin raised his eyebrows, at Martha, not Katie.

'I wish *you'd* wear scent,' said Martin to Martha, reproachfully. Katie wore lots. Martha never seemed to have time to put any on, though Martin bought her bottle after bottle. Martha leaped out of bed each morning to meet some emergency – miaowing cat, coughing child, faulty alarm clock, postman's knock – when was Martha to put on scent? It annoyed Martin all the same. She ought to do more to charm him.

Colin looked handsome and harrowed and younger than Martin, though they were much the same age. 'Youth's catching,' said Martin in bed that night. 'It's since he found Katie.' Found, like some treasure. Discovered; something exciting and wonderful, in the dreary world of established spouses.

On Saturday morning Jasper trod on a piece of wood ('Martha, why isn't he wearing shoes? It's too bad': Martin) and Martha took him into the hospital to have a nasty splinter removed. She left the cottage at ten and arrived back at one, and they were still sitting in the sun, drinking, empty bottles glinting in the long grass. The grass hadn't been cut. Don't forget the bottles. Broken glass means more mornings at the hospital. Oh, don't fuss. Enjoy yourself. Like other people. Try.

But no potatoes peeled, no breakfast cleared, nothing. Cigarette ends still amongst old toast, bacon rind and marmalade. 'You could have done the potatoes,' Martha burst out. Oh, bad temper! Prime sin. They looked at her in amazement and dislike. Martin too.

'Goodness,' said Katie, 'Are we doing the whole Sunday lunch bit on Saturday? Potatoes? Ages since I've eaten potatoes. Wonderful!'

'The children expect it,' said Martha.

So they did. Saturday and Sunday lunch shone like reassuring beacons in their lives. Saturday lunch: family lunch: fish and chips. ('So much better cooked at home than bought': Martin) Sunday. Usually roast beef, potatoes, peas, apple pie. Oh, of course. Yorkshire pudding. Always a problem with oven temperatures. When the beef's going slowly the Yorkshire should be going fast. How to achieve that? Like big bosom and little hips.

'Just relax,' said Martin. 'I'll cook dinner, all in good time. Splinters always work their own way out: no need to have taken him to hospital. Let life drift over you, my love. Flow with the waves, that's the way.'

And Martin flashed Martha a distant, spiritual smile. His hand lay on Katie's slim brown arm, with its many gold bands.

'Anyway, you do too much for the children,' said Martin. 'It isn't good for them. Have a drink.'

So Martha perched uneasily on the step and had a glass of cider, and wondered how, if lunch was going to be late, she would get cleared up and the meat out of the marinade for the rather formal dinner that would be expected that evening. The marinaded lamb ought to cook for at least four hours in a low oven; and you couldn't use that and the grill at the same time and Martin liked his fish grilled, not fried. Less cholesterol.

She didn't say as much. Domestic details like this were very boring, and any mild complaint was registered by Martin as a scene. And to make a scene was so ungrateful.

*

This was the life. Well, wasn't it? Smart friends in large cars and country living and drinks before lunch and roses and bird song – 'Don't drink *too* much,' said Martin, and told them about Martha's suspended driving licence.

The children were hungry so Martha opened them a can of beans and sausages and heated them up. ('Martha, do they have to eat that crap? Can't they wait?': Martin)

Katie was hungry: she said so, to keep the children in face. She was lovely with children – most children. She did not particularly like Colin and Janet's children. She said so, and he accepted it. He only saw them once a month now, not once a week.

'Let me make lunch,' Katie said to Martha. 'You do so much, poor thing!'

And she pulled out of the fridge all the things Martha had put away for the next day's picnic lunch party – Camembert cheese and salad and salami and made a wonderful tomato salad in two minutes and opened the white wine – 'not very cold, darling. Shouldn't it be chilling?' – and had it all on the table in five amazing competent minutes. 'That's all we need, darling,' said Martin. 'You are funny with your fish-and-chip Saturdays! What could be nicer than this? Or simpler?'

Nothing, except there was Sunday's buffet lunch for nine gone, in place of Saturday's fish for six, and would the fish stretch? No. Katie had had quite a lot to drink. She pecked Martha on the forehead. 'Funny little Martha,' she said. 'She reminds me of Janet. I really do like Janet.' Colin did not want to be reminded of Janet, and said so. 'Darling, Janet's a fact of life,' said Katie. 'If you'd only think about her more, you might manage to pay her less.' And she yawned and stretched her lean, childless body and smiled at Colin with her inviting, naughty little girl eyes, and Martin watched her in admiration.

Martha got up and left them and took a paint pot and put a coat of white gloss on the bathroom wall. The white surface pleased her. She was good at painting. She produced a smooth, even surface. Her legs throbbed. She feared she might be getting varicose veins.

Outside in the garden the children played badminton. They were bad-tempered, but relieved to be able to look up and see their mother working, as usual: making their lives for ever better and nicer: organizing, planning, thinking ahead, side-stepping disaster, making preparations, like a mother hen, fussing and irritating: part of the natural boring scenery of the world.

On Saturday night Katie went to bed early: she rose from her chair and stretched and yawned and poked her head into the kitchen where Martha was washing saucepans. Colin had cleared the table and Katie had folded the napkins into pretty creases, while Martin blew at the fire, to make it bright. 'Good night,' said Katie.

Katie appeared three minutes later, reproachfully holding out her Yves St Laurent towel, sopping wet. 'Oh dear,' cried Martha. 'Jenny must have washed her hair!' And Martha was obliged to rout Jenny out of bed to rebuke her, publicly, if only to demonstrate that she knew what was right and proper. That meant Jenny would sulk all weekend, and that meant a treat or an outing mid-week, or else by the following week she'd be having an asthma attack. 'You fuss the children too much,' said Martin. 'That's why Jenny has asthma.' Jenny was pleasant enough to look at, but not stunning. Perhaps she was a disappointment to her father? Martin would never say so, but Martha feared he thought so.

An egg and an orange each child, each day. Then nothing too bad would go wrong. And it hadn't. The asthma was very mild. A calm, tranquil environment, the doctor said. Ah, smile, Martha smile. Domestic happiness depends on you. 21 × 52 oranges a year. Each one to be purchased, carried, peeled and washed up after. And what about potatoes. 12 × 52 pounds a year? Martin liked his potatoes carefully peeled. He couldn't bear to find little cores of black in the mouthful. ('Well, it isn't very nice, is it?': Martin)

Martha dreamt she was eating coal, by handfuls, and liking it.

Saturday night. Martin made love to Martha three times. Three times? How virile he was, and clearly turned on by the sounds from the spare room. Martin said he loved her. Martin always did. He was a courteous lover; he knew the importance of foreplay. So did Martha. Three times.

Ah, sleep. Jolyon had a nightmare. Jenny was woken by a moth. Martin slept through everything. Martha pottered about the house in the night. There was a moon. She sat at the window and stared out into the summer night for five minutes, and was at peace, and then went back to bed because she ought to be fresh for the morning.

But she wasn't. She slept late. The others went for a walk. They'd left a note, a considerate note: 'Didn't wake you. You looked tired. Had a cold breakfast so as not to make too much mess. Leave everything 'til we get back.' But it was ten o'clock, and guests were coming at noon, so she cleared away the bread, the butter, the crumbs, the smears, the jam, the spoons, the spilt sugar, the cereal, the milk (sour by now) and the dirty plates, and swept the floors, and tidied up quickly, and grabbed a cup of coffee, and prepared to make a rice and fish dish, and a chocolate mousse and sat down in the middle to eat a lot of bread and jam herself. Broad hips. She remembered the office work in her file and knew she wouldn't be able to do it. Martin anyway thought it was ridiculous for her to bring work back at the weekends. 'It's your holiday,' he'd say. 'Why should they impose?' Martha loved her work. She didn't have to smile at it. She just did it.

Katie came back upset and crying. She sat in the kitchen while Martha worked and drank glass after glass of gin and bitter lemon. Katie liked ice and lemon in gin. Martha paid for all the drink out of her wages. It was part of the deal between her and Martin – the contract by which she went out to work. All things to cheer the spirit, otherwise depressed by a working wife and mother, were to be paid for by Martha. Drink, holidays, petrol, outings, puddings, electricity, heating: it was quite a joke between them. It didn't really make any difference: it was their joint money, after all. Amazing how Martha's wages were creeping up, almost to the level of Martin's. One day they would overtake. Then what?

Work, honestly, was a piece of cake.

Anyway, poor Katie was crying. Colin, she'd discovered, kept a photograph of Janet and the children in his wallet. 'He's not free of her. He pretends he is, but he isn't. She has him by a stranglehold. It's the kids. His bloody kids. Moaning Mary and that little creep Joanna. It's all he thinks about. I'm nobody.'

But Katie didn't believe it. She knew she was somebody al right. Colin came in, in a fury. He took out the photograph and set fire to it, bitterly, with a match. Up in smoke they went. Mary and Joanna and Janet. The ashes fell on the floor (Martha swept them up when Colin and Katie had gone. It hardly seemed polite to do so when they were still there.) 'Go back to her,' Katie said. 'Go back to her. I don't care. Honestly, I'd rather be on my own. You're a nice old fashioned thing Run along then. Do your thing, I'll do mine. Who cares?'

'Christ, Katie, the fuss! She only just happens to be in the photograph. She's not there on purpose to annoy. And I do fee bad about her. She's been having a hard time.'

'And haven't you, Colin? She twists a pretty knife, I can tell you. Don't you have rights too? Not to mention me. Is a little loyalty too much to expect?'

They were reconciled before lunch, up in the spare room. Harry and Beryl Elder arrived at twelve-thirty. Harry didn't like to hurry on Sundays; Beryl was flustered with apologies for their lateness. They'd brought artichokes from their garden. 'Wonderful,' cried Martin. 'Fruits of the earth? Let's have a wonderful soup! Don't fret, Martha. I'll do it.'

'Don't fret.' Martha clearly hadn't been smiling enough. She was in danger, Martin implied, of ruining everyone's weekend. There was an emergency in the garden very shortly – an elm tree which had probably got Dutch elm disease – and Martha finished the artichokes. The lid flew off the blender and there was artichoke purée everywhere. 'Let's have lunch outside,' said Colin. 'Less work for Martha.'

Martin frowned at Martha: he thought the appearance of martyrdom in the face of guests to be an unforgivable offence.

Everyone happily joined in taking the furniture out, but it was Martha's experience that nobody ever helped to bring it in again. Jolyon was stung by a wasp. Jasper sneezed and sneezed from hay fever and couldn't find the tissues and he wouldn't use loo paper. ('Surely you remembered the tissues, darling?': Martin)

Beryl Elder was nice. 'Wonderful to eat out,' she said, fetching the cream for her pudding, while Martha fished a fly from the liquefying Brie ('You shouldn't have bought it so ripe, Martha': Martin) – 'except it's just some other woman has to do it. But at least it isn't *me*.' Beryl worked too, as a secretary, to send the boys to boarding school, where she'd rather they weren't. But her husband was from a rather grand family, and she'd been only a typist when he married her, so her life was a mass of amends, one way or another. Harry had lately opted out of the stockbroking rat race and become an artist, choosing integrity rather than money, but that choice was his alone and couldn't of course be inflicted on the boys.

Katie found the fish and rice dish rather strange, toyed at it with her fork, and talked about Italian restaurants she knew. Martin lay back soaking in the sun: crying, 'Oh, this is the life.' He made coffee, nobly, and the lid flew off the grinder and there were coffee beans all over the kitchen especially in amongst the row of cookery books which Martin gave Martha Christmas by Christmas. At least they didn't have to be brought back every weekend. ('The burglars won't have the sense to steal those': Martin)

Beryl fell asleep and Katie watched her, quizzically. Beryl's mouth was open and she had a lot of fillings, and her ankles were thick and her waist was going, and she didn't look after herself. 'I love women,' sighed Katie. 'They look so wonderful asleep. I wish I could be an earth mother.'

Beryl woke with a start and nagged her husband into going home, which he clearly didn't want to do, so didn't. Beryl thought she had to get back because his mother was coming round later. Nonsense! Then Beryl tried to stop Harry drinking more homemade wine and was laughed at by everyone. He was driving, Beryl couldn't, and he did have a nasty scar on his temple from a previous road accident. Never mind.

'She does come on strong, poor soul,' laughed Katie when they'd finally gone. 'I'm never going to get married,' – and Colin looked at her yearningly because he wanted to marry her more than anything in the world and Martha cleared the coffee cups.

'Oh don't *do* that,' said Katie, 'do just sit *down*, Martha, you make us all feel bad,' and Martin glared at Martha who sat down and Jenny called out for her and Martha went upstairs and Jenny had started her first period and Martha cried and cried and knew she must stop because this must be a joyous occasion for Jenny or her whole future would be blighted, but for once, Martha couldn't.

Her daughter, Jenny: wife, mother, friend.